WITHOUT PARENTAL CONSENT

SHAE MARTIN WORTHY

WITHOUT PARENTAL CONSENT

His entire life was a lie

Worthy Publishing

This book is a work of fiction. Names, characters, places and incidents either are products of the author's imagination or are used fictitiously. Any resemblance to actual events or locales or persons, living or dead, is entirely coincidental.

Cover design by Worthy Publishing

Dedications

This book is dedicated to my daughter Ariel, who always inspired me. It's also dedicated to my mother and father, Barbara and Vonzell Nash who never let me give up on my dreams.

This book is dedicated in loving memory of my wonderful "Granny" Mildred McCloud Worthy, who always believed in me.

To the memory of Timothy Fitts, a wonderful fiancé and great loss who was truly the love of my life.

To my sisters Kim, Sheila, Dee Annamarie, Merideth, my brother Mickey, and my cousins Kenya, Kisha, DJ and Jarell, thanks for being so supportive over the years.

I love you all!

And thank you GOD Almighty for Your wonderful blessings and the gift of writing. I love You first and foremost.

Prologue

July 8, 1983

Victoria had known for the past week about the baby shower her friends were throwing for her. This was Garret and her first baby. She knew that Garret wanted a son, like most men. Secretly, she was hoping for a girl, although either one would be fine. All they really wanted was a healthy baby. A baby who'd only be the beginning of the many children they wanted to have.

All those wasted years, being married to other people. It didn't matter, because they were together now, after breaking up years before in high school. Somehow, fate had brought them through stormy marriages with other people, only to find their way back to each other. Garret had finished law school and was working at a good firm. They had their lives ahead of them.

The shower was a complete success. After the shower, Victoria was standing outside with her mother Anna and mother-in-law Jean when her mother remembered something she'd left in the restaurant, leaving Victoria alone with Jean.

Jean Marlow looked at her daughter-in-law intently. "You want to talk about it?"

"Oh, Jean," Victoria sighed. "What's wrong with me? I'm happier than I've ever been in my life, yet, I have such an uneasy feeling."

"You're just anxious. You and my son have waited a long time for such a precious gift. You'll see. Everything will be just fine."

"I'm going to hold you to that," Victoria smiled.

"Go ahead. It's a promise I'm going to keep."

"So, what are the two of you talking about so intently?" Anna asked, as she came out of the restaurant.

"Oh, just a little of this and a little of that," Jean said.

"I hope I wasn't interrupting," Anna stated.

"No. I was just giving our daughter here a few words of wisdom. And, on that note, I'm going to head home." Jean then hugged her daughter-in-law.

"I'd better get home, too," Victoria smiled. "I'm sure Gary's asleep in front of the TV."

"Why don't I drive you?" Anna offered.

"No, Mom, it's out of the way. Besides, I have my car. I'll be fine," Victoria insisted. "Marilyn is bringing the gifts by my house tomorrow. She told me I'd be too excited and try to get everything arranged tonight, and she's probably right."

"Marilyn's a wonderful friend," Anna said.

"Well, I'll see you tomorrow, Vicki," Jean said, hugging her again. Then she hugged Anna. "Anna, call me tomorrow."

"I will," Anna smiled. The two of them watched as Jean got into her car and drove off.

"Before you go, I have one more gift for the baby," Anna said.

"Mom, don't you think you've given me enough?" Vicki smiled.

"Never. I didn't want to give it to you in front of everyone. I'm not sure why I feel like I should give this to you tonight in the parking lot instead of waiting to give it to you later." Anna smiled as she gave her the box.

Victoria opened it to find her christening gown. "Oh, Mom!"

"I know you loved it, and it would mean so much to Daddy and me if you would christen your baby in it."

"It would be an honor," Vicki cried, hugging her mother. "Thank you so much!"

"Do you know how proud I am of you?"

~ ii ~

"Are you?"

"More than you'll ever know. I love you so much, Vicki!"

"I love you, too."

"Now, you go on home and get some rest!" Anna smiled. "And call me the minute you get there, okay?"

"I will."

"You be careful," Anna said, walking Victoria to her car.

"Bye, Mom," Vicki said, hugging her mom once more.

Victoria held on to her mother a little longer than usual, which made Anna uneasy. She was always so worried about her little girl. When Victoria had gotten safely into her car, Anna waved at her.

"Lock your doors!" Anna said as Victoria drove off, but, Victoria didn't hear her. Anna knew Victoria had a terrible knack of not locking her doors. Anna then got into her car and headed in the opposite direction.

*****

Victoria drove along, happy that the evening had been such a success. She couldn't wait to get home to Garret. He'd be so happy to hear about all the wonderful things they got for the baby. Marilyn was right. If Victoria had taken the things home, she'd be too excited to rest. Victoria smiled to herself as little Gary kicked her. She knew in her heart that she was going to give Garret a son. The next one would be a girl, but this was going to be a boy. Vicki was so deep in thought, until she almost ran the traffic light.

"The last thing I need is to have an accident in my condition."

The light seemed to hold forever. Vicki sat there, calmly tapping her fingers against the steering wheel. As she sat at the light on the nearly deserted road, Victoria screamed as a masked man jumped into the back seat of her car and held a gun to her. She'd not locked her doors, and now it seemed that she was going to pay for it.

~ iii ~

"Just drive," the voice whispered.

"O-Okay," Vicki cried. "P-Please don't hurt me!"

"Drive, dammit!" the voice demanded louder.

Vicki drove along, trembling the whole time. What did her assailant want? Was it money, was it the car? She would have gladly given him anything to save her life and that of her unborn child.

"Pull over and put the car in park," the assailant instructed, after making her turn onto a dark road. "And don't turn around."

"P-Please, take the car! Take my money! I don't care, but please don't hurt me!" Vicki cried once again.

Before Vicki could continue pleading for her life, she felt something cover her mouth. She tried in vain to fight. She couldn't breathe. Suddenly, everything went black.

*****

Victoria felt groggy, as she tried to open her eyes. She could hear voices around her, but couldn't understand what was being said. Everything was muffled and echoed. Who were these people? She felt such sharp pains in her stomach. She was in labor. Her baby was coming, but where was Garret? Who was in the room with her? She couldn't focus; all she could see was two figures looming over her. Why were they arguing? She felt as if she was being cut, but wasn't given anything for the pain. She weakly tried to scream out, but it was as if she was floating. She felt someone force her mouth open and stuff in a small towel to suppress her voice. She couldn't talk nor breathe. Her arms were tied. She tried to kick at her assailants, but they held her legs down. Who was doing this to her? Was her baby okay? As if on cue, she heard her baby cry. She tried to scream again, but couldn't. As she began to focus, she saw her assailants. Why were they doing this to her?

"No!" Victoria's muffled voice tried in vain to protest.

But it was too late; she could see the hate in her attacker's eyes. Someone up to this point that she'd trusted. Victoria knew she was going to die, as she saw the knife lunging towards her chest. For the few moments she lived, Victoria felt another stab, one after the other. She couldn't hold on. She felt her body dying slowly. At least the baby was okay. Or was he? Was it a boy as she'd always felt? Or would a girl grow up without knowing her mother?

"My baby," Victoria whispered, never getting a chance to see or hold her baby, as tears ran down her face. Victoria suddenly felt cold, as her body went limp.

Chapter
1

27 years later. . .

The well-dressed young man waited patiently as the elevator rose smoothly to each floor. Several people got off on the 7th floor, and the rest of them got off on the 14th, 15th and 18th floors. One man stood rigid as he continued his ascent alone. He held onto his briefcase, as he felt his palm slightly sweating with nervousness and anxiety as the elevator brought him closer and closer to his destination. He was attractive, 6' 2" and still maintained his athletic build after years of football and working out. His eyes were dark and purposeful, deeply defined, with thick, long eyelashes. His perfectly sculpted chin was hard and well maintained, with a well-groomed goatee. He closed his eyes and inhaled deeply as the elevator smoothly stopped on the plush 22nd floor.

As the doors opened, he exhaled purposely, slowly opening his eyes. His steps were purposeful, as he observed the day to day regime, with phones ringing, the usual hustle and bustle of any successful office. Starting his first day at such a successful law firm was just the beginning. Larson, Craig and Jacobs was a top law firm with clients from a corporate stature to criminal activities to bankruptcy to family law, employing 57 other attorneys. Cameron's specialty was criminal law, mostly dealing with capital murder cases, graduating the top of his class from Brooklander School of Law. After working for a year at a small firm in his hometown of Lariette Springs, Cameron was now about to embark on a new challenge with a new outlook on life.

"You can do this, Cameron," he whispered to himself as he took in the impressive surroundings.

He looked around and noticed the receptionist desk straight ahead. The woman sitting there was an attractive woman in her early twenties. Her face was perfectly made up, completely flawless and her hair was flowing freely down her back; exactly what the consensus would expect from a receptionist, who would be the first impression to anyone entering the firm. She was eye-candy in all its glory. He thought momentarily that this would be a conquest, until he noticed her left hand, displaying the telltale sign that she was married. He wryly thought that even he wouldn't go that far.

"Hi, can I help you?" the woman said, smiling in a flirtatious manner.

"Yes, I'm Cameron Spencer," he spoke up, looking at the name plate on her desk. Her name was Ginger Overton. She looked like a 'Ginger.'

"Hi, Mr. Spencer," the woman cheerfully greeted him. "Mr. Larson is waiting for you in his office." She pointed down the hall, tossing her hair ever so slightly.

"Thanks," Cameron smiled, looking back for several seconds to take in Ginger's looks. 'Too bad she's married,' Cameron thought to himself.

Cameron walked down the hall, where the phones seemed to fade into the background after entering through two large thick glass doors, only to come to the other receptionist area, where Mr. Larson's personal secretary was busy taking a message. He took this time to take in the opulent surroundings, thinking one day, this office could be his. When she noticed Cameron, she smiled and held her finger up in a motion that she would be with him momentarily.

"Yes, I will give Mr. Larson the message," she smiled. "Thank you, and you have a nice day, Mrs. Wellman." The secretary efficiently hung up the phone. "I'm sorry, Mr. Spencer, how are you today?"

"I'm fine. You know who I am?" he smiled.

"Ginger, the receptionist, called to let me know you were on your way. I'm Alison Jemison, Mr. Larson's secretary," Alison said, standing and holding out her hand. Alison was an older woman, very professional in her mid-forties. She wore her hair pulled back, with glasses efficiently positioned on her face.

"It's nice to meet you," Cameron smiled, flashing that flirtatious smile that made women melt. "You know, seeing you only confirms that there are beautiful women where ever I go in this firm."

Alison was about as plain as a woman could be, probably never really noticed by men, but Cameron always made it a point to let every woman think she was beautiful. It was a harmless fib worth it to boost a woman's ego.

"Thank you," Alison blushed. "I'll let Mr. Larson know you're here," Alison smiled, picking up the phone. "Mr. Larson, Mr. Spencer is here. Yes Sir." Alison hung up the phone. "Come with me, Mr. Spencer."

Alison led Cameron into another office to meet with Phillip Larson for the first time since his interview. Mr. Larson was one of the senior partners in the law firm and his reputation as a great criminal defense lawyer earned him respect in and out of the courtroom. He was in his mid to late fifties.

"Cameron, how are you, son?" Mr. Larson smiled, holding his hand out to shake Cameron's. "Have you settled in okay?"

"A little. I'm living out of boxes right now, because I haven't had time to unpack too much. I just moved into my apartment this past weekend because my father had been ill."

"I hope all is well now," Mr. Larson stated.

"Yes, Sir, he's fine."

"Will there be anything else, Mr. Larson?" Alison asked.

"Cameron, would you like a cup of coffee?"

"No, Sir. Thank you."

Mr. Larson smiled. "Alison, that'll be all for now."

"Yes, Sir," Alison smiled, giving Cameron a once-over as she walked out, closing the door. Upon final glance immediately before the door closed, Cameron gave her a little wink.

"Well, welcome aboard," Phil smiled. "I know you probably have a lot of questions about the firm, although we tried to inform you about everything you'd need to know. As a junior attorney, you have very little seniority. You will work closely with seasoned attorneys for quite a while, and when it's agreed that you're ready, we will allow you to head up cases as leading counsel."

"So, when do I get started?"

"Well, we're about to have a meeting in the boardroom. We have meetings every Monday to go over our new cases, to see where things stand, discuss strategies, et cetera. You probably know the routine."

"Yes, Sir. But, for obvious reasons, this will be quite different, Mr. Larson."

"Probably not as much as you think. And please, call me Phil."

"Okay, Phil. I haven't been to my office yet. What time will the meeting start?"

"It starts promptly at 9 a.m. Its 8:15 now, so go on to your office and get settled in." Phil reached to push the intercom button on his phone. "Alison, show Mr. Spencer to his office."

"Yes sir," Alison's voice came back over the speaker.

Cameron and Alison walked back down the hall, and through the glassed doors that led to the outer reception area again, making harmless small talk along the way. She introduced him to several people as they passed, and they all greeted him warmly. When he entered his office, it was small, about a fourth the size of Mr. Larson's office, but still larger than the one he had with Madison and Madison Law Firm. He placed his briefcase on top of his desk, and thanked Alison for showing him briefly around. The way she looked at him, he wondered if maybe he'd given her the wrong impression. She seemed nice enough, but very far from Cameron's type. Ginger was more his type, he thought to himself. He glanced around his office. With a couple of pictures, and his law degree of course, he could really make this office home. He knew from past experience that he'd probably be spending a lot of time there anyway, so he wanted it to be comfortable. He looked into his briefcase and pulled out his law degree. As he looked at it, he smiled and thought about his parents. They worked so hard to give him every possible opportunity to advance in life. He was not going to disappoint them.

He thought about the firm where he was previously employed. Madison and Madison was one out of only three law firms in the whole town. He was co-counsel on two capital murder cases with Paul Madison, who was a senior partner with Madison and Madison. As a seasoned attorney, Paul took Cameron under his wing and passed on almost 25 years of knowledge about death penalty laws and what it takes to get an acquittal for his client. Although Paul was a well-noted, experienced attorney, Cameron felt as if he'd never make a real name for himself if he stayed. So, after learning at the feet of a master in his field, Cameron knew it was time to move on. When he found out from a law school friend that Larson, Craig and Jacobs was looking for another attorney, he immediately went after the job. The timing couldn't have been better, especially after his breakup with Grace. Even though it meant relocating to another state, he was willing to do that, because this firm had been involved with many impressive, high-profile cases. This was the firm with whom to be associated.

He fleetingly felt a little guilty leaving his parents because they weren't getting any younger. He'd not spoken with his mom since Saturday. His phone wasn't to be connected until Wednesday and he'd been having problems with his cell phone, so he decided to call her from his office to let her know that everything was okay. She was constantly worrying about him, even as a child. It seems as if it had gotten worse since she found out that he was moving away.

~ 5 ~

Cameron was deep in thought when there was a knock at his door.

"Come in."

"Mr. Spencer? Hi, I'm Kristen Levine, your secretary," she smiled, holding out her hand to shake his. "I know this is your first day, and you probably want to get settled in, but I just wanted to see if there's anything you need and to introduce myself."

Kristen was an attractive woman. Cameron smiled at her, looking at her from head to toe as he slightly caressed her hand while shaking it. He sized her up quickly. She looked to be around his age, beautiful with a great figure.

"Um, no, nothing that I can think of. I'm just going to get myself together for the meeting this morning."

"Okay. My desk is right outside, so just let me know what you need. I'm sorry about not being at my desk when you came in a little while ago, but I was in the supply room. I've stocked your office with everything I think you'll need, but if there's anything specific that you want, please let me know so that I can get it for you."

"Thank you, Kristen," he smiled. He noticed her left hand. No ring. Now, this would be a strong possibility. *'Careful, Cameron. There's such a thing as sexual harassment,'* he thought to himself.

"You're welcome. Oh, and welcome to Larson, Craig and Jacobs."

"Thanks. Oh, Kristen, I do have one question. Where's the conference room?"

"The conference room is down the hall on your left. I'll show you when you're ready."

"Okay. Give me about ten more minutes, and I'll go anywhere you want to lead me," Cameron smiled.

Kristen blushed slightly. "I-I'll show you when you're ready, Mr. Spencer."

"Please, call me Cameron."

"Okay, Cameron," Kristen smiled. He eyed her body as she walked out the door, and especially admired the way her skirt hugged her form.

Meeting Kristen, Cameron was starting to think that maybe he'd been out of circulation long enough. A part of him was still trying to get over his love for Grace. He made a conscious decision not to fall in love again. Despite the fact that Cameron could have any girl he wanted, Grace Reed was his first real love. He had no idea that he wasn't her real love. They always promised each other that they would be together forever. There was no way she was cheating on him. After all, they lived in a town where the total population was 3,000. Surely, he'd have known. But, he didn't. That's why it came as such a shock when Grace eloped with Mark Jansen, who was from the neighboring town of Union Springs. All the time, Grace was seeing Mark and Cameron never knew. So much for instincts, he thought. She'd given his ring back to him, after she met with him to tell him about her marriage. She told him that it was no reflection on him, he just couldn't give her what she wanted. She felt as if he was destined to remain in Lariette Springs forever, right there with his mother.

Grace and Rebecca had never gotten along. He was beginning to think that his mom was right all the time about Grace. Mark was offered an internship after medical school at Marionette Medical Center in Bragston. When he wanted to marry Grace and take her away from Lariette Springs, she had to say yes. She said she wanted a man who was 'going places.' Cameron decided to show Grace better than he could tell her, so he moved on with his life, started fresh. The best place to start was here in Kerrigan. He looked around as he brought himself back to reality. He got up from his chair and went out to Kristen's desk.

"Kristen, I'm ready."

"Okay, follow me," Kristen said, rising from her desk. "You're not from here, are you?"

"No, I'm from Lariette Springs. It's a small town about three hours from here in Kentucky."

"Oh. No wonder I've never heard of it. How long have you been here in Kerrigan?"

"I just moved in over the weekend. A family crisis kept me from moving here sooner. Now, I'm living out of

~ 7 ~

boxes, trying to get settled in, and start a new job all at once."

"Well, if you need any help with anything, I'd be happy to come over and help you get settled in," Kristen offered eagerly.

"Thank you," Cameron smiled. "You know, I just might take you up on that."

"The offer stands whenever you're ready," Kristen smiled.

If Cameron wondered before, when he entered the conference room, he knew he was light years away from his humble career in Lariette Springs. The conference room was fairly large with chairs around a large, cherry wood oval table. There were oil paintings of each of the partners on one wall in the room. There was a slide projector, and a screen ascended into the ceiling. A flat screen television and DVD player rested in one corner of the room, and there were other chairs sitting away from the conference table.

People started to file into the room sparingly at first, some of which Cameron recognized from different conferences, high-profile cases, and even a few who'd written books. Promptly at 9 a.m., the partners arrived. To this date, Cameron had only met two of the partners, Phillip Larson and Alex Jacobs because when he interviewed, Matthew Craig was on vacation with his family. All the attorneys assembled around the table, talking amicably.

"Before we get started this morning, I'd like to welcome a new addition to Larson, Craig and Jacobs law firm," Phillip announced. "Cameron Spencer joined our firm and today is his first day. Welcome, Cameron."

There was a welcome applause around the room. Cameron stood and spoke a few words to his new colleagues, which were almost immediately forgotten.

"Now, let's get down to business," Phillip said, putting on his reading glasses. The meeting was productive, with everyone coming up to date on cases they were working on. No wonder this law firm was so lucrative. Before the meeting ended, Phillip brought up one more case.

"Indiana vs. Marlow," Phillip said. "Carl, what's the

status?"

"Not good, Sir. We've been working on this case for quite a while, but to be honest, I think it's a lost cause because we're running out of time. We only have a little over three weeks before the clemency hearing," Carl stated. Carl was a junior defense attorney, specializing in death penalty cases.

"What does Caitlyn think?" Phillip asked.

"As usual, Her Highness isn't here," Carl said sarcastically. "She seems to always have better things to do than to attend these mediocre meetings." There was a scattered chuckle about the room. From the way people responded, Cameron thought this Caitlyn person must be hell in high heels.

Phillip smiled slightly. "Has anything surfaced?" Phillip asked.

"Nope. I'd like to turn this case over to someone else. Maybe our new colleague would like a stab at it?" Carl asked.

Everyone looked at Cameron, who immediately stopped tapping his pencil. He looked around the table.

"Excuse me?" Cameron asked.

"I can't get anywhere, and Ms. Frazier and I are constantly at each other. Maybe you'll have better luck?" Carl smiled, shifting his eyes slyly to the colleague sitting next to him.

"Well, I don't know," Cameron said hesitantly.

"Oh, come on. You've been co-counsel on capital murder cases before," Carl smiled. "Unless you have something better to do than practice law."

"I guess I could look at it," Cameron said.

"Good," Carl said.

"Would you like to brief me on the case after the meeting?" Cameron said.

"I'll let Ms. Frazier do it, if you can find her. I'll drop the files off at your office because time is of the essence," Carl smiled.

Cameron got the sneaking suspicion that he'd been duped. Who was this Ms. Frazier? Was she that bad to work with? What was he getting himself into? Of course, he was

~ 9 ~

the new kid on the block, and could undoubtedly use the experience. His thoughts were interrupted by Phillip speaking again.

"So, is it agreed? Cameron will you be willing to take over as co-counsel on Indiana vs. Marlow?" Phillip asked.

"Of course," he said.

"Okay, good. I want constant updates on the case, okay?" Phillip stated.

"Yes Sir," Cameron responded, looking challengingly at Carl. *'Asshole,'* Cameron thought to himself. *'That's okay, you corporate kiss-ass. I'll be junior partner in a couple of years and a senior partner by five years.'*

"Now that's settled, so let's move on," Phillip said.

Phillip talked briefly about a few other issues, and then brought the meeting to a close. Some attorneys left, others stayed to have a cup of coffee, talking amicably amongst each other.

"Mr. Spencer?" a woman's voice called out from behind Cameron while he was sipping a cup of coffee. He turned around and almost dropped his cup, spilling just a little on his shirt. Somehow, hot coffee stinging his skin did nothing compared to what seeing this woman seemed to do. It took all of ten seconds for the memory of this woman who mesmerized Cameron so, to be embedded forever. She had the smoothest skin with full, pouty lips. Her hair was a cross between auburn and blond, and she had the most enchantingly beautiful eyes which were gray, with speckles of gold in them. She was dressed professionally in a brown suit, complemented by a silk blouse with a scooped neck. Her perfect legs were long and sleek, only to end with three-inch heel pumps. She held out her hand. "Hi, I'm Caitlyn Frazier," she said dryly.

"Hi. Nice to meet you, Mrs. Frazier," Cameron smiled, shaking her hand. As he looked at her, he quickly realized that Caitlyn's beauty surpassed every other woman at the firm; every other woman he'd ever laid eyes on.

"*Miss* Frazier," Caitlyn corrected.

"Even better," Cameron smiled under his breath.

"Excuse me?" Caitlyn asked.

"Nothing," he smiled. "I think we're going to be working a case together: Indiana vs. Marlow."

"So, Carl finally managed to weasel out of working with me," she commented. "It doesn't surprise me, though. He hates women, you know," Caitlyn leaned in and whispered. "It's that whole 'down-low' thing."

"Ah, so is that it?" he said. "And you would know this how?"

"Just a feeling I have," Caitlyn said. "But, I guess you'll have to do. Just keep in mind, this is my case, and we'll play it like I want to. Do we understand each other?"

"I'm not exactly just out of law school. I've been an attorney for over a year now and I don't need to deal with some arrogant, self-centered attorney who can't see beyond her mirror."

"Is that what you think I am?" Caitlyn laughed slightly. "Looks like you'll just have to learn. Be in my office in ten minutes to be briefed on the case." Caitlyn then turned and walked away, never waiting for a response from Cameron.

Cameron looked at Caitlyn as she left the room. She was feisty, without a doubt. "What a bitch."

"I see you've met our Ms. Frazier," a man spoke.

Cameron turned around to see who was talking. "Yes, I have. Is she always like that?" Cameron asked.

"Oh, you met her on a good day," the man smiled. "Hi, I'm Alan Smith, Domestic Law," Alan said, extending his hand.

"Hi Alan," he said, shaking his hand. "She must have ice in her veins. No wonder she's not married. Who would want her?"

"You'd be surprised," Alan chuckled lightly.

"Meaning?" Cameron asked.

"Let's just say that Ms. Frazier makes a lot of use out of that couch in her office," Alan laughed. "Don't get me wrong, she's easy on the eyes, and a real siren in bed from what I hear, but she's hell to work with," Alan smiled. "Good luck to you."

Alan then walked off, leaving Cameron to ponder his

~ 11 ~

statement. Cameron knew exactly what to do about her. He would get inside Caitlyn's head, win this case, and do everything he could to humiliate her in the process. Taking her to bed would just be an added bonus. Cameron's thoughts were interrupted when he was met by other attorneys coming up to introduce themselves personally, making small talk. Shortly afterwards, he begrudgingly made his way to Caitlyn's office. He knocked on her door.

"Come in," Caitlyn barked.

Cameron opened the door and closed it behind him. "Look, it's obvious that we're going to be working together. It's something we both apparently have to get used to. My suggestion would be that you make an attitude adjustment real quick," he said.

"Let's get one thing straight right now. I've been here for five years, and I've had some pretty high-profile cases. That hick-town crap you're used to doesn't even compare. So, let's stop the ego-trip you're on right now, because Larson, Craig and Jacobs is 1000 years ahead of, what was it? Madison and Madison? Husband and wife 'group' I assume," Caitlyn said sarcastically. "We use real computers here, not just pen and paper. And the telephones? They're not two cups attached by a string," she said sharply.

"Wow, you're pretty uptight. Are you just feeling threatened by me, or have you not gotten any lately?" Cameron snapped back.

"My sex life is none of your business!" Caitlyn shot back.

"I'm sure it would be if I were willing to oblige you," Cameron smiled.

"How dare you! I will not work under these conditions. Phil's going to have to take you off the case," Caitlyn said, picking up her phone. "Alison, get me Phil on the phone," Caitlyn snapped.

Cameron watched her beautiful form as she talked with her left hand on her hip as her right hand purposely held the phone. Cameron looked down her body, as her left leg was bent at the knee ever so slightly, bringing the tip of her heel off of the floor. He imagined what he would do to this woman. She had a lot of tension to get rid of, and he was just the man to do it.

"Phil, I can't work with Mr. Spencer. You'll have to assign someone else." Cameron listened as she talked to Phil. "What do you mean this is it? Look, just because several attorneys haven't worked out doesn't mean that I'm the problem! They're all threatened and jealous. Phil, you can't do this to me! I'll talk to Alex about this if I have to! What? Well, we'll see about this!" Caitlyn then slammed the phone down and sighed. She turned quickly to look at Cameron who immediately looked away from admiring her body. "What are you staring at?"

"Absolutely nothing," Cameron said sarcastically. "Now that you've finished ranting and raving like a spoiled two year old, can we get on with this case please? Who knows? You just might like me," Cameron smiled.

"I doubt that. But, your annoying idiosyncrasies aren't Mr. Marlow's fault. Unfortunately, we have to work together. So, let's get started. Are you familiar at all with the case?"

"That's better," Cameron smiled.

"Are you familiar at all with the case?" Caitlyn repeated with a heavy sigh. "It's a simple yes or no question."

"I remember reading about it in a couple of law books. A man was accused of murdering his wife, right?"

"Yeah, 27 years ago," Caitlyn said. "He was a corporate attorney."

"So, where do things stand?"

"He's had his final appeal and his execution date has been set for July 28th, with a clemency hearing fast-approaching on July 7th. So, if we're going to find evidence to clear our client, it has to be quick," Caitlyn stated.

"His original sentencing was over 20 years ago," Cameron stated.

"Exactly."

"So what are we supposed to be able to do that hasn't already been done?"

"Well, apparently, he's a good friend of Phillip's, and

~ 13 ~

he seems to think there's something out there that has been missed," Caitlyn sighed.

"You don't sound too optimistic," Cameron noted.

"When you read the files, you'll see why. I've been working on this case for a couple of months, and it doesn't look good."

"Have you talked to Mr. Marlow?" Cameron asked.

"Yes, I've met with him a couple of times. Phil came to me about the case three months ago. He refuses to give up on Mr. Marlow's case."

"There has to be something for Phillip to be so adamant about it," Cameron said.

"There is. He's thinking with his heart, not his head. Phil's had cases like this. He knows deep down it's a lost cause, but, he's such a good, loyal friend to Mr. Marlow. They were in law school together."

"So, why doesn't Phillip handle the case himself?"

"Oh, believe me, he has. How do you think Mr. Marlow has managed to appeal so much? Phil's called in favors all over the country. Unfortunately, his luck has just about run out. Plus, Phil's in bad health, and he'll probably be retiring soon."

"I didn't know that," he said. "And there you were just ranting away over the phone to the man, trying your best to get rid of me."

"Look, I'll work with you, but I don't have to like it. You're too cocky for me," Caitlyn observed.

"Cocky isn't always a bad thing," Cameron smiled slyly. "So, have you made any progress?" Cameron asked.

"No, not yet. Carl was supposed to be assisting me in this case, but he's been going against me at every turn. Phil insisted upon reassigning all of my cases to other attorneys so that I could give this one my undivided attention," Caitlyn said.

"He must think of you as a last resort," Cameron stated.

"What's that supposed to mean?" Caitlyn asked defensively.

~ 14 ~

"Well, it means that maybe because no one else has been able to do it, he knows that you can," Cameron said. "Boy, are you testy."

"I'm not testy; I just didn't like the way that sounded."

"Look, I didn't mean anything bad by it. Obviously you're good at this, otherwise you wouldn't be here."

"You're right. I specialize in capital murder cases. I've been doing this for almost five years, and I'm proud to say that all of my clients who faced capital murder charges have been acquitted."

"Impressive," Cameron shrugged.

"Of course it is. But, with this one I get the feeling my perfect record won't be so perfect anymore," Caitlyn shook her head. "I just don't think it's something winnable. This is pretty much a lost cause."

"Maybe it's not. Tell me what you know so far," Cameron suggested.

For the next hour, Cameron was quickly brought up to date. He had several files to read through, and opted to do that at home. Mr. Garret Marlow was accused of killing his nine month pregnant wife. When Mrs. Marlow was found, she'd given birth, but the baby was nowhere to be found. They decided to meet with Garret that week, to see if there was anything more he could add. After a while, Caitlyn's phone rang, and she remembered it was time for a previously-scheduled conference call.

"I'll leave you to your call," Cameron said.

"Okay. Go back to your office, read over the material, and we'll discuss this again tomorrow."

"You love giving orders, don't you?" Cameron observed.

"When they need to be given, yes, I do," Caitlyn said.

"See you later, Ice Princess," Cameron smiled, winking at her as he walked out. Her mouth dropped slightly at his statement.

Cameron took two boxes of the notes with him, heading back to his office. Kristen noticed the two boxes and immediately jumped from her chair, eager to assist him. She

~ 15 ~

got one of the boxes and carried it to his office while he carried the other one. As they walked along, they made small talk.

"Why don't I take you to lunch, since you've helped me with these boxes?" Cameron offered.

"It's just my job," Kristen blushed.

"Still, I insist," Cameron smiled. "That way, you can show me where the best restaurants are located."

"Are you sure?" Kristen asked.

"Of course, I'm sure," Cameron insisted.

"I'd be happy to," Kristen smiled.

"Then, it's settled. I'm going to read over some of this for a little while, and we'll go, shall we say, around 12:30?"

"That would be perfect," Kristen said.

"Great," Cameron smiled.

After settling the boxes in his office, he pulled out a few of the files on the case and for the next hour, Cameron read over some of his notes. He looked at his watch, noticing it was almost 12:30. Before he could get up from his chair, Kristen called to see if he was ready.

"I'll be there in just a minute," Cameron smiled.

Cameron then walked out to Kristen's desk as she was retrieving her purse. She stood quickly, as Cameron paid close attention to her low-cut blouse. He smiled as he thought of how much fun this was going to be. He found himself thinking that he'd much rather get to know this woman's body for lunch. As he eyed her, he seductively licked his lips, losing himself in thoughts of taking this woman right there on her desk. He was quickly brought back to reality when she spoke.

"I thought we'd go to Brockman's if that's okay," Kristen said.

"Wherever you want to go is fine," Cameron smiled.

"It's so pretty outside, and the restaurant is only a block away, so why don't we walk?" Kristen suggested.

"Sure," Cameron agreed.

Brockman's was located in the heart of downtown Kerrigan, and it was obviously very upscale. They thankfully

~ 16 ~

entered the building out of the summer heat. The air conditioning was a welcome change.

"So, Cameron Spencer, what do you think of Kerrigan so far?" Kristen asked, as she sipped her tea after placing their order.

"Actually, I just moved in this past weekend, so I don't have much of an opinion formed yet. I was supposed to be here two weeks ago, but my father was ill, so I was unable to be here before now. I know I was cutting it close, but sometimes things happen."

"I hope your father's better now," Kristen said.

"He's much better. He had a bad fall, and had to have surgery on his hip, but he's recovering beautifully. It happened about a month ago, about a week after I accepted the position here. Being an only child, I felt obligated to stay and make sure everything was okay."

"That's very sweet of you, to put your life on hold for the sake of your father. You must really love your parents."

"Who doesn't?" Cameron asked.

"You'd be amazed," Kristen smiled, shaking her head slightly.

"Sounds like there's a story there," Cameron observed.

"You could say that," Kristen shrugged slightly.

"Is it something you feel comfortable talking about?" Cameron asked.

"It's still a little complicated to tell people about," Kristen said.

"Hey, I understand if you don't want to. It's really none of my business," Cameron said.

Kristen looked at him and smiled. "No, you know what? Maybe it will do me some good to talk about it."

"They say it can be therapeutic," Cameron smiled.

"My father was pretty abusive to my mom, siblings and me," Kristen said.

"I'm sorry to hear that. Is your mother still with him?"

"She stayed right up until the end. The SOB died two years ago," Kristen said, with tears in her eyes. She suddenly regained her composure. "But, hey, we survived it, and we're all happier now."

"Why did she stay with him?"

"Where else would she go? After they got married, he made her quit her job, so she didn't work. He controlled everything. Face it, there was nowhere to run," Kristen sighed, as she stirred her tea dazedly.

"It obviously still haunts you," Cameron observed softly, placing his hand on hers.

"Not really. I'm over it, now," she smiled, looking at Cameron. "Why don't we change the subject? So, what do you think of Caitlyn?"

Cameron shook his head and sighed. "She's a pistol, that's for sure. How does anyone stand to be around her?"

"We don't have much choice," Kristen shrugged.

"What do you mean?"

"Caitlyn's a 'special case,' if you know what I mean."

"I don't follow," Cameron said hesitantly, shaking his head slightly.

"There are some of us who work hard to get where we are, and Caitlyn's no exception. In her situation, though, she worked harder on her back than in a classroom or courtroom," Kristen said.

"I heard another attorney mention something very similar earlier today."

"Exactly. She has a reputation. I've been at the firm for 7 years, and when she came in, she was mighty friendly with Alex Jacobs. He 'took her on' while she was in law school as a law clerk. They went out of town together, and worked a lot of late nights," Kristen said. "She started with the firm, and it's said that she didn't even pass the bar the first time. Yet, the partners allowed her to come in, provided she passed the next time. Well, she did, but barely, from what I hear."

"Maybe she's good in the courtroom," Cameron suggested.

"Does throwing up the first day you're due to be in court sound like someone who's good in the courtroom?"

"You're kidding?" Cameron asked, laughing.

~ 18 ~

"No, I'm not," Kristen chuckled, shaking her head.

At that moment, they were interrupted when their food was brought to the table. After the waiter left, Kristen continued to talk about Caitlyn.

"Caitlyn Frazier has slept her way to the top. She and Alex have been having an affair for the entire time she's been here, and before. I know I'm saying a lot of things that could get me fired," Kristen sighed.

"Look, don't worry. I won't say a word," Cameron smiled. "I just need to know what type of person I'm dealing with here. I'm obviously going to be working quite closely with her in dealing with this case."

"Just be careful. She'll cut you down as quickly as she can, because she hates being threatened."

"Why hasn't anyone been able to work with her on this case?"

"So, you heard about that?"

"I know that I was swindled by Carl, and I understand there were others," Cameron commented.

"There were three other attorneys, and she managed to alienate every last one of them. No one wants to work with her. She's vicious and cut throat. You'd think for someone who got this job by the skin of her nose based on her credentials, that she'd treat people better. But, because she's bedding one of the senior partners, she's confident that she can be such a bitch and get away with it," Kristen said.

"Have you been working for her the whole time she's been here?"

"No," Kristen shook her head. "I've only been working with her for six months. She's had two other secretaries fired. When they couldn't find anyone else who was willing to work with her, they asked me, and I gave it a shot. So far, I'm surviving."

"It'll only get better," Cameron smiled.

"Especially now that you're here," Kristen smiled back.

They continued their lunch talking amicably, with Cameron asking if she was still interested in helping him

~ 19 ~

unpack. She agreed of course, and they made plans for her to come over within a day or two. After leaving the restaurant, they walked back to the building where the firm was located. When he got back to his office, he phoned his mother to see how things were going.

"Hello?" The woman's voice on the other end was welcoming to his ears.

"Hi, Mom," he said, smiling just from simply hearing her voice.

"Cameron! I'm so glad you called. I was starting to worry about you."

"How are things at home?"

"Oh, they're fine. The house seems so empty without you here."

"How's Dad?"

"He's doing pretty good. He went to the doctor today, and the doctor told him that everything seems to be coming along beautifully. He just still has to take it easy. How are you, Son? Are you eating okay? Is the apartment in a good area?"

Cameron smiled at his mom's over protectiveness. "I'm eating fine. The apartment is in a very nice area. I wish you and Dad could come up here. You'd really love the city."

"Oh, Sweetheart, you know we wouldn't know where to fit in up there. Is your phone on yet?"

"No, it won't be on until Wednesday, but you can reach me on my cell phone. I have to have it replaced this evening because it's not holding a charge. That's why I haven't been able to call you from it since I got here."

"I understand, Dear. Have you made any friends?"

"I'm not in elementary school!" he laughed. "But, to answer your question, everyone here is very nice."

"I'm so happy to see you're settling in. You know your father and I are worried about you, being in such a large city all alone."

"Well, don't worry about me. I'm going to be just fine," Cameron reassured his mother once again.

"David called today to ask if I'd heard from you. He

told me that he'd not talked to you since you left."

"Let him know I'll call him as soon as I replace my phone. He and Linda are going to try to come up for a visit in a few weeks after I get settled in."

"Good. I wish you could have had someone like Linda. She's such a sweet girl. Nothing like Grace. I'm just glad the good Lord saw fit to get you out of that situation when He did. Thank goodness you didn't marry her!"

"Didn't we agree not to talk about Grace?"

"I know, Honey, but I just hate the way she hurt you."

"I know you do, but talking about it isn't going to help me get over it any quicker, so if you don't mind, can we please change the subject?"

"Of course, Dear. So, have they piled the work on yet?"

"Actually, yes. I've been assigned a case already."

"Well, that's good, Dear. I knew you'd do well. That firm is lucky to have you. We're really proud of you."

"I know, and I love you for it," Cameron smiled.

"I love you, too, Cameron," Rebecca said.

"So, where's Dad? I'd like to talk to him before we hang up."

"He's asleep, but I'll wake him. I know he'd want to talk to you."

"No, don't wake him. He needs his rest. I'll call him tomorrow."

"Okay, Cameron. Be careful, and don't work too hard!" his mom chided.

"I won't. I love you."

"I love you, too, Dear."

"Give Dad my love, and tell him I'll call him tomorrow."

"I will. Goodbye, Dear."

"Bye, Mom." After hanging up the phone, he looked thoughtfully at it before taking his hand off the receiver. He loved his mother, but he was truly glad to be away from her.

Cameron decided to get his office organized, so he went to the parking deck to get a box of things out of his trunk.

~ 21 ~

He'd brought along a hammer and nails just in case. He was just finishing up when Kristen called into his office to let him know she was leaving for the day, and to make sure he didn't need anything before she left. He wasn't used to someone being so attentive and beautiful. The secretary at the law firm he came from could learn a thing or two from Kristen.

On his way home, he stopped to have his cell phone replaced, which seemed to take all evening. He then stopped to grab a bite to eat, figuring it would be a long night going over things about the Marlow case.

Cameron started to look through the box once he got home while he was eating. While reading about the case, he learned a lot more in-depth information about Mr. Marlow and his wife.

He learned that Garret Marlow had been in love with Victoria in high school, but they'd gone their separate ways, each marrying other people. She'd been in an abusive marriage for two years and Garret was on the brink of divorce when she and Garret ran across each other again. Eventually, they both divorced their respective spouses and remarried each other. It also said that Victoria's first husband, Drake Fordham, was the first person to come to mind, but he had an airtight alibi at the time of the murder. He'd been in jail because of a fight he'd gotten into at a local bar.

The murder took place on Friday night, July 8, 1983, and Victoria was in her 9th month of pregnancy when she was killed. When her body was found, her wrists had been tied to a bedpost of a bed in a local hotel room. Her mouth was gagged. She was cut perfectly; an apparent c-section by someone who was very skilled, and the baby was removed from her womb. She had multiple stab wounds in the chest. Cameron's heart went out to this woman who was so brutally murdered. She'd been found two days after her murder on Sunday, July 10, 1983.

Victoria's husband, Garret had reported her missing after he had not heard from her for several hours. He didn't report her missing until 4:30 a.m. on Saturday, July 9, 1983. Garret stated that when he'd talked to her earlier, he'd known that she was going to be meeting with some of her girlfriends for a baby shower at a restaurant, but apparently, Victoria had left the restaurant by 9 o'clock and never got home. Garret didn't have an alibi, because he'd fallen asleep while watching TV, and didn't awaken until almost 4:30, when he realized his wife still had not gotten home. He called her best friend, Marilyn Fields, when he woke up to see if she knew where Victoria was, but Marilyn had not seen her since 9 o'clock. His mother and mother-in-law both stated the same thing when Garret inquired as to whether they'd seen Victoria. Victoria's mother stated that she'd called the house that night, but had not gotten an answer, so she assumed they were asleep and that Victoria had forgotten to call her after leaving the restaurant.

When Garret called the police, they told him they couldn't look for her until she'd been missing a full 24 hours. Garret stated that he and Victoria's father rode around for hours looking for her, after calling the police. According to the notes, Garret claimed that when he was about to leave to look for his wife, he accidentally touched the hood of his car, and noticed his car was still warm, yet he'd been home for over 10 hours and had not gone anywhere. He didn't think about it until later, because at the time all he could think about was finding his wife. Garret was unable to find his wife or her car after searching for hours. When they got back to Victoria's parents' home, Victoria's mother told him that she still had not heard from Victoria and that she had called all of Victoria's friends to see if they'd heard from her and no one had.

Victoria's body was discovered by housekeeping, who went to clean up the room after the man was due to check out, although the man who rented the room never returned the key. The hotel was only five miles from where Garret and Victoria resided. They also found that the hotel room had been paid for in cash for two nights' stay, by a man who matched Garret's description.

The hotel clerk positively identified Garret as the person who'd rented the room. Garret rented the room at 6 o'clock in the evening, and was alone signing in under an assumed name, George Mason. The hotel clerk stated that he remembered seeing Garret leave his room right after he'd checked in and taken his bag in. The hotel clerk didn't know what kind of car Garret was driving because he'd not seen it. The hotel clerk said he got off duty at 8 o'clock that night, and the next hotel clerk stated that he'd not seen Garret, but he'd been doing a night audit, so he wasn't at the front desk the entire night. Not to mention, the hotel rooms were accessible from the outside.

Several hotel guests testified to seeing Garret's car there around 9:30 that night, and one guest in particular remembered Garret taking off in a hurry around 3:30 a.m. He specifically remembered the time because he'd been in town on a business trip and his wife had called him at 3 a.m. because she was up giving their new baby his 3 a.m. feeding. He'd talked with his wife for about ½ an hour, and told her to hold on when he heard the car screeching off in a hurry. He described Garret's car as being the car to leave. Garret fervently denied ever being at the hotel.

When Garret's neighbors were questioned, they didn't recall whether Garret had been home that night, but one neighbor across the street from the Marlows specifically remembered neither Garret nor Victoria's car being there around 10 p.m. because he'd called Garret to invite him over for a poker game with a few friends, but didn't get an answer at his house. When he looked out to see if Garret's car was there, he didn't see either car. The Marlows had a garage, but they weren't parking in it because they were having some renovations done. He also stated that when his friends left the house, it was about 2 a.m. and neither Garret nor Victoria's car was there yet.

The police began to suspect Garret, and searched his car and house. They found a knife wrapped up in a shirt of Garret's in the trunk of his car, both with blood on them, and $10,000.00 in cash in a bedroom closet. Garret's fingerprints were all over the knife, which didn't come from Garret's house, and the blood type matched his wife's. Garret didn't know how the money got there, and concluded that someone was trying to set him up. It was also found out that Victoria

~ 24 ~

had taken out a very large insurance policy on herself for $250,000.00 in case something happened to her. Garret also had a large policy on himself for $500,000.00, but he was unaware that his wife had taken out a large policy on herself.

Garret was taken into custody, and bail was denied. He spent over two years in jail waiting on his case to go to court, only to lose, getting sentenced to death. Garret had no idea what ever happened to his baby, because they arrested him right after his wife's funeral. His baby's body was never found, and the prosecutor concluded that Garret must have sold the baby, because of the large sum of money found in the house. Garret didn't have an alibi for the night in question. Not to mention they found $10,000.00 in cash plus the murder weapon, and his wife had a large insurance policy on herself. Among other things, Garret's car was not at home during the time of the murder.

After reading for several hours, Cameron had no idea how he was going to clear this man, but he was going to try. Cameron decided to put everything up for the night and get some sleep. He'd been taking notes as he'd been going over evidence. There were pictures of Victoria's body amongst the evidence, and a picture of her taken by Garret when she was alive and pregnant. In the picture taken by Garret, she looked so happy and full of life. She was a beautiful woman, one who didn't deserve this.

Cameron found it hard to sleep that night after looking over the evidence. If there was evidence to support it, Garret could be cleared, but it wouldn't be easy. Worse than that, time wasn't exactly on their side. It wouldn't matter after Garret's execution. Exhaustion soon took over and he finally fell asleep around 3 a.m.

Chapter
2

When Cameron got to work the next morning, he immediately dove back into the Marlow case. The first thing they did was run the witness list through Vital Records to see if anyone came up as deceased. He knew it would take a couple of days to find out. He went over witness lists, and everything he could think of with a fine-tooth comb, to see if he'd missed anything. His first step was to find Garret's first wife. Maybe she could shed light on something that may have been missed. He knew he was grasping at straws, but he had to start some where. He also needed to track down the hotel clerks who'd been on duty that night, as well as the neighbor who lived across from Garret and Victoria. He also wanted to get in touch with the hotel guest who remembered seeing Garret's car leave the hotel that night. Cameron knew that this happened long ago, which meant it would be hard to find them.

Cameron also thought about getting DNA samples from the murder weapon. Maybe a stray hair or something was overlooked. That could possibly place someone else at the murder scene. DNA evidence was not even a factor so many years ago. Given the firm's resources, Phil wanted every available person to work on this case. He'd assigned a complete team of law clerks, paralegals and other clerical help to be at Cameron and Caitlyn's disposal. This was going to be tough, and he didn't think there would be enough time for he and Caitlyn to be prepared with enough evidence, especially with a clemency hearing date already set.

After quite a bit of research, Cameron went to Caitlyn's office after most of the staff had gone. He knocked on her door.

"Come in," Caitlyn said wearily.

"Hey," Cameron said, as he entered.

"What is it?" Caitlyn asked.

"I've been going over some things on the case, and I wanted to talk to you about it," Cameron said.

"Well? What is it?" Caitlyn snapped.

"Are you going to be a bitch throughout this entire case?" he asked, as he closed the door.

"How dare you?"

"Every time I say anything to you, you snap at me. To be honest, I'm sick of it."

"Who cares? You're nothing but a nobody attorney. I almost feel insulted having to work with you. You, on the other hand, should feel honored just to be in the same room with me," Caitlyn said, standing from her chair.

"Oh, yes, Ice Princess, I feel so honored to be in the presence of an attorney who's about as bright as a nightlight!" Cameron said sarcastically.

"What's that supposed to mean!?"

"That you don't deserve to even be at this firm sweeping the floors, let alone be on one of the most important cases in history!"

"Who have you been talking to?" Caitlyn asked, coming around her desk.

"Does it matter? You're the talk of this firm, so it doesn't matter who I talk to. All I get are sympathetic glances and forewarnings about what to expect from you!"

"Well, maybe you'd be better off not working on this

case with me!"

"Oh, no! I wouldn't give you the satisfaction of running me off! You can stomp and pout all you want! You're stuck with me!"

"Of all the arrogance!"

"Arrogance is right! You'll have to learn to live with my being there at every turn! Trust me, you'll be gone way before I will!"

"Is that what you think? Sweetheart, I've been here for five years, and four attorneys have come and gone. I'd never worry about my position, but you on the other hand, should be counting your days. I wouldn't get too used to that office, if I were you!"

"You know, you're right," Cameron sighed, looking around. "This office is larger, and in the corner, so, once you're gone, I'll move in here." Cameron then smiled as he looked at Caitlyn. "Thanks, Ice Princess, you keep digging your ditch a little deeper, and I'll be in your office faster than you can say 'Caitlyn's fired.'"

"You think they'd fire me over you?"

"Bedding someone can only go so far," Cameron laughed. "Sex gets old after a while, even with someone as beautiful as you. And I'm sure his wife would be quite interested in knowing about you. Let's face it, the minute she finds out, you're as good as gone."

Caitlyn laughed slightly. "And just who is it that you think I'm bedding?"

"What difference does it make? Whoever it is, I'm sure you don't have the scruples to at least make sure he's not married. Hell, the more married he is, the better, right?"

"I'm going to let that little remark slide. I'll let you have your digs, because that'll make it all the more pleasurable when you're out on your ass!"

"Tell you what, we'll go over this stuff tomorrow. You need to get home to your lonely bed and power tools to release some of that tension. I'm sure he's busy at home with his wife right now!"

"Get the hell out!" Caitlyn yelled, snatching the door

open.

"There may come a time when you won't want me to leave!" Cameron said, reaching up to caress her cheek lightly. She jerked away forcefully, slapping his hand away. "You have a good night, Ice Princess."

Cameron walked out, as Caitlyn slammed the door behind him. Cameron smiled as he looked at her closed door. He shook his head slightly as he walked away. Cameron then went to his office to gather his things for the evening.

That night after getting home, Cameron went over a lot of information he had on the case. Cameron did research on the DNA possibility. Cameron knew that all he needed was one good break. There had to be something that had been overlooked. He was up going over the case until almost one o'clock in the morning.

****

That Wednesday morning when Cameron woke up, his phone was thankfully on so he decided to call his mother before leaving for work. He knew if he didn't he'd never hear the end of it. He loved his mother, but a part of him felt as if he'd broken out of chains by moving away from home. She was a wonderful mother, but she wanted desperately to keep Cameron as a little boy, never wanting to let him grow up. If it weren't for his father, he would have been nothing short of a 'Mama's Boy,' but Evan Spencer taught him how to be a man.

"Hello?" Becky's voice boomed. Cameron marveled at how his mom seemed so cheerful so early in the morning. Cameron wryly thought to himself that she'd probably not had a drop of coffee.

"Hi, Ma," Cameron smiled.

"Hi, Cameron! I'm so glad you called! How are you?"

"I'm fine. My phone's finally on this morning. How are things at home?"

"They're okay. Your dad's up. Would you like to speak with him?"

"Yes ma'am, I would."

~ 29 ~

"Hello?" Cameron's dad sounded tired.

"Hi, Dad. How are you feeling?"

"I'm fine, son. Especially now since hearing from you. Mom told me you called the other day. She told me you were going to call yesterday, but when you didn't we figured you must have been busy. I hear you've been assigned a case already."

"Yeah, I have. It's a murder case. I can't really talk about it now, but it could mean a lot to my career."

"Well, Son, I know you'll do your best. How's everything else up there?"

"Everything's good. Look, I'll be coming home for the weekend in a few weeks. When do you go back to the doctor?" Cameron asked.

"Oh, in another week or so," Evan said. "Dr. Kirklin said I'm healing up just fine. I should be able to start driving again soon."

"That's great. I'm glad you're doing better," Cameron smiled. "Well, I really need to get going. Can I speak back to Ma?"

"Okay, Son. I love you," Evan said.

"I love you too, Dad," Cameron said.

"Hello?" Cameron heard his mom's voice.

"Mom, I just wanted to say 'bye' and that I'll see you in a month."

"Okay, Cameron. I can't wait. You make sure you're eating right, and don't stay up too late. You need to get enough rest. And try to eat breakfast in the morning. I know you won't eat right if I'm not there to fix it for you."

"I hear you. Look, I've really got to go. I love you."

"I love you too, Honey. Take care of yourself."

"I will. Bye, Ma."

Cameron hung up the phone and looked at the clock. He really needed to get going. He still wasn't quite used to the traffic in downtown Kerrigan. Cameron lived in Sheridan Falls, an area located on the outskirts of Kerrigan. He lived 15 minutes away from where his office was located, which wasn't very far. But considering rush hour traffic, a 15-minute drive could easily turn into 45 minutes.

When Cameron checked with Kristen about Caitlyn's whereabouts, Kristen told him that she wouldn't be in until 10 a.m. He instructed Kristen to let him know when she got in. When she arrived, he went to her office so that they could prepare for their meeting with Mr. Marlow. They were due to meet with him that afternoon. The information from Department of Vital Records had come back. Only two of their witnesses were deceased. That meant the rest of them were out there somewhere. When he walked into her office without knocking, she of course, was livid. He was getting just the response he hoped to from her.

"Don't you know how to knock?" Caitlyn snapped, looking up from a file she was reading.

"Well, good morning to you, too, Ice Princess," Cameron smiled.

"I don't have time for this, Mr. Spencer," Caitlyn sighed.

"Caitlyn, you seem nervous," Cameron said in a taunting tone, as he sat in a chair in her office.

"Nervous about what? I'm not the one who should be nervous; you, however, have reason to be."

"Let's call a truce long enough to get through our meeting with Mr. Marlow," Cameron suggested.

"Whatever," Caitlyn shrugged.

"Let's get started, shall we?"

"Fine. What did you find?"

"Well, I've been thinking about the possibility of DNA samples being taken from the murder weapon."

"How? The only DNA on the knife would be Victoria's blood."

"If the evidence hasn't been compromised, there could be stray hairs on the knife; anything to link someone else to the murder."

"That's really stretching it. You're saying on the off chance that a stray hair from the murderer ended up on the knife, we could try to find out who the real murderer is?"

"Exactly."

"DNA wasn't explored years ago as much as it is today," Caitlyn sighed, almost in agreement.

"Wow, you're in agreement with me?" Cameron asked in a surprised tone.

"Don't get too happy. It won't happen often. I still say you're not good enough to defend my dog in court." She was interrupted by Kristen calling into her office. Caitlyn turned and sighed heavily answering the phone. "What is it?" she asked in an annoying tone. "Oh yes, send them in."

"Send who in?" Cameron asked as she hung up the phone.

"Mr. Marlow's parents."

"I didn't realize his parents were still living," Cameron said.

"Yeah, and they've been quite dedicated. We'd scheduled this meeting last week," Caitlyn commented.

Cameron and Caitlyn met with Mr. and Mrs. Marlow for close to an hour bringing them up to date. From Mrs. Marlow's statements, she had her suspicions about Rachel, Garret's first wife and how she befriended Victoria.

Later, Cameron and Caitlyn drove to the firm's plane which took them to visit with Garret at the Indiana State Prison. It was a medium security prison, where all male death row inmates were kept. They were told to wait in a small room where they could consult with Garret. When Garret was brought in, he was wearing a bright orange prison uniform. He was in his early 50's but, stress and worry made him look a lot older. He was an attractive man who'd obviously been through a lot in his life. He seemed very pleasant, despite his circumstances.

"Hello, Ms. Frazier," Garret said.

"Mr. Marlow, this is my colleague, Cameron Spencer, who will be serving as co-counsel on your case," Caitlyn stated.

"Mr. Spencer," Garret smiled, and shook his hand.

"Hello, Mr. Marlow," Cameron said. "Sir, we wanted to consult with you about your case. As you are aware, your execution date has been set for July 28th, with an automatic

~ 32 ~

clemency hearing scheduled for Wednesday, July 7th," Cameron stated. "As you know, you are entitled to a clemency hearing three weeks before execution as a last attempt to offer any evidence crucial to your case. Now, there are four things that could happen at your clemency hearing. Number one, a complete pardon, which would offer complete absolution for the crime. Number two, a reprieve, which would offer temporary suspension of the punishment, which basically would give us a little more time to get to the truth. The third possibility is commutation, which could decrease the sentencing from death to life imprisonment. The fourth possibility would be complete denial, and you will be put to death by lethal injection."

"Well, I'm glad you're well informed about the legalities of a clemency hearing," Mr. Marlow smiled. "But, so am I."

"I apologize, Sir. I forgot that you used to be an attorney," Cameron said.

"Forgive my overly zealous colleague. He's still pretty new at this," Caitlyn chimed in.

Cameron fumed at how she took the opportunity to take yet another dig at him.

"No apologies necessary. He was just doing his job," Garret smiled.

"Mr. Marlow, is there anything you can recall from the night your wife was murdered?" Cameron asked.

"I don't know. I've replayed that night over and over and over again in my head. I know that I was set up, and I've lost over 25 years of my life because of this monster, and more importantly than that, my wife lost her life, and I have no idea whether my child lived or died. I don't know if I had a daughter or a son," Mr. Marlow stated. There were tears in his eyes as he spoke.

"Is there anyone who you know who'd hate you and your wife to this extent?" Caitlyn asked.

"I don't know. We never made enemies. I can't see anyone not liking Victoria; she was a wonderful woman. She was smart, beautiful, considerate. Everything I could hope

~ 33 ~

for," Garret stated.

"Mr. Marlow, I understand you were married before you and Victoria were married," Caitlyn stated. "What can you tell me about your first wife?"

"Rachel? She had a lot of problems," Mr. Marlow shook his head, thinking of his first wife. "She and I couldn't make it work after she found out she couldn't have children. It took its toll on our marriage, and we just decided to split up. She was understandably upset after I married Victoria, but she seemed to get over it quickly. She and I became good friends. She even offered to help with Victoria's baby shower."

"Have you ever been suspicious of your ex-wife's motives?" Caitlyn asked.

"Honestly, it crossed my mind at first, but I quickly dismissed the idea. Rachel had her problems, but she's not a killer. Even after what happened between us."

"You mean your divorce?" Caitlyn asked.

"No, I mean that Rachel came to me and tried to get me to leave Victoria on the night of my wife's baby shower," Garret commented. "She showed up out of nowhere, and I let her in, commenting that I thought she would be at the baby shower. She told me that she wanted for the two of us to talk about us, and how she was so much better suited for me than Victoria. It erupted into a small argument when I told her that I loved Victoria and I thought she understood that. She kept commenting that I wouldn't want Victoria when I realized how much weight she gained after the baby was born. At that point, I asked her to leave and never mention that conversation again. She then apologized, saying that she didn't mean anything by it, and she was just reminiscing because it was so close to what would have been our anniversary. She said she'd probably be leaving town soon, because she'd been traveling back and forth on a job she'd been working. She told me that it had taken its toll on her, and she needed to get on with her life. I didn't even realize she'd been working out of town until she said it that night. I remember that night that I was really out of it, almost groggy during the time when she was there."

~ 34 ~

"Did you happen to have anything to drink or eat in her presence?" Cameron asked.

"I had a beer, but that was it."

"Had you had too much to drink?" Caitlyn asked.

"No. I'd only had one before that," Garret stated. "Why do you ask?"

"Is it possible that Rachel might have drugged you?" Caitlyn asked.

Garret looked thoughtful for a few moments. "I never really thought about it."

"Did you see your ex-wife out?" Cameron asked.

"Come to think of it, no, I didn't," Garret said surprisingly. "The last thing I remember about Rachel being there was when she massaged my neck. I'd given her a glass of wine, because she said she wanted to toast our friendship. I went into the kitchen to get a glass of wine for her."

"Was she left alone with your beer?" Cameron asked.

"Yeah, she was. I was only gone for a minute though," Garret reasoned.

"It doesn't take long to slip something into someone's drink," Caitlyn argued.

"What happened next, Mr. Marlow?" Cameron asked.

"She handed me my beer when I got back into the den, and I gave her the glass of wine. She and I toasted, she sipped her wine, and I sipped my beer."

"And then what?" Cameron asked.

"Shortly afterwards, I started feeling really sluggish. I vaguely remember sitting down, and she offered to massage my neck like she did when we married," Garret stated.

"Then, I remember waking up in the den at a little after 4 a.m. with the TV still on. I got up to go into my bedroom, thinking that Victoria was there. She wasn't, and our bed had not been slept in. That's when I panicked and noticed that her car wasn't there. I immediately started calling around trying to find her."

"Where is your ex-wife now?" Cameron asked.

"I'm not sure. She came to visit me the first couple of months I was in jail. One day she came by in tears and told

~ 35 ~

me that she couldn't stand seeing me this way, and that she wanted me to forgive her if she never came to see me again. I told her I understood. She's written me a few letters since then, but she hasn't been back to visit."

"Do you still have the letters she's written you?" Caitlyn asked.

"Yes, I still have them. When you're in prison, especially on death row, you have very little to look forward to. So, letters are like a lifeline to the outside world."

"Can we see them?" Caitlyn asked.

"Sure. Guard, I need to go back to my cell to get something," Garret said to the guard.

When Garret left the room, Cameron looked at Caitlyn. "Well, what do you think?"

"I think it's a little strange that his ex-wife would befriend his current wife, when she's about to have a baby. That's a little odd. Remember? Even Mr. Marlow's mother wondered about it. I'm not saying it's impossible for the ex-wife and the current wife to tolerate each other, especially if there are children from the previous marriage. But, this wasn't the case. It's just a little strange for her to befriend the current wife so well. It just doesn't fit," Caitlyn said, shaking her head. "I get the feeling that if we find Rachel Marlow, we'll find Victoria Marlow's murderer," Caitlyn said. "I just don't understand why this wasn't explored years ago. I mean, the man felt groggy. The possibility was never explored that he'd been drugged."

"I agree. But, think about it: the DA wanted a conviction. He wasn't going to look at everything. I just can't believe Phil never looked into it. I wonder if he ever told Phil any of this?" Cameron stated.

"That's a good question. We do need to find out if Phil knew about Rachel's visit. But, now, to know that he was passed out before she even left? That gave her opportunity to put his prints all over the murder weapon."

Garret came back shortly after that. He gave the letters to Caitlyn.

"There's nothing really personal in any of them,"

Garret said. "The letters all came from a P.O. Box, so it may be a little difficult to trace them. The last letter I got from her was one I received over 25 years ago, back in 1984, about six or seven months after my arrest. We wrote each other once a week. To be honest, I'm not even sure if Rachel is still alive or not. After I was sentenced, I wrote to her at the address on the letters to tell her where I was serving my time. I never got a response from her, so I have no idea whether she received it or not."

"Are her parents still living?" Cameron asked.

"No, her parents both died years ago."

"Did she have any sisters or brothers?" Caitlyn asked.

"She had a brother, but I'm not sure if he's still living or not. His name is Roland Lyle, which is also Rachel's maiden name. Last I remember, he lived in Ohio, but I'm not sure where in Ohio. Like I said, it's been a long time ago."

"These letters are postmarked from Ohio," Cameron noticed.

"Yeah, I'm assuming that's where her job was from out of town. It makes perfect sense, considering that's where her brother was," Garret said.

"Maybe he's aware of her whereabouts," Caitlyn stated.

"Maybe, but, I've pretty much given up a great deal of hope of ever getting out. I've been here, in Indiana State Prison since January 20, 1986. That's the day I was convicted. Before then, I'd already served over two years in Cates County Jail because I was denied bail. I've missed thousands of days of my life that I'll never get back, each day knowing I'm that much closer to being put to death. That's a miserable feeling to sit day after day and wonder how it is that something like this happens to you when you know you never did anything wrong. I've lost everything, and I wonder sometimes if I'll ever be able to get my life together even if I do get out of here. It's not as if I can just pick up and start practicing law again."

"You never know, Mr. Marlow," Cameron said.

"Mr. Marlow, did Phil know about Rachel's visit the night of Victoria's baby shower?" Caitlyn asked.

~ 37 ~

Garret thought seriously, then shook his head slightly. "No, I never told him."

"Was there a reason you didn't tell him?" Cameron asked.

"Honestly, I never thought about the possibility of being drugged," Garret said, looking earnestly at Cameron. "I mean, I was a new attorney, and I was tired from working all day, I'd never had reason to believe Rachel would do something like that. I know I said the thought crossed my mind briefly, but, it just doesn't seem like something she'd do."

"Well, we're going to look into every possibility," Caitlyn said.

"Mr. Marlow, we're going to go, and one of us will be back in a few days to let you know what we've come up with," Cameron said.

Afterwards, Cameron and Caitlyn gathered their things and left, heading for the airport to catch the firm's plane back to Kerrigan. They were silent until Caitlyn had been driving for a few minutes.

"You know, Ice Princess, if Mr. Marlow's ex-wife is behind any of this, she's probably pretty relaxed by now that she'll never be caught," Cameron stated.

"Would you stop calling me that?"

"Sure, Ice Princess," Cameron smiled.

Caitlyn sighed. "You're hopeless. I'm not going to argue with you about it. But, you have a point about the first Mrs. Marlow. After 27 years, she's sure she's gotten away with it. Although, I hope we're not about to go blindly looking for the wrong person because time isn't exactly on our side. For once, there is something we both agree on."

"Well, I'm honored, Ice Princess. Mr. Marlow seems a little on the fence about the possibility that his ex-wife wouldn't do something like that. Remember? He said the thought crossed his mind briefly," Cameron reasoned.

"Yeah, I'm sure that he thought about the fact that jealousy can make people do a lot of things they may not do under normal circumstances. Think about it: Victoria Marlow was beautiful, loving, smart, and about to give Mr. Marlow the one thing Rachel Marlow couldn't: a child," Caitlyn stated.

"You have a point. When we get back to the office, I'm going to check with Jackson to see if he came up with anything else since we left."

Cameron and Caitlyn got back to the office just as most of the support staff was leaving. When Cameron checked in Jackson's department, he was still there, working on his computer.

"Have you come up with anything else?" Cameron asked him.

"Not really. I keep running into stumbling blocks. I've called the hotel where Mrs. Marlow was murdered, and they were very reluctant to even tell me anything. Said it took years to recover from the scandal behind her murder taking place in their hotel. But, I haven't given up on them," he commented.

"You'd better not. After all, your job depends upon this, Jackson," Caitlyn commented. She then looked at Cameron. "I'm going back to my office before I leave for the day. If the two of you do what you're supposed to, I might win this case. Goodnight." Caitlyn then walked out.

"Bitch," Jackson said, looking after her. He then looked at Cameron and shook his head. "Man, I pity you."

Cameron smiled as he watched Caitlyn walk down the hall. "Nah. I have special plans for Miss Frazier."

"What do you mean?" Jackson asked, smiling.

"Let's just say that our little ice princess will get more than she bargained for with me," Cameron smiled looking at Jackson.

"Man, you aren't important enough to get her into bed," Jackson laughed.

"You underestimate me."

"Would you care to put money on it?" Jackson asked.

"Name your price, but make it light on yourself," Cameron smiled.

"$100.00?" Jackson wagered.

"Come on, is that all you've got?" Cameron goaded.

~ 39 ~

"Well, I'm not a high-paid attorney like you. I'm just a little humble paralegal," Jackson shrugged.

"I suppose I shouldn't take too much of your money," Cameron said.

"Oh, I don't think I'll lose, but I never wager more than I can pay out of pocket right now," Jackson said.

"Fair enough. Any specific rules?" Cameron asked.

"You have exactly two weeks from today to get her in bed," Jackson smiled.

"You're giving me about thirteen days too many," Cameron smiled.

"That confident, huh?"

"Caitlyn's wound up like a mattress spring. She just needs someone to lay it down right to her," Cameron said.

"And you think you can do that in a day?"

"Yeah, I can," Cameron said. "But, we'll wager a couple of weeks." Cameron then held his hand out to shake Jackson's.

The two men then agreed to the bet, both smiling.

"Good luck, because you're going to need it. I suppose I can go ahead and make reservations at that expensive French restaurant for my girlfriend and me in a couple of weeks thanks to your upcoming financial contribution after I win our bet."

"The only French food you'll be eating is French fries after I take your money," Cameron laughed.

"We'll see."

"I'll see you tomorrow," Cameron smiled, walking out.

"See you then," Jackson said.

When Cameron walked towards his office, he smiled as he saw Kristen bending over to pick something up off the floor. Her tight skirt really hugged her. He gave her a long, satisfying glance. She looked around and smiled as she noticed him looking at her.

"See something interesting?" Kristen asked flirtatiously.

"Oh, just admiring the view," Cameron smiled, undressing her with his eyes.

"I hope the view is worth your admiration," Kristen said, walking towards him.

"Oh, it is, it is," Cameron said quickly. "So, uh, you still want to come by tonight to help me unpack?"

"Sure," Kristen smiled. "How about 7:30?"

"7:30 sounds good."

"Well, I need to go home to change. What's your address?"

"704 Sheridan Drive."

"Got it," Kristen said, jotting it down on a note pad. "That's only about two minutes from my apartment."

"Oh? Where do you stay?"

"Woodmere Manor."

"Oh, yeah. I pass by your complex everyday on my way to work and back home."

"How convenient," Kristen smiled. "Maybe we could carpool?"

"Maybe so. I'll see you later tonight," Cameron said, backing away from her desk, to his office.

"Tonight it is," Kristen smiled.

Cameron then went into his office, gathered his things and left. He got home, showered and changed before Kristen's arrival. He searched one of his boxes of belongings for something he felt could come in handy later on if things went as planned. He smiled as he looked at the box of condoms before placing them on his bedside table. Kristen arrived at his apartment promptly at 7:30. When she came in, she joked with Cameron about having a lot of boxes for someone who came with very little. Cameron explained to her that he collected model cars, and that he boxed them individually.

Cameron had a fairly large apartment for a single guy. He had two bedrooms, one of which was going to serve as his office. He figured he could have everything set up so that he could work at home a lot of nights. He'd purchased a fax machine which was set up on a separate phone line, and his computer was set up as well. His father had purchased a desk and chair for him, and it had been delivered earlier that day thanks to the apartment manager letting them in. The apartment came with a washer and dryer, for which Cameron was thankful.

They managed to get a lot of Cameron's things unpacked and put away, and then they ordered a pizza around 9 o'clock. By the time four hours had passed, they had the kitchen, living area, dining area, closets, bedroom and bathroom completely organized. His furniture was sparse, but they were still able to make the apartment look like home. Kristen suggested a few pictures on the walls, and she told him she'd go with him when he went to get living room furniture. She knew of a great place that sold good quality furniture at a reasonable price.

"Well, I guess I'd better be going. I've enjoyed tonight," Kristen said, noticing it was almost midnight.

"I'm glad you could come by to help. You've really got a decorator's eye. Maybe next time you come by it won't be as strenuous as it was this time, unless you want it to be," Cameron smiled.

"Meaning?" Kristen smiled.

"Oh, I think you know," Cameron laughed. He reached up to stroke her hair lightly. He leaned in slowly and kissed her.

She responded to his kiss, as if she'd been waiting on it all night. Cameron pulled Kristen closer to him, as their kiss grew more passionate. He felt himself swelling with desire for this woman. He'd not been with anyone in over a month, and he felt as if he was going to explode. Kristen was a beautiful woman. After a few moments, he lifted her into his arms and carried her to his bedroom. He quickly laid her on the bed, as he pulled forcibly on her shirt to quickly unbutton it. He noticed the black, lacy bra she was wearing, and how her breasts seemed to bulge out slightly, as if they were just waiting to be released. He found himself desperately wanting to enter her. He reached around and undid her bra. As he exposed her breasts, he gave her a satisfying glance as he roughly grabbed them with his hands. He buried his face between her breasts, quickly turning to take the right one into his mouth. As his hands caressed her body, he felt her

~ 42 ~

unzipping his pants and stroking his swollen manhood. He reached over to the bedside table for a condom. She stopped what she was doing when she noticed his pulling one from the box.

"What are you doing?" Kristen asked.

"What do you think?"

"I'm on the pill," Kristen said.

"That still won't stop me from using a condom. You should be glad," Cameron whispered. "It's to protect both of us."

"I-I don't like condoms," Kristen said, caressing his chest.

"I do," Cameron smiled.

"Maybe you could just pull out?" Kristen suggested.

"That's not my style," Cameron shook his head.

"Don't you trust me?"

"We just met a few days ago. I trust you, but I won't sleep with you without protection. I don't want any children right now."

"Well fine," Kristen said, sitting up. She reached to the foot of the bed and retrieved her bra.

"Where are you going?" Cameron asked.

"Home. I won't be with a man who doesn't trust me," Kristen said.

"Oh, come on. You don't have to leave," Cameron said, pulling her back towards him. "It's nothing personal. I just don't believe in unprotected sex," he soothed.

"You think I sleep around?" Kristen asked, looking at him accusingly.

"It's not that. It's just the way I was raised." Cameron then leaned in to kiss her on her neck. "Don't let this ruin our night."

"How do I sleep with someone who doesn't trust me?" Kristen whispered, clearly being drawn in by his seduction.

"Come on, let's get to know each other better before we start talking about unprotected sex. You want me, I know you do," Cameron whispered, as he reached up to cup her breasts.

He slightly turned her face towards him and kissed her. She responded to his kiss as he slowly pulled her back down on the bed. He quickly removed his pants as she removed her underwear. He immediately slipped on a condom, ready to enter her. As their passion grew more and more with every heated touch and kiss, he finally penetrated her.

"Oh, Cameron!" Kristen moaned.

"Oh, yes!" Cameron yelled passionately.

Their bodies were in perfect rhythmic motion as she called out his name. As his body moved against hers, he realized how much he missed the softness of a woman's body. He looked down at her as he moved in and out of her. Her eyes were closed as she licked her lips. She lifted her head to kiss his naked chest, and with one smooth motion, Cameron turned on his back as she straddled him. He never once pulled out of her. He was impressed at how she never broke stride, now riding him. He watched as her body moved up and down on him. Cameron withstood as much as he could, wanting the two of them to climax together. After many minutes of motion, he watched her as she climaxed first.

"Oh! You feel so good!" Cameron yelled, as he couldn't hold out any longer.

After several more minutes, he climaxed as well.

Kristen collapsed on his chest, with the both of them breathing hard. Both of their hearts were beating fast. He smiled as he placed his arms around her.

"Wow!" Kristen sighed quietly. "That was beautiful," she smiled, looking up at him.

"Did you think it wouldn't be?" Cameron smiled as he stroked her shoulder.

"The moment I met you I figured it would be great," Kristen said.

"Let's just keep this between us, okay?" Cameron suggested.

"Hey, I'm not one to kiss and tell," Kristen smiled.

"Good, because neither am I," Cameron said, as he moved her aside to get up.

She watched as his naked, well toned body walked into

the bathroom. He then turned the light on and closed the door. He removed his condom and flushed it down the toilet. He smiled as he looked in the mirror. Kristen would be a wonderful convenience. No commitment; just sex. As long as she didn't tell anyone at the firm, there wouldn't be any problem. He knew he'd never get serious with her. He got the feeling that Kristen had been around a few times. She was a beautiful woman; there was no disputing that. She just wasn't relationship material. Not that he was looking. He simply wanted a few good times. That's the way it had been since he and Grace split. He'd been with several others since that fateful night in February when she returned his ring. But, after his dad's fall, he'd been preoccupied with his father's health. Now that he'd started his new job and his dad was fine, he was ready to swing back into action. Kristen was the perfect jumpstart.

He left out of the bathroom and went back to the bed. Kristen had gotten under the covers and fallen asleep. He looked at her and shook his head as he sighed. He wanted for her to leave, but he figured just in case he got the urge in the middle of the night, she'd already be there. With that thought, he climbed into the bed next to her. She moved closer to him when she felt his naked body against hers. He put his arms around her as he felt the softness of her against his manhood. A few minutes later, he drifted off to sleep.

Chapter
3

The next morning, Cameron woke up and noticed that Kristen wasn't there. He looked around and realized that he heard the shower running. He smiled as he thought about the fact that he'd awakened again at 3:30 a.m. and she was eager to please him with another round of hot sex. He looked at his clock and noticed it was almost 7 a.m. He got up and slipped on a pair of boxers and went into the kitchen to start a pot of coffee. As he walked down the hall, he could smell the aroma of a freshly brewed pot. There was also bacon and eggs as well as toast. He poured himself a cup of the satisfying brew. He heard the water stop right after he looked outside of his door for the newspaper. He looked around as Kristen came out smiling wrapped in a towel.

"Well, good morning, Sleepy Head," Kristen smiled, as she walked seductively up to him to give him a long, passionate kiss.

"What a greeting," Cameron smiled as their lips parted. "So, you did all this?"

"I'd do anything for you," Kristen said.

With those words, Cameron backed away uncomfortably and sipped his coffee. He opened his newspaper to read the headlines. She watched him expectedly as he looked at her and smiled.

"I'm nothing without my morning coffee," Cameron explained, holding up his cup as he sat down in a chair.

"Oh," Kristen said. "I thought it was something I said."

"I just don't want this thing going too fast. Breakfast was sweet, but it really wasn't necessary."

"Well, it was just a gesture. I've not had sex that good in a long time. I figured the least you deserved was breakfast."

"But, you came over and helped me get organized. That was enough of a gesture for anything."

"I feel a bit strange standing here in a towel. Do you have a shirt I can borrow?"

"Sure," Cameron said, standing from his chair.

He went into his bedroom with her following closely behind and retrieved a shirt from a drawer. Kristen reached out for it, purposely letting her towel drop to the floor.

"Oops," Kristen giggled. "I suppose my hands are still wet."

"Is that what it is?" Cameron smiled, as he eyes roved her naked form.

He moved closer to her and reached behind her back, stroking the length of it. He then leaned down to kiss her. As he felt her naked body against his, he remembered the wild night she'd given him and longed to enter her again. He felt himself swelling once again just as he had a few short hours ago. She reached down and slipped his boxers off of him, claiming with her hand the manhood that was inside her a few hours before. As their lips parted, she stroked his neck with her tongue, raining kisses down his chest. He lifted her into his arms and carried her to the bed. This time, he didn't waste a moment before putting on another condom and entering her. He watched as her head went back with every stroke. He leaned down to passionately bite her neck as she cried out

~ 47 ~

passionately. Once again, they found themselves lost in their heated episode. After almost an hour, they both collapsed, exhausted.

"At this rate, we'll never get to work," Kristen said, snuggling close to him.

"You're right," Cameron said, moving away from her and getting out of bed. "I really need to take a shower."

"I suppose I should go. I still need to go home and get ready for work," Kristen said quietly.

"Yeah, maybe you should," Cameron said. "I'll see you at the office," he said in a monotonous tone. With that statement, he went into the bathroom to take his shower.

Cameron let the water wash away his senses for a brief moment. He thought about the fact that Kristen had fixed breakfast for him. She was a nice girl, but he didn't want her thinking there could be more than just the physical thing between them. There was nowhere else for them to go. He had nothing to look forward to with her. They'd known each other all of three days, and already they'd slept together. His father always taught him to know the difference between a one-night stand, a friendship with benefits, and the real thing. He smiled as he thought that Kristen would probably be a friendship with benefits. The bet he had with Jackson would strictly be a one-night stand, if he could get a hard-on with Caitlyn. Of course, he couldn't take anything away from Caitlyn's looks. She was a beautiful woman; but she was also a viper. Cameron always found it hard to be attracted to such a bitch. But, to stroke his ego more so than win the money, he'd sleep with her.

He then stepped out of the shower and into his bedroom with a towel around his waist. He noticed that Kristen was gone. He shrugged his shoulders. He was not about to get sentimental with her, because she would start to expect more. He looked at the clock on his bedside table and noticed that it was almost 8:30. That was the good thing about not having set hours. He got dressed and left out. He noticed the sun was shining brightly, so he pulled out his sunglasses and let the top down on his convertible. He rode past Kristen's apartment complex and smiled at his luck. She was almost too convenient. He kept going, and as he pulled up at a traffic light, he stopped right next to a beautiful woman who obviously had the same idea as he. She had the top down and her sunglasses on. He looked at her and she looked at him and smiled. When the light changed, she took off, waving at him. She had a vanity plate that said "AVAILBL."

"We'll see how 'available' she is," Cameron smiled, as he went after her. They ended up once again at another traffic light. "So, how available are you?" Cameron yelled.

"How ever much you want me to be," she smiled, as she drove off, making a right turn.

Cameron smiled as he continued straight ahead towards his office building, figuring he'd see her again at some point. He thought he recognized the car from one in his complex, which should make finding her easy. He pulled into the deck and parked. He got out and went into the building, immediately getting into 'attorney mode.' He walked by Kristen's desk and noticed she was there already. She smiled when she saw him.

"Good morning, Kristen," he said dryly.

"Good morning, Mr. Spencer," Kristen said, as her smile faded.

"You know, it's okay to call me Cameron," he said, in a businesslike tone.

"Yes, Sir," she said.

He went into his office and sat his briefcase on top of his desk. He sat in his chair and sighed. He pulled out the list of people that he and Caitlyn needed to see. He then went down the hall to her office. As he walked by Kristen's desk, he could feel her staring at him. He continued on his journey to Caitlyn's office. He knocked briefly, and then entered.

"Good morning, Ice Princess," he smiled, closing the door behind him.

"What, am I supposed to be grateful for that half-assed knock? I want for you to knock, wait for a response from me, and then follow my instruction from that point on, even if I tell you to trot back down to that broom closet you call an office.

~ 49 ~

Are we clear, Mr. Spencer?"

"Still didn't get laid last night either, huh?" Cameron smiled.

"Is there a reason you're here?" Caitlyn sighed.

"The list," Cameron said, holding it up as he sat in a chair. "We have a lot to do."

"You don't make the rules; I do. Now, I've already divided the list. You will see these people, I'll see the rest."

"Gee, Ice Princess, I suppose great minds think alike," Cameron said.

"Please," Caitlyn scoffed. "Comparing our minds is like comparing a genius to a retard."

"Oh, don't call yourself a retard," Cameron taunted calmly, looking at her. "That's such an insult to them."

"Take your list, and get the hell out of my office!"

"Such language! Please, Ice Princess, calm down. Tell you what." Cameron reached onto her desk and got a notepad. He wrote his phone number on it. "Here's my number, and when you're ready to work off some of that tension and frustration, why don't you give me a call?"

"I wouldn't call you if you were the last man on earth!" Caitlyn shot back.

"Well, since I'm not the last man on earth it means there's a safe bet you'll be calling me, huh?" Cameron laughed, as he tossed the notepad on her desk.

"Get out!" Caitlyn yelled.

"We'll compare notes later, Ice Princess." Cameron then stood and walked out of her office smiling.

He smiled and shook his head as he thought of how much he enjoyed rattling her. She was such an easy target. He looked at his list and decided to start with the neighbors in the community where Garret and Victoria used to live. Caitlyn was going to start with the people at the hotel.

He wasn't too familiar with the areas in the state yet, but he knew that the area where Garret and Victoria lived was a half hour's drive. His GPS would come in handy today. Stonehill Manor was an impressive community. It was an upper middle class suburb on the outskirts of Drennan City. It seemed to be perfect for raising children. There was a sign made of brick with gold lettering leading to the entrance. There were trees and beautiful landscapes. The roads were wide and clean. He knew that Garret and Victoria lived at 428 Wornash Circle, which was a cul-de-sac. When he found the street he was looking for, there were about 14 houses. Surely, someone must still live there that was there during the time of the murder.

"Where do I start?" Cameron asked himself.

He found the house that used to belong to Garret and Victoria. It was a beautiful 2-story home with a 2-car garage on the basement level. It was dark brick with columns in front. There was landscape lighting leading from the front porch down the sidewalk to the driveway. There was a 'for sale' sign in the front yard. This was a home, a home where Garret and Victoria should have been allowed to happily raise their child.

For reasons Cameron could not explain, his curiosity got the better of him, and he wanted to look around back. He pulled into the driveway, and noticed the gate leading to the back yard. There was a swing in back for a child, and another sitting swing. The covered deck stretched across the entire back of the house meeting up with what looked like a sunroom. The deck was large enough to have a grill, and three different sitting areas; one with a table and four chairs, another sitting area with a coffee table, and another area with a lounger and a glider. There was landscape lighting around a beautiful water garden that rested right outside of the sunroom.

Cameron wasn't sure why he wanted to see their home; he just felt he needed to see more than just what was on paper and pictures. This home gave him a sense of who Garret and Victoria Marlow were. Hearing the mailman brought Cameron back to reality. He remembered that he was a stranger, and the current owners of this house wouldn't appreciate his snooping around, even if the house is for sale.

"Thinking about buying it?" A voice from behind Cameron startled him. It was a woman in her late 30's to early 40's. She stood there with a gardening hat and gloves on talking to Cameron from the other side of the fence that went along the side of the driveway.

"Excuse me?" Cameron said.

"The house. I asked if you're thinking about buying it," the lady said.

"No, just looking around." Cameron walked over to the fence. "I'm Cameron Spencer." Cameron held his hand out to shake hers.

"Oh, one second," the woman said, removing her glove. She shook Cameron's hand and smiled. "I'm Amanda Warren. Were you looking for something or someone specifically?"

"Well, actually, I'm looking for someone who's been living in the area for at least 26 to 27 years," Cameron said.

"I beg your pardon?" Amanda said.

"I apologize if I'm being a little vague. I'm an attorney with Larson, Craig and Jacobs Law Firm in Kerrigan." Cameron pulled out a business card that had thankfully been sent to him a couple of weeks before. He handed the card to Amanda. She studied it.

"I've heard of the firm. What are you doing here, though?"

"I'm an attorney who's working for Garret Marlow." Cameron could tell by the woman's reaction that she was familiar with the case.

"Garret Marlow?" Amanda looked shaken.

"Are you familiar with what I'm talking about?"

"Yes, I know exactly what you're talking about. Mr. Marlow was accused of killing his wife."

"Were you living in the area at the time?"

"Yeah, I was," Amanda said.

"Is there anything you know about the night of the murder?"

Amanda looked thoughtful for a moment. "Mr. Spencer, would you like to come inside so we can talk privately?"

"Sure," Cameron said. Cameron moved his car over to Ms. Warren's driveway. When he walked into Ms. Warren's house, she led him to the living room.

"Have a seat. Can I get you anything to drink?" Ms. Warren asked.

"No, thank you, Ms. Warren," Cameron said, pulling out his notepad.

"Please, call me Amanda. I know you're wondering what kind of information I could possibly offer you about your client's case."

"Yes, that has crossed my mind. How well did you know the Marlows?" Cameron pulled out his tape recorder. "I'd like to record this if you don't mind."

"No, of course not. I knew them very well. I was 15 at the time of the murder. At that time, my parents lived here. They moved into a retirement home five years ago and left the house for me, my husband and our children."

"You said you knew them well."

"Yes. Mrs. Marlow was an angel," Amanda smiled. "She was so pretty and I'd never seen anyone happier about the prospect of becoming a mother. She'd even asked me about babysitting for her once the baby arrived."

"She must have really thought a lot of you."

"Yeah, she did. I could talk to her when I couldn't talk to my own parents," Amanda looked thoughtful. "My parents were very strict, but the Marlows were a young couple, who could relate to me. Mr. Marlow was great, too. He and I used to play ping pong in their basement, along with my boyfriend. He was like a big kid. He used to let all the kids in the neighborhood come over and play ball because he had a basketball goal in back. Their home was like a safe haven for the teenagers in the community. All of the parents trusted and respected them. That's why they were having the basement renovated. They wanted a hobby room, especially with their new addition coming."

"Tell me what you know about the night Mrs. Marlow was murdered."

"This has been plaguing my mind for years. It's always weighed heavily on my conscience," Amanda stated.

"What's been plaguing you?" Cameron asked.

~ 53 ~

"Well, the night Mrs. Marlow was murdered, I saw the man come back in Mr. Marlow's car."

"'The man come back'? What man?"

"It was around 3:45 that morning. I remember because my boyfriend at the time, who's my husband now, was walking me back home and I'd just told him that my dad would be waking up soon to go to work. I was on punishment for staying out past curfew a few nights before. So, I wasn't supposed to be with my boyfriend. I'd snuck out of the house around midnight to be with him. But, he had to park his car around the block so that my parents wouldn't hear his car pull up when he brought me home."

"You mentioned a man was driving Mr. Marlow's car."

"Yeah, when Jeff was walking me home, we noticed Mr. Marlow's car pulling into the driveway hurriedly. A man got out, ran to the car waiting on him and they left."

"There was a car waiting on him?"

"Yes. It was a rental car. It had one of those rental stickers on the back."

"You were able to see all of this?"

"My eyesight is perfect, and so is Jeff's. Besides, we were walking up the sidewalk, and we walked right by the car. The car had an out of state tag, and a sticker from Imperial Car Rental."

"Do you remember what state the tag was from?"

"It was from Illinois. I'll never forget what state it was from, but I don't remember the tag number. At first, we thought the man was Mr. Marlow, because the man could have passed for a brother, even a possible twin."

"How did you know it wasn't Mr. Marlow?"

"Well, for one thing, this man ran to the other car. Mr. Marlow had a limp. He sustained an injury in high school while playing football. He never ran anywhere. Plus, this man had basic features like Mr. Marlow, but it definitely wasn't him."

"And you're sure this man wasn't him?"

"Mr. Spencer, I couldn't be more positive. There was a woman driving the rental car. I mean, we're talking about being less than five feet away."

"But, it was dark. Are you sure you weren't mistaken?"

"No way. Besides, this man didn't wear glasses. Mr. Marlow wore glasses. Not to mention, if it were Mr. Marlow, he would have spoken to me and Jeff. He's witnessed our sneaking in late once before then, and he spoke. Then the next day, he sat both of us down and talked with us, telling us the next time, he'd tell our parents because it was just too dangerous to be out so late at such a young age. Jeff was only 16, and I was only 15."

"Maybe he didn't think about it because so much was going on at the time."

"No, that wasn't it. This man didn't even recognize us. Besides, unless Mr. Marlow was extremely good at faking it, he had a limp. This man didn't."

"Can you describe the woman who was driving the car?"

"Well, all I really knew was that she had long black hair. She had a scarf tied around her head."

"What kind of car was she driving?"

"It was a yellow 83 Charger. Oh, and I remember a baby crying."

"What did you say?"

"There was a baby crying. I never thought of that until now, but there was a baby in the rental car. The reason I just thought about it is because I remember telling Jeff that the baby was going to wake the whole neighborhood, with it being so quiet outside. The baby was screaming that loudly."

"Are your parents aware of all you know about that night?"

"No, they're not. I feel awful about it."

"Why didn't you ever come forward and tell anyone this?"

"I was young, and already in a lot of trouble. By the time I knew what was happening, I was being sent to live with my aunt Audrey in Wyoming because I was pregnant. I had the baby and my aunt raised her. In those days, young girls

~ 55 ~

didn't get pregnant out of wedlock. My dad is a minister, so certain things just aren't allowed," she smiled slightly. "When I returned, almost a year had passed and I didn't think it was relevant. Somewhere in the back of my mind, it always bothered me that I never said anything. It never occurred to me that it could be so important."

"Mrs. Warren, what you've told me may very well be the break we need. Would you be willing to sign a sworn affidavit?"

"I'll do anything I can to help. Mr. Marlow was a nice man. I don't think he would have killed his wife."

"Is there anything else you can think of to tell me?"

"Not right off hand. But, if I think of anything I'll call you."

"Thank you so much for your information," Cameron said, standing as he shut off his recorder. As he was about to leave, Mr. Warren came home.

"Honey, I'd like for you to meet Cameron Spencer," Amanda said. "This is my husband, Jeff Warren."

Cameron and Jeff shook hands.

"How do you do, Mr. Warren," Cameron smiled.

"Fine. Who are you?" Jeff asked.

"I'm an attorney with Larson, Craig and Jacobs Law Firm, and I'm here because I'm working on Mr. Garret Marlow's case."

"That's a name I haven't heard in a long time. What exactly can we do for you?"

"I've been talking with your wife, and she's been very helpful in giving me just the break I may need to help clear Mr. Marlow. I've asked your wife if she'd be willing to sign an affidavit, and she's agreed to it."

"I'm not sure why she agreed to it, but my wife won't be signing anything. We had nothing to do with it then, and we'll have nothing to do with it now," Jeff stated coldly.

"But, Honey, I've already told Mr. Spencer that--"

"I don't care what you've told him! You are not getting involved and that's that! Mr. Spencer, I think you'd better leave."

"Mr. Warren, your wife is a vital part to this case, and we really need her help."

"Look, Mr. Spencer, my wife dealt with the guilt for years for never coming forward, now that she's finally gotten over it, you want for us to dredge up these memories? We were teenagers!" Mr. Warren yelled. "We don't know who it was that got out of that car that night, but we're not going to put ourselves in a position to be bothered, or threatened or anything like that. We've got three children to think of. Amanda wasn't here during most of the time, because she was away having the baby we gave up while most of this was going on. Now, I will not have my home disrupted by some hotshot lawyer who thinks he can come in and get us to make his job easier. I'm sorry, but you'll have to find another way. Neither one of us will get involved on Mr. Marlow's behalf."

"Why, when you know that your testimony could very well help him?"

"Because we don't want any part of it! I don't need to explain myself to you! What I say goes, and that's all there is to it! Now, would you please leave our home!?!"

Cameron couldn't believe how rude and unhelpful this man was being. He looked at Mrs. Warren. He could tell that she was embarrassed by her husband's behavior. Cameron felt that he would probably be hearing from her anyway. Plus, he could subpoena her if he had to. She managed to help him, and give him a lead that he probably never would have gotten elsewhere, but he would still need her sworn statement. He couldn't produce evidence without having someone to corroborate his findings.

"Goodbye, Mrs. Warren. Thank you so much for your help," Cameron stated.

"You're welcome. And I'm sorry I won't be able to help you further."

Cameron left the Warrens' home thinking that Mr. Warren was obviously not an easy man to deal with. He smiled wryly as he thought Caitlyn should be the one dealing with Mr. Warren. He went over in his head all of the things that he and Mrs. Warren had discussed. Now, all he had to do was contact Imperial Car Rental in Illinois. Hopefully, there weren't too many of them.

He arrived back at the office at almost 2 o'clock. He'd called Caitlyn on her cell phone but had not gotten an answer. He thought to himself that she was probably ignoring his calls just to bug him. Cameron immediately went onto the Internet to see how many branches of Imperial Car Rental there were in the state of Illinois. When he pulled up the list, there were 37 branches across the state. This man and woman could have been at either one of them. After checking further, he was able to find out that there was only one open in 1983. It had been opened in 1982. He knew his focus should be that store. When he pulled up information in regards to that store, he noticed that the manager had been at the store since it opened in 1982. It stated that he started out as a car cleaner and eventually worked his way up to management. He didn't want to call; he felt it would be better to talk with the manager in person.

After printing out information about the car rental store in question, Cameron tried to contact Caitlyn again. He wanted to see if she'd had any luck with the hotel. When he finally reached her, she told him that she may have found something and that she would talk with him when she got back to the office. Cameron was really starting to feel confident that they might be able to clear Mr. Marlow after all. Caitlyn got back to the office shortly past three o'clock, and called Cameron's office.

"Yes?" Cameron answered.

"Get down here, now," Caitlyn snapped.

"Say please, Ice Princess," Cameron smiled.

The next moment, he heard her hanging the phone up. He smiled as he stood from his chair and walked to Caitlyn's office. He didn't knock.

"Alright, what do you want?" Cameron said, as he entered.

"Didn't we discuss the knocking thing this morning?"

"You called me, remember?" Cameron said, as he walked and leaned over her desk. "Or, was that phone call about my offer to you this morning?"

"In your dreams!" Caitlyn said, clearly uncomfortable with Cameron being so close. Cameron sensed her reaction to his being close to her. As he studied her, he realized that he would definitely win the bet with Jackson.

"We'll see," Cameron said, straightening up. "Those batteries only last so long."

"I'll buy out the store before calling you! Now, can we please get down to business?"

"Sure, Ice Princess," Cameron said.

"Thank you," Caitlyn sighed. She looked over her notes. "I met with Mr. Zeller and he was very helpful. He admitted to me that he lied years ago because he was having an affair, and the woman was at his hotel when his wife called. Mr. Zeller didn't actually witness Mr. Marlow leaving; the woman he was with did. A Ms. Sarah Forbes was with him, and she was looking out of the window while he talked to his wife. He put his wife on hold because Sarah was trying to get his attention and he was trying to get her to be quiet so his wife wouldn't hear her. He told me how to contact Ms. Forbes, who lives right here in Indiana."

"So, did you talk to her?"

"Yes, I did. She told me that she saw the car clearly when it left. She said that there was a man and a woman together, and that there was a baby with them," Caitlyn said.

"How did she know there was a baby?" Cameron asked.

"She heard the baby crying. She saw Garret's car clearly when it left and there was another car following it. The woman with the baby got into a Dodge, and Garret was in a Pontiac, which was what he owned at the time. She said the woman had a–"

"A scarf tied around her head," Cameron finished for her.

"Yeah, how did you know?" Caitlyn asked.

"I talked to a Mrs. Amanda Warren and she was very helpful. Very nice lady. Her husband is an asshole, but she was quite nice," Cameron commented, then he smiled. "You'd like her husband. You're two peas in a pod."

"Don't be a smartass," Caitlyn said. "Now, who is she, because I don't remember seeing Amanda Warren on the witness list."

"That's because she was only 15 at the time, and she never admitted to what she saw. She was the next door neighbor," Cameron said.

"What exactly did she see?"

"She saw something that just might be the break we need."

"Do I have to drag it out of you? What did she see?"

"She saw a man park Mr. Marlow's car in the driveway, then run to another waiting car. There was a woman driving the car, and she had long black hair with a scarf tied around it. Whoever this man was, he could pass for Mr. Marlow's brother, even a twin possibly. She also told me something that I never realized. Did you notice that Mr. Marlow has a limp?"

"Yeah, I noticed that when I first met him. Why?" Caitlyn asked.

"Well, the man ran to the car. Mrs. Warren told me that Mr. Marlow never ran because he was unable to. She also said that this man didn't wear glasses, and Mr. Marlow does. Now, the thing she told me that might be a good lead is that the car waiting on whoever this man was, was rented from Imperial Car Rental in Illinois."

"Really? Well, we need to check with the rental company," Caitlyn said.

"I'm way ahead of you. I've already researched it. I pulled the rental agency up on the Internet, and found that there are 37 stores in Illinois. But, there was only one back in 1983. I found the manager's name for that store. If Rachel Marlow rented a car from them, then your theory might actually be right: she's behind Victoria's murder."

"I know I'm right. But, we have to consider that she might have used an alias or she could have gotten someone else to rent the car."

"That's why we need the employees. Maybe this

manager remembers something about the time in question. Plus, Mrs. Warren said the car was a yellow 1983 Charger. How many yellow 1983 Chargers could have been rented during that time?" Cameron asked.

"Plenty, Einstein," Caitlyn said sarcastically. "That was a pretty popular car back then. I know, because my aunt had one."

"And here I thought you were raised by wolves," Cameron said.

"And I thought you were raised by cavemen," Caitlyn shot back. "If you get off the subject one more time--"

"Hey, here's a thought," Cameron said, cutting her off. "Maybe your aunt did it."

"Why you miserable son of a--" Caitlyn started.

"Okay, okay, Ice Princess. Calm down. It was all in fun," Cameron smiled, holding his hands up in a surrendering gesture. "But, in all seriousness, if we had a picture of Rachel, maybe we can track her down."

"You're the one with all the sense. How do you propose we get a picture? That's his ex-wife, so it's not as if he'd have her picture lying around."

"What about his parents' home? A lot of their things are stored there."

"Oh, yes, and Victoria would have had a picture of Rachel Marlow on the fireplace mantle right next to theirs, right?" Caitlyn said in a smart tone. "Use your head."

"You know, if you were anymore of a bitch, you'd be on all fours," Cameron said.

"How dare you!"

"I dare because you deserve it! Now, grow up and let's see if we can clear this man! His life is at stake, and all you can do is try and knock down any ideas I have!"

Caitlyn looked at him, stunned that he pushed back so much. He watched her and noticed that she finally seemed to realize that she was stuck with him, whether she liked it or not.

"Fine," she said. "I will not be thought of as unreasonable. Let's just clear our client," she sighed quietly.

Caitlyn and Cameron worked until late that night.

They were the only two still there at 11 o'clock that night. They were able to contact a lot of people, or at least leave messages for them. They'd accomplished quite a bit by the time they left for home. Caitlyn was able to track down Marilyn Fields, who stated that she always found it odd how Rachel befriended Victoria. Marilyn remembered that Rachel called to offer help with the baby shower, but Garret's mom didn't trust her. Marilyn said that Victoria was insecure when it came down to Rachel, but she had to trust in Garret's love for her, despite his history with Rachel.

Caitlyn suggested that they find out where Rachel was living during that time. After investigating, they found out that Rachel lived in an expensive apartment in Chadwick Manor. She was renting the apartment month to month, and after November, she'd moved completely. The landlord noted that she was never home. Whenever they went for routine inspections and exterminations, the apartment looked as if it wasn't being lived in. Her newspapers were always building up for a week at a time, and then, she'd come along once a week to collect them and check her mail, usually on weekends.

Cameron and Caitlyn were able to track down Rachel's social security number which revealed a lot about the first Mrs. Marlow. They found out that Rachel had worked for a doctor's office as a medical assistant. She'd only worked for them for a few months when she abruptly quit around the first part of March in 1983. There was no record of her working anywhere from that time on, yet according to Mr. Marlow, she had a job out of town.

Cameron and Caitlyn knew that Garret was paying alimony to Rachel, but they wondered how she was able to survive totally off of alimony and no other source of income. Records indicated that she received $1000.00 a month in alimony, yet her rent alone was $900.00. There was no other source of recorded income from March until she moved, but the manager of the building showed proof that she'd paid every month on time. Obviously, Garret was unable to provide alimony to her anymore once he'd gone to jail. Which means from August until November, she received no income

~ 62 ~

of any kind. There were too many questions still unanswered concerning Rachel Marlow. Where did she spend all of her time? Where was she working? How was she paying rent? It seemed as if they were unable to find anymore out about her life past her moving completely from her apartment in November. It occurred to them that maybe Rachel was working under an assumed name. Rachel Marlow's work record seemed to cease to exist after March of 1983.

Her job at the doctor's office still had a file on her, which was a big help. She'd never called them for a reference or anything. When Rachel's social security number was ran further, she came up as deceased. Apparently, she'd died in an automobile accident in 1984. This matched up with the time when her letters to Garret stopped. It was a little odd that no one in Rachel's family bothered to contact Garret about her death. There was a death certificate on file, which was filed in the state of Ohio. Cameron and Caitlyn felt as if they'd hit a dead end. It didn't mean that she didn't have anything to do with Victoria's death, but it did mean that it would be a little more difficult to prove his innocence.

Mrs. Warren's testimony could be valuable, but they still needed more. They had to prove beyond a shadow of a doubt that Garret wasn't the man who killed Victoria. Since there were obviously two people at the murder scene and at the Marlow's house, it could easily be stated that this woman was Garret's accomplice in the murder. She could have been a nurse or doctor which would explain the perfect c-section performed on Victoria. There were so many theories right now that could be shot down without the right evidence to back it up.

On Friday morning, they had a meeting with Phillip to let him know what they'd found out.

"Well, how are things going? Is there any hope of clearing Garret?" Phillip asked.

"It's going better than we'd hoped for, and I'm optimistic that we'll find enough evidence to clear him," Cameron stated.

"We've come up with several leads, now we just have

~ 63 ~

to follow up on them," Caitlyn added.

"Okay. Tell me what you've found out," Phillip said.

Cameron and Caitlyn explained everything they'd learned so far to Phillip. He was surprised they'd managed to make so much progress in such a short amount of time. They also explained Rachel's untimely death. They were actually more optimistic than ever.

"We can't exclude anyone as a suspect. Garret always seemed adamant that Rachel would never have anything to do with hurting anyone, but we can't be too sure. I didn't know Rachel, so I have no idea about what type of person she was. We became friends in law school, but, he and Rachel were over by then. I was a year behind Garret, but, he'd taken a year off. I didn't know him then, but when he returned, we were both 2L students, and that's when we became good friends. In fact, by the time we graduated, he was seeing Victoria," Phillip said. He then sighed. "So, is there anything else?"

"Sir, this case will take us out of town. We'll be going to Ohio as well as Illinois. These two states seem the most likely to have the evidence we need. If it's okay with you, Caitlyn and I would like to make travel arrangements to leave on Monday," Cameron stated.

"That's fine. I'll have Alison make all of your arrangements. The plane will be at your disposal if you need it."

"Thank you, Phil. Hopefully, we should be able to come up with something in time for the hearing," Caitlyn said.

"I feel confident that you will. Let me know your itinerary before you go. Give all of your information to Alison and she'll take care of everything. I'll be in and out next week, but you have my cell and home number to reach me in case anything happens," Phillip said.

"Whatever you feel is best, Sir," Cameron stated.

After his and Caitlyn's meeting with Phillip, the rest of the day was spent going over testimonies in Garret's previous trials, and making arrangements to leave. Alison contacted Kristen with hotel information. Since the beginning of the investigation was going to start in Lynbridge, they were going to be staying at the Levinway Suites located in downtown Lynbridge.

Most of Cameron and Caitlyn's calls had been returned by Friday afternoon, which unfortunately didn't lead to much more information. They still were not deterred by it because they'd accomplished quite a bit already. Now, it was time to clear Mr. Marlow, and not one day could be wasted in doing so.

Over the weekend, Cameron decided to make sure things were taken care of at home since he wasn't even sure exactly how long he'd be gone. He told his landlord that he'd be out of town for at least a week, and asked him to keep an eye on things while he was gone. Cameron made sure that the monitoring office for his security alarm knew his whereabouts while he was out of town. He didn't have to worry about plants, because he didn't have any, and he had no animals, so things would be fine during his absence. He called his parents to let them know that he had a case that would take him out of town. He was unable to talk with his father because he wasn't home. He didn't discuss the case with his mom, but he told her that he would be in Illinois. His mother, of course, was worried about him and asked a lot of questions. Cameron kept reassuring her that he would be fine and that they could reach him on his cell phone if necessary.

Later that Saturday night, he called Kristen, and she came over immediately. He wasn't sure how long he'd be gone, although he and Jackson still had the bet going. When she came over, they went right to it. He met her at the door in nothing but a pair of boxer shorts. Before she could get inside, he was removing her shirt and kissing her neck. Things were so passionate, until they had sex on his living room floor. As their naked forms lay there in the afterglow, Kristen snuggled with him.

"I don't want for you to leave," she pouted. "Especially being with Caitlyn."

"Being with her isn't exactly at the top of my list, but it's my job to find out the truth."

~ 65 ~

"I know. Why don't I come with you?" she asked, looking up at him.

"Because that would be suspicious, and Ice Princess would never go for it," Cameron said.

"It could be work-related."

"Have you ever gone out of town to work on a case?" Cameron asked, looking down at her.

"Well, no," Kristen said hesitantly. "But, Phil wants every available person on this."

"You also have three other attorneys who need your assistance. I won't be gone forever," Cameron reassured.

"A day away from you will seem like it," Kristen said, resting her head on his chest.

Cameron sighed and rolled his eyes as he held her. He was glad to get away, because this girl was starting to have expectations. He would miss having sex with her at his leisure, but he needed some breathing space. At work, they were strictly business, but in the bedroom, she was a siren, always ready to please.

Kristen stayed Saturday night, and they stayed in bed until Sunday afternoon. She got up and fixed lunch for Cameron. He stared at her as she put the dishes in the dishwasher. She was so easy, and she did everything he told her to. As he stared at her in a sexy lingerie, he realized that he was already starting to get bored with her. Kristen presented no sort of challenge to him. As he sat there watching her, his mind wandered to Caitlyn and what he would do to get her in bed. Now that would present a challenge. After breakfast, he began to make excuses so that Kristen would leave. No matter what he said, she had a reason for staying. After she got dressed, she even offered to pack for his trip. She was smothering him and he hated it.

"Kristen, you need to go home," Cameron sighed.

"What? You don't want me here?" Kristen asked.

"I just want to finish getting ready for my trip, and you're too much of a distraction," Cameron quickly covered.

"Oh," Kristen smiled. She walked towards him and placed her arms around his neck. "We could do something about that."

Cameron reached up to move her away from him. "Kristen, please," Cameron sighed in an irritated tone.

"Oh, come on," she soothed, trying to kiss his neck.

"Dammit, don't you get a hint!? I want to be alone!"

"But, why?"

"Because you are smothering me! I've tried to be nice, but you don't get it! Now, please leave!" Cameron said, walking to his door to open it.

"Is that all I am? Just a good lay, and then it's 'bye, bye, Kristen'?"

Cameron sighed as he closed the door. "You know that's not it. But, Kristen, I don't need for you to be like this. Give me the chance to miss you. Let me look forward to coming back home to you," Cameron said.

"Enough said," Kristen said tearfully, as she got her purse and walked to the door. She hesitated before opening it, as if she was hoping Cameron would stop her.

Cameron watched her, waiting for her to leave. He refused to stop her, because she was obviously getting mixed signals. He was starting to think that maybe he should reconsider sleeping with her. Kristen left and it was obvious that she was very hurt. Cameron sighed heavily as she closed the door.

"Finally," Cameron said.

He locked his door and went to the bedroom to do what he'd been planning to do all weekend. He now was at the last minute trying to get things together. As he packed, his phone rang. When he looked at the caller ID he noticed that it was Kristen. She left a message for him, which he ignored. The only way she would get the point would be for him to turn away completely from her. After packing, he got a good night's sleep. The flight wasn't a long one, but he needed to be alert when dealing with Caitlyn. They were due to meet at the airport that Monday morning at 7:30 a.m. For the first night over the past week, he was able to actually sleep peacefully.

Chapter
4

Cameron arrived at the airport promptly at 7 a.m. on Monday morning. He and Caitlyn were going to leave their cars in the secured parking lot until they returned. When Caitlyn got out of her car, he hardly recognized her. She was dressed in a pair of denim shorts with a purple Durman College School of Law t-shirt. She had her hair pulled back into a ponytail, and she didn't have on any makeup. She was so unlike the Caitlyn he'd gotten accustomed to seeing at the office. Cameron stared at her, thinking that even without makeup, she was a beautiful woman. He always made the excuse that without makeup, she'd look awful. Now, he knew that wasn't the case.

"Hello, Cameron," Caitlyn greeted him.

"Good morning, Caitlyn," Cameron said.

"I don't believe it. You called me 'Caitlyn' and not 'Ice Princess,'" Caitlyn said, half smiling.

"I didn't say I didn't know your name," Cameron smiled. "Here, let me help you with your luggage," Cameron said, getting one of her suitcases.

"Thank you," Caitlyn said. As they were getting her things, her cell phone rang.

"Hello? What? Is she okay?"

Cameron looked at her, as she seemed to be upset.

"No, call Dr. Patrick. You may need to take her in. I knew she looked as if she wasn't feeling well last night. I should have called him then," Caitlyn said, with tears in her eyes. "I'll come home." She paused as she listened. "But, she needs me. Please," Caitlyn whispered. Caitlyn closed her eyes and sighed. "Fine. Please, please keep me posted, okay? Make sure Cori knows I love her. We'll be in the plane soon, and I don't think I'll be able to use my cell phone. But, I'll call you back the moment we land, okay?" Caitlyn then smiled slightly. "I know. Thanks, Mom. I love you. Bye."

Cameron was watching and listening as she talked. She seemed almost human. He'd never heard that she had children, but whoever Cori was, she obviously wasn't feeling well. As the baggage helper helped them into the private plane, Cameron decided to take his chances and ask her what was wrong.

"Is everything okay?" Cameron asked.

"It's my dog, Cori. She's sick," Caitlyn said tearfully.

"What happened?"

"I-I don't know. She's not getting any younger, and I'm worried about her. She was diagnosed with arthritis last week, and it was advised that I put her to sleep. I couldn't do it," Caitlyn said, shaking her head.

"Well, that's understandable. You love her," Cameron said, as they sat in their seat.

"I have her daughter, also. Buffi's such a treat," Caitlyn smiled. Then her smile faded. "I don't know what she'd do without Cori. They've been together for four years."

"Don't worry, she'll be fine," Cameron soothed, touching her hand.

Caitlyn looked thankful, and then almost instantly, her demeanor changed. She quickly pulled her hand away.

"Look, don't try to be nice to me. We're here to work, not talk about my personal life!"

~ 69 ~

"Oh, so you have a personal life?" Cameron retorted.

"Listen, we are on this plane to solve a case," Caitlyn sighed. "You have your personal life, I have mine. Now, just leave me alone, okay?"

"Fine, Caitlyn. I just think since we're working together, and we'll be in a city where we don't know anyone, we should at least try to be cordial towards each other. Fair enough?"

"Whatever. Just don't ask me anything about my personal life. Are we clear?"

"Crystal," Cameron said. "I was only trying to be helpful because you were upset, but you don't have to worry about that happening again."

"Thank you," Caitlyn said, picking up a magazine.

Cameron looked at her, stunned that she could be so nice one moment and back to being a bitch the next. He shook his head and sighed. He then got up and went to another seat. At that very moment, the pilot announced that they were about to take off. He instructed them to fasten their seatbelts until they leveled off. They were told that the flight would take one hour, twelve minutes.

After almost an hour, Cameron, who'd been engrossed in reading about the case, looked in Caitlyn's direction. She was asleep with an open magazine resting on her lap. He got up from his seat, and retrieved a blanket to cover her. When he picked up the magazine, he noticed she'd circled an ad for a music instrument store. It was a picture of a Bastionne 450 clarinet. Cameron looked at the ad and wondered why she'd circled it. While he was looking at it, she awakened.

"What are you doing?" Caitlyn asked, snatching the magazine from him.

"You'd fallen asleep, and I was trying to cover you with a blanket," Cameron said. "So, why are you looking at a clarinet?"

"That's crossing the threshold from business to personal," Caitlyn reminded him.

"I was just asking a question," Cameron said. "You know, you don't have to be so cold. Why won't let anyone get close to you?"

"It's none of your business. Our plan is to save our client's life; I want to keep the focus on that."

Before Cameron could respond, the pilot came over the loudspeaker.

"We're beginning our descent into Illinois. Please fasten your seatbelts. The weather is partly cloudy, with a 30% chance of rain. Please turn off your phones and any electronic equipment," the pilot said.

"I couldn't pick up a signal on my phone anyway," Caitlyn muttered to herself as she removed the blanket to strap in.

Cameron then went back to his seat and strapped in, really puzzled by Caitlyn's attitude. He could tell that this was going to be a long trip. By the time they were actually able to get off the plane, it was after 9 a.m. Caitlyn called her mom about her dog but was unable to reach her.

Allison had made all the arrangements, and their rental car was available and waiting on them. Ironically, they rented from Imperial, which is the main reason they were in Illinois. After getting the car and finding their way to the hotel, it was almost 10 a.m. The rooms thankfully had access to a fax machine, and had everything set up for a laptop computer along with internet access. Once they got settled into their rooms, which were right next door to each other, Cameron called Imperial and spoke with the manager, John Stratman. He agreed to meet with them later, giving them directions to the branch.

They walked to the elevator in silence, until Caitlyn's cell phone rang. It was her mother calling her to let her know that her dog was okay. Caitlyn breathed a sigh of relief. Cameron marveled at how much she seemed to love her dogs. He almost felt sorry for her to know that her entire life was all about her pets. He wondered was she lonely, or was this the way she wanted it. As they drove along, Cameron looked at Caitlyn.

"What are you thinking about?" Cameron asked.

"I think I'm anxious to hear what Mr. Stratman has to

say. If the car was rented at his store, and he worked there at the time, he may be able to tell us something that could lead to the real killer. But, I'm afraid to get my hopes up. This may not even be the right store, so we need to keep an open mind."

"You're right. Okay, let's see, he said at the third light, turn right onto Jemison Drive," Cameron said.

"There it is," Caitlyn pointed.

They pulled into the parking lot full of stores and restaurants. When they entered the rental company, there was a bit of a wait because several customers were waiting to be serviced, and there were only four employees behind the main counter. Cameron and Caitlyn went to the counter and asked for the manager.

"I'm the manager, John Stratman. How can I help you?"

"Mr. Stratman, I'm Cameron Spencer and this is my colleague, Caitlyn Frazier. We spoke briefly on the phone."

"Yes, we did. Why don't you come into my office so that we can talk privately?" Mr. Stratman led them to a glassed in office. "Please, have a seat. Now, what exactly is it that I can do for you?"

"We understand that you've been here since this store opened up, and we hope that you might be able to help us with a case we're working on," Caitlyn stated.

"Like I told you one the phone, I'll try. What is it that you need to know?" Mr. Stratman asked.

"Back in 1983, which I know was quite a long time ago, do you remember much about the time you worked here during that year?" Cameron asked, pulling out his tape recorder.

"Boy, you're right. That was a long time ago. This place had only been open for a year. I know because I was one of the car cleaners at the time. What specifically are you trying to find out about?"

"During July of 1983, we have reason to believe that a 1983 Charger was rented from here and may very well be the car involved in a murder in Indiana. We have a witness who states that there was a sticker with Imperial Car Rental on the back of the car. We know that this was the only store that was open at the time. So, we're starting with you, especially since you've been here since the store opened," Caitlyn said.

"Well, that is true. I've been here for a long time. A 1983 Dodge Charger. What color was the car?"

"It was yellow," Cameron stated.

"During that time, we had several cars like that. It was a pretty popular car back then. But, we only had two or three in yellow."

"Do you remember anything odd about a rental during that time, or have record of the people who rented a yellow Charger during that month?" Caitlyn asked.

"Not that I can really think of. What exactly do you mean by 'odd'?" John asked.

"Anything out of the ordinary, maybe about the customer's behavior, or something left in the car, just whatever you can come up with," Caitlyn said.

"You know, now that you mention it, I remember cleaning up a yellow Charger, and there was a bloody baby's blanket left in the backseat. I think that was the same car I found the locket in also," John stated.

"A bloody baby's blanket?" Cameron asked.

"Yeah. I thought that was a little odd. It was almost as if a baby had been delivered on the blanket, or cleaned up with after being born. It kind of threw me off balance a little."

"What did you do with the blanket?" Caitlyn asked.

"Well, naturally, I threw it away. I remember telling one of the clerks about it, and she commented about how the couple seemed a little strange anyway."

"What did she mean by 'strange'?" Caitlyn asked.

"The woman was in a hurry, seemed real nervous. And the man was frazzled too. He waited in the car, but I was outside when they pulled up. He kept looking around, and glancing at his watch. I remember seeing the woman, because she had long, black hair and a scarf tied around her head. The best person to talk to about that is Deanna Lassiter. She was the one on duty when they returned the car."

"Deanna Lassiter? Do you know how we can reach

her?" Caitlyn asked.

"I sure do. I keep in touch with Deanna because we remained friends after she quit. Our families get together a lot, so I have her current address. Both of us started here at Imperial together. Actually, she works over at corporate because she'd left and come back a few years later."

"Mr. Stratman, you mentioned a locket. What was that all about?" Cameron asked.

"It was a really nice locket. It had a picture of a couple in it. I gave it to Deanna to put in the lost and found, and I don't know what happened to it after that. She may have thrown it away or something. We're not responsible for anything left in the cars, but as a courtesy, we give them up to a year to come back for valuable items."

"Is there anything else you remember about that particular incident?" Caitlyn asked.

"Not much. Deanna may remember. Why don't I give her a call and see if she's available to talk with you?" John suggested.

"That would be great. Thank you," Cameron stated.

John looked up Deanna's number in his rolodex.

"Okay, I have a number to her direct line at work. She should be there."

Cameron and Caitlyn waited patiently while John called Deanna. During that time, Cameron looked at Caitlyn. He marveled at her questions and professionalism. She really wasn't half-bad as an attorney. Cameron was brought back to reality as John explained everything to Deanna about the time in question, and asked if it was okay if he put Cameron and Caitlyn in touch with her. Soon after, he hung up.

"She's agreed to talk with you, and she told me it is okay to give you her number and address. She lives at 925 Krysteena Drive. Her phone number is 555-1992. I hope this helps you out with your case." He wrote down the information and gave it to them.

"More than you'll ever know. Did she say when would be a good time to call?" Cameron asked.

"Yeah, she said she gets off work at five and that if

you'd like you can come by her house. She wants for you to call her around 5:30, because by then she'll be home and she can give you directions to her house."

"Mr. Stratman, would you be willing to sign a sworn affidavit? Cameron asked.

"Of course I would. I have no problem helping out. Would I have to come to Indiana?"

"No. We'll prepare the affidavit tonight and bring it by along with a notary public to get your signature," Caitlyn said.

"I'll be here. Let me know if I can be of any more help," John said, standing to show them out.

"We will. Thank you so much. We'll see you tomorrow," Cameron said, shaking his hand.

When Cameron and Caitlyn left out of the rental agency, they decided to stop at an Italian restaurant located in the shopping center to eat. It took a lot of talking on Cameron's part, but she finally agreed to it. It was after 2 o'clock and against her better judgment, she realized she was hungry.

After their salads arrived, Cameron looked at Caitlyn.

"Now, this isn't so bad, is it?"

"I usually eat alone," Caitlyn commented, as she placed her napkin in her lap.

"And, why is that?" Cameron asked.

"Because it's my 'me' time, and I feel that no one else should infringe on that," Caitlyn said, then looking at Cameron with steely eyes. "Not even some wannabe hotshot charmer of an attorney."

Cameron smiled. "So, you think I'm a charmer?"

"Please, get over yourself," Caitlyn said, rolling her eyes. "The only reason I agreed to this lunch is because we have only one rental car, and you have the keys. I never said I'd make idle conversation with you."

"Would it hurt?" Cameron asked, as he took a bite of his salad.

"Talking gets people into a lot of trouble. You start to open up, and it comes back to bite you in the ass."

"How do you know that?"

~ 75 ~

"Because I've got enough bite marks to prove it."

"Hmm, may I see?" Cameron joked.

"Don't be crass," Caitlyn scoffed.

"I couldn't resist," Cameron laughed. "But, in all seriousness, maybe you talked to the wrong person," Cameron shrugged.

"Is that your explanation? I opened up to the wrong person?" Caitlyn then shook her head. "Wow, such words of wisdom."

"You know, you're not as cold as you want for people to think you are," Cameron observed.

"Oh? Why don't you tell me about me?" she said, putting her fork down.

"It's simple," Cameron shrugged. "You have a cold, hard exterior because you've been hurt before."

Caitlyn laughed. "And that sums me up? That's your 'analysis' of me? Maybe you should stick to law and leave psychology alone." Caitlyn then picked up her fork and resumed eating her salad.

"Didn't you know? Law is psychology. Think about it: what do we do all day but try and get inside people's minds? The judge, the jury, the witness. We anticipate it all, right down to whether we can win a case or not. I can read your mind, Ice Princess."

"Oh really?" Caitlyn laughed slightly.

"Yeah. I mean, like right now, you're uncomfortable because I'm getting too close to the truth. That's why you keep fiddling with your napkin," Cameron said, pointing to her hand, which was wringing her napkin nervously. "You were probably in love once, and he hurt you. So, you refuse to get close to anyone else."

"Well, well, well. You think you have it all figured out?"

"It's really not that hard," Cameron laughed slightly.

"So, what am I? The poster child for a broken heart? You see one, you've seen them all," Caitlyn shrugged. "But, let's be clear. Whatever I've gone through in my life, it will not get the best of me. I'm a strong woman who has held her own for a very long time. So, stop the psycho-analysis of me and let's talk about what we're really here for: clearing Garret Marlow."

"Caitlyn, I know why we're here. I just thought we should be more cordial towards each other."

"I don't have to be cordial towards you. All we have to do is save this man's life. Then, hopefully, in the future, we won't end up working together," Caitlyn sighed.

"Or, Phil could be so impressed at our teamwork, until he pairs us more often than not," Cameron argued.

"Oh, no, no, no, no," Caitlyn laughed, shaking her head in disagreement. "This is the first and only case you and I will ever be partnered on. I'll make sure of that!"

At that moment, their food arrived.

"Thanks," Cameron said to the waiter. Then he looked back at Caitlyn. "Why do you dislike me? Am I that much of a threat to you?"

"You're no threat. Haven't we had this conversation before?"

"But, I love your melodious voice when you disagree with me," Cameron smiled. "Come on, Ice Princess, if the truth were to be told, you can't keep your eyes off of me. Remember, I'm right next door in the hotel if you get lonely."

"There isn't that much loneliness in the world."

"You say that now, but tonight, when you're lying awake in that big, lonely king-sized bed, you'll yearn for me knowing that the only thing between us is a wall. Just to give you an idea, I sleep in the nude," Cameron whispered, smiling.

Caitlyn looked away quickly as he spoke. "Please, I'm trying to eat. I'd appreciate you not ruining my appetite."

"I'm not ruining your appetite. But, I have piqued your curiosity, haven't I?"

Caitlyn laughed, but never denied anything he was saying. "You know, you are unbelievable, Cameron Spencer. There are laws against some of the things you say. They call it sexual harassment."

"So, are you going to turn me in?"

"Keep bothering me, and I will," Caitlyn said.

~ 77 ~

"Fair enough. So, what shall we talk about next?" Cameron asked, as he took a bite of his meal.

"How about the case? We have a lot to go over," Caitlyn said.

"Not here in a crowded restaurant."

"I suppose you have a point. So, will you simply be quiet so that I can enjoy my meal?"

"Sure, Ice Princess."

At that very moment, Caitlyn sneezed.

"Am I allowed to say 'bless you'?" Cameron asked.

"Thank you," Caitlyn replied.

"Well, the Ice Princess has just a tinge of politeness," Cameron smiled.

"Don't push it," Caitlyn said. Then, she sneezed again.

"Could the ice princess be getting sick?"

"You wish. I wouldn't give you the satisfaction."

"That's more like it," Cameron smiled.

They continued the snide remarks over lunch, and before they knew it, it was 4:45. They decided to go back to the hotel and call Deanna Lassiter to see what input she had to add to their findings so far. She gave them directions to her house, and they agreed to meet with her at 7 p.m. Mrs. Lassiter lived only five miles away from the hotel, so they arrived sooner than expected. When Mrs. Lassiter opened the door, she seemed quite pleasant and eager to help.

"Please, have a seat. Can I get either of you a cup of coffee or anything?" Mrs. Lassiter asked.

"I'm fine," Cameron said.

"I'm fine, thank you," Caitlyn smiled.

"So, what can I do for you?" Deanna asked.

"Mrs. Lassiter, Mr. Stratman told us that you were the clerk on duty during the time in question. We're attorneys working on a murder case that took place 27 years ago, and we have reason to believe that a car rented from Imperial could have been used during that murder," Caitlyn stated, pulling out her tape recorder.

"John mentioned that. And please, let's not be so formal. You can call me Deanna. John said it was the car that

~ 78 ~

was rented by that strange couple. I'm not sure if it's who you're looking for, though," Deanna stated.

"Well, we'll soon find out. Can you describe the woman and man who rented the car?" Caitlyn asked.

"Let's see, if memory serves me correctly, she had long black hair, and for some strange reason, she was wearing dark shades," Deanna said.

"What was so strange about the shades?" Caitlyn asked, sneezing again.

"Bless you. For one thing, it was raining outside. And when she came in, she kept the shades on. It was as if they were more a disguise than anything else."

"What else do you remember about that day?" Cameron asked.

"She paid in cash. That was unusual, too. I mean, I guess these days, most places only take credit card reservations. Like I said, we wanted to promote business, so we accepted cash deposits. She wouldn't put anything on a credit card."

"You wouldn't by chance remember this woman's name, would you?"

"Oh, I'll never forget her name," Deanna stated. "It was Regina Matheson."

"Why do you say you'll never forget her name?" Caitlyn asked.

"Because I tried for months to contact her. She'd left a valuable locket in the car. Whenever someone pays with a cash deposit, we have to get five different relatives or friends, so that we can contact them, just in case they don't come back with the car. All I know is that I tried to contact her through the numbers she'd given. Each number I called was bogus. Either they didn't know her, or I could never reach anyone. I tried her number, and it, of course was out of service. Her ID probably wasn't real. We made a copy of it, but, chances are, she wasn't who she said she was. Back in those days, it was easy to fake a driver's license."

"There wouldn't still be a record on file with her information and picture, would there?" Cameron asked.

"I doubt if there's a picture of her on file, but that doesn't mean there's not a file on her at all. We always keep customers on our mailing list, like when we're running a special on a rental for weekends or holidays, etc. Usually, those lists are only kept for three or four years, and if they don't rent from us again, we discard their information. I'll check and see what I can dig up for you as far as a copy of her ID, but I seriously doubt if I find anything."

"We'd appreciate that. What ever happened to the locket?" Cameron asked.

"I pawned it," Deanna answered. "My manager told me that we'd done everything we could to contact her. He told me that I could get rid of it. We'd had it for over a year. I got $250.00 for it. That was a lot back then, so I'm guessing the locket must have really been valuable. Most pawnshops only give you a fraction of what something is really worth."

"What pawnshop did you use?" Caitlyn asked.

"I used Price Pawnshop on the corner of 30th Street and Keegan Avenue," Deanna told them. "It's still there, actually. It's one of the best pawnshops in Lynbridge. It's owned by the same guy, and he's always been fair. Chances are, the locket is long gone because it was beautiful. I think it had an inscription on back, but for some reason, I can't remember exactly what it said. Let's see, it said something about 'perfect forever' or something like that. It seems like there was more than that inscribed. Maybe Mr. Price remembers. But, then again, he sees so much, he probably won't remember much about it either."

"Do you remember anything else about Regina Matheson?" Caitlyn asked.

"Well, like I said, she had long, black hair. Come to think of it, she had an orange and yellow scarf tied around it. I mean, it was so obvious she didn't want people to recognize who she was. The man she was with waited in his car."

"How did you know she was with a man if he waited in the car?" Cameron asked.

"Because Ms. Matheson almost forgot her refund. She had actually left out of the store, and I had to run out to flag

~ 80 ~

her down to give her the refund. She had over $100.00 coming back to her. That alone was strange. No one ever forgets a refund. They seemed to be pretty well-to-do, considering the car the man was driving."

"What kind of car was it?" Caitlyn asked.

"It was a Corvette. It had a vanity plate on the back."

"Do you remember what the plate said?" Caitlyn asked.

"It said 'VARDEN 1,'" Deanna stated.

"Are you sure?" Cameron asked.

"I couldn't be more positive. It stuck with me because it was the same as my aunt's married name who stays in Colorado."

"Can you describe the man?" Cameron asked.

"He was a very attractive guy. I'd say at that time maybe early thirties. Smooth complexion, dark hair. Gorgeous smile. He smiled at me and thanked me for reminding them about the refund. He seemed friendly, but nervous, and the woman was downright impatient."

"What state was the tag from?" Caitlyn asked.

"It was from here, Illinois."

"Is there anything else you can remember?" Cameron asked.

"Yeah, they had a baby with them."

"Really?" Cameron asked. "Are you sure?"

"I couldn't be more positive," Deanna insisted. "Car seat laws weren't as strict as they are now, so when I ran to the car, the man was handing her the baby to hold. I mean, they were in a little two-seater car. When John told me about the baby blanket, I pretty much figured it belonged to the baby. The baby looked to be a newborn, so I assumed that maybe the baby had been delivered on it or something. Who knows? We see a lot of strange things."

"Deanna, would you be willing to sign a sworn affidavit?" Cameron asked.

"Sure, anytime."

"I'll be by tomorrow evening with a prepared statement for you to sign," Cameron said.

"That'll be fine. I'll be here after 5:30, or if you'd like,

~ 81 ~

I can possibly meet you somewhere on my lunch break."

"Let me know tomorrow what you'd prefer," Cameron stated.

"Thank you for your help," Caitlyn said. "I hope we didn't inconvenience you too much by showing up here this evening."

"No, not at all. I'm just glad I could help. When John called about it, I was telling one of my co-workers about how weird that whole incident was. It's probably one of the oddest situations I've encountered in all my years at Imperial."

"Well, we'd better get going," Caitlyn said, standing to leave.

"I hope that what I've told you helps."

"It really does. Thanks again," Cameron stated, walking behind Caitlyn. "And you'll call us if you find anything on file about her?"

"I sure will. I have both your cards, so I'll contact you as soon as I know anything else."

"You have a nice evening," Cameron smiled.

"Thank you, you do the same," Deanna smiled back, as they walked to the car.

"You know, Ice Princess, we actually might win this thing," Cameron stated, as they pulled out of the driveway.

"Against my better judgment, I'm inclined to agree with you. This is going to turn out to be a very enlightening trip. At this rate, we'll have enough evidence to clear Mr. Marlow in no time at all. So, who do you think this 'Regina Matheson' really is?" Caitlyn asked.

"I don't know, but I'd bet any amount of money that's not her real name. She's someone directly linked to Mr. Marlow. If only we had a picture of this 'woman with the long, black hair,' we might be able to show it to him to see if he recognizes her."

"It's quite possible she was wearing a wig. But, he may still recognize her despite that," Caitlyn said.

"I just hope we can get a picture," Cameron stated.

"Deanna said she pawned the locket at Price's Pawnshop located on the corner of 30th Street and Keegan

Avenue. It's been 26 years, so I seriously doubt that it's still there." Caitlyn sounded skeptical.

"It may be a long shot, but it can't hurt. You never know. Look at what these 'long shots' have led to so far."

"I'll decide by tomorrow if I think it's worth checking into. I for one am beat. I just want to lie down and get a good night's rest," Caitlyn said, yawning.

"So, the ice princess needs her beauty rest?" Cameron smiled, looking briefly in her direction.

"I don't need beauty rest. I'm just tired, that's all. Do you always have to be such a chauvinistic asshole?" Caitlyn asked sarcastically.

"Well, at least I know it's you. I hadn't heard a snappy comeback in a couple of hours, and I was starting to think you weren't the real Caitlyn," Cameron replied.

"Trust me, I'm still here. I wouldn't give you the satisfaction of going anywhere," Caitlyn responded.

They arrived back at the hotel just after 8 p.m., and Cameron walked Caitlyn to her room.

"I'll see you tomorrow morning," Cameron said.

"I suppose I don't have much choice. For now, I'm going to go in and take something for this headache you've given me." After that, Caitlyn sneezed.

"Bless you," Cameron said. "You know, you've sneezed several times today. You're not getting sick on me, are you?"

"Would you stop asking me that?" Caitlyn snapped, sneezing once again.

"Good night, Ice Princess," Cameron said.

After Caitlyn closed her door, Cameron shook his head and smiled. She was too mean and vindictive to get sick. He could probably get a lot done without her interference. He could only hope that tomorrow she'd be too under the weather to do anything.

Cameron decided to go downstairs to the bar. He still had so much on his mind. The case, his move, his family, his friends. And then there was Grace. When he and Grace started dating in high school, she was extremely popular. She was a cheerleader, very pretty, every guy's dream. Cameron was the envy of every guy at his high school for being with Grace. When he left to go off to college, Grace remained behind and decided to go to a two year college close to Lariette Springs, so they were separated during a lot of the time. Why she chose to end it with him after he'd finished law school, and after he'd proposed, Cameron would never understand. They'd actually started planning a wedding, or so he thought. Apparently, Grace wasn't planning much of anything, especially since she had no intention of marrying him.

At that moment, his thoughts went to Kristen. She was a nice girl on the surface, but Cameron was starting to think fatal attraction. He knew he was good in bed, but this woman was getting a little too attached entirely too soon. He didn't want anything serious with her. He didn't want her for a girlfriend, let alone consider her as wife material. She was too easy. There were a lot of beautiful women at that firm, and she was just the beginning. He had the feeling that Caitlyn would be his biggest challenge. But, she could be whipped. He was determined to get Caitlyn to the point of begging him for more and more. That was one bitch who desperately needed to be put in her place. And Cameron was just the man to do it. Cameron had been in the bar for over an hour when a woman approached him, interrupting his thoughts.

"Hello," she said, sitting next to him.

"Hi," Cameron responded.

"So, are you staying here in the hotel?" the woman asked.

"Yes, I am," he said. He looked at her. She was a very attractive woman with short hair, dressed provocatively.

"I'm Serena Felton," she said, holding out her hand.

"Nice to meet you, Serena. I'm Cameron Spencer," he said shaking her hand.

"Are you here on business, or is this strictly pleasure," Serena asked.

"Business," Cameron said.

"Oh. So how long are you in town for?"

"About a week. It depends on how long it takes for me to wrap things up," Cameron stated, as his eyes roved her from head to toe.

"Did your wife accompany you on this trip?" Serena asked. It was obvious she was interested in Cameron.

"No, I'm not married. Is this business or pleasure for you?" Cameron asked.

"Business. My company sent us here for a conference this week. It's being held here in the hotel," Serena said. "I'm so stressed. We've had a long day and I thought I'd come down here for a drink."

"You usually dress like that for work? Not that I'm complaining," Cameron smiled.

Serena laughed. "No, I went up to my room to change."

"I see. So, where's your husband?"

"No husband, at least not anymore."

"So, Serena, where are you from?" Cameron asked, as he sipped his drink.

"I'm from North Carolina. What about you?"

"I'm originally from Kentucky, but I live in Indiana."

"Indiana, huh? Nice state. So, what do you do Cameron?"

"I'm an attorney," Cameron stated.

"Oh, so you're here working on a case."

"Something like that. But, if you don't mind, I'd rather not get into it," Cameron said, turning more towards her. "I can think of a few other things I'd rather talk about."

"Oh? Like what?" Serena asked.

Cameron smiled as he looked at her seductively. "Oh, a little of this, a little of that," Cameron whispered, as he undressed her with his eyes.

"You don't waste time, do you?" Serena said.

"Procrastination is something I've never been famous for. Of course, there are some things I like to take my time in doing."

"What things would those be?"

"I'm better at showing my skills than telling you about

~ 85 ~

them."

"Is that so?"

"Of course, it is," Cameron shrugged.

"So, if I wanted to know more about you, I'd have to let you demonstrate your abilities," Serena said.

"Exactly," Cameron whispered. "But, not here. Maybe somewhere a little more private?"

"That would be nice," Serena smiled. "What room are you in?"

"I'm in room 724. Why don't you let me buy you another drink?" Cameron said.

"I'd like that," Serena smiled.

"Bartender, give the lady whatever she's drinking and I'll have another beer," Cameron said.

"I'd like another white wine, please," Serena said.

"Coming right up," the bartender said.

Cameron and Serena sat at the bar for a little while talking and flirting back and forth. Serena was 34 and she worked for Gorham Software. She was an executive who'd been with the company for eight years after completing graduate school. She told Cameron that she was divorced after a five-year marriage. Her husband was abusive physically and emotionally, and after dealing with it for five years, she finally had the good sense to get out of it. Cameron didn't go into details about the case he was working on, but told her that he and a colleague were there to try to gather information to clear their client. He never bothered to mention that his colleague was a woman. They sat there and talked until the bar was getting ready to close. It was the first part of the week, so the bar closed at 11 p.m.

"So, how about we go back to my room?" Cameron suggested. "We can get a nice bottle of wine."

"I'm game if you are," Serena smiled.

Just as they were getting up from their seats, Cameron's cell phone rang. He looked at it, but didn't recognize the number.

"Excuse me," he smiled at Serena. Then, he answered his phone. "Hello?"

"Cameron, why are you doing this to me?" Kristen was on the other end crying.

"What do you want?" Cameron whispered, giving a frustrated sigh.

"Please! Don't turn away from me! I miss you! I've fallen in love with you!" Kristen cried.

"We'll talk about this when I get home," Cameron said quietly, rolling his eyes.

"Maybe this isn't a good time," Serena said.

"No, no, wait," Cameron said to Serena, stopping her.

"Wh-who is that? Are you with another woman?" Kristen cried.

"You have to stop this. I'm hanging up now."

"I-I'll kill myself!"

"Kristen, please. Look, hold on." Cameron took the phone away from his ear. He looked at Serena apologetically. "I really need to take this."

"Tomorrow night, then? We'll meet down here, say 7:30?"

"That's perfect," Cameron said.

"Goodnight, Cameron," Serena smiled, kissing him on the cheek.

After Serena walked out, he went out onto the terrace. He was angry that Kristen had managed to ruin his night.

"Dammit, Kristen, what's wrong with you?!"

"Who is she, Cameron? Who are you with?"

"None of your damned business! I've had it with you! You need help!"

"Cameron, I need you! Don't do this to me!"

"Kristen, you have to calm down. I'm here on business," Cameron said. He didn't want for her to do anything to herself, or it would be on his conscience.

"Wh-who was the woman?"

"It was a potential witness," Cameron lied. "I'd finally gotten her to talk to me, and you might have just ruined that."

"I-I'm sorry. I just miss you so!"

"Kristen, I just left this morning. We were together most of the weekend."

"Until you put me out. I-I went and got a new cell phone number today, because you were ignoring my other one."

"Kristen, when I get home, I promise we'll spend some real time together. Just you and me," Cameron soothed. "But, if you want more from me, you have to trust me, okay?"

"Do you mean it?"

"Of course, I do," Cameron soothed. "I miss you, but I'm here on business. You have to let me do this so that I can hurry and get home to you. Now, will you let me do that?"

"O-Okay," Kristen sniffled. "I-I love you, Cameron."

"Okay, Kristen, I have to go now. Bye," Cameron said, hanging up the phone. He sighed as he shook his head. He was going to spend some time with her alright. Time to dump that loony. She needs to be in a padded room.

He went to his room afterwards and took a long, hot shower. He was starting to think that Kristen needed psychological help. He wondered how in the world he allowed himself to get tied up with such a crazy bitch. Given the choices, he'd prefer Caitlyn. At least she wasn't needy. She could hold her own. Now, Serena, there was a one-night stand in the making if he'd ever had one. She was perfect. They weren't even from the same state. He was half-tempted to call her room, but he decided to wait. When he stepped out of the shower, he noticed that he'd gotten five more calls, all from Kristen. She left messages asking him why he didn't say he loved her back. At that moment, he turned the ringer off on his cell phone. Then, he attempted to get a good night's rest. He didn't realize how tired he was until his head hit the pillow and he surrendered to a deep slumber.

Chapter
5

Cameron had left a wake-up call for 7 a.m., and when it came, he realized that he'd awakened entirely too early. It was as if he was starting to feel the repercussions from all the things he and Caitlyn had gotten done the day before. He found himself too tired to move and eventually drifted off to sleep once again. By the time he awakened, he'd slept an additional three hours, making it now shortly past 10 a.m. Jumping from bed, he took a quick shower. He went next door to Caitlyn's room, wondering why she'd not beckoned him. Once she opened the door, he had his answer. She looked awful, and he knew she was not feeling well.

"Ice Princess, if this is to turn me off, it's working," Cameron said.

"Oh, kiss my ass!" Caitlyn yelled, immediately before coughing.

"Now, now, now, we won't have such language," Cameron said, walking past her into her room.

"The only reason I'm not kicking you out is in hopes that you'll catch whatever I have, you SOB!"

"Even sick, some things about you don't change, huh?"

Cameron smiled.

"Is there a reason you're here?" Caitlyn sighed.

"I just thought I'd take care of the pawn shop lead."

"Do what ever you want! You don't need me to hold your hand! Besides, I'm too sick to even argue," Caitlyn sighed, throwing up her hand. "Just, get out!"

"Maybe I'll get you something to take, something that will knock you out," Cameron said.

"I've already taken something, thank you," Caitlyn said sarcastically.

"Too bad. I could think of a bottle or two of something I could give you," Cameron replied. "Where are your notes from yesterday?"

"Why?"

"Because I want to go over them," Cameron sighed. "Look, we're supposed to be on the same team. I'm not out to sabotage anything."

"You'd better not be. If I give you my notes, will you get out?"

"Gladly," Cameron said.

"They're on my desk."

"Thank you. I'm going to get these affidavits done and follow up on this lead, and I'll come by to check on you when I get back."

"Don't do me any favors," Caitlyn said, coughing.

Cameron shook his head as he closed her door after leaving out. He then went back to his room and prepared the affidavits. He contacted a notary public at the local courthouse and the two of them went together to get John Stratman's signature. He called Deanna and she was able to meet him on her break to sign her statement.

Afterwards, Cameron went back to the hotel to fax copies of the statements to Jackson. Cameron then left the hotel after getting directions to the pawnshop. He knew going to the pawnshop would be a long shot, but he had to see anyway if there was any chance of this being a productive visit. When he arrived at the pawnshop, he sat there for a minute trying to gather his thoughts. A part of him wondered what significance the locket would have, but, he had a nagging feeling that it was the key. When he got to the counter, the man behind it had not noticed his arrival.

"Excuse me," Cameron said.

The man turned to look at him. He was an older gentleman in his mid to late fifties.

"Yes? Can I help you?" the man asked.

"Is the owner here?"

"I'm the owner, Edward Price," he stated.

"Hi, I'm Cameron Spencer," Cameron said, holding out his hand.

"How do you do?" Mr. Price said, shaking Cameron's hand. "What can I do for you?"

"I'm an attorney with Larson, Craig and Jacobs Law Firm in Indiana," Cameron said, handing him his business card. "I'm investigating a case, and I've been told that an item that could prove helpful in our case may have been pawned here."

"When was it pawned?" Mr. Price asked.

"Around 26 years ago," Cameron said.

"26 years?" Mr. Price laughed. "You're kidding, right?"

"No, I'm not," Cameron said, shaking his head. "I know this is a long shot and there's a possibility that you have no idea what I'm even talking about. There was a locket that was pawned here by a woman, Deanna Lassiter. She was paid $250.00 for it. The locket had an inscription on it, something in reference to 'perfect forever.' Does any of this ring a bell?"

"'Picture perfect forever'?"

"Do you remember something about it?"

"Yeah, I remember that I was never able to sell it. It said 'Picture perfect forever, love, Gary.' No one wanted a locket with someone else's inscription. So, I was never able to sell it."

"What did you do with it?" Cameron asked.

"Believe it or not, I still have it. Wait just a minute." Mr. Price went to the back for a few minutes, returning with the locket. "I was pretty green in this business at that time,

~ 91 ~

and I gave the lady a lot more than I should have. I mean, it was worth the money, but it never occurred to me at the time that I wouldn't be able to sell it because it was inscribed with a personal message. So, I just chalked it up to a loss on my part. A lesson well learned." Mr. Price handed the locket to Cameron.

"It's very beautiful." Cameron opened the locket and saw a picture inside of Garret and Victoria.

Mr. Price noticed his looking inside the locket. "She's a beautiful woman, isn't she?"

"Yes, she is," Cameron said.

"I couldn't throw it away. Something wouldn't let me get rid of the picture."

"Well, I'm glad you didn't. It helps me a lot with my case," Cameron said.

"I don't know who it is," Mr. Price stated.

"It's my client and his second wife," Cameron said.

"Well, he's a lucky son of a bitch to be married to someone as beautiful as she is," Mr. Price laughed.

"Yeah, lucky," Cameron murmured.

Cameron turned the locket over and looked at the inscription. Then, he noticed something.

"What are these markings on it?"

"It's from this exclusive jeweler in Indiana. He swears that none of his work is ever duplicated." Mr. Price rolled his eyes. "I've seen his work before. He's a bit arrogant, but very talented."

"What's the name of his place?" Cameron asked.

"'Hallinger Fine Jewelry,' owned by Tyler Hallinger. It's located in Gavin, Indiana," Mr. Price said.

"How much would you be willing to sell this to me for?" Cameron asked.

"It's been so long. I tell you what, pay me $200.00 and you can have it. At least it won't be a total loss," Mr. Price stated.

"Do you take credit cards?" Cameron asked.

"Sure, I do."

As he waited, he looked up and noticed a clarinet in the

display case. It was just like the one Caitlyn circled in her magazine. He thought to himself that if she wasn't such a vindictive bitch, he would have gotten it for her.

"Is that a Bastionne 450?"

"Yes, it is," Mr. Price smiled. "Do you want it?"

"No, I was just wondering. Someone I know expressed some interest in one just like it."

"Well, it's here if you want it," Mr. Price said.

"I won't be buying it for her, that's for sure," Cameron smiled.

"Suit yourself," Mr. Price shrugged.

Cameron paid for the locket and left, informing Mr. Price that he may have more questions for him later. He went back to the hotel and called information to get the number to the jeweler. He called the jeweler and asked for Mr. Hallinger.

"Mr. Hallinger is not in at the moment," the woman stated.

"When will he be back?" Cameron asked.

"He'll be back in about an hour. Can I take a message for him?"

"Please have him to call Cameron Spencer at (513)555-9000, room 724. I'll be here waiting for his call," Cameron stated.

"Okay, I'll give him the message."

Cameron decided to go down to the restaurant in the hotel for a bite to eat. He was hoping he'd run into Serena, but he didn't. He assumed she'd be in meetings all day, so he didn't bother to try to seek her out. By the time Cameron went back to his room, he noticed the message light on his phone was blinking. He checked the message and immediately called Mr. Hallinger back.

"Hello?" A man's voice answered.

"Mr. Hallinger?" Cameron asked.

"This is Mr. Hallinger."

"Hi, I'm Cameron Spencer," Cameron said.

"Oh, yes, Mr. Spencer. My clerk told me you'd called and I'd called you back."

"Yes, I know. I was out of my room for a moment,"

Cameron stated.

"How can I help you Mr. Spencer?" Mr. Hallinger asked.

"I'm in possession of a piece of jewelry that was purchased from you at least 27 years ago."

"That's a pretty long time, although I do offer a lifetime guarantee. What seems to be the problem with it?"

"There's no problem with the locket, I was just wondering what you could tell me about it."

"Is this something that you personally purchased?" Mr. Hallinger asked.

"No, sir. I'm an attorney with Larson, Craig and Jacobs Law Firm there in Indiana."

"Yes, I know your firm. I know Phillip Larson quite well. He and I used to play golf together from time to time. How is he?"

"He's fine. I'm not in Indiana now, but I'm in Illinois. I'm working on a case and I needed to find out something from you about a locket that has your markings on it," Cameron said.

"I'd probably have to see it to be able to tell you about it. Does it have an inscription or anything?"

"Yes. It says 'Picture perfect forever. Love, Gary.' As I stated before, it would have been purchased over 27 years ago," Cameron said.

"One of the lockets I did for Garret Marlow?" Mr. Hallinger asked.

"You're familiar with it?" Cameron asked.

"Very familiar. Some of my best work. Gary and I were good friends before everything happened because we were in college together. I did the locket especially for him for Victoria. He gave it to her after he found out she was pregnant. He'd done one for his first wife, Rachel, too."

"Really?" Cameron asked. "So, there was one for Rachel, too?"

"Yes, but the one you're talking about was for Victoria. The one for Rachel had a different inscription. If I remember correctly, it said, 'To R, All the family I need. Love, G.' Gary wanted to cheer her up after they weren't able to have children."

"Are you sure about all of this?" Cameron asked.

"Of course, I'm sure. Gary was in his first year of law school when I did the locket for him, if I'm not mistaken. He was a good friend of mine, and I was just taking over my father's business. He and I were talking one day, and I suggested that I design something special for him to give to her. Wait a minute. Does this have something to do with Garret's case?" Mr. Hallinger asked.

"Yes, it does."

"Well, I'll gladly help in any way that I can."

"That's good to hear. You said his other wife had a locket that said 'To R, All the family I need. Love, G.'? Is that right?"

"Yes. Rachel really went off the deep end after she and Gary found out they couldn't have children. She was always a little strange, but Gary could never see any wrong in her."

Cameron was jotting all of this down as Mr. Hallinger spoke. Hopefully, this would just add to everything else and make his case stronger to clear Mr. Marlow. Cameron talked with Mr. Hallinger for a few more moments, wondering just how much more he knew about Rachel.

"Mr. Hallinger, did you know Mr. Marlow's first wife very well?" Cameron asked.

"Pretty well. I mean, we all were in college together. The things I could tell you about Rachel Marlow could send chills up your spine."

"What do you mean?" Cameron asked.

"Rachel was obsessed with Gary. I remember during our junior year they broke up for a while and he started dating someone else. My girlfriend at the time, Alice, told me in confidence that Rachel threatened the girl if she didn't stay away from Gary."

"From my experience in college, that type of cattiness is common among girls," Cameron reasoned.

"Not like this. According to Alice, this was much

~ 95 ~

deeper than spreading a bad rumor, or playing a cruel joke. Alice and Rachel were very close friends in college, but something happened to come between them and they had a terrible falling out."

"Do you have any idea what it was that came between them?"

"Alice would never say. I know that the girl Gary dated briefly left school. I'm sure it wasn't because of Rachel, but there were rumors."

"Rumors?"

"Yes. That Rachel had intimidated Jennifer into leaving school."

"That's giving Rachel a lot of power," Cameron commented.

"I know. That's why it's probably not true. Jennifer could have left for a lot of reasons, none of which had anything to do with Rachel. Jennifer was brutally killed a couple of weeks after she withdrew from college."

"Really?"

"Yeah. Jennifer and Gary were never that serious. She and Rachel were bitter rivals. She only went out with him to make Rachel mad."

"Looks like it worked."

"Probably better than Jennifer wanted."

"You're probably right. By the way, do you happen to have any pictures of Rachel?" Cameron asked.

"No, I don't. Gary doesn't have any?" Mr. Hallinger asked.

"No, and we can't seem to find a picture of her anywhere," Cameron said.

"If I'm overstepping, please let me know. But, what does a picture of Rachel have to do with Gary's case?"

"I'd rather not get into it right now. Thank you so much for your help. I'll be in touch with you really soon," Cameron told him.

"I'll be here," Mr. Hallinger said.

Cameron hung up with Mr. Hallinger and immediately got onto his computer to type up notes from his conversation with him. As he was working, he was interrupted by his phone ringing.

"Hello?" Cameron answered.

"Cameron?" Serena responded.

"Yes? Who is this?"

"It's Serena."

"Oh, hi, Serena. How are you?"

"Fine. I hope I didn't catch you at a bad time. Your conversation last night seemed pretty intense."

"It was nothing," Cameron said lightly.

"It didn't sound like 'nothing.'"

"Trust me, it's nothing that I can't handle."

"If you say so. I was calling because I was wondering if you still wanted to get together this evening for dinner."

"Sure, I still want to see you. I'll meet you down in the bar at around 7:30 this evening. Is that still good for you?"

"Yeah, that's fine. I'll see you then," Serena said.

After hanging up, Cameron thought to himself that he should be careful with this woman whom he knew nothing about. She'd be a good bedding partner, but he didn't want some obsessive fool like Kristen. He finished what he was doing on the computer, and then he showered and changed, meeting Serena promptly at 7:30. He was looking forward to the night, because he was sure he and Serena would end up in bed together. He smiled at himself as he looked in the mirror. He put on some of his best aftershave, and headed down to meet her.

Although he was anxious to get to the best part of the evening, Serena proved to be very good company, and the two of them stayed in the restaurant for well over two hours. The piano bar provided a relaxing atmosphere, which was just what Cameron needed. Serena was delightful, entertaining, and beautiful. After dessert, they both had a couple of drinks.

"So, why don't we continue this conversation in your room?" Serena suggested.

"I like a woman who gets right to the point," Cameron smiled.

"I know what I want, and I go after it," Serena smiled.

"I like that," Cameron smiled. He then motioned for the waiter. "Can I get the check please? And add a nice bottle of white wine to go to my bill."

"Yes, Sir," the waiter smiled.

Cameron paid for dinner and they left the hotel to head up to his room. They sat on the sofa in his hotel room and had a drink. Cameron excused himself to go to the restroom to make sure he had protection in case he and Serena ended up in bed. He went back to the sofa and they toasted with another drink Serena had waiting for him. They continued to talk for the next few minutes. Cameron hadn't had very much to drink, but he was starting to feel a little woozy. He'd always been able to hold his own when it came to drinking, but he was feeling this way after only two glasses of wine. Serena seemed to notice his unsteadiness.

"Cameron, are you okay?" Serena looked concerned.

Without warning, Cameron's vision became blurred, and his head was throbbing.

"Cameron? You don't look so good," Serena said.

"I-I don't feel very well," Cameron seemed to lose control of his senses.

"Cameron?" Serena called out to him in an echo.

Cameron felt as if he was in a cloud. He was fading fast and he couldn't seem to control it. The last thing he remembered was collapsing on his bed, and then everything went black.

****

Cameron awoke the next morning with the worst headache he'd ever experienced in his life, and he wanted to die to ease the pain. He tried groggily to remember where he was and what happened. He felt as if his head was ringing. Slowly, reality started to sink in and he realized that it wasn't his head that was ringing but his phone. He barely had the strength to answer it, but he eventually did.

"Hello?" Cameron answered.

"Cameron, where in the hell have you been?!" Caitlyn

yelled on the other end.

"Please don't shout. What time is it?" Cameron asked.

"It's 11:30 in the morning. I just hung up with Phillip. He's been trying to call you all morning. What floozy managed to distract you from answering your phone?"

"Wh-what? What are you talking about?" His head was starting to clear.

"Your boss, you idiot! Phil's been calling, I've been calling. I've been sick, and all you can find time to do is play around! You sound like you have a hangover. Serves you right!"

"Shut the hell up!" Cameron yelled, grabbing his head as he said it.

"Now, you listen to me, you--" Caitlyn started.

At that moment, Cameron hung up on her. His head was throbbing, and the last thing he needed to hear was Caitlyn's irritating voice. He looked towards his desk, and suddenly became alert. Cameron got out of bed, and noticed that all of his notes and tapes concerning the case were gone. It didn't take long after that for him to realize he'd been drugged. All of his information as well as Caitlyn's notes were gone. She'd even taken his computer. Then it hit him: Serena. She'd drugged him and stolen his information, but why? What connection could she have to the case? Cameron immediately called down to the front desk.

"Front desk," the woman answered.

"I'm trying to reach Serena Felton. She's a guest here in the hotel," Cameron said.

"Just a moment. I'm sorry, Sir, but we don't have a Serena Felton registered here in the hotel," the desk clerk said.

"Did she check out?"

"I'm sorry, but there's no record of her being here in the past either."

"Is there a conference for Gorham Software here in the hotel this week?"

"Yes, there is, but most of the guests for that group have already checked out."

"Thank you for your help." Cameron hung up the

phone, angry that he'd allowed himself to be set up.

This woman was obviously not who she said she was, and for whatever reason was trying to sabotage the case. This was the last thing he wanted to explain to Caitlyn. This would only give her the opportunity to rub it in that he was incompetent. His bigger concern was what would Phillip say when he finds out that all of his information had been taken. All of their files, everything that they'd brought with them was gone. Cameron had two boxes with him, and thank goodness he'd left some of his files at home. But, all of his leads, phone numbers, everything was gone. He immediately showered, dressed and went to Caitlyn's room. He figured he'd better get it over with. Cameron knocked at her door.

"Caitlyn," Cameron said through the door.

"Go away, you SOB! No one hangs up on me like that!" Caitlyn yelled through the door.

"Caitlyn, listen, it's important. It's about the case. Please open up. I need to talk to you," Cameron said seriously.

Caitlyn jerked the door open. "This better be good. I don't take too kindly to being treated with such disregard. Now, you have 30 seconds to say what you have to say. And an apology better be first!"

"Look, I'm sorry for hanging up on you, but we've got a real problem. Can I come in?"

"Hell no! Now, say what you have to say!"

"Please, let me in, Caitlyn," Cameron sighed calmly.

"Whatever," Caitlyn sighed, standing aside.

"I was drugged last night," Cameron said, as he sat quickly on the sofa.

"Drugged? By who?"

"By a woman I met in the bar."

"A woman?" Caitlyn gave a slight laugh. "Are you sure you're not just hung over?"

"Caitlyn, this is serious. I met her in the bar, and she seemed nice enough. We started talking, and we even met last night for dinner. Afterwards, we went to my room for a nightcap. At some point, she slipped something into my drink, because not long after, I became disoriented. I vaguely remember anything that happened before passing out. When I woke up, you were calling me on the phone this morning. The worst part is, she took all of my information on the case," Cameron said with a big sigh.

"What?! You idiot! Some woman comes along and bats her eyelashes, and you give her our whole case on a silver platter. Well, I'll let you be the one to explain to Garret Marlow when he goes for his lethal injection that he's losing his life so that you could have a romp in the sack!" Caitlyn yelled.

"Dammit, Caitlyn, that's not fair! I care about this case!" Cameron said, jumping to his feet. "I didn't know the woman was out to sabotage me! I never would have let my guard down!"

"A good attorney never does!"

"Look, we can sit here and argue about this all day, but it would be better if we thought of a way out of this mess," Cameron suggested. "Can we please work together and not snap at each other?"

"Oh? So, you want me to pull you out of this mess. I suppose you want for me to keep it from Phillip, too, huh?"

"Let's not tell him anything unless we have to."

"You self-serving bastard! You know how important this case is to Phil! I'm going to call him," Caitlyn said, picking up her phone.

"So, you finally did it? Finally, something to get rid of me! Well, go ahead! Why can't we work together? You keep going against me at every turn! All I'm asking for is a little time to figure this out," Cameron said, calming down.

Caitlyn looked at him. She sighed, as she put the phone down. "Fine, I won't call him. Not yet, anyway. Maybe it'll be good to have a noose around your neck that I can yank at any time. But, we do need to get our files. The only person I can think to call is Kristen. She can overnight them to us."

Cameron thought about Kristen. He'd treated her pretty shabbily, and now he was going to need a favor from her. Kristen was the last person he wanted her to call for help. Cameron quickly thought of a way to avoid having to deal with her.

"You know, Jackson knows more about what's going on," Cameron suggested.

"That's true. Well, let's call him," Caitlyn sighed. "Boy, you really know how to mess things up." Caitlyn shook her head as she dialed Jackson's number. "Hello, Jackson? Listen, I need a favor. Cameron--"

"Let me speak to him," Cameron interrupted, holding out his hand for the phone.

"Fine," Caitlyn sighed. "Jackson, Cameron wants to talk to you." Caitlyn gave Cameron the phone.

"Hey, Jackson," Cameron said.

"Hey, Cameron. Are you calling to tell me you won our bet?"

"Not hardly," Cameron smiled. "I need a favor. I need for you to ship overnight copies of everything we had on the Garret Marlow case."

"What happened?"

"It's a long story. All of our files were stolen last night, and as you know, we're in a pinch to try and clear this man. I'd really appreciate it if you could get this to us."

"Sure, it's not a problem."

"Thanks, Jackson. Oh, and by the way, keep this under wraps," Cameron instructed.

"You mean don't tell Phillip," Jackson clarified.

"Exactly."

"No problem. Give me your address."

Cameron then gave him the address to the hotel and instructed to send the package as deliverable only to Cameron or Caitlyn with a signature required. After hanging up with Jackson, he turned towards Caitlyn.

"I hope this works," Cameron sighed.

"Cameron, you've been an arrogant egomaniac from the moment I met you. And, although I'm sorry about this setback and what it could mean to Mr. Marlow, I think what happened only confirms that you aren't worth the paper your law degree is printed on," Caitlyn said calmly.

"I'll give you that one, Ice Princess. I slipped up. I trusted the wrong woman, and I'm paying a high price for it. But, what's your excuse for being such a bitch?"

"You haven't seen 'bitch' in me yet, Lover Boy. But, give it a little more time. When I finish giving you enough rope to hang yourself, you'll find out just how much of a bitch I can be!" Caitlyn said cruelly.

"I'm going downstairs to see what security can tell me about this woman. In the meantime, try to act like a human being and see what you can recall from previous interviews," Cameron said, walking to the door.

"You got yourself into this mess, you get yourself out!"

Cameron grabbed her by the arms. "Look, Mr. Marlow's life is at stake! Hate me all you want, but think about this man's life. Turn me in, report me, do whatever the hell you want after we clear our client! Now, get started on it!"

"You don't give the orders! You are in no position to be demanding. I'll work on this because of our client, but you stay the hell away from me!"

"You're so hard, so cold! You won't even let anyone get close to you! You know what? You've got so much to offer! Any man would kill for a woman like you, but you won't give them a chance!"

Upon impulse, Cameron pulled Caitlyn closer into his arms and kissed her hard on the lips. The kiss lasted all of ten seconds, but for the moment their tongues mingled, Cameron felt something that scared him. She fought briefly, but her body seemed to give in; she even gave a slight sigh. Then, she immediately pulled back. Caitlyn was stunned as she stared at him. She raised her hand to slap him, but he grabbed her arm, stopping her.

"You bastard! You disgust me!" Caitlyn yelled, jerking away from him. "Get out!"

Cameron then looked at her and gave a slight laugh. "Why do I even bother? Good riddance!" Cameron said, slamming out of the door.

Cameron then stormed down the hall to the elevator. As the doors closed on the elevator, he sighed as he leaned against the wall. Something in him suddenly became awakened when he kissed Caitlyn. He hated this woman. What on earth made him kiss her? She was mean, vindictive, evil, beautiful, feisty, and smart. Surely he wasn't developing feelings for this woman who drove him completely crazy. Cameron shook it off and laughed to himself. No, she wasn't his type. The kiss was just to teach her a lesson.

When he got down to the lobby, he asked to speak to hotel security to alert them to the fact that some of his property had been stolen. He described Serena, and they went down to view tapes from the night before. They could plainly see Serena on the tapes, and she was carrying a box, and there was a man with her who was also carrying a box. The surveillance tapes outside showed the two of them getting into a dark, late model Honda, but the tag was conveniently hidden. There was nothing distinctive about the car, and Cameron didn't recognize the man with Serena. She obviously knew exactly what she was looking for. They filed a report with the local police, but Cameron was told it probably wouldn't do much good. Without a tag number, and with the car being such a common color and model, the chances were slim that they'd ever find it. It could have been a rental, or they could be half way across the country by now. Serena probably wasn't even her real name.

Cameron went back to his room and pulled out his tape recorder, which thankfully had not been stolen. He retrieved some of the blank tapes in his briefcase, and began to recite what they'd learned over the past few days. It was hard without his notes, but he managed to recall quite a bit. As Cameron worked, he received a knock at his door.

"Who is it?"

"It's Caitlyn."

Cameron stood from his chair and went to open the door, ready to go another round with her. He noticed she had a bag in her hand.

"What do you want, Caitlyn?"

~ 104 ~

"Peace offering," Caitlyn said, holding the bag out to give to Cameron. "I went to the restaurant downstairs and got pastries for us."

Cameron looked at the bag, and then at Caitlyn suspiciously. "Why?"

"Because I want to try. I want to try to get along with you. I want to clear our client. And I know now that we need to work together to do this. If my stubbornness causes us not to clear our client, I'll never forgive myself. So, let's do whatever we have to do."

"Thank you, Caitlyn," Cameron smiled. "It was the kiss, wasn't it?"

"Get over yourself, Cameron," Caitlyn sighed. "So, what do you say? Can we call a truce?"

"Okay, truce. Please, come in," Cameron said, stepping aside.

The two of them sat down and picked up where Cameron left off. Apparently, she'd been working on some things as well. The two of them put their heads together and were able to get a lot done in a few hours' time. They were a day behind, but they worked hard to make up for it. It seemed as if the later it got, the more energetic Cameron became. In the back of his mind, he was still worried about who this Serena woman was, and her connection to the case. She looked too young to be the murderer herself, so who was she? Cameron looked at Caitlyn as they worked. He'd never worked with such a complex woman. Cameron ruefully thought about the fact that she had this real passion for her job, but she had a steel wall up that she wouldn't let anyone penetrate. As they worked, Caitlyn commented that they were out of coffee.

"I'll put on a fresh pot," Cameron offered. He then noticed he didn't have anymore, and he remembered seeing a pot in the concierge's lounge down the hall. He walked out of the room and down the hall into the lounge and poured two cups. When he returned, Caitlyn was lying on his bed, curled up and fast asleep. She looked like an angel lying there, and for reasons he couldn't explain, he wanted desperately to reach

~ 105 ~

out and hold her. Instead, he lightly stroked her face.

"I wish I could get to know the real you, Caitlyn Frazier," he whispered.

Cameron covered Caitlyn up with a blanket, and decided to bunk out on the sofa. He didn't want to wake her because he knew she was tired. She wasn't even completely over her cold yet. He suddenly felt an overwhelming sense of wanting to protect her. As he watched her sleep, he realized just how beautiful she really was. Cameron leaned back on the sofa, reading over some things, still pushing his brain trying to remember everything. He hated to admit to the fact that he was more distracted by Caitlyn than he wanted to be. As he worked, eventually, he started to drift off to sleep.

****

Cameron was awakened by the phone ringing the next morning. It was someone from the front desk informing them that they'd received the overnight package they were expecting, and the person who delivered was waiting on one of them to come downstairs. He looked over on the bed and realized Caitlyn was still asleep. She was obviously very tired since the phone didn't seem to disturb her. Cameron woke Caitlyn to tell her that the overnight files had arrived and he was going to go downstairs to pick them up. When he got down to the front desk, he was dismayed by what he saw next.

"Cameron!" Kristen smiled, rushing to hug him.

"Kristen, what are you doing here?" Cameron asked.

"Well, I overheard Jackson while he was talking to you, and I volunteered to bring the files personally to you. After all, I didn't want to take any chances that anyone would steal these, too. So, I got the company plane to fly me here," Kristen smiled. "Isn't this exciting? Now, we can be together for a couple of days."

"No, we can't," Cameron sighed wearily as he took her arms away from around his neck. "Why didn't Jackson come?"

"I-I thought you'd be happy to see me," Kristen said,

as her smile faded.

"This is not a joke nor is it a vacation!"

"I know it wasn't supposed to be that way, but, we're here together, so we may as well enjoy it."

"You don't get it, do you? I'm here on a case! Leave me the hell alone!" Cameron said firmly but quietly, noticing people were staring.

"Y-You don't mean that," Kristen said, with tears in her eyes.

"Oh, yes, I do. Now, I want you back on that plane heading back to Indiana. Thanks for the files, but Caitlyn and I can handle it from here. Now, go home!"

"Cameron, please," Kristen said.

At that moment, the elevator door opened, and Caitlyn stepped off.

"Kristen, what are you doing here?" Caitlyn asked. "Did Jackson push this off on you?"

"No, I overheard him talking to you, and I volunteered to come," Kristen responded.

"Good. I'm glad you're here. Can you stay and help us with a few things today? How soon do you need to get back?" Caitlyn asked.

"I can stay as long as you need," Kristen smiled, looking at Cameron.

"Good," Caitlyn said.

"Wait a minute. Who knows you're here? You have to get permission to use the plane," Cameron commented.

"Alex Jacobs did. Phil's out of the office for a few days, so you're safe," Kristen said. "I know you didn't want him to know what happened."

"Well, well, well, Cameron. Seems your 'secret' won't be a secret long," Caitlyn smiled. "Alex is going to tell Phil, you know."

"Whatever," Cameron sighed. "Look, let's just get these files upstairs."

At that time, Kristen got a room, and unbeknownst to Cameron, she wanted to make sure it was close to his room. Afterwards, a bellhop, who'd been waiting patiently nearby, loaded the files on a luggage rack and pushed the elevator button to take them up to Cameron's room. As they got on the elevator, Cameron was fuming. He was going to be stuck with Kristen for the next couple of days.

"I have a room right next to yours, Cameron," Kristen said lightly.

"So, who cares?" Caitlyn sighed, rolling her eyes.

"My thoughts exactly," Cameron said.

Kristen looked hurt by their callous words. Cameron looked at her, angry that she'd managed to ruin his entire trip. She was a clinging, nagging idiot and he hated the fact that he'd gotten involved with her at all. He felt he was finally starting to break through Caitlyn's wall, and now, here Kristen was.

Kristen went to her room to shower and change, while Cameron and Caitlyn did the same. They had a lot of work still left to do. Since he finished getting ready first, he started thinking about the fact that Deanna had told them that the sports car had vanity plates VARDEN 1. He decided to check with the Illinois State Department of Motor Vehicles to see what he could come up with. They explained to him that it would take a little time to research, but they would try to be back in touch with him by the end of the day.

Caitlyn, Kristen and Cameron spent the better part of the day once again going over evidence and making contact with other employees who worked at Imperial Rental. Deanna told them that she'd come up empty-handed concerning Regina Matheson, but she would continue to look. Cameron was starting to think their luck had just about run out, until the phone rang from the DMV, informing them that they'd found a match to the license plate. Apparently, it was registered at that time to Lawrence Varden, from Gavin, Illinois. They had an address, but also stated that the car it was registered to had been totaled. Cameron jotted down the address, and he and Caitlyn agreed to check it out the next day. Hopefully, Lawrence Varden would still live there, or at least someone who could tell them where he was.

Cameron watched Caitlyn, and noticed she seemed

tired. She yawned heavily, and decided that it was time for her to turn in. She stood up to leave Cameron's room.

"I suppose I should say goodnight. Kristen, don't let Cameron work you too hard," Caitlyn said.

"Oh, I'll be fine," Kristen said.

"Well, goodnight, you two," Caitlyn said, as she walked out the door.

"Goodnight, Caitlyn," Cameron whispered, staring after her as the door closed.

"Boy, I thought she'd never leave," Kristen said, standing to walk towards Cameron.

"What are you talking about?" Cameron asked, seemingly engrossed in something on Caitlyn's computer.

"I'm talking about the fact that we haven't had a moment alone until now," Kristen said, putting her arms around Cameron from behind him.

"Kristen," Cameron sighed. "Maybe you should go to bed, too."

"My thoughts exactly," she said, nuzzling his neck.

"I mean, maybe you should go to your room," Cameron said, getting up abruptly from his seat.

"Cameron, I'm starting to think that maybe you don't want me here," Kristen said.

"Gee, what gave it away?" Cameron said sarcastically.

"Cameron, I thought you loved me," Kristen said.

"I never said that. Kristen, you push too much. I don't love you; don't you get that? I couldn't get far enough away from you when I left. You need help," Cameron said.

"You slept with her, didn't you!"

"What? What in the hell are you talking about?"

"Caitlyn! You slept with that bitch!"

"Who I do or don't sleep with is none of your business!" Cameron yelled.

"It is my business because we're seeing each other and you are sleeping with me!" Kristen shot back.

"Not anymore! There's nothing between us, Kristen. We've never been 'seeing each other'! I don't want you!"

"If I can't have you, I don't want to live, Cameron.

Please don't leave me!" Kristen cried.

"Kristen, what's wrong with you?!"

"Cameron, don't leave me!" Kristen cried, rushing into his arms.

"I think you'd better leave," Cameron said calmly, moving her arms from around his neck.

"Cameron, make love to me," Kristen said, reaching up to caress his face.

"Are you out of your mind?" Cameron said, jerking away.

"Please, Cameron. I know you want me," Kristen said, leaning in to kiss his neck.

"No, you really need to go," Cameron said.

"Please. Can we call a truce?" Kristen whispered.

Cameron thought about Caitlyn, and when she came over to call a truce. As Kristen kissed him on the neck, he started to imagine her as Caitlyn. He started to think about that one kiss that seemed to haunt him. He wanted Caitlyn, and it had nothing to do with the bet. He felt himself swelling with desire for a woman who wasn't even in the room with him. Kristen misunderstood and thought he was desiring her.

"I knew you wanted me," Kristen whispered, as she stroked his manhood. "I can make you feel good, Cameron."

"Oh, Caitlyn," Cameron whispered.

Kristen stopped kissing him, and abruptly pulled back.

"What did you just say? Did you call me Caitlyn?"

Cameron looked at her and thought about it. "What if I did?" Cameron said. Cameron wanted desperately for her to leave.

"That's okay," Kristen smiled. "I forgive you. Make love to me, Cameron."

"Kristen, no," Cameron whispered.

"'No' means 'yes,'" Kristen said, as she undid his pants.

Cameron was still seeing Caitlyn as Kristen caressed him. He was starting to give in, because until that moment, he didn't realize how much he really wanted Caitlyn. He closed his eyes and imagined himself caressing Caitlyn. He roughly

~ 110 ~

pulled Kristen's face towards him and kissed her hard. He then pushed her hard against the wall, and ripped away her blouse. She seemed to enjoy it, as he imagined her as Caitlyn. He forced her skirt up as he pulled out his manhood. Immediately afterwards, he pushed her underwear aside to expose her, entering her hard. She moaned with pleasure, as he tore her bra away, raining fiery kisses down her chest, as he took a hardened nipple into his mouth. He thrust against her hard, over and over again. He felt himself giving way faster than usual, all the time imagining Caitlyn.

"Oh, Caitlyn! Caitlyn!" Cameron yelled.

Kristen didn't seem to care, for she continued to let him imagine she was Caitlyn.

"I'll be Caitlyn for you, Baby! That's right, give it to me! I'm Caitlyn!"

At that moment, Cameron felt himself climaxing. "Oh, Caitlyn!" Cameron was breathing hard as his heart was racing. When he opened his eyes, reality started to sink in as he realized he'd just had sex again with Kristen. He pulled away from her quickly, as he buttoned and zipped his pants.

"Oh, God! What have I done?" he groaned, holding his head.

"I knew you wanted me," Kristen smiled, placing her hands on his chest.

"Get away from me, you psycho!" Cameron yelled, backing away from her.

"Cameron, you wanted me. We just made love. Don't deny your love for me," Kristen pleaded.

"Made love? Please! I've never made love to you! I've simply been having sex with you. I said another woman's name! I imagined myself with her! Don't you have any pride!? Get the hell out!"

"Cameron, don't do this to me! I-I'll kill myself!"

"Well, put us all out of our misery and just do it! The world would be a lot better off! Now, get the hell out!"

"Don't deny it! P-Please don't make me leave! You love me! You just don't know it yet!"

"You need to get on a plane back to Indiana! You are

~ 111 ~

not well, and I don't want anything else to do with you! Now, get out of my room, and leave me alone!" Cameron said, pulling her roughly.

"You think you can just put me out!? You can't get rid of me that easily!" Kristen said harshly. Then she smiled, "after all, I might have gotten pregnant tonight!"

"You've been trying to trap me! You conniving bitch!" Cameron yelled. He pushed her against the wall. "You take your ass back to Indiana, and leave me alone!"

Suddenly, there was a knock at the door. "Cameron, open the door. Is something going on in there?" Caitlyn asked.

Cameron looked fiercely towards the door. "Everything's fine, Caitlyn."

"Are you sure? Where is Kristen?"

"I'm here. I'm okay, really. We're just having a difference of opinion," Kristen said.

"It sounds like more than that. What's going on in there?" Caitlyn insisted. "Open the door."

Kristen buttoned her blouse back as Cameron got himself together. He then opened the door. "I thought you turned in for the night," Cameron said.

"I was about to," Caitlyn said slowly, looking from Cameron to Kristen. "What was going on in here?"

"Nothing," Kristen smiled.

Cameron watched Caitlyn, as he realized that she obviously heard them. She looked at Kristen angrily, but she maintained her composure.

"Um, Kristen, I think it would be best if you return to Indiana tomorrow. I'll call and have the plane come back to pick you up," Caitlyn said calmly.

"No! I want to stay here! You two need me!" Kristen protested.

"You've been a big help today, and we really appreciate it, but I think its best that you go back to Indiana first thing tomorrow morning," Caitlyn said.

"I agree with Caitlyn," Cameron said.

Kristen glared at Cameron. She pursed her lips together, as she reached for her bag resting on the chair.

"Fine. Why wait!? Why don't I leave tonight!"

"Suit yourself," Caitlyn shrugged.

"You stupid bitch! This is all your fault!" Kristen yelled. She pulled her arm back forcefully and tried to slap Caitlyn. Cameron stopped her by grabbing her arm.

"Kristen! Get a hold of yourself! Now, you need to go back to Indiana," Cameron said, holding her arm.

"Let go of me!" Kristen yelled, jerking away from Cameron. "You haven't heard the last of me! You think you can just sleep with me and end it like this!? Oh, no, it's not over yet! I'll sue you for sexual harassment!"

"Kristen, you've been throwing yourself at Cameron since day one. I've seen it," Caitlyn sighed calmly.

"You don't know what you're you talking about!" Kristen said, looking fiercely at Caitlyn.

"You've been unprofessional, and you've totally humiliated yourself by chasing behind a man who has told you he doesn't want you. Now, you will be back on that plane tomorrow morning, is that clear? Otherwise, I'll reveal a lot of your little secrets."

"You haven't heard the last of this. You'll pay," Kristen spit out. Then she looked at Cameron venomously. "You both will." At that moment, she stormed out of the room and slammed the door.

"I don't know what to say," Cameron sighed. "I really owe you."

"Oh, you've done quite enough. I can't believe you were stupid enough to get involved with a subordinate! And of all people, Kristen? Didn't you know better!?" Caitlyn yelled.

"It didn't start out that way," Cameron started to explain.

"I'm sure it didn't. A pretty face and nice figure is all it took for you. My God, Cameron what were you thinking!"

"I'm sorry, Caitlyn. I didn't mean for things to go this far. Tonight was a mistake. I thought she was--" Cameron then stopped mid-sentence.

"You thought she was what?" Caitlyn asked.

~ 113 ~

"Never mind. It doesn't matter."

"What were you about to say?"

"Just forget it," Cameron said.

"Cameron, your personal life is your business. Far be it from me to pry, but when it compromises a very important case, I have to speak up."

"You're right. I've been very unprofessional, and I really want to apologize for that," Cameron said. He reached out and gently took Caitlyn's hand. "Sometimes, I don't think I'm worthy of being on this case with you. You're a phenomenal lawyer," Cameron whispered passionately.

Caitlyn looked at Cameron with tears in her eyes. "I-I heard you having sex with Kristen."

"How much did you hear?"

"I heard you calling my name, Cameron," Caitlyn sighed, closing her eyes.

"You did?"

"Yes, I did. What made you do that?" Caitlyn asked softly.

"Because I've been feeling something for you every since I kissed you. I-I was picturing myself with you," Cameron said.

"I don't even know what to say," Caitlyn said. "I thought you hated me."

"Honestly, I don't know what I feel. I know you're beautiful, you're smart, and you irritate the hell out of me," Cameron said, chuckling slightly. Then, he looked at her deeply. "But, then, I look into those beautiful eyes of yours, and I see something deeper." Cameron reached up to gently stroke the side of her face.

She closed her eyes as he touched her. A tear ran down her face, as she slowly reached up with a shaking hand to cover his hand that caressed her. "I-I can't give in to this," Caitlyn whispered. "You just had sex with another woman, and now you're revealing all these feelings for me. I-I have to go."

At that moment, she rushed from the room. Cameron stared after her. He was attracted to her. Caitlyn already had a very hard wall to tear down. Now that she knew about his affair with Kristen, she'd never give him a chance. He was so angry with himself for being so stupid. Worse yet, it was possible that Kristen might have become pregnant. He had only been careless with one other woman and that was Grace. He was so impulsive with Kristen because he imagined her as Caitlyn. Had he been in his right frame of mind, he never would have had unprotected sex with Kristen. Now, he might have ruined things with Caitlyn before they started. Caitlyn rocked him to the core, and he couldn't even control it. He sat on his bed and sighed. As he sat there, he thought long and hard about what he wanted. He saw something in her that no one else had been able to see. The problem would be getting through to her that he was serious about his feelings. He gave a frustrated groan as he wondered why she should believe him after he just slept with their secretary. He wouldn't blame Caitlyn if she decided she never wanted to get involved with him. He's not even sure where these feelings for Caitlyn surfaced. His mind was tired as he leaned back on his bed and covered his face with his hands. Eventually, Cameron became tired and fell asleep, as his thoughts were overpowered by dreams of Caitlyn.

Chapter
6

On that Friday morning, Cameron and Caitlyn made sure that Kristen got back on a plane to Indiana. She wasn't happy about it, but she didn't have a choice. Once they were able to get rid of her, they got directions to the address they were given for Lawrence Varden, which was over an hour away. They didn't want to call, because if this was someone directly linked to the murder, they would be giving them a head-start to cover any evidence, although it's doubtful that there would be any evidence left to hide. Still, Cameron and Caitlyn didn't want to tip their hands too early, so a surprise visit would be more beneficial to them. Hopefully, this Larry Varden could lead them to Regina Matheson. Cameron had been driving along in stifling silence, and he knew Caitlyn obviously had something on her mind that she wanted to say.

"Caitlyn, are you okay? You've been extremely quiet."

"I'm just thinking, that's all," Caitlyn said.

"Anything you want to talk about?" Cameron asked.

"Maybe it's better if I keep my mouth shut," Caitlyn said.

"About what? What's bothering you?"

"Cameron," Caitlyn sighed. "I really don't want to get into it."

"I thought we agreed to try and get along. You've been as icy and cold to me as ever this morning. Now, would you mind telling me what your problem is?"

"There's a lot wrong with me! Kristen? Of all people in this world, you chose to carry on an affair with her?"

"Look, I had no idea she was as unstable as she is. She seemed like a nice person. Believe me when I tell you that I regret ever getting involved with her."

"Well, it's a little late. She's not going to let this drop, and you could be in a world of trouble by the time we get home," Caitlyn argued.

"Don't you think I've thought about this all night? I regret all of this! I wish I'd used my head in dealing with her."

"Oh, you were using your head alright; just not the right one!"

"Did you have to go there? I know sleeping with her was the biggest mistake of my life, so I don't need for you to rub it in!"

"Cameron, since we've been on this trip, you've managed to be drugged and have all of our important files stolen by someone who has an uncanny interest in the case, only to have the copies delivered by a psychopathic sex maniac who is willing to sleep with you while you call out another woman's name."

"And I'm sure it didn't hurt your ego to hear it was your name!"

"Oh, get over yourself! If it weren't for your overgrown ego and your libido, you might actually be able to solve this case without screwing up so much!"

"Screwing up? Lady, if it weren't for me, we wouldn't have half the information we do and you know it!"

"You are unbelievable! You just won't admit it, will

~ 117 ~

you?"

"Admit what?"

"That you can't win this case without me! You're nothing but a skirt-chasing son of a bitch and I hate working with you!"

"Same, here, Sweetheart! I can't believe I ever thought you could be anything close to human!"

"And I can't believe I thought you had half a brain! I should feel insulted being with such a third-class lawyer!" Caitlyn rolled her eyes and gave a frustrated sigh. "I have got to be paying for something pretty bad in my past life to be dealing with you!"

"Let's face it, you haven't been an angel in this life either!" Cameron shot back.

"I hate you, Cameron Spencer! You are arrogant beyond belief! There's a woman somewhere who has all of our information on this case. What ever possessed you to trust this woman? Was she *that* pretty?"

Cameron could hear the jealousy in Caitlyn's voice. "So, now we're getting to the truth! You're jealous! You want me!" Cameron laughed.

"Want you?" Caitlyn scoffed. "I don't even want to be in the same room with you!"

"Well, we'd have to be in the same room, otherwise it could be difficult," Cameron retorted.

"You're disgusting!"

"And you love it! I'm the best thing to happen to you. You lead a pathetic, lonely life, and I'm the most exciting part of you," Cameron laughed.

"How dare you! You're nothing more than an incompetent attorney! If you weren't trying to chase in behind some woman, we'd still have all of our vital information. I should have known better than to let you have my information. If you would have left everything in my room where it was, it would never have gotten stolen! You told me you were going to go over evidence in your room, but you failed to mention that you had plans with a woman. What was that all about? Was all the talk about working just a smokescreen so that I wouldn't know?"

"Why would I care if you knew? You don't own me! I may be co-counsel on this case, but you are not my boss! So, stop flattering yourself!"

"And just how is that flattering myself!? You know, I had you pegged right! You're just another arrogant attorney who can't see beyond his own self importance!"

"What in the hell does that make you?! Last I checked you also had a law degree! And I actually care about my clients! I don't worry about the prestige of winning, or the embarrassment of losing," Cameron roared.

"I care about my clients! People see a woman who takes her job seriously as some sort of man-eating bitch. You've led a sheltered life that in no way prepared you for the real world! What do you know about life anyway?! I still don't see why Phillip allowed Carl to give such an important case to you. I've been here for almost five years and it's taken this long to get recognized for my true ability. You walk in off the street and get one of the most talked-about cases in the country!"

"So, now the truth comes out! You're jealous of me on so many levels! Phillip lets me have the case, practically off the street, and you're mad because you've had to prove yourself for the past few years! Be happy that Phil trusted you with this one, because you know how important it is to him! But, just for the record, I've proven my ability to handle this case, and any other case as well."

"Yeah, and being a man doesn't hurt!" Caitlyn shot back.

"Being a beautiful woman doesn't hurt, either. Of course, from what I hear, most of your success came from lying on your back!"

"You miserable bastard! When we get back, I'm calling Phillip to tell him I want you off of this case! I'm head counsel and I don't have to work with you!"

"That's what you think! Remember, you called Phil already and tried that once before. Face it, Caitlyn. You're stuck with me! Everyone at the firm was right!" Cameron

~ 119 ~

yelled.

"Go to hell, Cameron!" Caitlyn yelled.

"Being with you has got to be a close second to what it's like!"

The rest of the trip was spent in complete silence, each fuming over their argument. Cameron found 4258 Lakeland Hills Drive. They arrived at a beautiful home in a secluded, very well-to-do area. From the looks of it, Deanna was right in assuming the person driving the car was wealthy. Cameron pulled up the long driveway that circled around a beautiful fountain. Cameron and Caitlyn both got out of the car in silence. When Cameron rang the doorbell, the housekeeper answered.

"Yes, may I help you?" the housekeeper asked.

"We're looking for a Mr. Lawrence Varden?" Cameron said.

"Dr. Varden is at his office. Would you like to leave a message for him?"

"No, that's okay. We'll check with him later," Caitlyn said, before Cameron could respond.

The housekeeper closed the door, and Caitlyn turned to go back to the car.

"Why did you do that?! Are you just determined to ruin this case?" Cameron said, once they'd gotten into the car.

"I did it so that she would not call him and let him know we were looking for him. If we started trying to find out where his office is located and flashing our business card, she's going to clam up. This way, we'll call information for his office phone number and address, and go directly there. Even a wet-behind-the-ears 1L law student would know that!"

Caitlyn used her cell phone to call information and got the address to Dr. Lawrence Varden's office. Then, she entered it into the GPS system. When they found the office, it was located in the hospital's Professional Office Building. Cameron and Caitlyn took the elevator to the fourth floor to find suite 406. When they got there, Caitlyn and Cameron approached the front window and told the receptionist who they were and that they needed to talk to Dr. Varden. While

Caitlyn was talking to the receptionist, Cameron looked around the office and noticed a painting hanging on the wall. The man bore an uncanny resemblance to Garret Marlow. While they waited, Cameron pointed out the picture to Caitlyn.

"My God, they could pass for twins!" Caitlyn whispered.

"Ma'am, sir, would you please come this way?" the receptionist interrupted.

When they entered the office, they realized this was clearly not the person they were supposed to see.

"I'm Dr. Varden, can I help you?" he said, shaking their hands.

"I'm Caitlyn Frazier, and this is my colleague, Cameron Spencer," Caitlyn said. "I'm sorry Dr. Varden, but we expected someone older."

"Well, I'm 36, is that not old enough?" Dr. Varden smiled.

"No, you misunderstand. We were expecting an older gentleman. You clearly cannot be the person we're looking for," Cameron said.

"Who exactly are you looking for?" Dr. Varden asked.

"We're looking for Lawrence Varden, who should be at least in his mid-sixties." Cameron said.

"Oh. You're looking for my father?" Dr. Varden said, surprised.

"Yes, that's quite possible," Caitlyn said.

"My father was killed some years ago. I'm now partner with his former colleague, Dr. Franklin. I'm Dr. Larry Varden, Jr."

"How long ago was your father killed?" Cameron asked.

"My father has been dead for almost 25 years. He was in a terrible car crash."

"I'm sorry to hear that," Caitlyn said.

"Listen, I have several patients waiting. I really need to know what this is concerning or I'm going to have to ask you to leave."

"We're attorneys from Larson, Jacob and Craig Law

~ 121 ~

Firm in Indiana, and we're working on a murder case that your father may have been involved in," Caitlyn stated.

"Excuse me?" Dr. Varden asked. "My father? Involved in a murder?"

"It's quite possible. We have reason to believe that he may have had a connection to a woman we are trying to locate," Cameron stated.

"A woman? What woman?" Dr. Varden asked.

"Rachel Marlow?" Caitlyn asked, hopeful.

"No," Dr. Varden shook his head. "That name's not familiar."

"What about Regina Matheson?" Cameron asked.

"Regina Matheson?" Dr. Varden looked as if he'd seen a ghost. He clearly knew exactly who they were talking about. "Now, that's a name I know, although I haven't heard it in a long time," he sighed.

"So you are familiar with Ms. Matheson?" Caitlyn asked.

"Yeah, she used to work here, for my father. She was a receptionist here for about three or four months. That woman caused more problems when she was here than you can imagine. Why are you looking for her anyway?" Dr. Varden asked.

"We believe she may have played a part in a murder that was committed 27 years ago. We're representing the man who was convicted of the murder. Do you know what ever happened to Ms. Matheson?" Cameron asked.

"She quit, and I have no idea where she went. I was glad when she left. I mean, I was only nine years old at the time she worked here, but I knew enough to know that she was up to no-good."

"Why do you say that?" Cameron asked.

"For one thing, she and my father were having an affair."

"Are you sure?" Caitlyn asked.

"Very sure. I remember the day I found out something was going on between them. I'd scored the winning home run at my baseball game, and I was so excited about it. The first

~ 122 ~

person I wanted to tell was my dad. I ran into his office all excited, and caught them kissing. My father yelled at me about it, but later apologized."

"Did your father ever mention anything about helping her to deliver a baby?" Caitlyn asked.

"No, he never did. To be honest, suspecting her of murder is not a far cry from what I'd expect to hear about her."

"What do you mean?" Caitlyn asked.

"The woman was pure evil," Dr. Varden said, shaking his head. "She was always up to something. I caught her going through my dad's private file cabinet once, which was always strictly off-limits. When I told my dad, she of course denied it, and told me in private that she was going to be my new mom one day and I'd better respect her or she'd have me shipped off to a military school. I told to her that I already had a mom, and she and my dad were never going to split up. She told me that there's always a way. She even made the comment that my mother was dispensable, and that my dad was waiting to get rid of her like yesterday's trash."

"What was your response to that?" Cameron asked.

"What could I say? I was nine years old. I told my dad about it, and he tried to tell me that I misunderstood her, and I couldn't see the good in her because of what I'd witnessed. He was totally blinded by her, and had she just not all of a sudden disappeared, she probably would have killed my mom. I was always suspicious of her; my sister and I both were. At the time, my sister was only eight years old, but she always would ask questions about why Dad liked Ms. Matheson so much. We were adults before I ever told her what I'd witnessed."

"Did your mother know that he was having an affair?" Caitlyn asked.

"No, she never did. She went to her grave believing that her husband was faithful to her; at least she never said anything to me if she suspected something."

"How long has your mother been deceased?" Cameron asked.

"For almost two years. She never remarried after my

father died."

"Did she know Ms. Matheson?" Caitlyn asked.

"She'd only met her two or three times, once at a July 4th picnic, another time at an office party, and I think she may have seen her one other time also."

"Dr. Varden, you mentioned that Ms. Matheson 'all of a sudden disappeared.' What did you mean by that?" Cameron asked.

"She just left. One day she was here, the next day she was gone. To be honest, if you want to know about Ms. Matheson, you need to ask Lauren Jordan," Dr. Varden suggested.

"Who's Lauren Jordan?" Cameron asked.

"She's a nurse who works here who was very close to Regina Matheson."

"She's still employed here?" Caitlyn asked.

"Yeah, she's been here the longest. She could probably tell you everything you need to know."

"Where is she?" Cameron asked.

"Hold on, I'll check." Dr. Varden called out to the receptionist. Shortly after that, there was a knock on the door.

"Dr. Varden, you wanted to see me?" An older woman poked her head in the door.

"Yes, Lauren, this is Cameron Spencer and Caitlyn Frazier. They'd like to talk to you if you have time. You can use my office to speak privately, because I have patients to see. Mr. Spencer, Ms. Frazier, it was a pleasure meeting you. If you have any other questions or concerns, you're welcome to call me." Dr. Varden gave them a business card, shook both their hands and then left.

"What can I do for you?" Lauren asked.

"We're here with questions about Regina Matheson. What can you tell us about her?" Caitlyn asked.

"Regina Matheson? I haven't seen Regina in years. Why are you inquiring about her? Is she in some sort of trouble or something?" Lauren asked.

"We'd rather not get into the specifics right now. We're trying to locate her, and we need to know what you can tell us about her," Cameron stated.

"My God, it's been over 25 years since I've talked to Regina. When she quit and left abruptly, she never called me or anything."

"What do you know about her? At this point, we're desperate. We represent the person who was accused of murder and we have reason to believe that Ms. Matheson may have had something to do with framing him," Cameron said.

"If you'd told me that when I first met her, I'd tell you that you were out of your mind, but as time went on, it's not that far-fetched to believe that she'd do something like that," Lauren stated.

"Why do you say that?" Caitlyn asked.

"When Regina first started here, I'd only been a nurse for about a year," Lauren started. "In fact, this was my first and only nursing job. She always seemed so timid, and I befriended her when she started. She and I used to go to lunch together all the time; we did everything. Then, after about three months, she started to change. She was always talking about this being just a stepping stone for her, but I always thought she meant career-wise, until we had a very odd conversation one day," Lauren said.

"What was the conversation about?" Cameron asked.

"Well, Regina told me that in order to get what she wanted she had to 'remove certain obstacles.' She stated that she'd been cheated out of something in her life, and she was determined to make the people who cheated her pay for what they'd done. This bothered me a little, but I didn't take her literally. Then, one day, I confided in her that my husband and I were going to have a baby. We were pregnant with our first child. I'll never forget that day as long as I live. I'd never been so scared before in my life." Lauren suddenly looked shaken.

"What happened?" Caitlyn asked.

"We were the only two people in the break room having lunch," Lauren said. "It was raining that day so we'd decided not to go out to eat. I was so happy because we'd been trying to have a baby for a while. When I told Regina

~ 125 ~

that I was pregnant, her eyes were so cold towards me. Then she slammed me into a locker and said, 'Not you, too! Even you're betraying me! You lousy tramp! Everyone gets a baby but me!' I must say, I was scared out of my mind. Then, she all of a sudden calmed down and apologized. I had a bruise on the back of my head from when I hit the locker."

"Did you ever report what she'd done?" Cameron asked.

"No, because she was so apologetic afterwards, and she tearfully begged me not to say anything."

"You didn't think there was something seriously wrong with someone who would react like that to your being pregnant?" Caitlyn asked.

"Of course I did. But, considering she'd slung me into a locker, I didn't want to alienate her," Lauren reasoned. "I mean, who knows what else she was capable of doing? At that point, I started to distance myself from her. The day she left and didn't come back, she made the comment to me that she was going to take her baby and move away. The statement shocked me, because she'd never mentioned a baby, and she also had gotten so angry at the mere mention of my being pregnant. I wondered what she meant, but that's all she would say."

"She never said where she would move to?" Caitlyn asked.

"No, just that she wanted to move somewhere secluded in the country, and get away from it all."

"Dr. Varden has mentioned that Ms. Matheson and his father were having an affair. Is there any truth to that that you're aware of?" Cameron asked.

"You know, that's not surprising," Lauren stated. "She never actually told me herself, but I know that she was a little too close for her to be his employee. She was always going into his office, staying long periods of time. I've heard that they've gone away on weekends before. In fact, they'd gone away the weekend before she quit. She didn't tell me, but there was a buzz around the office that the two of them had gone away together."

"Ms. Jordan, you wouldn't happen to have a photo of Ms. Matheson, would you?" Caitlyn asked.

"No, I don't," Lauren said, shaking her head. "The hospital personnel might. I mean, she worked for the hospital and they have to take photos of all new employees."

"Where's personnel?" Cameron asked.

"It's on the first floor in the main hospital. You mentioned this is about a murder. What exactly happened?" Lauren asked.

"We're defending a man who was accused of killing his nine month pregnant wife over 25 years ago," Caitlyn stated. "The baby was never found."

"If that's the case, my advice would be to definitely locate Regina," Lauren agreed. "She probably knows something about it. Especially for her to suddenly start talking about a baby that she'd never mentioned before. Regina really took me by surprise after all the strange things she started doing and saying."

"Is there anything else you can remember? A mention of other relatives or friends? Anything you can think of at this point?" Cameron asked.

"I remember her mentioning that she had relatives in Ohio. Come to think of it, I remember Regina having a confrontation with a woman here one day," Lauren said.

"Who was the woman?" Caitlyn asked.

"She was a patient of Dr. Franklin's. She apparently knew Regina, but she kept calling her Rachel," Lauren said.

"Are you sure about this?" Cameron asked.

"Yeah. The woman was taunting Regina about something she'd done in her past and how she wasn't going to let her get away with it."

"Do you remember this patient's name?" Caitlyn asked.

"No," Lauren shook her head. "I wish I did, but it was so long ago."

"Do you remember how the woman looked?" Caitlyn asked.

"I remember her having a medium complexion, kind of

~ 127 ~

slender build. I think they went to college together."

"Why do you say that?" Cameron asked.

"Because she kept referring to Regina as her sorority sister. But, the way she said it was menacing, like she was being sarcastic. It was as if Regina had done something to her, like maybe they'd been friends at one time or another."

"And you're sure that she called her Rachel?" Caitlyn asked.

"Yes. I couldn't be more pos–" Lauren stopped.

"What were you about to say?" Caitlyn asked.

"Cramer! That was the woman's last name, Cramer," Lauren said.

"How do you remember?" Cameron asked.

"Because Regina kept calling her Crabby Cramer. I don't know her first name, though. I'm not even sure if she's still a patient of Dr. Franklin's. I didn't see her any more after that day. I remember Regina telling her that she'd kill her if she ever referred to her as Rachel again, that Rachel no longer existed. Ms. Cramer told her that she'd have to pay her for her silence about what happened, and that she'd be in touch."

"What did Regina say after that?" Caitlyn asked.

"She told her she'd see her dead first before giving her a dime. Then, the woman mentioned something about that hefty inheritance she got after her parents' house was sold, and she wanted her part of it. She then stated something about keeping her secret all those years for free, now it was time to pay up."

"Did she say what this secret was?" Cameron asked.

"No, but whatever it was obviously was pretty serious," Lauren said. "I'm sure there was so much more to the story than what I heard."

"Did the woman mention what Rachel's last name might have been?" Cameron asked.

"No, she didn't," Lauren stated.

"Ms. Jordan, you've been a tremendous help to us. Here's our card if you think of anything else," Caitlyn said.

"Okay. I'll see what else I can remember," Lauren said.

"We're staying at the Levinway Suites in Lynbridge if you need to reach us," Cameron said.

"Can you tell us how to get to personnel?"

"Sure. I'll take you over there. It's not very far."

"Before we leave, we'd like to get a sworn affidavit from you," Cameron said.

"That's fine," Lauren smiled.

Caitlyn and Cameron walked to personnel, accompanied by Lauren. She introduced them to an office clerk. The office clerk explained to them that employees from that many years ago who were no longer employed, their records were filed away, and it would take a while to find the information needed. All she was able to tell them was that she was employed there from March 6, 1983 to July 11, 1983. The employee helping them also stated that she wasn't sure if there would be a picture or not, because that was around the time they'd just started taking pictures with ID badges. She told them that she would check and have to get in touch with them later. Although this was not what Cameron and Caitlyn wanted to hear, they didn't have much of a choice, so they asked if there was a conference room they could use at the hospital to prepare an affidavit. The woman in personnel directed them to a small room that contained a printer so that they could hook their computer to it. They thankfully had someone who worked in personnel who was a notary public, so they were able to get Mrs. Jordan's signature and witness without any trouble. Those tasks complete, they decided to return to the hotel, now with even more linking Rachel and Regina.

They didn't have very much to say to each other when they arrived back at the hotel. Caitlyn went to her room, and Cameron went to his. Cameron was in his room going over some of the files on the case, when it occurred to him: the picture they saw at the doctor's office. It prompted him to call Dr. Varden to find out who that was on the picture. He talked directly to Dr. Varden who told him that the picture was one of his father. He'd had it done in his honor some years ago. Cameron started to realize that the witnesses had gotten Garret and Dr. Varden mixed up. Dr. Varden had to be the man Amanda Warren saw. That was the only explanation. After all, these two men could almost pass for twins. Cameron was still angry with Caitlyn, but he felt the need to share his theory with her. He went to knock at her door.

"I thought we decided not to talk to each other," Caitlyn said, standing at the door, not letting him in.

"It concerns the case," Cameron stated, pushing past her.

"I don't remember inviting you in!" Caitlyn yelled.

"Too bad. Look, put your silly pride aside and let's do what we can to solve this case. Is that agreeable with you?" Cameron asked.

"'Silly pride'? Trying to belittle me isn't the best way to get on my good side," Caitlyn said.

"What ever made you think I wanted to get on your good side? I'm starting to think that you don't have a good side."

"There are a lot of sides to me that you'll never have the opportunity or pleasure to know."

"I beg to differ. Why don't you just admit how you feel? There's nothing wrong with being attracted to me," Cameron said.

"Being attracted to you comes with consequences, as I can see from Kristen."

"Kristen is a special case," Cameron said, walking towards her. He could sense how uncomfortable she was with his being so close. "But you, you're different."

"Different how?"

"Caitlyn, it's time we stopped kidding ourselves. Let's face it: as much as I hate to admit it, I happen to think you're a wonderful attorney, and probably the most beautiful woman I've ever seen."

With that statement, he reached up slowly, and gently stroked her cheek. Caitlyn moved something in him. He still wasn't quite sure what he felt for this woman, but he was starting to realize that it was much more than just a begrudging respect for a fellow colleague. This wasn't even about sex.

"Cameron," Caitlyn whispered. Her eyes seemed to pierce into his soul.

Cameron stared at Caitlyn, taking in all the beauty of this woman, knowing he could no longer resist. . . . .

Cameron leaned in slowly, afraid that if he moved too fast she would fade away. In what seemed like an eternity, their lips met for the second time, only this time, there wasn't any anger. It was passion. When Cameron kissed her, his body burned with desire to have her completely. He caressed the small of her back, all the time wondering if he could get any closer to this woman he longed for. He ran his fingers through her hair, slightly pulling it back to expose the curve of her neck. He caressed her neck with his tongue, running a hot trail of kisses to her ear. Cameron felt his manhood rising and knew that he wanted more than anything to make love to Caitlyn.

He knew that she felt the same way, too, by the way she responded to his kiss. Their lips seemed to be made for each other, acting on a passion that had been developing since the first moment they laid eyes on each other. A passion only fueled by the fiery confrontations they'd had since the day they met. Cameron pulled away just slightly, and looked deeply into her eyes. Their eyes communicated for them, because never a word was spoken. Caitlyn smiled slightly, and looked seductively at him, as she unbuttoned his shirt. She was obviously finally ready to give in to what she was feeling for him. Cameron started to undo her blouse, wondering how he'd managed to wait as long as he had. He exposed her bra, and at that very moment, lifted her into his arms and carried her to the bed. He'd never felt skin as soft and delicate as hers, and she smelled so sweet, like a combination of jasmine and strawberries. He caressed her bare stomach, and moved his hands up to cup her breasts. They were ignited by the passion they felt for each other, until the phone rang, bringing them out of the paradise they'd found together. Caitlyn jumped slightly.

"Let it ring," Cameron whispered.

"It could be about the case," Caitlyn said, sitting up.

Much to Cameron's dismay, she answered the phone. "Hello? Oh, hi Phillip." She stared at Cameron. "Why did I call? Well, just to give you an update about the case. We seem to be making some headway. We'll probably be leaving here in a couple of days heading to Ohio. How's Mr. Marlow? Good. Well, tell him that we're working as diligently as possible to try to save him. Okay. We'll talk with you soon. Bye, Phil." Caitlyn hung up the phone.

"So, what were you really calling him about? You were actually going to ask to have me taken off the case?" Cameron asked.

"I was upset." Caitlyn placed her hand on his thigh.

"You didn't waste any time, did you?" he asked, standing up to button his shirt.

"Cameron, please don't be that way. You and I have been at each other's throats since we met. But, maybe we can solve this case together."

"Do you really mean that? No more fighting? No more going against each other at every turn?"

"Can I be completely honest with you?" Caitlyn stood up and faced him.

"Please do," Cameron said.

"Sometimes, I think I do want you off of the case, but not for the reasons you're thinking."

"Why don't you enlighten me then?"

"I hate to admit this, but there has been a growing attraction between us since we met, and to be honest, it was getting to be a little too much for me to be around you. Look at what almost happened a few minutes ago. I mean, you called out my name when you were with Kristen. I don't know how I could even consider something with you after knowing you've had an affair with our secretary. How do I get past that?" Caitlyn whispered tearfully, looking into Cameron's eyes. "Besides, we have to stay focused on what we're here to do. We cannot get caught up in sex. Mr. Marlow is counting on us because his life depends on it. Am I making any sense?"

"Yes, you are. But, Caitlyn, I've heard a lot of

unscrupulous things about you since I joined," Cameron argued. "I'm willing to forget about what I heard if you would give me the chance to get to know the real you."

"Cameron, I know there's a lot you don't know about me. I'm almost sure that most of the information you have received was from Kristen, right?"

"Some of it was," Cameron agreed.

"Then, that should tell you something. But, to ease your mind, I'll tell you a little more about my life," Caitlyn sighed. "Alex Jacobs is my uncle."

"What? Are you serious?"

"Very much so," Caitlyn said.

"Why didn't you say so?"

"Because you'd think I got this job because of him. I got this job based on my own merit. I'm sure you heard that I didn't pass my bar exam the first time. My stepfather had a heart attack and I had to leave the exam early. It wasn't that I didn't pass, it was that I was unable to finish so I had to wait and take it the next time it was offered. No one would believe I scored the second highest score on my bar exam, or that I graduated at the top of my class. My uncle has been harder on me than anyone. He doesn't take any slack from me, and he's the first to reprimand me if I do wrong. I suppose a part of me resents the fact that he seems to be so much more lenient towards the other attorneys, but there's no room for error on my part."

"That's because he's proud of you. You represent him more than anyone at the firm, and he's determined that you represent him well. He sees something in you, and knows that if he pushes you, you'll not let him down," Cameron explained.

"I suppose I never thought about it like that," Caitlyn smiled.

"You have a beautiful smile," Cameron said.

"Thank you," Caitlyn blushed. "Cameron, I do want for us to get along. We're probably going to be working on a lot more cases together, and I'm tired of being known as the worst bitch in heels. Or, as you would call me, the 'Ice

Princess,'" Caitlyn said.

"I suppose I liked poking at you, just to get you riled up. I'm sorry for giving you such a hard time when we met."

"I'm sorry for being so awful to you," Caitlyn said.

"I understand now, Caitlyn. Maybe we can be friends?" Cameron said, extending his hand.

She reached out to shake his and smiled. "Friends. It'll be nice to have one of those at the firm for a change."

"So, no one at the firm knows you're Alex's niece?"

"No. The senior partners know, but that's it. They didn't know for the first three months I was there. I asked my uncle not to say anything, and to let me get a shot at getting the job on my own," Caitlyn said. Then she smiled. "We had a deal that if I'd not found work at a firm in six months, that he'd guarantee me a job at his firm. I'd sent out resumes and recommendation letters all over town. When I was called in to interview, I was afraid that my uncle had said something, but he assured me that he'd not. So, I interviewed, and got a job offer."

"That's noble, but it seems like maybe you made it harder on yourself," Cameron commented.

"No, I didn't. I got the job just the way I wanted to. I didn't want the question mark hanging over my head as to whether I got the position because I was really qualified or because of my uncle. As it stood, it worked out quite well."

"You should really be proud of yourself," Cameron said.

"Thank you. It means a lot hearing that from you," Caitlyn said.

Cameron stared at her. She was so beautiful. She'd hardly ever smiled since they met, but Cameron noticed how her eyes seemed to twinkle, and how perfect her lips were. With that thought, he leaned in to kiss her again. Caitlyn didn't resist, as he lifted her in his arms. He really wanted her, and he couldn't resist her any longer. He gently laid her on the bed, as he rained kisses all over her body. He reached over to take the phone off the hook, because he didn't want any more interruptions. He ached to enter her as he undressed her. They were ignited by the build up of passion, and were ready to know each other as lovers. Cameron wanted to take it slow with this woman. He didn't want to cheapen it. As they kissed passionately, learning each other's bodies for the first time, there was a knock at the door, interrupting them. They tried desperately to ignore it, in hopes that whoever it was would go away.

"Ms. Frazier," the voice from the other side called out.

They immediately stopped kissing, and both sighed heavily. She looked at Cameron.

"They're not going to go away. I'm sorry." Caitlyn sat up and pulled her shirt on. "Who is it?"

"It's hotel security."

Caitlyn sighed as she stood from the bed. After buttoning her shirt completely, she opened the door.

"Yes? What can I do for you?"

"We managed to get a tag number from the vehicle that the person used who stole your merchandise. We tried to call, but the line's been busy. We also tried to reach Mr. Spencer, but there was no answer." The security manager looked past Caitlyn, and saw Cameron buttoning his shirt. "I didn't mean to interrupt, but Mr. Spencer stated that this was quite important."

"It's okay," Caitlyn assured him. "So, who was the car registered to?"

"It was a rental, but it was rented by a Preston Greer. Does that name sound familiar to either of you?"

"No, it doesn't," Caitlyn said shaking her head.

"Do we have an address?" Cameron asked, joining in.

"We're still working on it. How much longer will you be here in the hotel?"

"No more than a couple of days," Cameron said.

"We should have something by then. Once again, I'm sorry to interrupt," the security manager stated.

"It's okay," Cameron said.

After Caitlyn closed the door, she looked at Cameron. She gave a heavy sigh as she shook her head.

"Obviously, you and I aren't supposed to be together

~ 135 ~

tonight."

"You think that's why we keep getting interrupted?" Cameron asked.

"It's possible. Maybe it's for the best. We can't get sidetracked. I'll make a deal with you. First, we have to clear Mr. Marlow, and then we can see where things go. Is that okay?"

"I don't suppose I have much of a choice, do I?"

"No, you don't," Caitlyn smiled. "Now, let's see if we can clear our client."

Caitlyn and Cameron worked non-stop, trying to come up with something that they may have missed before, gathering lists of people to talk to in Ohio. Somewhere, there had to be a photo of Regina Matheson. Cameron had instructed one of the paralegals to go to Garret Marlow's parents' home to look for a picture of Rachel. When Cameron talked to her afterwards, she told him that she'd come up empty-handed. The only pictures she could locate were of Garret and Victoria.

They were working on the theory that Regina was really Rachel and that she'd murdered Victoria, all the time framing Garret. She had the perfect motive: Victoria had her ex-husband, and was about to give Garret the one thing she never could, a child. It was obvious now that Rachel's name was connected with Regina since according to Lauren, this woman referred to her as Rachel. There was no way this could have been coincidental.

Chapter
7

Cameron and Caitlyn decided on that Saturday to enjoy the day, get a little sight-seeing in while they were in Illinois. Business-wise, there was very little they could do that they hadn't already. There were so many wonderful, historical things to see, so he took pictures of everything in sight to send to his parents. His mom and dad had barely ever been outside of Kentucky, although Cameron had always tried to get them to go on a well-deserved vacation. They decided to go to a nearby park for a picnic. Cameron couldn't remember when he'd been as relaxed and content as he was at that moment. He lay back on the blanket and looked up at the sky while Caitlyn sat out their lunch. He started to remember times in his childhood, which made him smile. Caitlyn looked over at him and smiled.

"What are you thinking about?" Caitlyn asked.

"I'm thinking about when I was a little boy and how I used to try to figure out what shapes the clouds were," Cameron said.

"Tell me about your childhood," Caitlyn said, lying

~ 137 ~

next to him, propping her head up with her arm.

"I had a great childhood," Cameron smiled. "My mom and dad are loving parents, and they never neglected me. I mean, it was a little boring growing up with no brothers and sisters, but my mom always made sure I never had time to think about it. She and I used to go on nature hikes together, we went fishing, everything."

"Your mom likes to fish?" Caitlyn asked.

"Oh, she's a pro at it. She's better than my father or me any day," he said. "My dad bought me my first fishing rod when I was only seven. But, going fishing was really a special time for my mom and me. We have a fishing pond on our land where my mom and I would go. We've had more talks there than I could ever even count. My father and I were always close, but my mom, she's my rock. Although in many ways, as much as I confide in my mother, my father knows more about me than she does, because she worries a lot. My dad and I talk about other things in my life that are important, you know, like those father-son things that I don't want to worry her with."

"You mentioned it was boring with no brothers or sisters. Do you think you would have been as close with your parents as you are now if there were siblings?" Caitlyn asked.

"I'd like to think I would but, probably not," Cameron shrugged. "I mean, I have the next best thing to having a brother: my best friend David Kimbrey. He and his wife Linda live in Lariette Springs. They have a horse ranch that his parents left him when they died. He and Linda love it, and according to them, they want to grow old and gray right there on Kimbrey Ranch," Cameron smiled.

Caitlyn smiled. "How long have the two of you been friends?"

"Since we were five years old. We met in kindergarten when we got into a fight over who was going to push Linda on the swing set. We both had a crush on her, even at five years old," Cameron smiled. "He still jokes with me today about how he 'stole my girl' in kindergarten. After he finished beating me up, the teacher made us make up. He offered me ½

~ 138 ~

his peanut butter and jelly sandwich as a peace offering, and we've been best friends ever since. I honestly don't know what I'd do without him. We were inseparable throughout grade school and high school. When we graduated, I went off to school and he stayed and went to school locally. He, Linda and Grace would come up and visit me sometimes when I couldn't get home for the weekend. Although we're still good friends, it's nothing like it used to be."

"That's understandable. You're both adults now, which adds a lot more responsibility to your lives than you had before. Friendship can survive the distance if it's important enough to you. I don't know if I've ever had a best friend, I mean someone I could confide in about anything and everything," Caitlyn said. "You mentioned Grace. Who's she?"

"Grace was my fiancée," Cameron sighed.

"What happened?"

"She felt like I couldn't give her what she wanted," Cameron shrugged nonchalantly. "She was seeing this guy who lived right in the next town. He'd gotten a residency in one of the best hospitals in the state, and he wanted to 'take her away' from Lariette Springs. Never mind the fact that she was wearing my ring. So, they eloped, and she broke the news to me on Valentine's Day of this year. Needless to say, Valentine's Day won't be the same for me from now on. The most romantic holiday of the year, and she tells me she just married another guy."

"I know that must have been a difficult time for you," Caitlyn said.

"Yes, it was. My mom saw through Grace from the beginning. She told me that Grace was no good for me. I guess I should have listened. But, we live and learn. So, how about you? Do you have a 'past'?"

"Not an interesting one. I dated a guy pretty seriously in high school, but it was downhill afterwards. He went off to school, and we tried to keep a long distance relationship going, but, eventually he wrote me a 'Dear Jane' letter ending it with me. Then, he got married six months later because the girl he was seeing was pregnant."

"Man, that must have been rough," Cameron sighed.

"Yeah, it was. My guess is, she was in his life all the time, probably there telling him what to write in the cowardly letter he sent me. I was totally devastated, because I really thought we had a future together. Then the way I found out about the wedding was so hurtful and cold. At least Grace told you and you didn't hear it through the grapevine like I did. Since he didn't have the decency to tell me himself, I found out from his cousin. His cousin thought I already knew, and I didn't. I think I cried for two weeks."

"I'm sorry you went through something like that. It's not a good feeling, that's for sure."

"People rarely understand why I'm like I am, but it's been hard to let myself get close again to anyone. I dated a guy briefly last year, but he was threatened by the fact that I made more money than he did. He constantly complained about it, but was also always asking for money to 'help him out' with his bills. My track record with men has left a lot to be desired," Caitlyn said. "So, I tend to throw myself into my work because it keeps me going. That's why everyone at the office thinks I'm the worst thing in high heels."

"Caitlyn, you have the chance to change things at the office. Alex Jacobs being your uncle isn't anything to be ashamed of. But, you've got a wall up that needs to be torn down. Let's face it. We can't make it in this world without someone to lean on. At least try to get along with others. People are more receptive than you think."

"I don't know if that's true. When I first started, I tried. But, no one wanted to get to know the real me. You know they think I'm having an affair with my uncle?"

"I heard about that. But, you can make that right," Cameron reasoned.

"Why should I have to explain myself? Why can't people just accept me? You expect for me to believe it will be better when they find out that Alex Jacobs is my uncle? No, at that time, they'll find something different to talk about. Instead of me bedding him, I'll have everything because of my

~ 140 ~

uncle. Don't you see, Cameron? I can't win either way."

"That's not true, Caitlyn. You've already earned your place in the courtroom. Your impeccable record has nothing to do with bloodlines. People realize that. They begrudgingly respect you. But, you've got to open up. People talk because you're so hard. If you'd bend a little, you'll find that people are more willing to give you the benefit of the doubt than not."

"I suppose you're right. It is kind of hard being a loner," Caitlyn commented. "None of the female attorneys invite me to lunch, none of the secretaries invite me, none of the clerks invite me. I'm just usually on my own. I had one good friend, Marie, who worked there, but she left when she had her baby a few months ago. She made the decision to be a stay at home mom because her husband wanted her to. I envy that. I mean, to have that trusting, caring relationship where you both have an agreement about raising a family. I asked Marie if she felt she was giving up a lot, after all, she was a very good attorney with a very prestigious firm. Her response was that no job would ever be more important than her husband and child. That's commitment."

"Well, obviously Marie saw something in you. How often do you talk to her?"

"Usually once or twice a week. She's got a lot going on, so we rarely get together. She is truly one of the closest friends I have and the only one besides you who knows Alex is my uncle," Caitlyn smiled. "I'm her baby's godmother."

"She must have a lot of trust in you," Cameron smiled. "I mean, to name you her baby's godmother is a phenomenal way to say she thinks a lot of you."

"Not nearly as much as I think of her," Caitlyn said. "She's truly one of a kind. Maybe you'll get to meet her one day."

"You mean like getting together socially; you and me, her and her husband?"

"Actually, I meant that she comes by the firm sometimes, and you'll probably get to meet her then."

"I liked my idea better," Cameron smiled.

"I'm sure you did," Caitlyn laughed. "One step at a

~ 141 ~

time, okay?"

"One step at a time," Cameron repeated.

Suddenly, there was an awkward silence between them that seemed to last an eternity. When their eyes locked and neither could seem to look away, it was obvious that they felt an attraction to each other, a fact that they'd proven the night before. Cameron tried hard to fight what he was feeling for this woman. He'd melted her defenses, and she'd melted his heart. At that moment, he wondered what this could possibly lead to. He noticed her nervously fumbling with the bracelet she was wearing.

"That's a beautiful bracelet," Cameron observed.

Caitlyn smiled. "Thank you. My grandmother gave it to me for my 18th birthday, and I treasure it. But, the clasp is loose and I keep checking it to make sure it's still on my arm."

"Why don't you put it away until you can get it fixed?" Cameron suggested.

"Because it keeps me connected to her. I'd hate to lose it. It was the last gift she gave me before she died, and I never go anywhere without it."

"What kind of charms are on it?"

"Well, my grandmother always encouraged me to follow my dreams," Caitlyn smiled. "When I was 18, I didn't know what I wanted to major in while in college, and I had no idea what I wanted to do with the rest of my life." Caitlyn held out her arm. "So, she gave me this bracelet with seven charms: one of the scales of justice for law, one of the happy and sad masks for acting, one of the medical staff for medicine, one of an apple and ruler for teaching, one of a novel for writing, and one of a chef's cap. And last but not least, there's one of an angel for two reasons: first, she told me I'd always be her little angel, no matter what I did in life, and second she said it's a way of having my guardian angel with me at all times. The bracelet was her way of telling me that the sky was the limit and I could be anything I wanted. It had a profound impact on my life, so, I majored in education and went to law school."

Cameron smiled. "Sounds like you had a wonderful

relationship with her. I never knew my biological grandparents on either side."

"Really?"

"Yeah, my mother's parents died years ago, before I was ever even born; and my real father died before I was born also and he was an orphan. The only grandparent I ever had any knowledge of was my stepfather's mother, who passed away two years ago," Cameron stated.

"Were you close to her?"

"Not as close as I would have liked to have been," Cameron admitted.

The two of them sat there and talked until the sun set. It was a beautiful evening. Moments like this made Cameron almost forget the real reason they were there. They arrived back at the hotel that night, showered and changed so that they could go out to dinner.

They decided to go to a restaurant called Blakely's that came highly recommended by the concierge at the hotel. There was a lounge area for those who had to wait on a table. The lounge was lavishly decorated along with an elegant cherry wood curio cabinet, filled with precious antiques.

Cameron and Caitlyn were seated after waiting a few minutes. Luckily, they were seated at a table that had a breathtaking view of the city. The restaurant had a veranda, and since it was on the 65th floor of the building, the city seemed to twinkle below them. Cameron couldn't think of a more romantic place to be with Caitlyn, and he knew he would always remember it fondly. As they were sitting there, the pianist started playing *Heaven Smiled On Us*, and Caitlyn smiled.

"What are you smiling about?" Cameron asked.

"I used to love to play that song on my clarinet."

"I noticed you circled a clarinet in a magazine on the plane," Cameron smiled.

"Yeah, I had one just like it when I was younger," Caitlyn reminisced. "My biological dad bought it for me, but, he had a gambling addiction and eventually sold it. I was heartbroken."

"I'm sorry," Cameron said, reaching out to cover her hand. "So, are you hoping to find one again?"

"Yeah, I'd like to, but I can't seem to find one," Caitlyn replied.

"What about the ad?"

"That wasn't a sales ad. It was an ad about the history of music, and the clarinet I love just happened to be in one of the pictures," Caitlyn shrugged. "It's pretty rare, and I'll probably never find one like it again."

Cameron smiled as he thought about the pawn shop. He knew exactly what he needed to do. He looked around and noticed there were several people dancing.

"Would you like to dance?"

"I'd love to," Caitlyn smiled.

Cameron stood and took Caitlyn's hand, guiding her to the dance floor. As they danced, everything around them seemed to fade away. They were the only two people in the world as far as Cameron was concerned. He wondered where had she been all of his life. He ran his fingers gently through her hair, and relished in the moment of being close to her. Cameron could feel Caitlyn's heartbeat, which seemed in perfect rhythm with his own. Her skin was so soft against his hands, and he wanted to remain that way forever; just the two of them, with him holding her close. They stayed there until almost midnight, yet for Cameron, time had stood still. Cameron wondered was he fooling himself by believing that Caitlyn felt the same way for him. He'd tried his best to stay focused on what they were doing there, but Caitlyn was quite a distraction for him. As they sat down for dessert, Cameron ran his fork distractedly through his cake.

"What's wrong?" Caitlyn asked.

"Just thinking," Cameron said.

"About what?"

"About the fact that you and I are starting to get close and how I may have already ruined it," Cameron commented.

"I don't understand."

"My affair with Kristen. There could be some serious consequences behind it," Cameron said.

"Like what?"

"Well, I feel like it'll keep you from getting too close to me. I get the feeling she's been trying to trap me, and the other night, she might have succeeded."

"What's that supposed to mean?"

"I can't believe I'm about to tell you this, but, I was so weakened by thinking about you, I actually had unprotected sex with her, so, if she's pregnant, I'll have no one but myself to blame. I can't have a child with someone like her."

"But don't you see? You can't," Caitlyn said, shaking her head as she took a bite of her dessert.

"What do you mean?"

"There are things you don't know about Kristen. We had an attorney, Eric Taylor, who left the firm last year because of her. She had an affair with him, and then threatened to turn him in for sexual harassment if he didn't leave his wife for her. The affair lasted for a few months, and then she made sure his wife found out. She sent his wife a video tape of the two of them together in Eric's own house. She was thinking his wife would leave him, and that she'd have him all to herself. The only way he kept his marriage was to leave the firm."

"Why would he be dumb enough to let her tape them having sex in his own home?"

"He didn't know it was being filmed. She had one of those little camcorders that was hard to spot. She went over there, knowing his wife was out of town on business, supposedly to take him some files he'd left. She ended up seducing him and filming the whole thing. Apparently, she tried to trap him by getting pregnant," Caitlyn said. "When he refused to leave his wife, she had a bad abortion. Cameron, Kristen can't have children."

"What? Are you serious?"

"Very serious."

"How do you know this? Did she confide in you?"

"No, she didn't," Caitlyn sighed. "Eric did. He and I went to law school together, and we were good friends. Eric and I were working on a case together when he suddenly left.

When I asked him about it, he told me what happened. Kristen's notorious for ruining lives, Cameron."

"I had no idea. I never would have gotten involved with her had I known."

"Well, you live and learn. But, it's in the past now. Just try to put it behind you, get yourself tested and get on with your life," Caitlyn suggested.

"Tested? Do you really think--"

"I'm not saying anything to scare you, but, Kristen's a bed hopper. If I'm understanding you, the other night in the hotel was the only time you were unprotected, right?"

"Right," Cameron agreed.

"But, it only takes once. Just for your own peace of mind."

"And yours?" Cameron smiled slightly.

"Actually, yes. If things move forward with us, I want to know that everything's okay."

Cameron thought back to his last time with Kristen, and how he imagined he was with Caitlyn. This was truly a remarkable woman sitting before him. He looked at her, and reached across the table to hold her hand again.

"Thanks for being a friend," Cameron smiled.

"It's nice to have you as a friend, Cameron," Caitlyn smiled.

They sat there for the next few minutes enjoying their dessert and coffee. When they got back to the hotel, Cameron hated for the evening to end. He wanted to be with Caitlyn, even if it was just to hold her. But, they both knew that if they were in a compromising position, they would give in to what they were feeling. They ended the night with Cameron giving Caitlyn an innocent kiss on the cheek. They needed to pack anyway since they were going to be leaving the next afternoon.

****

The next afternoon, they left the hotel and caught the firm's plane to Ohio. They'd found out as much as they could in Illinois; now they needed to contact some of Rachel's relatives. After renting a car, they had a nice dinner that night and decided to turn in early. They had a pretty long day ahead of them.

Early that Monday morning, they used GPS to get directions to the address they'd tracked down as belonging to Roland and Miriam Lyle. When they arrived, it was obvious that they came from very humble means. Their house was an older home in what was not considered the best area in town. They lived on the outskirts of Caldmill, Ohio, which ironically was one of the best areas in Ohio. Cameron knocked on the door.

"Yes?" an older woman answered the door.

"We're looking for Roland Lyle," Cameron stated.

"Who are you?" the woman asked.

"I'm Cameron Spencer, and this is my colleague, Caitlyn Frazier, and we're attorneys with Larson, Craig and Jacobs Law Firm in Indiana. We'd like to speak with Mr. Lyle if possible."

"My husband's resting right now. What is this all about?" The woman still didn't let them in. Instead, she talked through a dirty screen door.

"We're working on a case concerning Garret Marlow, and we'd like to talk with Mr. Lyle concerning his sister, Rachel."

"Rachel? The last person in the world my husband would want to talk about is Rachel. I already told the other woman the same thing! Now, would you please leave?"

"Ma'am, if we could just talk with the two of you for-" Caitlyn started.

"I said NO!" the woman slammed the door in their faces.

"Well, that went well," Caitlyn sighed.

Cameron decided not to give up. He knocked at the door again. "Mrs. Lyle, we're not here to cause trouble, but it's important that we talk to your husband," Cameron yelled.

"If you don't leave, I'll call the police!" she shouted back.

"Please do. That way we can all talk together!" Caitlyn

said.

After that, Mrs. Lyle reluctantly opened the door and let them in. As they were walking in, Mr. Lyle rolled into the room in a wheelchair.

"Miriam, what's all the yelling in here?" he asked.

"These people are here about Rachel," she said.

"Rachel? What's this all about?" Mr. Lyle said.

"Mr. Lyle, I'm Cameron Spencer and this is Caitlyn Frazier, and we're working on Garret Marlow's case. We understand that his ex-wife Rachel is your sister."

"Rachel's dead. So, what could you possibly want to know from me?" Mr. Lyle said.

"Do you remember much about the time when your ex-brother-in-law was convicted of murdering his second wife, Victoria?" Cameron asked.

"Remember it? I'll never forget it," Mr. Lyle said. "Pardon our manners. Please, sit down."

"Thank you," Cameron said. "Would you mind if we record this interview?" Cameron asked.

"No, please do. What do you want to know?" Mr. Lyle asked.

"Did you have any contact with your sister during that time? We have several letters that she sent to Mr. Marlow from Ohio, and we're trying to find out if it's at all possible that she had something to do with framing her ex-husband," Caitlyn stated.

"Oh, she probably did. After what Rachel did to me and my family, I'd never put it past her. Why do you think I'm in this wheelchair?"

"Excuse me?" Cameron asked.

"Rachel tried to kill me and my wife. Unfortunately, she succeeded with killing our daughter, Lisa."

"What happened?" Caitlyn asked.

"We were all here one night, and Rachel and the baby had been living with us, for oh, I don't know, maybe six months or so, when she started raging out at us—"

"Wait a minute." Cameron interrupted Mr. Lyle. "Are you saying she had a baby with her?"

~ 148 ~

"Yeah, her baby. Cutest little boy I'd ever seen," Mr. Lyle smiled at the mention of his nephew.

"He was the son she had after she supposedly re-married," Mrs. Lyle said.

"What do you mean 'supposedly'?" Cameron asked.

"Rachel showed up on our doorstep one day saying she'd had her baby, and her husband was still overseas, in the Air Force," Mrs. Lyle rolled her eyes. "She didn't want to take the baby over there, so they wanted to stay with us. We never met this 'husband' of hers, and he didn't even come to her funeral. For one thing, we never could find him. My guess is, she got knocked up by some guy and didn't want Roland to know. So, she made up some story about a husband overseas," Mrs. Lyle said. "She'd somehow blown all the money Roland gave her from the sale of their parents' home."

"How much money was it?" Caitlyn asked.

"$50,000.00. Back then, that was quite a bit, but my little sister blew it all on something that she probably didn't need. She was extremely wasteful. She didn't think there was any end to money, and she spent lavishly."

Cameron and Caitlyn looked at each other. Cameron wondered if maybe she had to go through with giving Ms. Cramer the money.

"Did you know anyone by the last name of Cramer who knew your sister?" Cameron asked.

"Cramer? You mean Alice Cramer?" Mr. Lyle asked.

"We don't know her first name," Caitlyn said.

"Alice Cramer and Rachel were best friends in college. They fell out a year or so before Rachel came to stay with us," Mr. Lyle said.

"What did they fall out about?" Cameron asked.

"I'm not too sure, but I'd bet my bottom dollar that my little sister was at fault," Mr. Lyle said, shaking his head.

"Do you know where Alice Cramer lived?" Caitlyn asked.

"I remember her being from Illinois, which is where Rachel and Garret went to college. They were all students at Premington University."

"Was Rachel in a sorority?" Cameron asked.

"No, she wanted to be. She tried out for a sorority, but her temper flared too much for her to ever get through initiation, so she was cut from the process during the first week."

"Was Alice in this sorority?" Caitlyn asked.

"Yeah, Alice got in," Mr. Lyle stated.

"Maybe Rachel was jealous of that," Cameron suggested.

"No. They remained friends after that. Something else happened to come between those two years later, although I'm not sure what," Mr. Lyle stated.

"Mr. Lyle, you were telling us that one night she started raging out at you. What was that all about?" Caitlyn asked.

"My wife could probably explain it better than I can," Mr. Lyle said.

"I'd been cleaning up, and I went into Rachel's room to vacuum," Mrs. Lyle started.

"There was a notepad lying on the floor, so I picked it up to put it on her bed. It was some sort of checklist. It had something scribbled on it about getting rid of the heavy weight. I shrugged it off, and continued vacuuming. Later that night, after our daughter, Lisa had gone to bed, Rachel, Roland and I were sitting downstairs in the den. Rachel was feeding the baby and we were watching TV." Mrs. Lyle seemed very emotional all of a sudden.

"Are you okay?" Caitlyn asked.

"This still brings back very bad memories for my wife and me, so just bare with us," Mr. Lyle said, reaching over to cover his wife's hand.

"We understand. Take your time," Cameron said.

"I commented to Rachel, jokingly of course, about the notepad and what it said," Mrs. Lyle sniffled. "All I said was that she was being silly trying to lose weight. In fact, it was hard to believe she'd ever had a child given her size. She went completely crazy on me. She stopped feeding the baby, and jumped up and tried to attack me. Roland jumped up and pulled her off of me. She started shouting at me telling me I had no idea what I was talking about and she was the wrong person to ever cross or say something like that to. She also said that if I ever said something like that again, she'd kill me. I was totally stunned, because I honestly didn't mean anything by it. If anything, it was a compliment because I remembered how hard it was for me to lose weight after having our child."

"I couldn't believe my sister could do something like that to my wife," Mr. Lyle sighed. "I told her she needed help, and that she had to leave. I told her she had to pack her things and be gone the next day. She told me I'd regret it. I told her to go upstairs and calm down. I'd never seen my own sister look at me with so much hatred in her eyes. I thought I knew her, but had I known at that moment just how sick she really was, I never would have let my guard down. She took the baby and went upstairs. When my wife and I went to bed, we had no idea what she was really up to." Mr. Lyle became tearful.

"What happened next?" Caitlyn asked.

"A little later, I woke up because I smelled smoke. Our house was engulfed in flames." Mr. Lyle looked dazed as he spoke. "I tried to open the door, but it was hot. I managed to convince my wife to climb out the window to safety and go next door to call 911. I needed to get to our daughter. I went into the bathroom in our bedroom and drenched a blanket in water, and tried to open the door again. I managed to get into the hallway, and to my daughter's door. She wasn't in there, so I was praying she'd gotten out. I kept calling her name, but she never answered. The smoke was thick and choking, and I was blinded by the flaring flames in front of me. I could hear my house collapsing under me. I went to Rachel's room and she and the baby weren't in there. All I could do was pray that my family had gotten out safely. I tried calling their names again, then I was knocked unconscious by a piece of wood. The next thing I remembered after that was being in an ambulance, and Miriam leaning over me crying. I had third degree burns on my arms, and both my legs had to be amputated because they'd been crushed under wood and

~ 151 ~

debris. Our daughter had apparently gotten up to go to the bathroom, and never made it out."

"I'm sorry that this caused so much pain for you. But, did Rachel and the baby perish in the fire also?" Cameron asked.

"No, because she started the fire," Mrs. Lyle said.

"Well, what happened to her?" Caitlyn asked.

"Rachel was so busy trying to get away after what she'd done, her car was found crashed, and blown up. Her body was burned beyond recognition. The baby was never found in the car. In other words, she got exactly what she deserved after what she did to us," Mrs. Lyle said.

"Rachel was so evil, so cynical; she even disabled our fire alarm so we couldn't get out in time," Mr. Lyle said, his voice shaking. "We lost everything because of her. Our home, our daughter, all of our belongings, everything. It was ruled arson, so our insurance wouldn't re-build. Our health insurance eventually ran out because I had to be hospitalized for so long. We were barely able to give our daughter a decent burial. I couldn't even be at my own daughter's funeral. I was confined to a bed for a long time, so my wife had to identify Rachel's remains."

"How did you ID her if she wasn't recognizable?" Caitlyn asked.

"I had to identify her jewelry. She didn't have any dental x-rays on file that we could find, so I identified the body as hers. It was her car, her jewelry, and at the time, I was totally concerned with my husband's health and dealing with the fact that I'd lost the only child I'd ever have," Mrs. Lyle said.

"What happened to the baby when your sister died?" Caitlyn asked.

"We don't know," Mr. Lyle said.

"For all we know, she could have left the baby on someone's doorstep. She'd flipped out completely," Mrs. Lyle said.

"We didn't have the resources to try to find the child, because it took everything we had just to survive. I was placed

~ 152 ~

on disability, and we had to move from the area where we lived. We were reduced to meager means, and it's been hard on us ever since," Mr. Lyle said.

"Rachel took a lot away from us after we opened our home to her. She was Roland's sister, for God's sake! She was an unredeemable monster," Mrs. Lyle said.

"Mr. Lyle, the baby she had most likely wasn't hers. Your sister was unable to have children," Cameron said.

"I had no idea. But, how's that possible? Rachel was pregnant once before, while she and Garret were together," Mr. Lyle commented.

"Are you sure?" Caitlyn asked, surprisingly.

"Yeah, I'm sure. She called me all excited about it. But, she lost the child. She never mentioned that she couldn't get pregnant again. In fact, I distinctly remember her saying that they'd have a baby someday," Mr. Lyle said. "She always gave the impression that everything was okay. But, she and Garret split up shortly after that."

"Did you know that Victoria Marlow was pregnant when she was killed?" Cameron asked.

"Yes, I remember them mentioning it on the news, but there was never any other talk about it. I just assumed the baby died with Victoria, and Rachel never said anything."

"When Mrs. Marlow was killed, her baby had been taken from her womb by C-section," Caitlyn said. "The baby was never found."

"What?" Mrs. Lyle said.

"We have reason to believe that Rachel Marlow had something to do with Victoria Marlow's murder, and that she possibly had taken the baby."

Mr. Lyle looked stunned. "Are you telling me that was Garret and his wife's baby?"

"It's quite possible," Caitlyn said.

Mr. Lyle sighed. "Well, the timing would be about right. She showed up here a few days after everything happened. Oddly enough, she wasn't even the one who told me about Garret. The next day after she got here, we saw it on the news about Garret being arrested a few days before for the

~ 153 ~

murder of his wife. I asked her had she known anything about it, and she said she had no idea about it. She seemed so sincerely concerned; she even asked if we could watch the baby while she went to Indiana to visit Garret."

"How often did she go to see him?" Cameron asked.

"Oh, maybe once every couple of weeks. It didn't last long; only for a couple of months," Mr. Lyle commented.

"Do you have any pictures of your sister?" Cameron asked.

"No. All of our things were destroyed in the fire. Rachel and I had so many pictures that we'd taken together, during happier times," Mr. Lyle said. "All of our photo albums, special memories, everything, gone. Maybe that's a good thing. I don't know if I could stand to look at a picture of her after everything she cost me. I do have her diary from years ago. After we sold our parents' house, apparently, the new owners were going to do some major renovations to it. In doing so, they ran across Rachel's diary in a window seat in Rachel's room. We have it because it was sent to us after the fire by the real estate agent who handled the sale of my parents' home. She'd had it for over a year but had forgotten to send it to us. Otherwise, it would have been destroyed in the fire as well."

"Can we see the diary?" Caitlyn asked.

"Sure. You can have it," Mr. Lyle said, rolling over to a table. He retrieved the diary from the drawer and handed it to Caitlyn. "Maybe this will help a little."

"Thank you. Are you sure you want to part with it?" Caitlyn asked.

"Trust me, I don't want or need any reminders of Rachel. I never threw it away, but I should have a long time ago. As long as I don't have to see her face, I'm fine," Mr. Lyle stated bitterly.

"We understand. Unfortunately, a picture is just the thing we need. We've been unable to find a picture of your sister, and you were pretty much our last hope," Cameron said.

"Why do you need a picture of her?" Mrs. Lyle asked.

"We have witnesses who we'd like to identify her, but

we have no record on file. Even DMV can't seem to help us. Their records only go back so far, and apparently, your sister hasn't tried to get a driver's license in the past 25 years."

"Well, that would be hard to do since she's dead," Mr. Lyle commented.

Cameron and Caitlyn looked at each other.

"Is there something you're not telling me?" Mr. Lyle asked.

"Nothing relevant at this point," Cameron said.

"Did Rachel ever talk of anywhere she may have wanted to go, or move to?" Caitlyn asked.

"Not that I can remember," Mr. Lyle said. "She liked our hometown of Little Brook, which was a country area here in Ohio, about an hour from here. She used to always want to move back there, but that's about it from what I can remember."

"Do you still have relatives in that area?" Cameron asked.

"No, we don't. Our parents are no longer living, and Rachel and I were their only two children. Any relatives we have that were there have either died or moved away. It was a small town. Most people tended to move away instead of making a life for themselves there. A lot of the older people remained, but that was about it."

"My husband and I are just making it day to day. Rachel still haunts us, though. I don't know what else we could possibly tell you," Mrs. Lyle said.

"Believe me, you've told us a great deal already. More than you'll ever realize," Caitlyn said.

"By the way, what was the baby's name?" Cameron asked.

"Richard Lyle. She gave some excuse about wanting to keep the Lyle family name and Richard was our father's name," Mr. Lyle said. "I think the only person Rachel ever really loved was our father."

"Why do you say that?" Cameron asked.

"Well, everyone knew she hated Mama; everyone except me and Dad," Mr. Lyle stated. "We never wanted to believe there was any bad in her. We always came to her defense. What we didn't know until later was that she purposely made life hell for our mother. She was jealous of her. She even tried to have our father believe that our mother was having an affair."

"Why would she do that?" Cameron asked.

"Rachel was obsessed with being close to Dad," Mr. Lyle explained. "She didn't want anyone in his life but her, and that included Mama. After I went off to the service, she started planting telltale signs of Mama's 'affair.' I was gone, now she wanted Mama gone. It almost worked, too. In fact, our parents separated for a few weeks. They soon realized what Rachel had done. Mama wanted to have Rachel committed, to get some help for her, but Dad wouldn't hear of it. His little girl was not going to some institution. So, they didn't do anything about it."

"And that didn't make Rachel stop?" Caitlyn asked.

"No, not at all. If anything, it made her more determined. When Rachel couldn't get rid of Mama one way, she had to try another. Obviously, getting her out of the house didn't work, so she had to resort to more desperate measures."

"What do you mean?" Caitlyn asked.

"She actually pushed Mama down the stairs, causing her to lose her baby."

"Your mom was pregnant and Rachel pushed her down the stairs?" Cameron asked.

"Yeah, only about three or four months," Mr. Lyle said.

"And that still didn't prompt your father to get help for her?" Caitlyn asked.

"No way," Mr. Lyle shook his head. "Rachel cried and said it was an accident; that she'd lost her balance and knocked into Mama by mistake. Mama wrote to me after it happened, and she told me that she was becoming more and more fearful of my little sister everyday. She just couldn't understand why Dad and I couldn't see the evil in Rachel."

"So, why would she make her mom lose her baby?" Cameron asked.

"For one thing, she hated that baby, and another thing, Rachel felt that Dad had betrayed her by having another baby with Mama."

"'Betrayed' her? She was his daughter. Why would she feel that way? It's almost like you're saying Rachel was in love with your father," Cameron said.

"In a way she was," Mr. Lyle shrugged. "I don't think it was in a sexual sense, but in her eyes, she was Daddy's 'little girl' and no one was supposed to replace that. They did everything together and she believed everything he ever said to her. He, of course, loved his daughter. Somewhere in Rachel's mind, there was the thought that Dad couldn't love her completely if there were other people just as close to him in his life. And, you can't get much closer than a wife and his other children. So, we're the ones she was threatened by."

"Why didn't she ever do anything to you as a child? I mean, you were their child also," Caitlyn said.

"Because I was a boy. Not only that, I spoiled her just as much as our father did. Besides, I was closer to Mama than I was to Dad. So, she wasn't as competitive with me for Dad's affections. No, it was our mom. She was the 'other woman' in Dad's life. She was afraid that this other baby would be a girl, and she'd be put in the shadows forever."

"You said that your parents are dead now. How did that happen?" Cameron asked.

"Daddy had a heart attack about 29 years ago, and Mama died six months later in her sleep."

"So they died a couple of years before your house was destroyed," Caitlyn said.

"Yeah, that's about right," Mr. Lyle nodded. "They were constantly worrying about what Rachel was up to. They sent her off to college when she graduated from high school a year after Mama's miscarriage. Mama was still terribly afraid of what she would do. Rachel met Garret while in college. Mama was relieved because she thought that now Rachel would have a focus somewhere else and maybe get her life together. They got married about a month after they graduated, but their marriage didn't last but a little over two

~ 157 ~

years, and then they got a divorce. Garret started law school right after they graduated college. She miscarried about a year after they got married. Garret even took a year's hiatus from law school, but by then, their marriage was deeply in trouble. They were together for that year he sat out, but, during that time, they divorced. Rachel moved home for almost a year after her divorce, but she started raging out again, and Mama and Daddy told her she had to get help. She was under a psychiatrist's care briefly, and then she moved back to Kerrigan. She wanted to make things work with Garret, but by that time, he was already seeing his second wife."

"What was her reaction to his romance with Victoria?" Cameron asked.

"Oh, she didn't like it. She didn't like it at all. She called and told Daddy that she wanted for him to 'make Victoria go away,'" Mr. Lyle stated.

"What did she mean by that?" Caitlyn asked.

"Knowing Rachel, nothing good, that's for sure," Mr. Lyle shook his head. "Daddy tried to talk a little sense into her and told her that if it was meant for her and Garret to get back together, things would work out eventually. She got angry at Daddy for telling her that, and she told him that she'd handle things herself."

"What did she do?" Cameron asked.

"Nothing at the time. We figured she was just blowing smoke, trying to get her own way. Things were pretty quiet for a while, until Garret called me once and confided in me about Rachel."

"What did he say?" Cameron asked.

"He told me that he'd had a little too much to drink, and he almost slept with Rachel a few weeks before he was to marry Victoria."

"But, nothing happened?" Cameron asked.

"He was in love with Victoria," Mr. Lyle said.

"Sounds like you and Garret were pretty close for him to confide in you about something like that," Cameron observed.

"Actually, we were," Mr. Lyle smiled slightly.

"Ironically, that call kind of caused a rift in our friendship. When he called, he was more or less complaining that my sister was complicating his life. Well, she's still my sister, and I defended her. I told him that maybe he was giving her mixed signals and he should stop rubbing it in her face about the fact that he was about to marry again. I told him to stay away from her if he'd decided to move on with another woman. He told me that Rachel was pursuing him, and I told him to man up about it and own up to the fact that he never loved my sister."

"What was his response to that?" Caitlyn asked.

"He said I was being blinded by Rachel just as he had been. But, he had always loved Victoria. From the way he sounded, I honestly believe that even if my sister could have gotten Garret to sleep with her, it wouldn't have stopped him from marrying Victoria."

"So, Rachel was trying to stop the wedding," Caitlyn said.

"Of course, she was. She had Victoria fooled. She befriended Victoria, tried to find out her weaknesses so that she could use them against her. No matter what my little sister did, she couldn't prevail. They got married, and apparently a few months afterwards, ended up pregnant."

"What was her reaction to Victoria's pregnancy?" Cameron asked.

"That's the odd thing about it. She never told us that Victoria was pregnant. She called and said she'd gotten married and was over Garret," Mr. Lyle stated. "I didn't find out that Victoria was pregnant until they mentioned it on the news after her murder."

"She was supposed to be married to the guy in the military," Mrs. Lyle said. "She said they eloped, and that he would be shipping out but she would remain in the States. She said they kept it quiet because his parents didn't care for her. They'd supposedly been married for a few months when she called telling Roland she was pregnant and due in July."

"And you never met this husband of hers?" Caitlyn asked.

"No, never did," Mr. Lyle said, shaking his head. "We

didn't see her until she showed up on our doorstep with the baby."

"Which was right around the time of Victoria's murder," Cameron reiterated.

"Exactly," Mr. Lyle agreed.

"Well, we've taken up enough of your time, and we're very sorry for all that you've gone through," Cameron said. "Here's our card if you think of anything else." He passed the card to Mrs. Lyle.

"Okay," Mrs. Lyle said, reading it. "And I want to apologize for earlier. I shouldn't have been so rude."

"It's perfectly understandable. We had no idea how much you'd gone through, and had we known, we would have been a little more sensitive about coming here like we did," Caitlyn said.

"You know, Rosemary might have a picture," Mr. Lyle suggested.

"Who's Rosemary?" Caitlyn asked.

"Rosemary is our cousin. She was kind of slow, but was always crazy about Rachel. She always thought that Rachel could do no wrong. She used to come and visit us during the summer when we were younger."

"Where was she from?" Cameron asked.

"She was from a little town in Kentucky called Lariette Springs."

"Lariette Springs?" Cameron asked surprisingly.

"Yeah. Her mom was our mom's sister, Jacqueline," Mr. Lyle clarified. "Little Rosemary has always been on disability because she had trouble learning. Never worked as far as I knew. She was really kind of sad when we were younger, because Rachel treated her terribly. But, she didn't understand. She thought Rachel was only looking out for her best interests. Funny, I've not heard from them in a long time."

"What's Rosemary's last name?" Cameron asked.

"Faulkner," Mr. Lyle said.

"That's not a common name," Caitlyn commented.

"Yeah, especially in a little town like Lariette Springs,

there shouldn't be that many," Cameron said.

"You know the town?" Mr. Lyle asked.

"I'm from there," Cameron stated.

"Well, you may be closer to the truth than you think," Mr. Lyle said.

"You might be right. We really appreciate everything you've told us," Cameron said, standing to leave.

When they left the Lyles' home, Cameron was beginning to like Rachel less and less. She'd already proven to be a pretty awful person, but the things she did to her own family were unbelievable. A part of Cameron hoped that Rachel was still alive so that she could be brought to justice. So far, it seemed as if she'd already murdered at least two people, maybe three. She'd possibly murdered Victoria and her own niece, and most likely, she'd murdered whoever was found in her car. She'd obviously attempted at more than that. This was a woman who let nothing stand in her way when it came down to what she wanted. They might be able to get an order to have Rachel's body exhumed to do a DNA test, but, what would that prove? That still doesn't make her the murderer of Victoria. That would have only meant she faked her own death.

They went back to the hotel and called Phillip. They suggested that Phillip run a check on Richard Lyle, Rachel's son. They also told him to try and locate Alice Cramer, who went to college with Garret and Rachel. They had enough already to establish doubt, but would it be enough to clear him in time? They knew that the key was finding Rachel Marlow, if she was still alive. This woman was conniving in the worst way and had managed to evade punishment for 27 years. She wasn't going to go down without a fight, that was obvious. Now, they had to find proof that she was still alive. Cameron and Caitlyn also prepared affidavits for the Lyles to sign. They went back to their house with a notary public to get their signatures that evening. When they got back to the hotel, they went over what they knew so far. They knew that Rachel Marlow had a terrible temper, and so did Regina Matheson. They knew that Rachel worked out of town somewhere, and

Regina worked for Dr. Varden during the same time. They knew that Dr. Varden and Regina Matheson rented the car and were at the hotel, plus they had a baby. They also knew that Rachel Marlow showed up at her brother's home with a baby. Plus, according to Ms. Jordan, Regina had relatives in Ohio. Most compellingly, Regina was called Rachel by an obvious nemesis from her past. This linked her to Rachel more than anything else. The key was finding this woman who has been presumed dead. They couldn't continue looking for her beyond Lariette Springs because they had so many other issues to deal with concerning the case.

Early Tuesday morning, Phillip called to let them know that there were 61 Richard Lyles across the country, but none of the dates of birth matched anywhere near the date of the Richard Lyle in question. He also told them that the Alice Cramer that went to college with them had been missing since sometime in 1984. She almost seemed to vanish in thin air. The last place she was seen was somewhere in Kentucky, where her credit cards had been used. After talking to Phillip, Cameron and Caitlyn read Rachel's diary for some sort of clue. From Cameron's past experience, he knew that a mentioned name could be a big clue to where a person would turn for help. Cameron was amazed at how sick this woman truly was. He began to read its contents:

'Date: April 12, 1969
Dear Diary,
Well, another day passed and he still didn't say he loved me. Maybe he doesn't anymore. What's wrong with me? Why can't I get what I want from him? He's trapped between me and her, and doesn't know what to do. I have to win his heart completely. I have to get her out of the way, have him all to myself. If I can't get what I want soon, I'll have to take that bitch out, by any means necessary.'

"Who do you think she's referring to?" Caitlyn asked.
"Any normal teenager, it would sound like it's just some boy, but with her, you never know," Cameron

~ 162 ~

commented. "Of course, no normal teenager, would say anything like 'take that bitch out.'"

They continued to read the diary, only to find out that she was referring to her father. She made mention of the fact that her mother was carrying a baby, and that she would really be out in the cold if there was another baby. She mentioned how stupid Rosemary was and how every time she went to that boring town of Lariette Springs to spend time with her she took advantage of her and got Rosemary to do whatever she wanted. She mentioned how she would convince Rosemary to steal money from her parents and give it to her. She called Rosemary a simple twit who had the IQ of a dog. Rachel was calculating from her teenage years. No doubt, Rachel had opportunity, motive, desire and a devious enough mind to pull off murdering Victoria and framing Garret. They were banking on all of the evidence they had so far being enough to establish doubt. For the first time since Garret Marlow was convicted, there was doubt because it looked as if someone else had a motive.

Cameron and Caitlyn unanimously decided that they'd go to Lariette Springs. They decided to use the rental car instead of getting the plane to come back. To think that the answer to this case could lie in Cameron's own hometown. They had several hours' drive ahead of them, and he didn't want to waste a moment.

Chapter
8

Wednesday morning, around 1 a.m., they left for Kentucky. Cameron always preferred traveling late at night because there was less traffic on the road. Caitlyn and Cameron discussed the case detail by detail, with Cameron hoping that he'd not forgotten anything after their setback the week before. Around 7 a.m., they stopped for a leisurely breakfast at a very nice restaurant. Afterwards, they continued on their journey. Cameron thought a lot about this Rosemary. He wondered if Rachel had contacted her. Given Rosemary's admiration for Rachel, she'd do anything Rachel told her to, including helping her cover for murder.

They arrived in Cameron's hometown by 10 a.m. Cameron's home was a beautiful house that sat on 150 acres of land. He was very proud of where he was from and he wanted to share all of it with Caitlyn. Cameron still had his key, but he decided not to use it. They weren't expecting him, so they might think it was someone trying to break in. It felt good being home again, even if it was for just a couple of days and to investigate a case. Cameron parked the car and he and

Caitlyn got out and went to the backdoor. He could see his mom through the window washing the breakfast dishes. He rang the doorbell. Rebecca opened the door.

"Cameron!" she exclaimed. "I didn't know you were going to be home!" She hugged him and started to cry. "Come in! Come in!"

"How are you, Ma?" Cameron asked.

"Great, especially now!" Rebecca said, hugging him again.

"Mom, I'd like for you to meet my colleague, Caitlyn Frazier. She's an attorney at the firm where I work. Caitlyn, this is my mother, Rebecca Spencer."

"Hi, Mrs. Spencer. How do you do?" Caitlyn smiled and held out her hand.

"Hi, Caitlyn. It's nice to meet you," Rebecca smiled, shaking her hand. "Well, come on in and sit down. Why didn't you tell me you were coming home?"

"I wanted to surprise you."

"Well, this is the best surprise I've had all year!"

"Where's Dad?"

"Out in his workshop. You know he can never keep still. He's building something, of course. Are you hungry? Let me fix you something to eat."

"No, we had a big breakfast."

"You mean you had a big breakfast before getting here? Now, how can I spoil my son and his friend if you won't let me cook a big meal for you?"

"Don't worry. You'll have time. We'll be here for a couple of days," Cameron said.

"So, what brings you here?" Rebecca asked.

"We're working on a case, and our trail has led us here," Cameron said.

"Oh? What's the case about?" Rebecca asked.

"It's a long story. We'll talk about it later," Cameron smiled.

"Your dad's going to be so happy to see you. I'm going to go out and get him," Rebecca said.

"No, let me go. I want to surprise him, too."

"Okay. While you're doing that, Caitlyn and I will get to know each other better," Rebecca smiled.

"Okay." Cameron smiled.

Cameron walked out to his father's workshop, which was his father's little domain of contentment. Building things always had a way of helping his father relax. He especially needed that now since he was unable to work. When Cameron opened the door, his dad didn't even hear him come in because he was preoccupied by his latest creation.

"Hi, Dad," Cameron smiled.

Evan Spencer stopped what he was doing to look around and find his son standing there. "Cameron! How are you son?" Evan smiled and hugged his son.

"I'm fine. The question is, how are you?"

"Oh, I'm fine. If I can get your mom and Dr. Kirklin to stop fussing over me, I might actually recover with my sanity intact," Evan laughed.

"Dad, they do it because they're concerned about you. We all are." Cameron then looked at Joseph, one of their faithful ranch hands who had been with them for years. "Joe, how are you doing?"

"I'm fine, Mr. Cameron, just fine," Joe smiled shyly. "And you, Sir?"

"I'm great. You're looking well," Cameron said. "My parents aren't working you too hard, are they?"

"Never that, Mr. Cameron," Joe smiled.

Cameron then looked at his father. "So, what has your doctor said lately, Dad?"

"He says I'm healing up just fine, but I won't be able to do the work I was doing before. You know I hate working in the office. Jim has always been better at that than me. He offered to buy me out, but you know me, I wouldn't hear of it. I'm going to prove Dr. Kirklin wrong. I'll be back out there, you'll see. So, how are things going for you?" Evan asked.

"I'm fine. We're here investigating a case, so we'll be here until Friday."

"'We'? Who's 'we'?"

"My friend Caitlyn came with me." Cameron

immediately smiled.

"Oh. So you brought your girlfriend home so Mom and I could check her out?"

"Believe me when I tell you, this woman is not my girlfriend. She's an attorney at the firm where I work. You know, when I first met her, she had ice in her veins," Cameron smiled.

"And now?" Evan asked slyly.

"Let's just say I think I'm starting to melt it a little," Cameron laughed.

"Ah, so that Spencer charm is hard at work?" Evan laughed.

"Without a doubt. Sometimes, I think it's more of a curse than charm," Cameron sighed.

"What makes you say that?"

"Dad, I had a real fatal attraction on my hands," Cameron shook his head.

"Damn, you just got there a couple of weeks ago," Evan said in a surprised tone.

"Yeah, but that was long enough for her to develop a fixation on me."

"So, you laid it on her, huh?"

"A little too well," Cameron said. "I slept with her a few times, and she became obsessive. Even came to Illinois while we were there."

"We Spencer men have a knack for affecting women that way," Evan chuckled.

"I know," Cameron smiled.

Evan could tell Joe was a little flustered listening to them. Joe had always been shy and a little slow. He lived on the ranch in a small house. He'd been working for his parents for almost 15 years.

"Joe, why don't you go on to the store and get the horse feed?" Evan said.

"Yes, Sir," Joe said, leaving out of the shop.

"You know Joe's shy, so I guess he got a little embarrassed about what we were saying," Evan said.

"Dad, he's over 50, so I think he can handle it,"

Cameron smiled.

"Yeah, but I don't know if Joe's ever even had a woman," Evan sighed.

"Come on, are you serious? Never?"

"From what I've gathered about him, he hasn't," Evan shrugged. "But, I could be wrong. Now, why don't you tell me why you're really here."

"Well, the reason we're here is because of a case which has led us to Lariette Springs."

"Well, this is a pleasant surprise despite the reason," Evan commented.

"I probably won't have much time to visit. This case will keep me pretty busy."

"Can you talk about it? You said it led you here. What's going on?" Evan asked.

"It's an old murder case. This guy we're defending was wrongly accused of killing his wife. He's been given the death penalty. He's appealed to the highest court and they're upholding his death sentence," Cameron sighed. "Now, Phillip wants for us to find evidence to prove him innocent and get a pardon from the governor. We've found some pretty compelling things, but I'm not completely sure that the governor would see it that way. We may not be able to find enough in time," Cameron commented.

"Are you sure the guy didn't do it?" Evan asked.

"Yeah. Pretty sure. He's a nice guy and he's lost 27 years of his life because of this thing."

"That doesn't make him innocent," Evan commented.

"I know, Dad. But, if you knew what we've found out over the past few days, you'd know he didn't kill his wife. He had this ex-wife who was a complete bitch, and it seems she's somehow connected to the murder. The things this woman has done would bring you to tears."

"That bad, huh?"

"Terrible. This woman tried to kill her brother and his family, her mom, and I seriously believe she killed the victim."

"So, where is she?" Evan asked.

"She's dead supposedly," Cameron answered.

"What do you mean by that? Do you have reason to believe she's not dead?"

"A part of me does. I don't know, Dad," Cameron shook his head. "He was a great guy to her, and they divorced because she couldn't have children and she went through this deep depression because of it. He did everything he could, but I believe that deep down his second wife was the one he wanted to be with. He and his second wife were high school sweethearts, and over time, they drifted apart. When he met his first wife, things kind of kicked off from there. The two of them got married, she found out later she couldn't have children, even though according to her brother, she was pregnant at one point but lost the baby. And, get this: she shows up at her brother's house with a baby within a week after the murder saying it was her baby. I guess that was just another lie she told. My client did everything he could to make her happy. Even had this locket with a special message engraved on it. I have this feeling that finding that locket could be the key, but that would be like trying to find a needle in a haystack."

"Well, what did the locket say?" Evan asked.

"'To R, All the family I need. Love, G.' It was supposed to be a locket he gave her after they found out she couldn't have children. I'm not saying that's the only way to end a woman's pain over something like that. But, he did try to make things as easy on her as possible after the disappointment of not being able to have children. We believe she's behind his second wife's murder and she stole their baby."

"So, why did this case bring you home?"

"Well, she has relatives right here in Lariette Springs," Cameron said.

"Relatives? Do these relatives have names?" Evan asked.

"Yeah, their last name is Faulkner. There's Rosemary, the daughter, and Jacqueline, the mother. I haven't heard mention of her father's name yet. Apparently, they lived here in Lariette Springs. Do those names sound familiar?"

"No, they don't. Do you have an address?"

"No, we don't. Rosemary's slightly retarded, and apparently thought the world of Rachel. We get the feeling that if Rachel were going to turn to anyone for help, it would be the Faulkners," Cameron said.

"You may be right. Where's your mom?" Evan asked.

"She's in the house with Caitlyn. Are you okay?"

"Yeah, I'm fine. Let's go on in the house for a little while," Evan smiled. "It's really good to have you home." Evan placed his arm around Cameron and they walked out together.

When they returned, Caitlyn and Rebecca were in the living room looking through old photo albums. They were laughing like old friends. "Oh, hi, Cameron. I was just showing Caitlyn some of your baby pictures," Rebecca commented.

"I should have known not to leave the two of you alone," Cameron smiled.

"You were a cute little boy," Caitlyn smiled. "There's nothing wrong with your mom being proud of you."

"Cameron gets embarrassed whenever I show off his pictures," Rebecca said.

"You're just being a proud mom," Caitlyn smiled.

"Okay, enough about me. Caitlyn and I have a lot of work to do while we're here," Cameron said.

"How about if I fix an early lunch for all of us? I haven't had to cook for more than two people since you left. I'll fix all your favorites," Rebecca said.

"Caitlyn, is that okay with you?" Cameron looked in her direction.

"Sure, that's fine. We can get started after that," Caitlyn smiled.

Cameron and Caitlyn went out to the car to get their luggage. Rebecca went up to prepare the guest room for Caitlyn and to get Cameron's old room ready for him. When they came back in, Cameron's dad asked to talk with him privately for a few minutes. Rebecca came down and got Caitlyn to show her where she would be sleeping. Rebecca was always such a gracious hostess. Despite the fact that Cameron had shown up unexpectedly on her doorstep with a friend didn't bother her one bit, and Cameron knew it. He knew she'd be accommodating. When they went upstairs, Cameron and his father took a walk out by the pond. Cameron decided to break the silence.

"Dad, what's wrong? You've been preoccupied since I got here. Are you sure you're being honest with me about your health?"

"No, that's not it. I assure you, my health is fine. I'm just concerned about this case you're on, that's all," Evan commented.

"Why? I've been on murder cases before and it's never bothered you," Cameron said.

"I always worry about you. You've grown into a fine young man who I'm proud to call my son, even if I'm not your biological father," Evan said.

"Where is all of this coming from?" Cameron asked.

"Just thought I should let you know how much you mean to me," Evan smiled. "Now, about this case you're on. You mentioned something about a locket being the key to your case. Why do you say that? What makes this locket so unique?"

"It's one of a kind. There's not another one around like it," Cameron said. "My client had one made exclusively for his wife; both wives. The lockets were different in some ways, and had different inscriptions. This jeweler, Hallinger in Indiana doesn't duplicate his work. The locket for Rachel, who was my client's first wife, was the one I mentioned earlier. The one for Victoria, his second wife, said 'Picture Perfect Forever, Love, Gary.' Now, I have the second locket, but the first one is probably with Rachel. Her brother never mentioned if it was among her jewelry that his wife identified when she ID'd Rachel's body. I believe that Rachel Marlow faked her death and is living somewhere happily ever after. My guess is, she'd never part with a locket that meant so much to her."

"Her brother's wife identified her body? When did this

~ 171 ~

woman die? Couldn't his wife just look at her face and tell whether it was her or not?" Evan asked.

"No, see that's the thing. Rachel was 'conveniently' burned beyond recognition in a car explosion. And, there were 'conveniently' no dental records for Rachel. This all happened around 25 years or so ago in Ohio."

"Why couldn't her brother identify her body?" Evan asked.

"Because he was on the brink of death himself. Rachel, his own sister, burned down his house while he, his 12-year old daughter and his wife were there asleep. She even disengaged the fire alarm so that they wouldn't get out in time. Her sister-in-law got out and her brother was saved, but their daughter perished in the fire. I would love to catch this woman and put her behind bars for what she's done. She's not capable of loving another human being. The things she's done are unforgivable," Cameron shook his head.

"Do you have the locket with you? I'd love to see it," Evan said.

"Why are you so interested? I mean, I don't mind, but you've never taken such an interest in my cases before. What's going on?" Cameron asked.

"Nothing. I'm just taking up a new hobby," Evan smiled. "I've nothing better to do, so I'd like to know as much about what's going on with you as possible. Plus, you say this family might live here in Lariette Springs. Maybe I can do some asking around for you."

"Don't stress yourself over it. That's why Caitlyn and I are here, to see if we can find them."

"Well, if there's anything I can do, just let me know."

Evan looked really worried and Cameron couldn't understand why. He really felt that his dad wasn't telling him something, but his dad was quite stubborn about telling when something was bothering him. Cameron and Evan walked back to the car, where Cameron had all of his notes about the case. He looked in his briefcase and retrieved the locket.

"Here it is. It's really quite beautiful," Cameron commented.

"This is the locket your client gave his second wife?" Evan asked, looking at it.

"Yeah, it is. My guess is, the other one is probably similar in some ways, because the jeweler has some unique way that he designs his jewelry."

Evan opened the locket and saw the picture of Garret and Victoria. "Who's this?"

"That's Garret and his wife who was murdered. She's really beautiful isn't she?"

"Yes, she is," Evan murmured.

"I know she's a beautiful woman, but why are you staring at the locket like that?" Cameron asked.

"I thought about getting something like this for your mom. Do you know how I can get in touch with this guy?" Evan asked.

"I have his number written down. I think that would be great for you to do something like that for her," Cameron said, looking in his wallet for the number. He wrote it down on a slip of paper and gave it to his dad.

"Thanks. Don't tell her, okay? Just in case, don't mention that we had this conversation."

"Dad, why are you being so mysterious? What's going on with you?" Cameron was starting to get suspicious.

"I want to surprise her, that's all. Do you have a problem with me doing something nice for your mother?" Evan asked.

"No, sir, I don't. I guess that's just the attorney in me coming out. Let me know what Mr. Hallinger says when you talk to him, okay?"

Evan looked deep in thought. "Can you be sure it wasn't among the jewelry identified by her brother's wife? I mean, maybe he didn't mention it because he didn't think it was relevant," Evan suggested.

"You're right. I didn't think about that. Of course, if it's there, it could mean she faked her death, knowing that would be one item that would prove that it was her. But, if it's not there, then there's no doubt that she's alive somewhere."

Cameron looked in his briefcase and located Roland

~ 173 ~

Lyle's number and called him from his cell phone.

"Hello?" Mrs. Lyle answered the phone.

"Mrs. Lyle? This is Cameron Spencer."

"Hi, Mr. Spencer. How are you?"

"I'm fine. I don't mean to disturb you, but you stated that you identified Rachel's jewelry."

"Yes?"

"Was there a necklace with a locket on it that had 'To R, All the family I need. Love, G' inscribed on it?"

"No, there wasn't. Now that you mention it, Rachel never went anywhere without that necklace. She had it on the night of the fire."

"Are you sure?"

"I'm positive. All that was found was the ring that belonged to her mother, and a bracelet Roland had given to her for her birthday. Her watch was found also, but that was it. There was no locket among her things. Does all of this mean something?" Mrs. Lyle asked.

"It might. Is it possible the locket could have been lost?" Cameron asked.

"It's highly unlikely. Rachel loved that locket. She felt that it was her connection to Garret. If there was anything that should have been found on Rachel's body, it should have been that necklace."

"Thank you so much, Mrs. Lyle. If I have anymore questions, I'll call you."

"That'll be fine. Would you do us a favor?"

"What's that?"

"I get the feeling that you think Rachel is alive. If so, will you let us know?"

"Of course I will."

"We appreciate it," Mrs. Lyle stated.

Cameron hung up his phone, and looked at his father. "The necklace was not found among her things. She has to be alive. According to Mrs. Lyle, Rachel never went anywhere without her necklace, because she felt it connected her to Garret somehow."

"So what do you do now?" Evan asked.

"I do what I've been doing. Try to find Rachel Marlow and clear Garret Marlow of this whole ugly mess. It's quite possible that she's been here in Lariette Springs."

"That would be something," Evan muttered.

"What do you mean?" Cameron asked.

"Nothing. Now, why don't we go on inside? You'd better put this away. It's evidence, right?" Evan said, handing the locket back to Cameron.

"Yes, it is," Cameron said. As they walked in, they could smell the aroma of some of Cameron's favorite foods cooking. He knew his mom was going to go overboard, as usual. It was good to be home. Before sitting down to eat, there was a knock at the back door. Cameron opened it to Joe.

"Hi, Joe," Cameron smiled. Cameron stepped aside to let him in. "Come in."

"Hi, again, Mr. Cameron," Joe smiled shyly, taking his hat off as he walked in. "I came to give Mr. Spencer the receipt for the horse feed."

"Come on in. We're all in the dining room. I want you to meet a friend of mine," Cameron said, leading him to the dining room. "Caitlyn, this is Joseph Waters, our ranch hand."

"Hi, Joseph," Caitlyn smiled.

"Hi, Miss Caitlyn," Joe blushed. "Uh, Mr. Spencer, I wanted to give you the receipt for the horse feed," Joe said, not wanting to stare too hard at Caitlyn.

"That's okay, Joe, her looks stunned me too the first time I met her," Cameron smiled, patting Joe on the back.

"Cameron!" Caitlyn blushed.

"Well, it's the truth. She's beautiful isn't she, Joe?" Cameron asked.

"Yes, Sir, she is," Joe smiled, still shying away from Caitlyn.

"Cameron, leave him alone," Rebecca smiled. "You're always into mischief. You're making the poor girl blush."

"Thanks, Joe. Go get everything stored away and get started on cutting that south pasture," Evan instructed.

"Yes Sir," Joe said. "It was nice meeting you, Miss Caitlyn."

"Nice meeting you, too, Joe," Caitlyn smiled.

Soon after, Joe left out to the house to get back to work. Not much later, Cameron, Caitlyn and his parents sat down to lunch talking and laughing about Cameron's childhood. His dad was rather quiet, but no one seemed to notice except Cameron. Before Cameron knew it, his mom brought Grace into the conversation.

"I hear Grace is about to have a baby," Rebecca said.

Cameron immediately stopped smiling. "Ma, I really don't want to talk about her."

"I'm sorry, Dear, but you've done so much better than her anyway. Caitlyn, I think you're wonderful for my son," Rebecca smiled. "Did he ever tell you about Grace?"

"Um, actually, he mentioned her once or twice." Caitlyn was clearly uncomfortable talking about Cameron's ex-fiancée.

"Rebecca, please," Evan said.

"No one wants to talk about Grace. So can we please just drop it?" Cameron said.

"I'm not trying to open old wounds, I just think I should tell Caitlyn how much better she is for you than Grace was. Grace broke Cameron's heart, and I was so worried that he'd never get over her. I'm glad he met someone like you. I knew she was wrong for him from the start, but some things people have to find out on their own," Rebecca said, shaking her head.

"Can we please not talk about this now?!" Cameron yelled.

He pushed his chair back and stormed out of the dining room. Cameron went outside to calm down. He wasn't sure why he reacted that way to the mere mention of Grace. Was he still in love with her? Surely not after the way she treated him. He walked out to the white fence that surrounded the stable where they kept the horses to admire the scenery he'd grown to love over the years. He watched Joe from a distance as he was working. Caitlyn came out shortly afterwards to find him. He was so deep in thought, until he didn't notice her presence until she placed her hand on his shoulder.

"Hi," Caitlyn said, leaning against him. "Are you okay?"

"Yeah, I'm fine. I'm sorry for storming out like that. I just still prefer not to talk about her, and I don't know why my mom doesn't seem to understand that. I know she made you uncomfortable, and I hate that."

"I'm a big girl, I can handle it," Caitlyn soothed. Cameron turned towards her. "Besides, your mom has been very kind to me. I see why you love her so much. I was only uncomfortable because I thought you might be. I know that you had a life before you ever joined the firm. Look, Cameron," Caitlyn sighed. "We know that there's something between us, and I'm still not sure how I should feel about that. But, I need to know, are you still in love with Grace? Because if you are, married or not, she will still have you and the two of us don't stand a chance," Caitlyn said.

Cameron looked at her deeply and stroked her hair. The sunlight beamed against the side of her face. Her hair was blowing softly in the wind, and her beautiful eyes stared back at him. Looking at her now, Cameron wondered if he ever loved Grace. After all, Grace never brought out feelings like this in him. He knew everything about Caitlyn by simply looking into her eyes. He could never read Grace like that. He knew it was unhealthy to compare the two of them, but he also knew that he didn't want to make the same mistakes. Caitlyn was perfect for him. What he felt for her, the passion and the connection was instantaneous, although both of them were too stubborn to admit it. He was beginning to fall hard for this woman, and it helped to put things in perspective for him. Caitlyn smiled and closed her eyes as he stroked her cheek. Then, their lips met. He pulled her into a deep embrace and kissed her passionately. He caressed her, hugging her tenderly as their lips hesitantly parted.

"I only want to be with you, Caitlyn. Grace is definitely my past," Cameron whispered. "I am no longer in love with her."

"That's all I needed to hear," Caitlyn smiled.

They kissed passionately again, both trying hard not to

give in to the desire they were feeling for each other. Cameron wanted desperately to be with her, but he had to have self-control. Cameron's breathing was labored.

"We'd better stop," he whispered, pulling away.

Caitlyn looked at him lovingly. "Come on, let's go back to the house so you and your mom can iron this all out. She was so upset knowing that she'd angered you."

"I didn't mean to snap at her. I owe her an apology. She didn't raise me to treat her that way," Cameron said.

Caitlyn and Cameron walked hand in hand back up to the house. When they walked in, Cameron immediately apologized to his parents, especially his mother.

"I'm the one who's sorry, Cameron. I never should have gone on and on about her. That was unfair to you. Can you forgive me?" Rebecca asked.

"There's nothing to forgive. I know you only want what's best for me," Cameron said, hugging her.

"I really do. Caitlyn, you're so sweet. Thank you for being there for my son," Rebecca reached out and touched Caitlyn's hand.

Caitlyn marveled at how close Cameron and his family were. She'd never had that. She always knew her mother loved her, but by the time she had someone she could call a real father, she was an adult. She felt cheated and a little jealous of Cameron's life with his family. Cameron looked at Caitlyn. He smiled at her and wondered what she was thinking at that very moment. He was satisfied knowing that he was surrounded by the people he cared about most in the world.

Cameron decided that since he was in town, he'd give David a call. David was glad to hear he was in town and he insisted that the two of them come over for dinner that evening. He gladly accepted, explaining to his mom his reasons for not being there for dinner. His parents always thought the world of David and his wife Linda, and surprisingly enough, she thought it was a great idea. Usually, his mom would have told him to invite David and Linda over.

After lunch, Cameron and Caitlyn decided to go to the

courthouse to try to dig up some sort of information on Rosemary Faulkner. When they got there, they found out that her parents were killed in May of 1985 in a car accident, and shortly afterwards, Rosemary disappeared. They were able to get her address, and decided to see if she had any personal belongings, pictures, anything that could lead them to Rachel Marlow.

As they were about to leave the courthouse, they ran into George Stapleton, police chief of Lariette Springs. Like everyone else in Lariette Springs, he knew Cameron and his family quite well. Even though he and Cameron were often defending opposite sides of the law, he and his wife Mary had often had dinner with Cameron and his family. Ironically, Grace was George's niece, but even with that fact, it had never put a strain on the friendship between Cameron's parents and the Stapletons. George had often voiced his concern and dismay over the fact that Grace had treated Cameron so terribly.

"Hi, George," Cameron smiled, extending his hand.

"Cameron! How are you?" George smiled.

"Great. This is my colleague, Caitlyn Frazier."

"How do you do?" said Caitlyn.

"Ms. Frazier," George smiled, tipping his hat slightly.

"You know, George, maybe you're just the person I need to talk to about something," Cameron said.

"Sure, what is it?" George asked.

"We're here trying to locate a woman by the name of Rosemary Faulkner. Apparently, she lived here in Lariette Springs."

"Faulkner? Wasn't she the daughter of James and Jacqueline Faulkner?"

"Yeah. We just found out a little information, including the fact that her parents were killed years ago," Cameron said.

"Yeah, they were. A few months after that happened, Rosemary disappeared. Poor girl was slightly retarded, never really had been on her own. She's been on the 'Missing Persons' list for over 20 years. Unfortunately, she has never

~ 179 ~

been found."

"Yeah, that's what we just found out. She was an important link to a case I've been working on," Cameron said.

"I'm sorry, Cameron, but if Rosemary was an important link, you've probably hit a dead-end. But, I'll see what I can find out. It's been a cold case for years, but I'll pull up the preliminary report."

"Who reported her missing if her parents are dead?" Cameron asked.

"Her job. She worked at the local daycare center as part of one of those work programs for the mentally challenged. When she didn't report for work for a few days, someone went to her house, and there was no sign of her. All of her things were still there, but no one ever heard from her again. She lived all alone in the house that belonged to her parents, which she probably shouldn't have been allowed to do."

"Did she live off of Hwy. 210 on Wilkerson Drive?"

"Yeah, she did. Don't know what's there by now," George said, shaking his head.

"We're going out there to look around," Cameron commented.

"Do you need me to send one of my officers out there with you?"

"No thanks, we'll be fine," Cameron smiled.

"I'll gladly help in any way I can," George offered.

"Thanks, George. I appreciate it."

"No problem," George smiled. "I'll get that report to you tomorrow morning."

Cameron and Caitlyn left the courthouse and traveled several miles to find the deserted house that belonged to the Faulkner family. It was a large log cabin by a small lake. It was obviously once a beautiful place, and could be very nice if it was fixed up. The front porch stretched across the front and around two sides of the house. When they walked onto the porch, the front door had a broken window. Cameron carefully reached in and unlocked the door, trying to avoid cutting himself on the broken glass. He slowly turned the knob, having no idea what they'd be walking into.

"Stay close," Cameron said to Caitlyn, holding her hand as they went in.

"You don't have to tell me twice," Caitlyn said.

The dust nearly choked them as they entered the large living area. The heat was stifling, obviously from being closed up for a long time. The floors creaked as they walked. The furniture was covered with white sheets, yet a lot of the drawers were opened and things scattered out on the floor. There were cobwebs throughout the house. Caitlyn screamed when a small mouse scurried across the floor. They went into one of the bedrooms, and everything was in disarray. It was obvious that someone had been looking for something. Maybe Rachel had been there trying to find anything that would link her to the family. Maybe vandals had broken in. The house had been empty for so long, until it was hard to say. They saw a desk in the living room covered with papers. That would be the best place to start. There were old receipts and utility bills. They looked through everything, as Caitlyn accidentally knocked some things off onto the floor. As she leaned down to retrieve them, she glanced in the direction underneath the desk and noticed a white envelope taped to the bottom of it, far towards the back.

"Cameron, look," Caitlyn said.

"What is it?" Cameron asked leaning down with her.

Caitlyn retrieved the envelope from underneath. She opened the envelope and there was a note that looked to be written by a child.

"What does it say?" Cameron asked.

"It looks like it was something written by Rosemary, because her name's at the bottom," Caitlyn said. She then read the letter out aloud:

'Dear who ever find my note,

She want to hurt me bad. I scared of what she gonna do. Rachel is mean now. I thought she was nice, an she not nice. She mean mean mean. I saw her kill that man when he axd for more mony. Rachel got mony from wut Ma and Pa left

~ 181 ~

me to pay him for fixin her frend car. I dont no much, but I dint no braks cos so much mony to fix. Rachel always bin the smart wun, so if she say it tak ten thosend dolers to fix the braks, then that how much it cos. I scared now, caus she told me not to breth a word of wut I saw. How can I breth words. Wut if she kil me? Did I do sumthin wrong? She told me to never ever say I no her name Rachel. She told me to call her Elen Harwud. That not her name. Her name is Rachel. She help me wen Ma an Pa died. The acsident was bad, and Rachel help me. She sined evrythin for me, caus I not real smart. She told them she was Elen my sister and I had to tel them that she was. I dont worry much caus Rachel make shur I eat an have cloths an have a hows. She handal all the mony. Ma and Pa lef me some mony. A lot of it. Now Rachel not nice to me no more. She sed she kil me if I told. I dont no what to tel. She kil that man and push him in the wel owt bak. I so scared sometime he comin owt of the wel to get me. Rachel sed he wud if I was bad an dont do what she say. Help me. Rachel so mean!!!!
Lov
Rosemary'

"Man, Rachel was something else. How could she do that?" Cameron asked.

"Not much about Rachel surprises me," Caitlyn commented. "We have to contact the police. At least Rosemary was smart enough to hide this letter."

"So, now we need to add Ellen Harwood to the list. That was obviously an alias Rachel used as well as Regina."

"Wait a minute. The brakes. Dr. Varden. Wasn't he killed in a car accident?" Caitlyn said.

"Yeah, he was. I wonder was that what happened to him. If Rachel paid someone $10,000.00 to do a 'brake job,' that had to be it. We both know it doesn't cost $10,000.00 to repair brakes," Cameron stated.

"I guess it would if they were tampering with the brakes to cause an accident," Caitlyn said.

"We'd better get George on the phone," Cameron said,

pulling out his cell phone.

They called George, who came over with several officers and forensics. They went around to the well located in back of the house. It was covered, so forensics explored it while wearing protective wear. At this point, they had no idea what to expect. Cameron and Caitlyn stuck around until after they could find out if there was actually a body at the bottom of the well. After a couple of hours, and trucking equipment combing the area of the well, they indeed found a badly decomposed skeleton. The skeleton had on a man's set of clothes, looking to be a mechanic's jumper. This new information fit into the facts Rosemary had written in her letter. Cameron and Caitlyn gave George the letter as evidence but asked to get a copy of it as soon as possible. It would take time to find out who the body belonged to. It obviously had been there for many years. Rachel had no end to her danger. All of these facts really fascinated Caitlyn a little. She wasn't expecting all of this to turn up during their investigation. They stayed at the Faulkner cabin until after 6 p.m., and left when George told them he'd be in touch.

When they returned to Cameron's parents' home, Rebecca and Evan were out. Cameron asked Caitlyn if she still felt up to going to dinner at David and Linda's house. She insisted that maybe it was just what the two of them needed. They showered and changed before leaving for David and Linda's. Despite everything that had happened, Caitlyn told Cameron how much she still was enjoying getting to know more about his life.

"I know we're here on business, but it's so peaceful," Caitlyn said.

"I know. I wouldn't trade it for anything," Cameron said.

"So, why did you come to Kerrigan? It seems that this life had to be pretty good."

"I needed a change. It wasn't the lifestyle exactly, but the need to at least try something different, to find out what I really wanted in life. I don't regret my decision to move away, but this will always be home for me."

"I can respect that. Not to pry, but as much as your mom likes to have people around, why didn't they have more children?" Caitlyn asked.

"I don't know. I remember when I was little, I would always tell them I wanted a little sister or brother, and my mom would tell me that if it's meant to be, it'll happen. But, unfortunately, it never did. I've asked my mom since I've been an adult if she regretted not having more children. She told me no. So, I left it at that," Cameron said.

Caitlyn smiled. "So, what time did you tell David we'd be there?"

"I told him by 7:30. Why?"

"Well, I wanted to stop and get a bottle of wine or something."

"That's really sweet of you," Cameron smiled. "You know, here in Lariette Springs, we don't have much, but we actually have one of the best places to buy wine in the entire state of Kentucky," Cameron said.

The two of them stopped to purchase a bottle of wine before venturing on to David's house. When Cameron pulled into the driveway, David and Linda were out on the front porch waving.

"Cameron, how are you?!" David exclaimed, hugging him.

"I'm fine, how are you guys?" Cameron smiled.

"We're doing good. Man, it's good to see you! I know you've only been gone a couple of weeks, but it feels like a lot longer than that," David said.

"Come over here and give me a hug!" Linda said.

"Linda, how's it going?" Cameron said, hugging her.

"Everything's great. The big city treating you well?" Linda asked.

"It's been really good to me. Guys, I'd like you to meet my colleague and friend, Caitlyn Frazier," Cameron said.

"Hi, Caitlyn. I'm Linda, David's wife." Linda shook Caitlyn's hand.

"And I'm David, Linda's husband obviously," David smiled, shaking her hand next.

"It's great to meet you both," Caitlyn smiled. "Oh, we brought this for you two." Caitlyn handed them the bottle of wine.

"Thank you," David smiled. "Well, come on in you two. We've got a lot to talk about."

"If you're not about to tell me I'm about to be an uncle finally, I don't want to hear it," Cameron said.

"Is that right? I guess you'd want to hear about this twice then," Linda smiled.

"What?" Cameron said confusedly. Then, it dawned on him what she was saying. "Twins? Are you expecting twins?" Cameron asked.

"Yeah. We found out last week that we were having twins," David said.

"When did you find out you were pregnant?" Cameron asked.

"Actually, I'd suspected it for a few weeks, but I wanted to know for sure. So, I went to the doctor and he confirmed it," Linda said.

"How far along are you?" Caitlyn asked.

"I'm four months."

"Congratulations to you both," Caitlyn smiled.

"Thank you," Linda smiled.

"Four months? When did you find out? Because I've only been gone almost two weeks," Cameron said.

"We actually just found out the Monday right after you left. She was already 15 weeks and we didn't know it," David said.

"I am so happy for you two," Cameron said.

"Why don't we all go into the living room?" Linda suggested.

"Cameron, how about a beer?" David offered.

"Sure, thanks," Cameron responded.

"You decorate beautifully, Linda," Caitlyn said, looking around.

"Thank you. Keeping the house clean with David is a full-time job in itself. Once the babies come, I'll hardly have time for myself. But, I'm really looking forward to it. So, how long are you guys here for?" Linda asked.

"Until Friday. We need to get back to Indiana fairly soon," Cameron said.

"Is this business or strictly a friendly visit?" Linda asked.

"A little of both. We're working on a case, so we're staying with Mom and Dad," Cameron said.

"How are your parents doing?" David asked, handing Cameron his beer.

"Thanks," Cameron said, taking the beer. "They're fine. Dad's still recovering from his surgery. He seems so preoccupied and I'm really worried about him."

"What do you think is going on?" David asked.

"I'm not sure. I was just talking to him about a case I'm working on and he seemed so distant all of a sudden. Oh, by the way, have you ever heard of a woman named Rosemary Faulkner? She's supposed to be from here," Cameron said.

"Rosemary Faulkner? Did she attend school with us?" David asked.

"No. I'm guessing she'd be in her fifties."

"No, I've never heard of her. Why do you ask?"

"She's a cousin of the woman we're trying to track down. We've just found out that she's from here," Cameron said. "I talked to George Stapleton earlier and afterwards, Caitlyn and I went to Rosemary's house. She apparently disappeared many years ago. We found a letter obviously written by her, saying that she was scared for her life and how this woman Rachel had killed a man and dumped him into the well."

"What?" David asked, astonished.

"Sad part is, she was right," Caitlyn chimed in.

"How did you find out for sure?" David asked.

"When we read the letter, we called George out, and he brought forensics with him. They investigated the well, and sure enough, just like Rosemary's letter stated, there was a body in there," Cameron stated.

"You guys saw the body?" Linda asked, wrinkling her nose.

~ 186 ~

"Oh, yeah, and I'll tell you, TV makes it a hell of a lot more glamorous than it really is," Cameron laughed.

"I'll bet," David laughed. "Was it badly decomposed?"

"Come on, David. It was a 20 plus year old corpse. What do you think?" Cameron joked.

"Point taken," David smiled. "So, what did George say?"

"He told us that he'd get in touch with us when they positively ID the guy. We're not grossing you out, are we, Linda?" Cameron asked.

"Remember, I live with David. If I can clean up after him, I can handle anything," Linda laughed.

"You've got a point!" Cameron laughed.

"Do you hear them, Caitlyn?" David laughed, looking in Caitlyn's direction. "He's just jealous because I stole Linda from him. Did Cameron ever tell you how I wooed Linda from him?"

"Yeah, when you were five," Caitlyn smiled.

"Five, fifteen or twenty-five, I still have more charisma!" David laughed.

"In whose fantasy?" Cameron laughed.

"You know it's the truth!" David laughed, standing up. "Come on, let's eat."

"Just like you to change the subject when I'm winning," Cameron laughed as they stood to go into the dining room.

The four of them had a nice dinner, as Caitlyn and Linda talked about the babies and their arrival. They reminisced about their days in school, as Caitlyn felt like she was a part of it all by the animated details they gave of their adventures. It was a wonderful visit, and they all hated to see it end. But, Cameron and Caitlyn knew they had a lot of work ahead of them the next day, so they wanted to get back to Cameron's house to get a good night's sleep.

"I'll call you later," Cameron said to David.

"Okay. Caitlyn, it was great meeting you," David said.

"It was nice meeting you too," Caitlyn smiled.

"Let's try to get together again before you leave,

~ 187 ~

okay?" Linda suggested.

Cameron and Caitlyn rode along as Caitlyn commented how nice David and Linda were. They arrived at Cameron's parents' home and got out of the car laughing about one of the anecdotes David had shared with Caitlyn. Before they could even enter the house, they heard shouting. Cameron quickly unlocked the door to find his parents screaming at each other. They were too involved in their argument to hear him come in.

"Dammit, Rebecca, I asked you a question! Answer me!" Evan shouted.

"How dare you? How could you ask me something like that?! You have to be out of your mind to even say such cruel things to me!" Rebecca yelled.

"Oh, please! I will not keep living like this!" Evan shot back.

"Mom, Dad! What's going on here!?" Cameron asked.

"Oh, honey, I'm so sorry you had to hear that," Rebecca said, running to him. "Your father and I are having a disagreement."

"What's this all about?" Cameron asked.

"Cameron, there are a lot of things you need to know," Evan said. "There's something I need to tell you, Son."

"Dad, what is it? What's going on here?" Cameron asked.

"Cameron, your father's not in his right mind right now. Evan, please, our son is preoccupied. Don't bother him with our petty disagreements," Rebecca said.

"No, Mom, if Dad has something to say, I want to hear it," Cameron said.

"Cameron, listen to me. There's something you need to know, Son," Evan said. His breathing became labored. "I-I need t-to tell y-you something–" Evan's speech became slurred, and he wavered. His left side seemed to give out and he suddenly fell to the floor.

Chapter
9

Dad! Dad! What's wrong? Caitlyn, call 911!" Cameron was shaking his father, trying to bring him back. Evan seemed totally unaware of anything, as if he couldn't talk. He was unable to form words. Cameron figured out that his father was having a stroke. "Mom! Will you please help me? Dad! Wake up!" Cameron continued to try to bring his father back, while Rebecca just watched, as if she suddenly was oblivious about what was going on around her. Unfortunately, besides calling 911 there was very little Cameron could do for his father. Shortly after that, Evan blacked out.

"Cameron, what's the address?" Caitlyn shouted from the phone.

"38 Castleberry Way, Route ten. The Spencer Ranch," Cameron said. "Tell them to please hurry!"

"What else can I do to help?" Caitlyn asked after hanging up the phone.

"Check on my mom," Cameron said.

"Mrs. Spencer? Mrs. Spencer? Are you alright?"

Caitlyn was shaking her slightly. "Cameron, she's in shock."

Rebecca stood there, staring at Evan lying on the floor. The four minutes it took the paramedic to get there seemed like forever to Cameron. He was ever so thankful that they came back when they did. It was obvious from looking at his mother's reaction she wouldn't have been able to do anything. The paramedic arrived and after stabilizing Evan, explained that he'd had a massive stroke, probably a result of a burst aneurysm and had to be treated immediately. They were concerned about Cameron's mother also, who was indeed in a state of shock. She finally seemed to come around, and said she wanted to ride in the ambulance with Evan. They rushed him to Ludwick Memorial Hospital, which was 15 minutes away. Cameron and Caitlyn followed in their rental car.

Cameron wondered what was really going on between his parents, and knew that he had to get to the bottom of why they were arguing. Right now, all he wanted to do was make sure his father was going to survive. So many questions were racing through his head. In all the years he could remember, he'd never even witnessed an argument of any kind between his parents. The two people he saw tonight were complete strangers to him. They were talking as if they hated each other and Cameron had no idea why. Caitlyn interrupted Cameron's thoughts.

"Cameron, do you want me to drive?"

"No thanks, I'm fine. I can't believe this. What if my dad doesn't make it?" Cameron sighed.

"Don't think like that," Caitlyn soothed.

"They said the stroke was massive. That could kill him."

"Let's just hope for the best and see what the doctor says. Your dad strikes me as a strong man. He'll pull through. What do you think he was trying to tell you?"

"I'm not sure. He seemed preoccupied earlier today. Maybe he wasn't feeling well," Cameron said.

"What do you mean 'preoccupied'?" Caitlyn asked.

"I was talking to him about the case and he became very distant, asking a lot of strange questions. You don't think

~ 190 ~

he knows Rosemary do you?"

"Don't you think he would have told you? I mean, why would he hide it?"

"You're right. I just wish I knew more about what was going on with him."

Shortly thereafter, they pulled up at the hospital emergency room. Ludwick Memorial was an excellent hospital, but was the last place Cameron wanted to see again.

"I thought I was finished with this place after my father's fall a couple of months ago. Now, here I am again, but this time it's a lot more serious," Cameron sighed. "Come on, let's see if we can find out what's going on."

Cameron opened his door. He was feeling numb, as he prepared himself for the worst possible news. Cameron and Caitlyn walked through the automatic doors leading to the emergency room. Rebecca was talking to a nurse.

"All I know is, he and I were having a disagreement, and he suddenly fell to the floor and was unable to talk," Rebecca was crying. "Will he be okay?"

"It's really too soon to tell, Mrs. Spencer. We're doing everything we can for him," the nurse stated. "We need all of the medications he's currently on, and we can find out his allergies from past medical records. I'm going to direct you to the clerk who will explain to you about an advanced directive," the nurse said.

"I understand you have to inform me about it, but, my husband has already made it clear that he doesn't want to be put on life support if it comes to that. He has a living will," Rebecca stated.

"Dad has never wanted to be a burden, not that he ever would be. But, he's adamant about not being put on life support if there is no hope for recovery," Cameron said.

"It's something we discussed in detail but never really thought we'd have to consider. I guess that's why it's always best to discuss these things," Rebecca said.

"Okay, well we have all we need. Take your insurance card to the admitting clerk, and she'll take care of you from there," the nurse said. "Someone will be out to talk to you

~ 191 ~

momentarily."

Cameron went with his mother to the admitting desk and gave all of Evan's information to her while Caitlyn waited in the waiting area. After they went back to the waiting area, Cameron went to get coffee for his mom, Caitlyn and himself. He felt that it was going to be a very long night. Cameron began to think about the argument that had ensued, and needed to know more about what was really going on.

"Mom, what was going on? What were you and Dad arguing about?" Cameron asked.

"It's personal," Rebecca stated dryly.

"Are you sure? It sounded as if there was something that Dad wanted me to know, something he was trying to tell me. What is it?" Cameron asked.

"Cameron, leave it alone! Stop asking so many questions!" Rebecca yelled.

"Mom, I know you're upset right now, but I feel I have a right to know," Cameron stated.

"You're right, Sweetheart. I'm sorry I yelled," Rebecca sighed. "Your father and I were arguing about selling the house. He doesn't want to sell, but I'm ready for something smaller. I thought about a little condo, maybe in Kerrigan," Rebecca said.

"You want to sell the house? Mom, you love that house," Cameron said.

"Yes, but 150 acres? It's getting to be too much. Your father's not as well anymore, and all of the upkeep is falling onto me," Rebecca stated. "I know we have hired hands to take care of the horses and land, but, it's still too much for me."

"I guess I never thought about it that way," Cameron commented.

"It's been a back and forth thing lately. But, after you moved, I realized that I wanted to be close to my son. Besides, this way, I can still take care of you," Rebecca smiled.

"Mom, I'm not a little boy anymore. You and Dad need to think about yourselves. Travel a bit, buy a place on the beach, but don't feel as if you have to take care of me."

"But, I love to take care of you," Rebecca said.

"Thanks, but I'll be fine," he hugged his mother. "I'm going to go check and see if they can tell us anything yet." He went to the nurse's station to inquire about his dad's condition.

"I'm sorry sir, they're still in with him. The doctor will be out as soon as he can to talk to you," the nurse said.

The entire day's events reeled through Cameron's head, and he wondered was his mother telling him the entire truth. A disagreement about the house? That was an explosive argument about something else. Rebecca wasn't telling him everything. Cameron wandered back to the waiting room and sat next to Caitlyn. Rebecca had fallen asleep.

"Any word yet?" Caitlyn whispered.

"No, nothing yet. I'm sure this whole thing has stressed my mom out. She must be going through hell right now," Cameron said.

"She's a strong woman, Cameron. She'll be fine, and so will your dad," Caitlyn said.

"I hope so."

"It's just a good thing we came back when we did," Caitlyn said.

"I couldn't agree more. Thanks for keeping me sane," Cameron smiled. They sat there for almost another ½ an hour chatting back and forth when two doctors came out.

"Mrs. Spencer?" the doctor said.

Cameron nudged his mother gently to wake her. "Mom, the doctor's here," Cameron said.

"Hello, Mrs. Spencer. I'm Dr. Moreland, the ER physician. This is Dr. Farrington, the neurosurgeon on call. I called him in to evaluate your husband," the doctor said.

"How's my husband?" Rebecca asked.

"About as well as can be expected. Your husband has suffered a subarachnoid hemorrhage, better known as a stroke. We have him stabilized, but right now, it's too soon to tell what's going to happen," Dr. Farrington said.

"What could have caused this?" Cameron asked.

"Stress, more than likely. But, because of what the

~ 193 ~

tests show, it looks as if he's had an aneurysm for some time, but it apparently didn't show up before. He was in the hospital recently, and they did several tests because he was complaining about headaches," Dr. Moreland said.

"Headaches? Dad never complained about headaches," Cameron stated.

"According to his chart, he did. It's not totally unusual that something like this wouldn't show up in previous tests, but since he was complaining about headaches, it's a little surprising. There are times these things can happen practically over night, which tells me that maybe his headaches had nothing to do with the aneurysm because it should have shown up before now. We also noticed some leakage of some of the smaller blood vessels in his brain. Has he been taking a great deal of medication lately? Maybe much more than the recommended dosage?" Dr. Farrington asked.

"Are you trying to say my husband was on drugs?" Rebecca asked defensively.

"No, Mrs. Spencer, but, the leakage that showed up is the type that usually indicates some sort of over dosage or possible drug use. I'm not accusing your husband of anything, but I still have to ask. This still would have happened even without the leakage."

"Well, just for the record, Evan never used drugs. And as far as his medication, from what I know, he always took only the prescribed amount," Rebecca said.

"Okay. I understand your being upset, but I needed to know. We'll be running drug panels on him anyway, especially considering all of the medication he's been on lately," Dr. Farrington said.

"What's going to happen to my father?" Cameron asked.

"It's really hard to say this early. I've scheduled an MRI to be done tonight, so that we can evaluate what's going on," Dr. Farrington stated. "The amount of bleeding will determine the severity of his cerebral hemorrhage. Not to alarm you, but, in many cases, people with cerebral hemorrhages die because of increased pressure on their brain.

But, those who live tend to recover much more than people who've had strokes caused by a clot."

The doctor went on to explain exactly what Evan's chances were in regards to his recovery. After listening intently, Cameron was worried. The news was not good, and he felt pessimistic about his father's chance of survival. He looked at his mother, noticing the concerned look on her face. This was going to be hard on her, and Cameron had to do everything he could to be supportive.

"In other words, even if my husband survives, he will never be the same again?" Rebecca asked tearfully.

"I'm sorry I don't have better news for you Mrs. Spencer, but his stroke was massive. Like I said, there is some hope because of the kind of stroke he had. The next couple of days will be critical in whether he lives or not. After that, I'm afraid he has a long fight ahead of him in his recovery. We've got him stabilized, if you'd like to see him briefly before we take him to MRI and then transport him to intensive care," Dr. Farrington said.

"So what happens now?" Cameron asked.

"Well, we operate," Dr. Farrington said.

The doctor went on to explain in great detail about the surgical procedure that Evan would require and the expected recovery time for such a serious condition. He also explained to them the fact that Evan would now require repair on his hip once again, because it was injured during his collapse.

"Thank you, Dr. Farrington, Dr. Moreland," Cameron said, putting his arm around his mother. "Come on, let's go see Dad."

"I'll wait here," Caitlyn suggested.

"We'll be back in a few minutes," Cameron said.

Cameron and his mother walked into Evan's room. He was still in the emergency room for the time being. He looked weak and helpless hooked up to several monitors and machines. Cameron looked at him from head to toe. He had a face mask on to help with his breathing. He had tubes in both arms and probes on his chest to monitor his heart rate. There were probes even attached to his head, to monitor brain activity. Cameron was shaken by the fact that this once strong, capable man who'd always taken care of his family now depended on his family to take care of him. Cameron knew that he could never desert Evan. Rebecca cried softly, touching Evan's hand.

Cameron thought back to so many special memories he'd made with his father, and how his father had always been there for him. He'd given him advice on women, school, careers, everything. Cameron honestly didn't know what he'd do without him. He was the only father Cameron knew. He couldn't miss what he never had, because his real father was killed in a car crash before he was even born. He never even saw a picture of his real father, because all of the memories his parents had made together were destroyed years before in a tornado. Evan had always been a real father to him, and had they not made the decision to tell him the truth, he would have gone on believing that Evan was his natural father.

He knew that the only thing he could do for his father was to pray. His father had always been a pillar of strength, and Cameron depended on him. Now, it was up to Cameron to take care of his mother. Evan's motionless body lay there, not knowing what was going on around him. He felt there were still so many things left for he and his father to do together.

He began to blame himself for ever leaving home. Maybe had he stayed home, none of this would have happened. His parents might never have argued because the issue about selling the house never would have come up and his father might not have had a stroke. He knew deep down that it was silly to feel this way, but he couldn't help it.

Cameron was giving serious thoughts to moving back home. He felt obligated to finish the job he'd started for Mr. Marlow, and he would honor his commitment. One way or the other, the Marlow case would be settled in a few weeks. He wondered if Phillip would understand his need to take care of his family. He voiced his suggestion to his mother.

"Mom, I think I'm going to move back home," Cameron said.

"Oh, Cameron. That would be wonderful. It could just

be you and me," Rebecca smiled, hugging him.

"I think it's best to help Dad recover," Cameron said.

"Well, as it stands now, we don't know what's going to happen to your father," Rebecca said. "But I really need you here to support me."

"We hope Dad pulls through. Isn't that what you want, too?" Cameron felt surprised at even having to question his mother's loyalty to his father.

"Of course, Dear. I love your father. But, I want to be prepared for the worst possible outcome," Rebecca said.

"I understand that, but Mom, you talk as if you just know Dad's going to die," Cameron said.

"Sweetheart, it's not that. No one wants your father to pull through more than I do, but, we have to be realistic after what the doctor said."

Cameron soon realized he was just stressed about the entire situation. He knew his mother loved his father. No amount of arguing could come between those two. The two of them stayed for a few minutes more, only to be interrupted by a nurse coming in telling them it was time for Evan to go for his tests.

"He'll be in the intensive care unit afterwards, and once he's settled in, you'll be able to visit with him briefly. He's going to be in ICU-9," the nurse said.

"Thank you," Cameron said.

Soon after, the assistant and a tech from radiology came in to get Evan. Cameron and Rebecca stood aside and watched helplessly as they wheeled him out of the room. They went back to the waiting room to join Caitlyn who'd been leafing through a magazine.

"How's Mr. Spencer?" Caitlyn asked, standing.

"Not good. They're taking him for tests now, and then he'll be going to the intensive care unit," Cameron said, feeling a sense of fear he'd not felt since childhood.

Cameron wasn't accustomed to not being in control. They stayed in the waiting room a few minutes more and then went to the fourth floor, which is where Evan would be once he finished with his tests. There was a waiting room there for

~ 197 ~

family members, and Cameron noticed the hours were restricted. He thought about the fact that his mother would probably want to stay.

"Mom, if you want me to, I can go home and get some things for you," Cameron suggested.

"No, that's okay. I'll be going home tonight," Rebecca stated.

"Going home? You're not going to stay with Dad?" Cameron asked.

"Not tonight, Dear. I'll be back bright and early tomorrow. That way, I can go home and get my things together myself, and not bother you," Rebecca said.

"It's really no problem," Cameron said. "Dad needs us here, and I think you should be here with him."

"I said no! Your father won't change tonight. He won't even know I'm here! Now, I'm going home. Are you going to drive me, or do I need to call a cab?" Rebecca asked.

Cameron was clearly shocked by Rebecca's attitude. "I can't believe you! Mom, what's wrong with you? Dad's holding on for dear life, and you're so callous about it!" Cameron was almost shouting.

"Cameron, calm down," Caitlyn said calmly.

"No, I won't calm down! Within the past few hours, my father has had a near-fatal stroke and my mother couldn't seem to care less! I think I have reason to be upset right now!"

"Cameron Spencer, don't you take that tone with me!" Rebecca yelled. "I'm tired and stressed out and I want to go home!"

"Is everything okay here?" a nurse asked.

"It's fine. My son will be staying with his father tonight, but I'll be back in the morning," Rebecca said.

"That's fine, but please keep it down," the nurse said.

"We apologize for the commotion," Caitlyn said. "Everyone is just under a lot of stress right now."

"I understand that, but we have other patients and family members to consider," the nurse stated.

"We'll be quiet. Cameron, why don't you come with me to get some air?" Caitlyn suggested.

"Fine. Mom, I feel like I don't even know you anymore," Cameron said walking off.

Rebecca stood there with tears in her eyes, as her only son looked at her with such repulsiveness. Cameron and Caitlyn went out to the veranda on the third floor. Cameron stared out blankly, wondering why it seemed as if there was so much more going on than he knew about. His mother was totally out of character, as if she didn't care. There was definitely something wrong, and he was determined to find out what it was. Caitlyn interrupted his thoughts. She placed her hand on his shoulder from behind him.

"Cameron, I know things are not looking good right now, but it will get better," Caitlyn soothed.

"I just don't see how things could get better. My father might die, and my mother doesn't seem to give a damn. Why is this happening?" Cameron asked.

Caitlyn gently put her arms around him and leaned her head on his back. "Life just does things like that to us sometimes. It's nothing you did, it just happened."

"Maybe I should have stayed home, never moved to Indiana."

"And what would that have solved? It would have only delayed the inevitable, if it would have done that. Cameron, if your father was meant to have a stroke, he would have had it whether you still lived here or not. If it's meant for him to pull through, he will. Stop second-guessing yourself. You're a great attorney who went out to have a successful career. It's not your fault for having a life beyond your parents' home."

"But, Caitlyn, you don't know my relationship with them. They depend on me. What would have happened had I not been around tonight?" Cameron asked.

"But you were around. There's a reason we came when we did, and maybe this was it. Hey." Caitlyn turned him to face her. "Don't beat yourself up. I'm here for you, and I'm not going anywhere."

"You don't know how good it makes me feel to hear you say that," Cameron mustered a smile. He gently pulled her into a tender embrace. "It's amazing that a week ago, we couldn't stand each other. Now, I don't know what I'd do without you. Thank you, Caitlyn for everything."

"There's no need for thanks. Let's just get your mom home, and I'll come back up here to the hospital with you."

"Would it be terrible if I asked you to stay with my mom tonight?" Cameron asked. He knew he was asking a lot since Caitlyn and his mom hardly knew each other.

"No, it wouldn't be terrible. I'd love to stay with your mom. She probably doesn't need to be alone right now, anyway."

"Something's not right with her. I don't know what it is, but something's terribly wrong," Cameron said.

"She's just upset. You'd be amazed what people will say and do when they're upset. Give her time to let reality sink in. She'll be okay," Caitlyn said.

"You're right. Well, let's get back in here to see if we can find anything else out," Cameron sighed. He was starting to feel the pressures of the day's events, as his body felt worn out. Caitlyn placed her arms around him, and he placed his around her, as they walked slowly towards the elevator.

When they got to the fourth floor, Cameron saw his mother, and she was crying. He immediately regretted all the terrible things he said to his mother, then he started to panic, wondering if the news about his father was worse. He rushed to his mother's side.

"Mom, is everything okay? It's not Dad, is it?" Cameron asked ominously.

"No, son. There's no change. I just hate the way things were left between you and me," Rebecca said.

"Mom, I'm really sorry about what I said before. I was just upset, and I didn't know what else to do. I shouldn't have taken my anger out on you," Cameron said.

"That's okay, Dear. As long as you and I are okay now and you won't leave me," Rebecca said strangely.

"Mom, I'd never leave you. Look, Caitlyn and I are going to take you home, and she's going to stay with you and I'm going to come back up here to the hospital for the rest of the night," Cameron said.

"Okay. Caitlyn, are you sure you don't mind?" Rebecca asked.

"No, I don't mind at all. I just want to be here for you," Caitlyn said, hugging Rebecca.

"You're so sweet," Rebecca said.

They decided to wait until Evan came back to the floor so that Cameron could talk with the doctor.

"Doctor, how does it look?" Cameron asked.

"Pretty much exactly like we expected. He has some bleeding, but I'm a little more optimistic than I was earlier. He's still not out of the woods yet, but it's not as severe of a bleed as I initially thought. I have to be honest with you, the next 48 hours will be critical, and we'll just have to wait and see. Why don't you all go home? I'll have the nurse call if there's any change. It'll be at least another hour before you can see him."

"I'm going to take my mother home, but I'll be back afterwards," Cameron said. "Last time we were here, there were rooms that family members could rent. Is there one available for tonight?" Cameron asked.

"Sure. I'll have the clerk call over and reserve one for you, so that it'll be ready by the time you get back. He's getting the best of care," Dr. Farrington reassured. "I've contacted Dr. Kirklin, and he'll be back tomorrow morning. He was able to shed light on a lot of things concerning your dad."

"Thank you so much, Dr. Farrington," Rebecca said, shaking his hand. "I'll be back tomorrow morning."

"That's fine. Like I said before, it's fine if you all want to stay home tonight," Dr. Farrington suggested once again.

"I'd feel better if I were here, just in case," Cameron said.

"No problem," Dr. Farrington smiled. "I'll see you in a little while."

Caitlyn and Rebecca walked to the main lobby, and Cameron went to bring the car around to pick them up. Rebecca settled herself in the backseat as Caitlyn sat up front next to Cameron. The three of them rode in silence for the first few minutes, until Rebecca interrupted.

"Cameron, I need to stop at the drug store to pick up a prescription," Rebecca said.

"Okay. I'll go in and get it for you," Cameron said.

"No, that's okay. I want to talk to the pharmacist about something," Rebecca responded.

"Are you sure?" Cameron insisted, as he pulled into the drug store parking lot and parked his car.

"Quite sure. You and Caitlyn sit here while I go in. It'll only take a few minutes," Rebecca said, getting out of the car. "I'll be right back."

Cameron and Caitlyn discussed the entire day's events, reeling over the fact that they'd not only discovered a body, but also rushed to save his father's life.

"How are you holding up?" Caitlyn asked.

"I'm not sure right now. It's been a difficult day for me."

"I can only imagine, Cameron. How about if I go back to Indiana in a day or two and work on the case? You stay here and take care of your family," Caitlyn offered.

"Are you sure you want to?" Cameron asked.

"Of course. Mr. Marlow's hearing is coming up, and you don't need to be bogged down with it right now. We have so much evidence at this point, until we should be okay. I'll stay until after your father's surgery tomorrow, and then I'll fly back to Indiana."

"You're wonderful, Caitlyn," Cameron smiled, stroking her hair. "I don't know how long things are going to take, because now they've got to go in and do surgery on his hip again. I don't know when they're planning to do that particular surgery, but I need to be here."

"I understand completely," Caitlyn smiled. "I'll call the airline when we get to your house."

"Maybe the firm can send the plane for you," Cameron suggested.

"I talked to Phil earlier and he said that the plane is booked for the next week, and that if we needed to get back, to

~ 202 ~

take a commercial flight and charge it to the firm," Caitlyn said.

"Did he mention anything about Kristen?"

"No, he didn't. Let's not even worry about her right now. We have enough to deal with," Caitlyn said.

"You're right," Cameron sighed. "This has been a hell of a day, huh?"

"That's putting it mildly," Caitlyn said calmly.

Around that time, Rebecca came back to the car. "I'm sorry it took so long, Dear," Rebecca smiled.

"That's okay. We were just talking. Did you find everything you need?" Cameron asked.

"Yes, I did." Rebecca looked from Cameron to Caitlyn. "Is everything okay?"

"It's fine. We were just going over some things about the case," Cameron said. "Caitlyn is going to fly back in a day or two to try and wrap things up, and I'll stay here with you."

"Oh, I'm glad," Rebecca smiled. "You've been very vague about this case. What's it about?"

"It's an old murder case. We'll talk about it later. Right now, I just want to concentrate on Dad's recovery," Cameron said.

"What ever you think is best, Dear," Rebecca said.

They rode along the rest of the way in silence, each lost in their own thoughts. Cameron looked at Caitlyn, who sat quietly with a tired look on her face. Cameron wanted desperately to reach out to her, but somehow, he felt she was a million miles away. They pulled into Cameron's parents' driveway, and Cameron helped his mother out of the car and into the house.

"If either one of you needs me, I'll have my cell phone on the entire time," Cameron said.

"Cameron, call me later. I'm going to call the airline to see what time I can get a flight out either tomorrow or Friday," Caitlyn said.

"Okay," Cameron said, hugging her, then hugging Rebecca.

"I'll walk you out," Caitlyn offered.

"Goodbye, Dear," Rebecca said.

"Bye, Ma," Cameron said, walking out the door.

Caitlyn walked Cameron to the front door silently. Cameron looked at her.

"Hey, what is it?" Cameron whispered, holding her hand.

"It's nothing," Caitlyn said.

"You know, I've figured out when something's wrong with you. But, I won't push if you don't want to talk about it," Cameron said.

"It isn't that. It's just that I have a lot on my mind right now about the case and everything that's happened today. You just go on back to the hospital. I'll be fine here, and I'll keep a close eye on your mother," Caitlyn said.

Cameron stared into Caitlyn's eyes. Spontaneously, he kissed her lightly on the lips and smiled. "I'll call you later," Cameron said.

Cameron drove to the hospital with the day's events going through his head. His mother wasn't taking this well, and he honestly didn't know what he'd do if anything happened to her. She was so out of character earlier, and Cameron realized that even the best of people have a breaking point. Rebecca had come to hers. Rebecca was truly a remarkable woman. He could only hope to be married to someone half as wonderful as his mother. His thoughts immediately went to Caitlyn. Was Caitlyn the one? Was she anything like his mother? Was she the woman he was supposed to spend the rest of his life with? He and Caitlyn started out on a very bumpy road, but, he'd come to rely on her beautiful smile, and he didn't think he'd be able to imagine her not being in his life. Cameron smiled at the twist of fate, and how a woman he despised was becoming his best friend. She was becoming someone he was falling for fast. Was it love? Was it lust? He desired her, but he knew it was something deeper than that. He wasn't sure if he was ready to call it love yet, but he was developing very strong feelings for her.

Cameron pulled into the parking garage at the hospital and went to the fourth floor. Almost an hour passed since

~ 204 ~

they'd left the hospital, and Cameron wanted to know if he could go in to see his father.

"Sure, Mr. Spencer. I'll call back to the nurse and make sure it's okay to send you back," the clerk said, calling to his father's room.

"Thanks," Cameron said.

"The nurse said it's fine to send you in. He's in Room 9, which is right down the hall on left," the clerk said, pointing him in the right direction.

Cameron walked slowly, because he had no idea what to expect. He wanted to be strong for his father, but he didn't know how he could hold up after everything that had happened. He slid the glass door back leading to his father's room. All Cameron could hear was the sound of the many machines and monitors hooked up to his father. The nurse was checking his vital signs.

"How is he?" Cameron asked.

"He's a little more stable, but we're not out of the woods yet. We have a lot to do, so I can only let you stay back here for a few minutes," the nurse said.

"I understand," Cameron said.

Cameron stared disbelievingly at his father, wondering would his father ever gain all of his faculties if he pulled through. His father was restless enough after having hip surgery; this would surely be frustrating for him. Cameron knew that he had to do whatever necessary to see that his father received the best of care. He didn't want to relent to the idea that his father might not pull through. He looked at the monitors and realized that machines were possibly keeping his father alive. No longer could Evan take for granted the breathing he'd done on his own for his entire 56 years. Evan now lay there, helpless, with endless tubes and probes monitoring every bodily function. Cameron felt uneasy relying on technology built by man to keep his father alive. He knew this was an arrogant attitude to take, as if his father was above being saved by modern technology, above being reduced to relying on a machine for dear life. Then he realized there must be some hope because if not, legally, he would have

~ 205 ~

to be taken off life support.

"It's okay to talk to him," the nurse said. "It can be very therapeutic."

"Really? I felt as if I'd be wasting my time," Cameron said.

"No, sir. Encouragement from loved ones can sometimes be the best medicine."

Cameron looked thoughtfully at his father. "Dad? Can you hear me? It's me, Cameron." Cameron looked at the nurse.

"I'll leave you for a few minutes," the nurse smiled, leaving the room.

"Thank you," Cameron smiled back. He looked back at his father. "Dad? Dad? Can you hear me?" Cameron sighed, wondering was this really doing any good.

"How are you holding up?" Dr. Farrington asked, walking into the room.

"The bigger question is, how is my dad?"

"Right now, your father's holding his own."

"Is my father going to pull through this?"

"Cameron, I wish I could make you a promise, but I can't right now. We'll just have to see how things go tomorrow. Your dad's past medical history doesn't exactly work in his favor. I think you should be prepared for anything," Dr. Farrington said. "We're not going to operate on his hip tomorrow. Dr. Grayson was here while you were gone, and he ordered several tests to see what the damage looks like. According to those, we'll schedule his orthopedic surgery for some time next week."

One problem compiled on top of the other. His hip, the stroke; everything was taking its toll on Evan Spencer. He knew that if his dad didn't make it, he'd have to be there for his mother, which would mean moving home. He suddenly realized what this would mean for him. His life would once again change drastically. He'd met a wonderful woman and he really enjoyed working at Larson, Craig and Jacobs, but his first obligation had to be to his family. His mother and father had always provided every opportunity available for him, and he refused to turn his back on them. What could he do? There was only one thing to do: take care of his mother. If that meant putting his life on hold, then so be it.

Chapter
10

Cameron paced back and forth into the wee hours of the morning, worrying about his father, and especially his mother and how she would handle it if she lost her husband. Eventually, Cameron went to his room and showered. He decided to lie down to try and sleep, and left word to be awakened at 7 a.m., which was only four hours away. The wake-up call came much too quickly, as Cameron got out of bed and called to check on his father. The nurse told him there was no change, and that he'd be going in to surgery around 12:30 p.m. Cameron decided to try and call his mother around 8 a.m. He wanted her to sleep as long as possible because he knew she needed her rest. It took a long time, but she finally answered.

"Hello?" Rebecca answered.

"Mom? Hi, its 8 o'clock and I just wondered what time the two of you coming to the hospital," Cameron said.

"I'll be there as soon as I get dressed," Rebecca said.

"Where's Caitlyn? Is she still asleep?" Cameron asked.

"No, she's awake and in the shower. Do you want for

me to have her to call you when she gets out?" Rebecca asked.

"No, it's okay. I'll just see her when you get here," Cameron said. "How are you doing?"

"Oh, I'm much better. I feel as if everything's going to be okay. I'm very optimistic about your father," Rebecca said. "Sweetheart, last night, you mentioned that you'd be willing to come home. Did you really mean that?" Rebecca asked.

"Of course I did. You and Dad mean the world to me."

Cameron's heart sank. His mother was now counting on him to do just that. He realized that maybe he should have thought things through before saying that to her the night before. Now, it was too late.

"I'm so glad, Son. I don't know what I'd do without you. Now that your father's on the brink of death, I don't think I can make it a day without you."

"We'll discuss it later," Cameron suggested.

"You're right. We have all the time in the world to discuss our future. Will you be in your room or on the unit by the time we get there?" Rebecca asked.

"I'll be on the unit by then. Visiting time will start at 9:30, so I'd better let you go so that you can be on your way," Cameron said. "I'll see you shortly."

"Okay, Son," Rebecca said.

Rebecca and Cameron hung up, and he got dressed and left his room heading to the unit's waiting area. He was restless, and it seemed as if time had stood still. There was still another 30 minutes before visiting time. Shortly after that, his mother and Caitlyn arrived.

"Hi, Mom," Cameron said, hugging her. Then, he hugged Caitlyn. "Hi, Caitlyn. Thanks for coming back with my mom."

"Anytime. I called the airline, and the earliest I can get a 12:45 flight is Monday afternoon," Caitlyn said.

"The day after a holiday?"

"I know. I was lucky to get that. Most people travel the days around the holiday."

"Well, that gives us a couple of days to get everything

~ 209 ~

together before you leave," Cameron commented.

"Cameron, don't worry about it. I can handle everything," Caitlyn insisted.

"I have to do something to keep my mind occupied," Cameron said.

"I understand," Caitlyn smiled.

"Cameron, have you heard anything yet?" Rebecca asked.

"Not so far. I'm waiting until we go in before I talk to the doctor again. No one called me, so I assumed everything was still the same. Dad's surgery is scheduled for 12:30 today, so hopefully, we'll know something before then. How are you feeling?" Cameron asked.

"I'm fine. It's been rather hard dealing with everything that's going on. Did you rest okay?" Rebecca asked.

"Yeah, I rested fine. I really hope Dad pulls through this. The doctor said Dr. Grayson will schedule his hip surgery once he evaluates the tests they ran last night."

"Your father's a strong man. I'm sure he'll be just fine," Rebecca said.

Cameron was restless with all the waiting. They still had another 15 minutes before visiting time. "Does anyone want a cup of coffee?" Caitlyn asked.

"Thank you, Dear. Two sugars and one creamer please," Rebecca said.

"Cameron, do you need anything?" Caitlyn asked.

"No thanks," Cameron smiled.

"I'll be right back," Caitlyn said.

"Mom, I wanted to talk to you again about Dad," Cameron said.

"What about him, Sweetheart," Rebecca said.

"Do you really think we should let Dad remain a DNR? I know his situation is critical, but miracles happen every day."

"Cameron, if Evan is meant to come out of this, he will. His being a DNR isn't going to prevent that from happening. Your father never wanted to be a burden on us. Look at what's going on with him. I mean, not only is his health further complicated by the fall he took last night, but

~ 210 ~

he's in really bad shape otherwise. How are we going to take care of him?"

"Financially, we're doing quite well," Cameron reassured.

"I'm not talking about that," Rebecca said, shaking her head. "I mean, what kind of life will he have? He'll probably be wheelchair-bound for the rest of his life. He'll never be the man he used to be. I just think that instead of putting him through that torture, we should let him leave peacefully if he wants to."

"Are you suggesting we shouldn't have consented to the operation?"

"Honestly?"

"Yes," Cameron nodded.

"I think we are only subjecting your father to a life of misery and degradation of his manhood. Is that fair? Is it fair to do that to any man?"

"I understand what you're saying, but, I'm not ready to lose him yet," Cameron said.

"Well, neither am I, but we don't have a right to hold on to him for selfish reasons," Rebecca commented.

"You're right," Cameron sighed.

"No matter what happens, it'll always be you and me. We just have to be here for each other regardless of how things turn out for Evan," Rebecca said, hugging him.

They sat there quietly in the waiting room for a few minutes more when Caitlyn returned. Cameron was deep in thought when there was an announcement that visiting time was about to start. Cameron, his mom and Caitlyn went to his father's room to visit. While they were there, Dr. Kirklin came in to talk to them along with the orthopedic surgeon who would be once again operating on Evan.

"Cameron, Rebecca, you know Dr. Grayson," Dr. Kirklin said.

"Yes, how are you, Doctor?" Cameron said, shaking his hand.

"I'm fine. As you know, I'll have to go back in to correct some of the damage caused by your father's collapse.

That, of course, will not be done today. We've scheduled it for early next week. Dr. Farrington is already in surgery operating on another patient and will not be available to talk with you until after he's finished operating on Evan, but we'll keep you posted," Dr. Grayson said.

"Thank you, Doctor," Cameron said.

The three of them visited with Evan a little longer, and Rebecca signed all of his surgical consent forms, seemingly not totally comfortable with doing so. They waited in the waiting room for what felt like an eternity while his father was in surgery. Cameron decided to call Phil while they waited, so he and Caitlyn went back to his suite to call and check in. Cameron tried Phil on his direct line.

"Hello?" Phil answered.

"Phil, hi. This is Cameron."

"Cameron. Caitlyn told me that things were going well. When will the two of you be back?"

"Well, we've run into a problem, or at least I have anyway."

"What's wrong? Have you run into a dead end on the case?"

"No, not really. In fact, we've had some wonderful leads. But my father has taken ill again."

"What happened?"

"He's suffered a massive stroke last night. He's in surgery now as we speak."

"Cameron, I'm really sorry to hear that. How are you handling things?"

"About as well as can be expected. I'm really worried about my mother. She's not dealing too well with my father being so sick. Obviously, I'll need to be here for the next few days."

"Of course, I understand. Caitlyn's been head counsel on the case for a little while, so she should be able to handle it on her own from here. When do you think you'll be able to get back here?"

"From the looks of things, I'm not sure if I'll be able to get back in time for the hearing next week. Phil, I'm sorry to

~ 212 ~

have to say this, but after I finish with the Marlow case, I may have to resign from the firm. Right now, my mother needs me desperately, because I'm all she has. My father's barely hanging on, and I just can't desert her," Cameron stated.

"Cameron, I'd hate to lose you so soon, but I know that these things do come up. Why don't you just take a family medical leave of absence?" Phil suggested. "That way, your job will still be here, and you can still take care of your family. Do you think that would work better for you?"

"Maybe. I'll let you know. While I have you on the phone, Caitlyn wants to talk with you."

"Okay, put her on. And Cameron, don't worry about anything. I'll keep you and your family in my prayers," Phil said.

"Thanks, Phil," Cameron said. Then he handed the phone to Caitlyn.

"Hi, Phil," Caitlyn said. "Everything's just fine. I was able to get a commercial flight, so I'll be home Monday afternoon. With everything we've gathered so far, I think we have a really good chance of getting a full pardon, at the very least a reprieve."

Caitlyn continued to brief Phil on the investigation and what the defense would argue to clear Garret. Shortly afterwards, Caitlyn hung up with Phil. Cameron looked at her intently. Caitlyn reached over and held his hand, smiling at him.

"You've been like a lifesaver for me, Caitlyn," Cameron smiled.

"I wouldn't have it any other way. I wish I could do more for you."

"You are, just by being here," Cameron smiled. He slowly leaned in to kiss her gently on the lips. As they sat there, their kiss became more passionate, as Cameron leaned Caitlyn back on the bed.

"Cameron, we have to stop this," Caitlyn said, pulling away from him.

Cameron sighed as he sat up. "What's wrong with me? I mean, we made the decision not to give in to our feelings

~ 213 ~

right now. After all that's happened, I can't believe how distracted I am by you." Cameron tried unsuccessfully to wipe the tired lines from underneath his eyes.

"Right now, you have a lot of emotions to deal with. You're confused, hurt, tired. Everything's taking a toll on you. Stop beating yourself up," Caitlyn soothed.

"You're the only calm in my storm right now, Caitlyn," Cameron whispered.

Caitlyn leaned gently on Cameron's shoulder, as he placed his arm around her. He wanted terribly to tell her how much she truly meant to him, but now wasn't the time. After a few more quiet moments together, they decided to go back to the main hospital to see if there was any word on his father. When they got back, Rebecca was reading a magazine.

"Has there been any word on Dad yet?" Cameron asked.

"No, not yet, Dear. What happened to the two of you?" Rebecca asked, looking from Cameron to Caitlyn.

"We called Phil to let him know what was going on," Cameron said.

"And it took both of you to do that?" Rebecca asked.

"We both needed to talk to him," Cameron stated. "What difference does it make?"

"I just wanted you here in case the doctor came back," Rebecca said.

"But, the doctor hasn't been back," Cameron snapped.

"Cameron," Caitlyn said calmly.

"Sweetheart, I didn't mean to upset you. I just wondered what happened to you, that's all," Rebecca reasoned.

"I'm sorry, Mom," Cameron sighed. "I'm just tired. I shouldn't take my frustrations out on you."

"That's okay, Dear. We're all tired after last night," Rebecca said, placing her hand on Cameron's.

As they sat there, Dr. Farrington came in to talk to them. He looked tired, as he had an unreadable expression. Cameron didn't know what to think. Was it good, was it bad?

"Rebecca, Cameron," Dr. Farrington said. "This is my

nurse practitioner, Charlotte Mims."

"Ms. Mims," Cameron said, shaking her hand.

"How is he, Dr. Farrington?" Rebecca asked, holding her breath.

"He came through surgery extremely well which was quite surprising. Your husband is a strong man. He still has a very long and hard fight ahead of him, but I feel confident that he will make a full recovery. Now, he's going to have to have many months of therapy if there's ever a possibility of becoming himself again," Dr. Farrington said.

"When can we see him?" Rebecca asked.

"Well, he'll be in recovery for a couple of hours, so you probably won't be able to see him until later tonight."

"How long will he have to be in intensive care?" Cameron asked.

"Oh, I'd say three or four days, maybe more. It's strictly up to how well he progresses," Dr. Farrington said.

"What's next?" Rebecca asked.

"Now, we wait to see how things go. He'll be monitored very closely. Dr. Grayson is planning to go back in to repair his hip injury on Monday."

"Will that cause problems, considering everything he's gone through?" Cameron asked.

"He'll be fine. We need to do it now, because once he's awake, he'll have to start physical therapy. The sooner we go back in and repair what's wrong, the sooner he can be on the road to a full recovery," Dr. Farrington reasoned.

"Dr. Farrington, thank you for everything you've done for my father. We've been so worried about him," Cameron said, shaking his hand.

"It's all a part of the job," Dr. Farrington smiled. "Initially, I was worried he wouldn't make it, but now, I'm confident that he will be just fine."

After Dr. Farrington left, the three of them decided to go out to a restaurant to eat. His mother loved seafood, so that's where they went. As they sat there, Cameron looked at the two most important women in his life and had the overwhelming feeling that the time would come when he'd have to choose between them. Why couldn't he have the best of both worlds? He thought a lot about his father and the progress he would have to make over the next few months, and knew that his mother couldn't do it all alone. Things were challenging enough when his father fell a few weeks before, but now to compile a stroke on top of that was probably the worst thing that could happen. His parents weren't getting any younger, and now was the time for him to repay them for all they'd done for him all of his life. They stayed at the restaurant for almost two hours, and then made the trip back to the hospital to visit with Evan. When they got there, Dr. Farrington was examining him.

"Well, I see you all made it back," Dr. Farrington smiled.

"We just went out for dinner. How's he doing?" Cameron asked.

"He's still unconscious, but that's to be expected. As long as we can keep him with as little stress as possible, he should pull through okay. He's got a long fight ahead of him, but he should be able to make a full recovery," Dr. Farrington said.

"Thank you, Dr. Farrington," Rebecca said. "How long can we visit?"

"We have to limit the time you're with him to only 20 minutes. That's just while he's up here. Once he's strong enough to be moved to a regular room, you can stay with him as long as you like," Dr. Farrington said.

"Thank you, doctor," Cameron said.

Shortly afterwards, Dr. Farrington left. The blinds were drawn to Evan's room, but there was not a nurse with him at the time. Evan was still connected to several monitors and tubes. Rebecca looked at her husband.

"He looks so fragile lying there. Are they sure he's going to be okay?" Rebecca asked.

"Mom, don't worry. Dad's very strong. He'll be just fine. Maybe when he gets out, the two of you can go on a little vacation somewhere. The sunshine will do him a lot of good."

"Cameron, Caitlyn, would you two mind terribly if I

had a few minutes alone with Evan?" Rebecca asked.

"No, of course not. We'll be right outside. Plus, I need to call David to let him know that Dad's okay. I'd called him earlier to tell him about what happened."

"Okay, Dear. I'll be right here when you're done."

Cameron kissed his mother on the cheek and the two of them left the room. As they were walking out, the nurse was about to go in.

"Um, my mother wanted a few minutes alone with my dad if that's possible," Cameron said, stopping her.

"I won't be in the way. I just have to change his IV bag and administer some medication to him. She won't even know I'm there," the nurse smiled.

"Thank you," Cameron smiled back.

Maybe that would be better. Just in case his mother had any questions, the nurse would be there. Cameron and Caitlyn went to the waiting area after he called David to let him know about Evan. They sat there discussing their plans for the next few days.

"I'll head back Monday afternoon, and I'll be at the hearing to present our new evidence. You take your time here, and I'll see you when you can get home," Caitlyn said.

"Caitlyn, I may have to leave the firm," Cameron said solemnly.

"I heard you telling Phil that, but I won't accept that. You're a good attorney, Cameron. Don't do this to yourself," Caitlyn pleaded.

"You don't understand, Caitlyn. I'm all they have. I can't desert them," Cameron argued.

"And no one's asking you to. You have a life to lead. You can be here for your parents and still live your life. It's only fair. They didn't raise you so that you could put your life on hold the moment a crisis arose," Caitlyn stated.

"I think this is a little more than a 'crisis,' Caitlyn. We're talking about my father's health, and let's face it, things don't look too good," Cameron said.

"But, the doctors seem optimistic."

"Yeah, for now. Look, no one wants for my father to

~ 217 ~

get better more than I do, except maybe my mother. But, what if I'm not here and something happens? I'd never forgive myself. Dad's going to have to go through months of rehabilitation before he's back to himself. And even with that, he may never be fully functional again."

"I've never heard you speak so pessimistically before," Caitlyn observed.

"I don't know that I've ever been this pessimistic in the past. I don't know, maybe it's the case compiled on top of everything else," Cameron sighed.

"Don't worry about Mr. Marlow. I'll do everything I have to in order to clear him," Caitlyn reassured.

"I know you will," Cameron smiled, touching Caitlyn's hand. "There's just something about this case."

"What do you mean?"

"I don't know. I can't quite put my finger on it, but I just feel so drawn to it. I know it doesn't make sense. I'm a lawyer, for God's sake. Cases like this come along everyday," Cameron sighed.

"Maybe this is different because it's down to the wire. Mr. Garret has served 27 years for a crime he didn't commit. That would touch anyone with a conscience."

"Yeah, anyone except Rachel Marlow," Cameron commented.

"I don't think that woman even has a conscience," Caitlyn sighed.

Shortly afterwards, there was an announcement that the visits would be over in another five minutes. Cameron and Caitlyn decided to check on Rebecca. The nurse was still in the room. Rebecca looked frustrated, as she told Cameron she'd be outside in the waiting area. Cameron sat there with his father for a couple of minutes talking with him, as Caitlyn stood vigil beside him. The nurse came over to the bedside.

"Mr. Spencer, is your mother okay?" the nurse asked.

"She's just under a lot of stress. Why do you ask?" Cameron asked.

"Because she literally bit my head off for coming in here. I explained to her that I'm just doing my job, and it's very important that I take care of her husband's needs. She kept insisting that she be left alone to visit with him. Sir, I'm not trying to be indifferent, but your father just came out of surgery, so he has a lot of needs right now. I have to be with him practically the whole time."

"I understand. My mother's been dealing with a lot over the past 24 hours. I'll talk to her and see if she's okay," Cameron stated. "My father's well-being is the most important thing right now, so don't worry about my mother."

"I'm sorry she was so upset. Please apologize to her. Just let her know that I have to take care of him so that she will have all the time in the world to spend with him. It's for his own good."

"It's okay. Thanks for letting me know what's going on. We probably won't be here for the last visit, because I have some business to take care of. My mother hasn't been feeling well, so she probably will want to go home."

"Yes Sir. Once again, please apologize to your mother for me."

"Do you want for me to check on Rebecca?" Caitlyn offered.

"No, we can do it together," Cameron said, standing from his seat. The two of them returned to the waiting room, and noticed his mother had so much bitterness in her expression.

"Mom, what's wrong?" Cameron asked.

"That stupid nurse wouldn't leave me alone with my husband! My own husband! I don't need a baby sitter! Did you send her back in there to be with me?!" Rebecca was extremely upset.

"No!" Cameron yelled. "Mom, what is going on with you? The nurse was simply doing her job. Dad has to be her first priority, not whether you have 'alone time' with him. I'm liking less and less of what I've been seeing of you lately. It's almost as if you don't want for Dad to get better. Like you want for him to die. Is that it? Do you not care about what's important for Dad's recovery? If that's the case, then you are not the woman I thought you were! You've become so callous

~ 219 ~

about things, almost disappointed that he made it through surgery alive."

"It's not that, Cameron. It's just that I really need to reconnect with your father, and I may never have a chance again. Life is so short as we can see, and I wanted to be alone with him, to hold his hand and comfort him."

"And you can still do those things," Cameron reassured. "But while he's in intensive care, the nurses are there around the clock. They understand that you love your husband. Don't judge them too harshly. The nurse wanted for me to apologize to you about the fact that you were not able to be alone with him. But, like she said, she has to take care of him now so that you can be alone with him later."

"You're right, Dear. I don't know what's wrong with me. Are you ready to head home?"

"Yes, I am. Caitlyn and I have some things we need to go over before she leaves Monday concerning this case we're working on," Cameron commented. "Caitlyn, are you ready?"

"Sure," Caitlyn smiled.

Since Caitlyn and Rebecca came together, Caitlyn volunteered to drive Rebecca's car back for her, and Rebecca rode with Cameron.

"When are you going back to Indiana, Cameron?" Rebecca asked as they drove along.

"I'll be here at least another few days. At least until Dad comes out of the second surgery and we know he's going to be okay," Cameron stated.

"Son, why don't you go on back to Indiana with Caitlyn for a few days and turn your notice in? Your father will be fine."

"Mom, don't try to be strong for me, I'm here for you. I've already talked with Phillip and he's in agreement with my being here," Cameron said. "Not to mention, the reason we came here was to find someone who may be vital to our case."

"And who would that be?" Rebecca asked.

"Rosemary Faulkner. Have you ever heard of her?"

"No, I haven't. Who is she supposed to be?"

"She's the cousin of our client Garret's ex-wife. She

could be the missing link," Cameron said. "I asked George about her, and he said that she's been missing for over 20 years, shortly after her parents' fatal car accident. So, it looks as if we're at a dead end."

"Well, Son, I know just about everyone in this town, and I've never heard of a Rosemary Faulkner," Rebecca said. "But, if George says she's been missing for over 20 years, then that's probably the reason."

"You're right. I figured if anyone could help, it would be you or Dad. Why does everything have to happen at once? Dad gets sick, and we're trying to race against time to save a man's life."

"I just think you should go back and wrap things up in person," Rebecca said. "I need you too much! If your father doesn't make it, who will be there for me?" Rebecca started to cry. "Is this case more important to you than me?!" Rebecca was almost hysterical.

"No, Mom, of course not. Our client's final hearing is coming up next week. After that, it'll pretty much be over, unless we're lucky enough to get a reprieve, which would give us a little more time. At this point, I'll be happy with that," Cameron said as he pulled into the driveway.

Caitlyn was immediately behind them, as she pulled the car into the garage after using the remote to let it up. Caitlyn then got out of the car and walked out the side door to Cameron's car in the driveway after letting the garage down.

"I just don't like it! I don't like it at all!" Rebecca cried, as she was getting out of the car.

"I had no idea you were this worried about me," Cameron commented.

"I'm always worried about you. You're my only son, and I don't know what I'd do if I ever lost you. Promise me, that you'll always be here, no matter what happens," Rebecca said, as Caitlyn gave the keys to her. "Thank you dear."

"You're welcome," Caitlyn smiled.

"Mom, I'll always be here for you. I'm not going anywhere," Cameron insisted as they walked into the house.

"You say that, but can you absolutely promise me that

~ 221 ~

you'll always be here?"

"I promise, I'll be here. Where is all of this coming from? Why do you feel like I'll leave you? Do you think something is going to happen to me? Is that it?" Cameron asked.

"Yes, or maybe you will just stop loving me one day," Rebecca said oddly.

"I'd never stop loving you. Why would you even say something like that?"

"I don't know. Some children leave the nest and never think twice about their parents. What if you marry and have a family of your own and forget about me?"

Cameron looked at Caitlyn when Rebecca made that statement. Caitlyn looked surprised that Rebecca would say such a thing.

"Rebecca, Cameron will never stop loving you," Caitlyn reassured.

"You don't know that," Rebecca said. "What if he got angry with me about something and never spoke to me again? Then I died from a broken heart?"

"There's nothing in this world that could ever make me stop loving you. Nothing will come between us. I'm your son, your flesh and blood. You've raised me, taken care of me. I'll always be here for you," Cameron reassured. "Believe me, you'll never die from a broken heart, at least not from me. I'll never break your heart."

"You're the only one who could. No one else really matters," Rebecca stated.

"What about Dad? Doesn't he matter?"

"Of course he does. But, right now, we don't know your father's fate. I just need to know that I'll always have you. So, will you please go back to Indiana to quit your job, pack up your things, and come back so that we can be a family again?" Rebecca asked.

"You really want for me to give up my job?" Cameron asked.

"I think it would be for the best. You're a bright attorney. Madison and Madison would love to have you back.

They didn't want for you to leave, remember? Or you could open your own firm," Rebecca suggested.

"Let's talk about this tomorrow, when you've gotten a good night's rest," Cameron said. He could tell that Caitlyn felt that Rebecca was manipulating him by the frustrating look she had on her face.

"No, I'm going to do the laundry," Rebecca stated.

While she was busy doing the laundry, Cameron and Caitlyn went into the den to go over what they were going to argue at the hearing, and which witnesses would be able to be there. After going over everything for a few hours, Rebecca informed them that she was going to turn in for the night. When Rebecca had gone to bed, Caitlyn and Cameron went to sit on the front porch.

"Gosh, it's so quiet here," Caitlyn smiled. She leaned on Cameron as he put his arm around her.

"I know. I wouldn't have it any other way," Cameron smiled.

"Cameron, I've been thinking," Caitlyn said.

"About what?"

"About what you said earlier, and how much your mother really depends on you," Caitlyn said.

"What do you mean?"

"I wonder about your closeness with her," Caitlyn started.

"'Wonder'? There's nothing to wonder about. I love her, but she's my mother and you're my–"

"Your what?"

"Never mind," Cameron blushed.

"I think I know what you were going to say," Caitlyn said.

"Is it wrong for me to want to be here for her?" Cameron asked. "I owe my parents my life."

"I know you think you do. But, not in that way. I mean, I love my mother, but that dedication you have to yours, that connection the two of you have, it's almost surreal in many ways."

"You think it's too good to be true?" Cameron

~ 223 ~

challenged.

"In a way. We all want that kind of connection to our parents to a certain extent, but Cameron, you are this woman's life." Caitlyn sat up straighter.

"You say that like it's a bad thing." Cameron took his arm from around her.

"Maybe it is. Think about it, Cameron. She wants for you to quit your job, to come and take care of her. Is that fair to you?"

"Caitlyn, my parents have given me everything I needed and pretty close to everything I've wanted. They taught me to be responsible. Part of that responsibility is to be there for them in their time of need."

"Did they say that to you? Does your father feel the same way?"

"No, they've never told me to do such a thing. But, my mom's afraid now. She's going through something that I'm sure she never thought she'd endure. We can't predict these things. I have to be here for her, no matter what. If you can't understand that, then maybe you're not the person I thought you were," Cameron snapped.

"Cameron, I don't mean to anger you, but you've got to be realistic," Caitlyn reasoned.

"The reality is, my father's sick, my mother needs me, end of story," Cameron said.

"So, that's it? You just throw in the towel to your own life, after all your hard work to become a successful attorney?"

"I can open my own practice, I can go back to my old firm. My life doesn't have to end because I came home. It'll just take on a different direction."

"'Different direction'? It's a little more than that, Cameron. You left that firm for a reason. You left Lariette Springs for a reason," Caitlyn argued. "Are you sure you're ready to be reminded of those things that pushed you away from here in the first place?"

"Are you referring to Grace?"

"No, not necessarily," Caitlyn shrugged.

"Well, good. Because she's my past."

"And what about me, Cameron? What am I?"

"Caitlyn, I can't even think about that with all that's going on," Cameron sighed. "This isn't about us or you. It's about my family. They have to come first. I care about you, but, honestly, I can't put my feelings for you ahead of my family. I just won't do it. Either you accept that, or you don't."

"So whatever could have been between us, you're just shrugging it off?" Caitlyn spit out.

"Are you willing to move to Lariette Springs?! Are you willing to give up your life in Kerrigan in order to be with me?"

"Dammit, Cameron, stop making this all about you and your wants and needs! I'm trying really hard to understand, but you expect for me to just give up everything for something that may not even work out!"

"Well, I guess I know where things stand between us, and maybe it's a good thing we didn't go any further than we have," Cameron said.

"What are you saying?"

"I'm saying that I'm coming back home. Maybe you are the person I thought you were when we first met! Good luck to you and your life, Caitlyn, because I won't be a part of it!" Cameron said. Getting up from his seat, he stormed into the house.

Caitlyn followed him inside. "Don't you walk away from me! We're not finished talking about this!"

"Oh, yes, we are! I'm finished with it. You go back to Indiana, get the hearing done, and I'll come back by the end of the week to wrap things up. I'm going to bed!" Cameron then stormed up the stairs.

Caitlyn stood there, morosely thinking about the fact that she was about to lose the man with whom she'd fallen in love. Her pride wouldn't let her go after him, so she went back into the den and packed up all of the files for the case. She looked on the table and saw the keys to the rental car and decided upon impulse to go for a drive.

Chapter
11

Cameron's mother didn't wake him, so he slept until 10:30 that morning. When Cameron woke up, he took his shower and dressed. When he got downstairs, his mother had breakfast ready for him. She seemed so happy and content as she sat at the kitchen table. Cameron had not seen her this calm and relaxed in a while. It was nice seeing her more like herself again.

"Why didn't you wake me?" Cameron asked.

"Because you needed your sleep," Rebecca smiled.

"Where's Caitlyn?" Cameron asked as he fixed his breakfast.

"She had to run an errand. She'll be back soon," Rebecca said, standing to get the juice out of the refrigerator.

"I really need to apologize to her."

"Why?" Rebecca poured him a glass of juice.

"We had a terrible argument last night, and I said some things that I didn't mean."

"Do you want to talk about it?" she asked, passing him the glass.

"Thanks. I'd rather not, Mom," Cameron stated.

"I understand, Dear," she smiled, sitting back down.

"I don't want for you to think I'm shutting you out, it's just something that I need to talk over with her first."

"Cameron, there's no need to explain. You've fallen in love with her, haven't you?"

"I think so," Cameron smiled. "I feel like I'm being pulled in two different directions," he said as he sat down.

"What do you mean?"

"I mean, I need to be here for you, but at the same time, I want to be with her, have a life with her," Cameron said.

"Cameron, I would never be one to tell you how to live your life, but, if this girl is too selfish to understand about your wanting to be here for your family, then maybe you should re-think your relationship with her. Your father and I really need you now. It won't be forever," Rebecca reasoned.

"I know that, but Caitlyn doesn't see it that way. Maybe I'm expecting too much from her. I mean, she and I have only known each other for a few weeks. Does it really happen this fast?" Cameron sighed.

"Do you really want my opinion?"

"You know I value your opinion," Cameron smiled.

"Don't rush things," Rebecca said, reaching out to touch her son's hand. "You've got your whole life ahead of you. Caitlyn's just one girl. She seems nice enough, but what do you really know about her? Don't limit yourself to revolving your life around her. We don't want another Grace on our hands," Rebecca said, shaking her head.

"But, she's nothing like Grace."

"Of course, she isn't, Dear. But, she may have some hidden agendas that you may not be aware of. How does she get along with the other attorneys in your office? She strikes me as a little standoffish if you ask me. You need someone who's warm and caring."

"Well, honestly, when we first met, she was a real viper. I thought she was the worst person to ever walk the earth," Cameron commented.

~ 227 ~

"Maybe that first impression is the one that you should stick with," Rebecca suggested.

"No, she's really not that bad," Cameron disagreed.

"Well, if she's not that bad, she has to put your needs first," Rebecca said.

"But isn't that a little selfish? We have to be able to compromise," Cameron reasoned.

"Of course, you do. But, a woman should follow her husband to the ends of the earth if necessary. Is she willing to relocate here for you and the sake of your family? I think not," Rebecca laughed slightly.

"We're not living in the Stone Ages. Is it right of me to ask her to give up her career? I always vowed never to do that."

"But, you're not. You're simply asking her to compromise," Rebecca reasoned. "The two of you can practice law right here in Lariette Springs. We could build you a house on the land. But, if you want my opinion, I don't think you should apologize to her. She's not worth it, Son. If you apologize now, you'll live your life trying to always yield to everything she wants. Your father and I aren't getting any younger, and we really need you now. But, I don't want to stand in the way of your happiness. If Caitlyn's worth leaving us, then I think you should do it."

"Don't you think you're overdoing it a bit?"

"Oh, Cameron. I just want you to see all sides of this. No woman should make a man turn his back on his family. Am I overdoing it by saying your father's deathly ill, or that I'm not getting any younger? What have I stated besides the facts?" Rebecca argued.

Cameron smiled. "You almost sound like an attorney."

"My Lord, is that good or bad?" Rebecca laughed.

"It's good. You put up a good argument, and you're right."

As they sat there talking, Caitlyn came back. The two of them looked in her direction as she came in the door.

"I'll leave the two of you alone," Rebecca smiled, as she stood to leave the room.

~ 228 ~

"You don't have to leave," Caitlyn said.

"No, I think it's best. Cameron, I'll be upstairs if you need me." Rebecca then left the room.

"So, what kind of errand did you have to run?"

"I just wanted to get a head-start on a few things for the hearing, that's all."

"Oh." There was a stifled silence between them as Cameron stood from his chair. "So, are you hungry?"

"No, I ate already. Your mom is an early riser. She already had breakfast ready when I got up."

"She's used to doing that," Cameron smiled. Then, his smile faded as he stared at her.

"I'm sorry," they both said in unison.

Caitlyn smiled slightly. "You first."

"Caitlyn, I was a complete jerk for what I said last night. I had no right to talk to you that way. I just wish you could understand," Cameron said.

"I do understand, Cameron. I understand that you have to be here for your mother and father. I'm just not ready for that. I care a lot about you, but I can't leave my life in Kerrigan."

"I have to respect that, don't I?" Cameron asked.

"I'd like for you to."

"Enough said. So, what do we do now?"

"We admit it's over before it ever gets started," Caitlyn smiled gently.

"Just like that?"

"What other choice do we have? You have to be here for your family, and I have to go back to my life in Kerrigan. Damn shame. You're a hell of a good kisser," Caitlyn smiled, shaking her head.

"Is that all you'll miss about me?" Cameron smiled.

"No, that's not all. I'll miss the friendship we've developed over the past few days. I know we got off to a bad start, and I really regret that we didn't get to know each other better from the beginning. I'll miss the thought of what could have been. Boy, I was really a bitch to you," Caitlyn smiled slightly.

"No, you challenged me. It was intriguing. I've never had a problem having a woman in my life, but you, you were different," Cameron said. "It was almost like wanting something I couldn't have. But, it goes further than that."

"How much further?"

"Let me put it like this. When you're ready to settle down to a quiet life, let me know," Cameron stated.

"Only to find out you've married and had a couple of kids? I don't think I can put myself through that," Caitlyn smiled.

"So, this is it?"

"Yeah," Caitlyn nodded slowly. "I'll fly home Monday to get everything ready for the hearing. I hope I see you when you come back."

"I don't know if that's such a good idea. I might not want to leave," Cameron smiled.

"Maybe that's the point," Caitlyn smiled. "Cameron, I really do understand, okay?"

"I know. You just don't want that kind of life for yourself," Cameron shrugged.

"Can I at least get a hug?" Caitlyn asked.

"Anytime," Cameron smiled, pulling her into a deep embrace.

He held on to this woman for dear life and didn't want to let go of her. This would be one of the hardest things he'd have to do, but he didn't have a choice. He turned to smell her hair as he caressed her back, pulling her closer. He knew if he didn't let her go now that he never would. Reluctantly, Cameron pulled away from the woman he'd grown to care about. He desperately needed to change the subject.

"I want to go and visit my father. Would you care to join me?"

"Of course," Caitlyn smiled. "Is your mom going?"

"I don't know. I'll check," Cameron stated.

He backed away from her, still holding her hand. He caressed it, eventually letting go. His heart sank as he walked away. He felt as if he was walking away from his lifeline. At that very moment as he let go of her hand and looked into her eyes, he realized without a doubt that he'd fallen in love with her. It hurt everything within him to give up on the two of them so easily. He just didn't see what choice he had considering his obligation to his family. Cameron went upstairs to his mother's room, and knocked before entering.

"Mom?"

"Yes, Cameron?" Rebecca answered. She was lying on her bed.

"We were about to go to the hospital. Do you want to come along?"

"No, Sweetheart. I'm really tired, so I think I'll sit this one out. If I feel up to it, I'll go up there later this evening."

"Okay. Get some rest, and I'll see you when we get back," Cameron said.

"Give your father my love," Rebecca stated.

"I will."

Shortly thereafter, Cameron and Caitlyn headed for the hospital. They rode along in complete silence, both seemingly a million miles away. Cameron wondered was he about to make the biggest mistake of his life. When they got to the hospital and he saw his father again, he realized he was doing the right thing. He kept reassuring himself that he has to make this sacrifice for his parents, because he knew his parents would do it for him. His mother had no idea that Evan's health would fail him the way it has.

After leaving the hospital, Cameron and Caitlyn went back to his parents' home to continue preparing for Garret's hearing. Jackson was helpful with getting things done in Indiana. After several diligent hours of work, Cameron's cell phone rang.

"Hello?" he answered.

"Is this Cameron Spencer?" the woman asked.

"Yes, it is. Who is this?" Cameron asked.

"Don't worry about that. I have vital information that you need," the caller stated.

Cameron suddenly recognized the voice. "Serena? Is this Serena?" Caitlyn looked surprisingly in Cameron's direction.

"Yes, it is."

"What do you want? How did you get this number?"

"Remember? You gave me your card when we had dinner."

"Haven't you caused enough trouble?"

"Cameron, what does she want?" Caitlyn asked.

"I don't know. That's what I'm trying to find out," Cameron stated.

"Cameron, I have vital information that could clear your client," Serena said.

"Why should I believe you after what you did?" Cameron asked.

"I'm sorry about Illinois," Serena said.

"I suppose it would be asking too much to expect you to return my files," Cameron stated sarcastically.

"I'll do better than that. I'll provide you with the piece of evidence that can totally exonerate your client," Serena said.

"And I'm supposed to trust evidence provided by you? You've lost complete grip of all of your senses if you think I'll trust anything you have to say!" Cameron yelled.

"I'm being completely honest with you. Look, I could've kept my mouth shut, but I'm trying to do the right thing."

"A little late for that, don't you think?" Cameron said.

"No, I don't think so," Serena disagreed.

"What's this supposed new evidence?" Cameron asked.

Caitlyn looked strangely at Cameron, wondering what Serena could be saying to intrigue him so. After all, this was the woman who drugged him and stole important information pertaining to their case.

"I know for a fact that your client didn't kill his wife," Serena said.

"How?" Cameron asked.

"I want to meet with you," Serena said.

"No, not until you tell me what proof you have," Cameron stated.

"Not over the phone," Serena said.

"Where are you?" Cameron asked.

"I'm in Indiana. Your office told me you were still out of town. I won't trust this information with anyone else," Serena stated.

"I won't be back until next week," Cameron told her.

"I have to meet with you," Serena insisted. "Isn't your hearing next week?"

"Yes it is. My colleague, Caitlyn Frazier will be there on Monday."

"What about you?" Serena asked.

"Serena," Cameron sighed. "I'm tired of this. What's this all about?"

"It's about Lawrence Varden and his part in Victoria's murder," Serena acknowledged.

"What? How do you know Lawrence Varden?" Cameron asked.

"He's my father," Serena said.

"He's your what?" Cameron asked, astonished.

Caitlyn looked at Cameron. "What did she say?" Caitlyn asked.

Cameron held his hand up slightly, shushing Caitlyn.

"He's my father," Serena repeated. "I have his journal, and in it, he'd written some astounding things years ago."

"Why should I believe you?" Cameron asked.

"I-I have to go. I'll contact you again," Serena said, in a rushed tone.

"Serena, wait." Cameron tried to stop her from hanging up, but he was too late. Cameron looked at his phone and went back through the ID showing the last call's phone number.

"What did she say?" Caitlyn repeated, waiting anxiously on Cameron's response.

"She said she's Dr. Varden, Sr.'s daughter and she has a journal of his that can vindicate Garret."

"You're kidding?"

"No. That's what she said," Cameron shrugged. "I'm going to call the number back," Cameron said, using his cell phone. From the area code, he knew she was really in Indiana like she said. Cameron waited and waited, as the phone

~ 233 ~

continuously rang. He hung up, realizing it was probably a payphone or something untraceable. "No answer."

"You don't believe her, do you?" Caitlyn asked.

"I don't know. This woman has lied before."

"Exactly. I say we don't put too much merit into what she says," Caitlyn said.

"What if she's telling the truth?"

"What if she's not?"

"Don't we owe it to Garret to find out?" Cameron argued.

"We also owe it to him not to go off on wild goose chases a few days before his hearing," Caitlyn reasoned.

"I know you're right, but I get the feeling she was telling me the truth," Cameron said.

"So, how do we find out?" Caitlyn asked.

"We call Dr. Varden, Jr." Cameron found Dr. Varden's card and dialed his number.

"What are you going to say?" Caitlyn asked.

"I'll ask him about his sister," Cameron said, as Dr. Varden's phone rang.

"Hello?" Dr. Varden answered.

"Dr. Varden? This is Cameron Spencer."

"Yes, Mr. Spencer," Dr. Varden responded. "What can I do for you?"

"Didn't you tell us you have a younger sister?"

"Yes, I do. Why are you asking about Serena? She was only eight when Regina was around. She couldn't help you."

"You don't think she knows anything about Regina?"

"No, I don't. Leave Serena out of this. She can't help you," Dr. Varden insisted.

"Okay, Dr. Varden. I won't try and question her," Cameron said.

"Thank you. I hope you find Regina and bring her to justice for whatever it is you think she did, but please leave us out of it from this point on," Dr. Varden said.

"I understand your reluctance to get involved," Cameron stated. "You have a good night, Dr. Varden."

Cameron then hung up the phone.

"Well?" Caitlyn asked, waiting.

"He does have a sister named Serena," Cameron sighed.

"But, do you think *this* woman is really his sister?" Caitlyn asked.

"It could explain her involvement and interest. We know the woman's too young to be the killer, but she obviously has a vested interest in what we're doing," Cameron reasoned. "I think it might help to meet with her."

"I don't know if I agree with you, Cameron. Right now, we have more important things to do," Caitlyn said.

"You're right. But, if Serena calls back, I'm going to arrange to meet with her."

"Suit yourself," Caitlyn said, in a frustrated tone.

Cameron looked at Caitlyn. He saw a hint of what she was when they first met. Maybe she hadn't really changed after all. He shook his head and laughed slightly.

"Caitlyn, you don't have to control everything, you know," Cameron said.

"I resent that!"

"You shouldn't. The moment something doesn't go your way, you act like a spoiled child who's had her favorite toy taken away."

"You know what, Cameron, your arrogance is unbelievable!" Caitlyn yelled.

"No, you're unbelievable! You're nothing but a lonely, jealous woman who can't let herself get too close to other people," Cameron commented.

"How dare you? I hate I confided in you about anything!"

"Dammit, Caitlyn! Admit it! You don't trust this woman because I had dinner with her! If it were anyone else, you'd be the first one to want to see what she has to say!"

"Of all the arrogance!! Is that what you think?!"

"Yes, it is!"

"Do you remember the woman drugging you? Stealing our files?! Any of this ring a bell?!"

"Oh, please! You would have been against her if she'd never done any of those things!"

"And you can forgive her like that?!"

"I'm trying to clear our client! If she has information, I damned well want to hear it!"

"I can't believe you!" Caitlyn yelled. Then, she threw up her hands. "You know what? You do what ever you want! I'm going to bed!"

"Goodnight!!" Cameron yelled.

Cameron was livid. How could she be so closed-minded? Caitlyn was jealous and didn't want anyone in Cameron's life that she considered a threat, despite the fact that she'd made it quite clear that she wasn't willing to give up her life in Kerrigan for a life with him in Lariette Springs. Was he being overbearing expecting her to give in to his wishes? Did that make him any better? Cameron was tired of thinking about it. He went upstairs to shower and go to bed.

******

The sun was shining brightly causing Cameron to wake with a start. He looked at the clock and noticed it was 8:35 a.m. The visit would be starting in 55 minutes. He immediately got up to get ready to go to the hospital. He knocked at his mom's door, and peeked in when she didn't answer. Her bed was already made up. He went down the hall and knocked on Caitlyn's door.

"Come in," Caitlyn murmured. She was packing her things.

"What are you doing?" Cameron asked, entering her room.

"I'm packing. I'm leaving today," Caitlyn said, continuing to pack.

"I thought you couldn't get a flight until Monday?" Cameron asked.

"I can't. I'll take the rental car. I need to get away from here," Caitlyn commented.

"Caitlyn, please listen to me," Cameron said, going

~ 236 ~

further into the room.

"No, Cameron," Caitlyn sighed. "There's nothing else left to say. You're going to handle this case the way you want, and despite the fact that I'm head counsel, I don't have a say in the matter."

"That's not true, Caitlyn. I just think we should be open to what Serena has to say."

Caitlyn stopped packing. "Even at the risk of her possibly setting you up?"

"We won't go blindly into anything," Cameron reassured. "We just need to see what she's talking about."

"I don't trust her," Caitlyn whispered.

Cameron was standing close to Caitlyn. He brushed his finger lightly against her cheek. How could he love someone so much who drove him so crazy? He smiled slightly, thinking about the fact that no matter how crazy she made him, he didn't want to live without her. She closed her eyes, as a tear ran down her cheek.

"Don't, Cameron," Caitlyn sighed, gently moving his hand from her face. "Don't you see? I can't have you confusing me this way."

"I'm not trying to confuse you, Caitlyn," Cameron sighed. "I want for us to try and work through this disagreement."

"Working through it is doing it your way," Caitlyn said.

"Caitlyn, I'm not trying to undermine you. I just want us to be reasonable."

"Are you saying I'm not being reasonable?"

"No, I just think you're focusing on what happened in Illinois, and you're being a little too over-cautious."

"I think I have reason to be," Caitlyn said.

"We'll go together and meet with her, or make her come to the firm, where there will be plenty of people. How about that?"

"Fine," Caitlyn sighed. "You're determined to do this, aren't you?"

"Garret's life depends upon our finding out as much as

~ 237 ~

we can about what happened to his wife."

"Okay," Caitlyn smiled. "We'll do it your way."

Cameron smiled at her, and without thinking, he leaned in to kiss her. He pulled her close, as their kiss grew more passionate. She didn't pull away from him, and he could tell by her body language that she wanted him as much as he wanted her. As they kissed, Caitlyn backed slowly to her bed, as he walked with her, then Cameron gently pushed her down on it. His hands roamed her body, anxious to know her in every way. They'd come so close to making love before, and here they were again. Caitlyn then pulled away from him.

"No, Cameron. We can't do this," Caitlyn whispered, sitting up on the bed.

"Why do you keep pushing me away?" Cameron whispered, as he sat up beside her.

"Because we always almost make love under extreme circumstances. The first time we were almost intimate, was right after an argument. The second time was the day of your father's surgery, and now here we are again, right after an argument. If we're going to do this, I want it to be right," Caitlyn said.

"So, what are we going to do? Do you want to try this? Do we really have a chance?"

"I don't know, Cameron, but I don't think I can let you go without at least trying to find out," Caitlyn said, touching his face.

"I still can't commit to staying in Kerrigan," Cameron whispered. "At least not until we know what's going to happen with my father."

"I know, and I can respect that. We'll just take it one day at a time," Caitlyn smiled.

"It's my kiss again, isn't it?" Cameron smiled playfully leaning on Caitlyn.

"That and a few other things," Caitlyn smiled flirtatiously, playfully pushing him away.

"Hey, whatever works," Cameron laughed. He put his arm around her, and kissed her lightly on the cheek. "I think we're going to be okay."

"I hope so. I'm trusting you with my heart. Just don't break it," Caitlyn said.

"I'm doing the same thing, Caitlyn," Cameron said. He then glanced at his watch. "I guess I'd better get going. I'm going to see Dad. Do you want to come?"

"Sure," Caitlyn smiled. "My luggage can wait, since I'll be here until Monday."

"I'm glad you changed your mind. Have you seen my mother?"

"She left early going to the store, I think. She said she was going up to the hospital as well to visit with your father, so we'll probably see her there."

"Good. I've been really worried about her lately," Cameron commented.

"What do you mean?"

"She's just been acting as if she's not feeling well," Cameron said.

"She's going through a lot. I mean, your father's sick, and she's worried about you. That's a lot on a person. I see why you have to be here for her."

"I'm glad you understand," Cameron smiled. "Come on, let's go."

Cameron and Caitlyn then left, heading for the hospital. When they got there, Rebecca was indeed waiting to go in and see him. She was surprised that Cameron had decided to come to the early morning visit.

"Hey," Cameron said, kissing his mother on the cheek.

"Cameron, I didn't expect to see you here," Rebecca said.

"I decided to come on early, because I knew I'd have a hectic day ahead of me," Cameron stated.

"Well, I'm sure your father appreciates the fact that you're here," Rebecca smiled.

Shortly afterwards, there was an announcement that the visits were about to start. The three of them went in to visit with Evan. Cameron looked at Evan and wondered how such a strong man could be reduced to needing someone to take care of him. Maybe his mother was right. Were they doing him an injustice by allowing him to have an operation? Evan was a proud man, and he hated the thought of being a burden on anyone. After staying there during the entire visit, the three of them left.

Rebecca insisted upon going ahead with the Independence Day cookout the next day, so she had quite a bit of shopping to do. Cameron and Caitlyn went back to his house to work on Garret's case. He tried in vain several times to reach George. He left several messages for him, anxious to find out what he found on the Faulkner family. They worked all day, with Rebecca getting home later that afternoon. She insisted on cooking a big meal for them, which was welcome since the two of them had not eaten all day. They ate and eventually called it a night after working a little more.

****

The next day, Cameron, Caitlyn and Rebecca awakened early to get prepared for their company. Cameron insisted upon going to the hospital first, so the three of them went to the first visit. Evan still wasn't responsive, but the doctors still didn't seem too worried. He'd be going back to surgery the next day for his hip. Cameron decided that according to Evan's progress, he would leave Tuesday so that he could be there for the hearing. This would only be provided that Evan was doing well enough for him to leave town.

That afternoon, David and Linda came over. George and his wife Elizabeth also came over as well as Evan's dearest friend and business partner, Jim and his wife Ann. Several neighbors 'dropped by' for a visit that lasted the entire afternoon. The 'small gathering' resulted in having almost 30 guests there for the holiday. Rebecca loved every moment of it. She made sure there was plenty of food and drinks for everyone. Most of them brought different dishes, trying to make things easier on Rebecca. Cameron appreciated the help they all were to them, and it eased his mind a little knowing that she would have them for the few days he'd have to go back to Indiana. Cameron looked at Caitlyn, wanting desperately to steal a few private moments with her. She was going to be leaving the next day heading back to Indiana. Since they'd met, they hadn't had any time apart, whether arguing or otherwise.

He motioned for her, and she joined him after grabbing two beverages for them. The two of them walked off hand in hand down towards the stables. They spotted George looking deep in thought while watching the horses as he sipped on a beer. Cameron and Caitlyn walked up to him.

"Hey, George. Did you get my messages yesterday?" Cameron asked.

"Hi, Cameron, hi Caitlyn. Yes, I got them," George sighed. "But, Liz had me running around all day yesterday and I didn't get a chance to call you back."

"Did you find anything out?" Cameron asked.

"Yeah, I did. Cameron, I wish I had something concrete for you, but, we have no idea what happened to Ms. Faulkner. She disappeared back in October of 1985 and no one has seen her. Her parents were killed in May of 1985. I have the reports that were filed in my car," George said.

"Can we get them?" Cameron asked.

"Sure," George said. The three of them walked to George's car, away from the crowd. They could still hear the distinct social murmurs of the guests in the distance. George gave Cameron the reports.

Cameron read over them briefly. "It says here that she told co-workers that her cousin was trying to kill her. Why didn't anyone take her seriously?"

"Cameron, you have to remember, Rosemary was slow, almost child-like," George reasoned.

"And children are some of the most honest people I know," Cameron said.

"True. I must admit, more people should have taken her seriously, but back then, no one would listen. Rosemary had an active imagination," George said, shaking his head.

"What do you mean?" Caitlyn asked.

"She kept saying her cousin had this 'real gold' locket to give her and that it was worth a million dollars," George

~ 241 ~

chuckled slightly.

"A locket?" Cameron looked stunned. "Rachel promised her the locket."

"What locket was she referring to?" Caitlyn asked.

"I don't know," George shrugged. "Probably just another part of her overactive imagination."

"No, it wasn't," Cameron murmured. "In order to get her to do things, Rachel promised her that she would give her the locket," Cameron surmised.

"What locket? Cameron, what are you talking about?" Caitlyn asked.

"The other locket. The one Garret gave Rachel," Cameron said.

"I wasn't aware he'd given Rachel a locket," Caitlyn said, shaking her head. "I knew there was some talk about the one left in the rental car, but we never saw it and Mrs. Lassiter wasn't totally sure about the inscription."

"I have the locket he gave Victoria," Cameron said.

"What? Why didn't you mention it?" Caitlyn asked.

"I thought I did. I'm sorry, Caitlyn, it must have slipped my mind. I got it at the pawn shop, which was during the time when you were sick," Cameron said.

"Where is the locket now?" George asked.

"It's in my briefcase in the house. The pawn shop was unable to sell it because it had a personal inscription on it," Cameron said. "I contacted the jeweler who designed it, and he informed me that he'd made one for Rachel as well."

"Can I see the locket?" George asked.

"Sure. I'll go and get it," Cameron said. "I'll be right back." Cameron went into the house and looked in his briefcase to retrieve the locket, realizing he'd noted about the locket, but it was among the notes Serena had stolen, which is why he forgot to mention it to Caitlyn. "Here it is."

"It's beautiful," George said. "But, this doesn't help much with the locket Rachel probably had."

"Maybe it does. Apparently, the one that Hallinger designed for Rachel was very similar to the one he designed for Victoria. Plus, he remembered the inscription on

~ 242 ~

Rachel's," Cameron stated.

"What did the inscription say?" George asked.

"It said, 'To R, all the family I need, Love, G,'" Cameron said.

"What? Let me see that locket," Caitlyn said, retrieving the locket from George.

"Look at the markings on this one," Cameron showed Caitlyn. "Those are the special markings this jeweler uses to authenticate his work. Plus, as you can see, there's the inscription he made to Victoria."

"'Picture perfect forever, Love, Gary,'" Caitlyn said softly. "This still doesn't prove anything about the locket Rachel has."

"It proves that Rachel had a locket very similar to this one with a special inscription on it," Cameron reasoned.

"But, she could have pawned it," Caitlyn argued.

"It's doubtful. I get the feeling that if we find that locket, we'll find Rachel," Cameron said.

"I don't see it," Caitlyn said, shaking her head. "How can finding Rachel rest on this locket?"

"Think about how in love Rachel was with Garret," Cameron stated. "She wouldn't have gotten rid of it. I even called Rachel's brother back, and his wife told me that it wasn't among her things identified and she also said that Rachel had it on the night of the fire."

"When did you talk to Mrs. Lyle?" Caitlyn asked.

"The same day we arrived here. Dad and I were talking about it, and he suggested that maybe it was with her things. I called Mr. Lyle, and his wife answered the phone. She told me that if there was one thing that should have been found on Rachel it was the locket."

"'To R, all the family I need, Love G,'" Caitlyn repeated. "How can Hallinger be sure that's what the inscription said? It's been almost 30 years ago."

"Hallinger was a good friend of Garret's, so he remembered it quite well," Cameron commented. "He told me quite a bit about when they were in college together. Come to think of it, he mentioned his ex-girlfriend, Alice, was a good

~ 243 ~

friend of Rachel's. I wonder if it's Alice Cramer?"

"Well, I don't know. You seem to be the one with all the secrets," Caitlyn said sarcastically.

"I'm sorry, Caitlyn. I guess I forgot about the conversation I had with Hallinger because it happened shortly before the incident with Serena," Cameron said.

"Is there anything else I need to know?" Caitlyn asked in a frustrated tone.

"No, I think that's about it," Cameron said.

"It can't be the locket," Caitlyn sighed.

"Caitlyn, what's wrong?" Cameron asked.

She looked solemnly at Cameron. "Nothing. I'm just stressed out about all this, that's all," she smiled slightly.

"Are you sure that's all?" Cameron asked.

"Yes, it is. Why don't you put this back in your briefcase?" Caitlyn said. "We'd better join the others. George, thank you so much for everything you've done. You've helped us more than you know."

"I wish I could have done more," George said, walking with them.

"Oh, by the way, did they ever positively ID the body found in the well?" Cameron asked.

"Not positively, but they believe it's Oscar Lucas, a mechanic from many years ago. Oscar was kind of shady, and a mean SOB," George said. "But, right now, there's nothing definite. We should know a positive ID in a few days."

"No great loss to society, huh?" Cameron said.

George shook his head and laughed. "No, not really."

Everyone was at their home until almost 9 p.m., which was longer than usual. By the time they finished cleaning up, it was after 11 p.m. Rebecca eventually went to bed, leaving Caitlyn and Cameron up. They decided to go out onto the deck for fresh air so that they could unwind. Cameron looked at Caitlyn in the moonlight, and noticed how troubled she looked. Her whole demeanor had changed, just since earlier at the cookout. Cameron had to break the silence.

"Thanks so much for all of your help today," Cameron smiled.

"You're welcome," Caitlyn said in a monotonous tone.

"Caitlyn, please talk to me. What's wrong with you?" he asked.

"I can't talk about it now," she murmured.

"Maybe you should talk about it."

"Cameron, leave it alone. Please trust me on this."

"Trust what? You won't tell me anything."

"It's better this way," she reassured.

"Caitlyn–"

"Cameron! Please let it go!"

"Fine! You know, these little mood swings of yours are ridiculous!"

"You really need to leave it alone," Caitlyn said calmly. "I'm going to bed. I need to be at the airport by 11 a.m. Goodnight, Cameron."

"Goodnight, Caitlyn," Cameron sighed.

He was starting to think he was losing his mind. First Rebecca's mood swings, now Caitlyn's. He chauvinistically wondered if the problem was hormonal. He wondered if he'd ever be able to survive marriage if this was a constant expectation. He refused to let her bother him any longer. It had been a long day, and tomorrow his father would be going back into surgery for the second time in a few short days. The last thing he needed was to be worried about Caitlyn's little tantrums. He went upstairs to shower and get ready for bed.

He was feeling restless, so went back downstairs into the den and sat down to watch TV after grabbing a cold beer from the refrigerator. As it stood, he found himself not paying attention to anything that was on. He sat there thinking about the argument he'd had with Caitlyn, and how much he still wanted to be with her despite that. Cameron tried in vain not to stress his tired mind about it. He eventually dozed off in his father's recliner for much desired rest.

The next day, Cameron awakened to find himself covered with a blanket. He smiled as he realized his mother had probably come down in the middle of the night and covered him up. He went into the kitchen and noticed a note that Rebecca had left, stating she was going to the hospital to be with Evan before his surgery. He looked at the clock and noticed it was almost 7:30 a.m. He went to his room and got ready to go to the hospital. He'd found out that Evan's surgery was scheduled for 10:30, and he'd be going to pre-op at 9:30. Caitlyn's flight was due to leave at 12:30. He wasn't sure if she'd welcome his taking her to the airport, and he almost decided not to ask. But, since women don't come with an instruction manual, he realized that she probably would be expecting him to ask, and would be upset if he didn't. One of these days, Cameron was going to learn what makes a woman tick, if the mystery was ever to be solved. He decided to be a man about it. He inhaled deeply before knocking on Caitlyn's door.

"Come in," Caitlyn responded.

As he walked in, Caitlyn was packing her things again.

"Hey," Cameron smiled.

"Hi," Caitlyn said dryly, as she continued what she was doing.

"I'm going to visit Dad before his surgery, and I'll be back in time to take you to the airport," Cameron stated.

"I can call a cab," Caitlyn shrugged.

"No, it's not necessary. Why don't you take the rental car and turn it in at the airport? I can use my dad's car while I'm here," Cameron offered. "Maybe you can come by and see Dad on the way to the airport."

"No, thanks. I hate long goodbyes. To be honest, I'd prefer to take a cab," Caitlyn said, never once looking up at Cameron.

"Whatever, Caitlyn," he sighed. "Will you at least call me to let me know you made it home safely?"

"Sure," Caitlyn shrugged nonchalantly as she continued to pack. "Goodbye Cameron."

"Lock the door behind you," Cameron said. "Goodbye, Caitlyn." He then closed the door.

Why was she being this way? He thought she'd changed after opening up to him. He was disappointed knowing that he'd fallen in love with a woman who seemed to be everything he thought she was when they first met. He was

~ 246 ~

starting to question his judgment in women. At least he'd not bought her an engagement ring. As he drove along, he thought a lot about Caitlyn. It seemed that he and Caitlyn were just too out of sync to make it work. It didn't stop him from loving her though. When he got there to visit with his father, the nurse told him his mother had been there, but she had to go home for something. Cameron was worried, and wanted to make sure that everything was okay, so he went to call Rebecca on her cell phone.

"Hello?" Rebecca answered.

"Hey, where are you?"

"I had to come back to the house," Rebecca said.

"Why?"

"I left my medication, and I really need it," Rebecca stated. "I just pulled into the driveway, so I'll be back shortly."

"We must have just missed each other," Cameron said.

"Probably so," Rebecca responded.

"Caitlyn probably hasn't left yet."

"How's she getting to the airport?"

"She's going to call a cab. Her pride wouldn't let her allow me to take her," Cameron sighed.

"We women are a tough bunch," Rebecca said lightly. "I'll be back within an hour."

"I'll see you then," Cameron said.

About half hour later, Cameron's cell phone rang. "Hello?"

"Hey, Cameron. How's everything? Have they started on your dad's surgery yet?" David asked.

"Not yet. Still just waiting right now. Mom went home for her medication, but she'll be back soon."

"Why don't Linda and I come up there and keep you company?" David offered.

"I appreciate that. I could use all the support I can get right now."

"That's what I'm here for," David said.

"Thanks, David. I'll see you guys in a little while," Cameron said.

After hanging up, Cameron was told that he could visit his father. Before doing that, he called his mom to check on her, but she didn't answer the phone. Afterwards, he went into his father's room. He sat there talking to him as if he were still awake. He told him all about how he was feeling about the way Caitlyn was treating him.

"What do I do, Dad? I love this woman, but I have to be here for you and Mom," Cameron sighed. "What am I talking about? It's not as if you can give me advice about what I should do," Cameron smiled. He looked at his father. "I miss you, Dad."

Cameron touched his father's hand, as a tear rolled down his face. He watched this man who was invincible, lying before him now on the brink of death. For the state of vulnerability his father was in, ironically, he'd survived because he was a strong man with a will to live. Evan seemed to be fighting really hard to come back. After he came out, he went into the waiting room. Cameron tried to occupy his mind while he waited for word on his father. He watched TV, read through several magazines, anything to make the time pass. Not long after that, David and Linda showed up. Cameron was really concerned about his mom. He didn't know why she'd not returned yet.

"Hey, you two," Cameron smiled.

"Hey, Cameron. Where's Rebecca?" David asked, looking around. "Is she still not back?"

"No," Cameron sighed. "When I called her earlier, she said she was home because she had to get her medication. She should have been back by now. She's not answering her phone. I'm a little worried."

"You want me to go to the house to check on her?" David offered.

"Would you mind? I'd feel a lot better if I knew she was okay," Cameron stated.

"Consider it done."

"Sweetheart, I'll stay with Cameron," Linda said.

"Okay, I'll be back as soon as possible," David said. By the time David got to the elevator, Rebecca was stepping off of it.

"Mom, are you okay?" Cameron asked.

"Yes, I'm fine. Just had a couple of other errands to run," Rebecca smiled.

"I wondered what happened to you," Cameron smiled. "Was Caitlyn there at the house?"

"No, she'd already left. You know you have to be at the airport two hours before, so I probably had just missed her. Any word on Evan yet?" Rebecca asked.

"No, nothing yet," Cameron answered.

"You know, I've been doing a lot of thinking. Maybe you should go on back to Indiana tomorrow. Your father will have had both surgeries, and you need to turn in your notice. There's no need in waiting," Rebecca reasoned.

"Are you sure you're okay with that?" Cameron asked. "I mean, I really feel that my place is here for the next few days. Caitlyn's going to handle the hearing, so I can stay."

"Sweetheart, you don't need to baby sit me," Rebecca laughed lightly. "I'll be fine for a few days."

"Yeah, Cameron. If you have business you need to take care of, I'll be here for your mom," David offered.

"I know you will. Mom, we'll talk about it tonight," Cameron said.

They'd all been sitting waiting on word about Evan when Cameron noticed his mother. She seemed as if something was really bothering her.

"What's wrong? Are you worried about something?" Cameron observed.

"Of course I am. My husband is in surgery again. That's enough to worry any woman."

"It just seems like it's something more than that. Are you sure everything else is okay? You know you can talk to me about anything," Cameron stated.

"Everything's fine, honey," Rebecca reassured.

"I'm worried about you. I think all of this is taking its toll on you, and it has me wondering if maybe you need to get more rest," Cameron suggested.

"Cameron, I'm a little fatigued, but nothing that a good

~ 249 ~

night's sleep won't cure. I just want to take care of your father and always have you with me. But, if you must know, I had a bad dream last night that I'd lost something important to me," Rebecca commented oddly.

"Do you think it was a premonition about Dad?" Cameron asked solemnly.

"I don't know, Dear," Rebecca sighed.

Shortly afterwards, the doctor came in to talk to them. They were relieved to find out that Evan pulled through surgery with flying colors. They felt confident that he would probably be coming out of it in a day or two. They were told that they could visit with Evan in another hour or so. By this time, Cameron had gotten used to the routine. The four of them sat there for another 45 minutes before the nurse came out to let them know that they could see Evan. He was still hooked up to several monitors. The nurse explained that he would be monitored closely for the next 24 hours, but hopefully would wake up pretty soon. Cameron and his mother were both very tired, so they decided to go home after making sure everything was okay. They said their goodbyes to David and Linda and left the hospital. By the time they got home, they noticed that there was a Fire Marshall's vehicle, and smoke coming from where the cabin was located. They immediately got out of their cars.

"Steve, what's going on?" Cameron asked the Fire Marshall.

"Hey, Cameron. It seems that that old cabin of yours burned down," Steve said. "How are you, Mrs. Spencer?"

"I'm fine. Steve, what was the cause of the fire?" Rebecca asked.

"Oh, who knows? We'll know for sure in a few days. That cabin's been there for a few decades so it could have been faulty wiring. I hope you didn't have anything too important in there," Steve said.

"No, we didn't," Rebecca said. "Just a couple of old fishing rods and things like that."

"I can't believe the cabin's gone," Cameron said.

"Well, thankfully it didn't spread any farther, like to

the main house. Luckily, one of your ranch hands saw the smoke and knew something was wrong," Steve said.

"Where's Joe?" Cameron asked.

"I don't know. I've seen several of your ranch hands, but I haven't seen him," Steve shrugged. "He may not have been here when it happened."

"Not to mention he doesn't have a phone. We've got to get Joe a phone, Mom," Cameron sighed.

"He's been out all day. His truck has been gone since this morning because I think your dad had some things for him to take care of today that he's known about since before your dad got sick," Rebecca said.

"Is there anything we need to do?" Cameron asked.

"No, that's about it. I'll have a report pretty soon. We've put it out pretty good, but there's still a little smoke from the site. It's nothing to be alarmed about," Steve said.

"Good," Cameron said.

"We'll have someone back out here early tomorrow to get started with the investigation," Steve said. "I know you've probably been at the hospital all day. How's Evan doing?"

"About as well as can be expected. He had surgery today, so we'll know more soon enough," Cameron said.

"Well, we're praying for him," Steve said. "I'll check on you tomorrow. For tonight, try to get some rest."

"We'll try our best," Cameron said. "Thanks for everything, Steve."

"Goodnight, folks," Steve said as he got into his car.

"I wonder where Joe could be?" Cameron asked, as he and his mother went into the house.

"You know Joe. He's such a loner. Your dad probably had him pretty busy. He's got more work ethic than any of the other hands who work on the ranch. I know he has a sister over in Calston County. Maybe he's visiting her for the day. He'll turn up soon enough," Rebecca assured. "Come on, I'll fix us both an early dinner."

"You seem a lot more relaxed today, Mom," Cameron observed. "I mean, Dad's surgery, the cabin burning down. That's a lot for one day."

"Sweetie, I have every confidence in your dad's surgeons, and as far as the cabin, let's face it, we haven't used that place in years. I never had the heart to go out there anyway without you," Rebecca said.

"If you say so," Cameron said. "I'll help you fix dinner."

"You'll do no such thing. Sit down and relax. I'll take care of everything," Rebecca insisted.

As his mom worked in the kitchen, Cameron sat in the den to watch TV. It was hard for him to concentrate, because as he looked around morosely, he realized that Caitlyn was truly gone. When his mother called him in to the kitchen to eat, Cameron didn't seem to have much of an appetite.

"You're not eating very much," Rebecca observed.

"I'm not as hungry as I thought I was," Cameron responded.

"Cameron, is something on your mind?"

"Not really, just thinking," Cameron said.

"About what?"

"Caitlyn should have gotten home by now and she hasn't called," Cameron commented.

"What time was her flight supposed to get to Indiana?" Rebecca asked.

"Around 2:30 this afternoon."

"Maybe she'll call soon," Rebecca said.

"I wouldn't count on it," Cameron murmured.

"Is everything okay, Dear?"

"I think you were right about Caitlyn. She's definitely not the one for me," Cameron sighed.

"Oh, Sweetheart. What happened?"

"She really is this cold, distant prima donna who I don't even know."

"Well, you said that she was not a nice person when the two of you first met. First impressions are usually the right ones," Rebecca stated.

"We've done nothing but disagree since we met. She's selfish, and she's keeping something from me."

"What do you think it is?"

~ 252 ~

"I don't know, but I don't have time for games. I want a woman who will be honest with me about where we stand. She's not telling me the whole truth, and it's frustrating."

"Well, don't you think its better that you find out now that later? I know you cared about this girl, Cameron, but you can do a lot better. Plus, you've only known her a few weeks. You haven't given yourself time to figure out whether you really want to be with her or not," Rebecca reasoned.

"I know what you're saying is true, but it doesn't stop it from hurting."

"Oh, Cameron," Rebecca said, placing her hand on his. "I never want for you to hurt or be disappointed. I hate that she's doing this to you."

"It doesn't matter at this point. She's back in Indiana now. I'm going to go back, pack up my things and come home. Obviously, Kerrigan is not the place for me," Cameron sighed.

"You'll find your place, Sweetheart. Who knows? Maybe it's right here," Rebecca smiled. "You know I'd love for you to stay here and open your own practice. You could do so well in Lariette Springs, as well as in surrounding areas. I only want your happiness, Cameron. Your happiness is all that matters to me."

"You really are the only one who is truly in my corner," Cameron smiled. He looked on the kitchen counter. "Is that Caitlyn's cell phone?"

Rebecca looked at the phone. "I suppose it is. She must have left it. Well, you could mail it to her or take it to her when you turn in your notice," Rebecca suggested.

"That's odd that she'd forget it," Cameron said.

"Not that odd, Dear. Women forget things sometimes. Her hands were probably full when the cab arrived, and chances are, she sat it down and forgot to pick it back up."

"I asked her to call me when she arrives. If she has the decency to do so at some point, I'll let her know that it's here," he stated.

"My, my. She really has you bitter, doesn't she?" Rebecca observed.

~ 253 ~

"More than you'll ever know," Cameron sighed. He then looked at his mother and smiled. "Why don't we change the subject?"

"Will do," Rebecca smiled. "So, tell me about this case you've been working on," she asked as she took a bite of her food.

"It's been an unbelievable case. Our client, Garret Marlow, was accused of murdering his wife, Victoria years ago. At the time, Victoria was pregnant. Garret was accused because he had no alibi. He'd been home all night asleep. They found her body a couple of days later in a hotel where she had been brutally murdered after having her baby."

"Oh! How awful! That must have been terrible for him!"

"Yeah, it was. He was the only suspect, but we've come to believe that his ex-wife, Rachel might have had something to do with it. She was ruthless. She hurt so many people in such unforgivable ways. She even tried to hurt her own mother," Cameron said.

"What? Why would anyone do something like that?" Rebecca asked.

"Supposedly because she felt her mother was coming between her and her father. She tried to kill her brother and his wife. Unfortunately, she succeeded at killing their 12 year old daughter. An innocent child, died for no reason at all," Cameron shook his head. "It's heart-wrenching."

"This Rachel sounds awful," Rebecca commented.

"She is. I pity anyone who knows her. She seemed to destroy everything and everyone that she came into contact with. Although she's presumed dead, Caitlyn and I believe she's still alive somewhere. Probably living everyday happily ever after with no conscience about what she's done."

"Well, at least this case is about over. This woman sounds dangerous," Rebecca said.

"She is. You know, every time we discover something new about her, I like her less and less."

"Maybe she's just misunderstood. Just never had the love she needed."

"But, she destroys everyone who she stands a chance to get love from. Her mother, her brother, her niece, her ex-husband, everyone. She's unredeemable."

"What do you think is the real drive behind her doing those things?"

"My opinion is that she's narcissistic and evil. To tell you the truth, she deserves execution."

"That's a little harsh, isn't it, Son?"

"No, I don't think so. I'm so glad to have a mother like you. I'd never want anyone like her in my life, for any reason."

Rebecca gave a slight smile. "Well, you don't have to worry about that. I'm about as far from being like her as you can get."

"That's the truth!" Cameron smiled. "Look, if you don't mind, I don't want to talk anymore about the case. Besides, it seems as if a decision will be made soon anyway," Cameron said. "I mean, his clemency hearing is the day after tomorrow. If our evidence isn't strong enough, he dies in three weeks from lethal injection."

"Oh, how sad!"

"Yeah, it is. I just hope we can save him," Cameron murmured.

"I know you'll do your best," Rebecca smiled.

Rebecca and Cameron talked for a long time after that about other things as they ate. The day was starting to wear in on Cameron, and after helping his mother clean up, he went up to shower and get ready for bed. He noticed that he still didn't have any messages from Caitlyn. He tried to call her, but didn't get an answer so he decided to leave a message for her. He knew she was angry, but she wouldn't be this careless about calling. Cameron was starting to get worried. He called Phillip at home to see if he'd heard from Caitlyn.

"Phil, I hate to disturb you at home, but I'm a little worried," Cameron stated.

"What is it, Cameron?"

"Caitlyn left today, but she's not called. She was supposed to be checking in. I just have a strange feeling."

"What time was her flight?" Phil asked.

"She should have been back several hours ago. Her plane should have landed at 2:30 p.m. I mean, it's almost 9 o'clock."

"That is strange, because Caitlyn's usually not this careless."

"I just don't understand why she hasn't called."

"Did you try her cell phone?"

"She left it here," Cameron stated.

"Did you call her mother's home?" Phil asked.

"I don't know her mother's number. I tried to check her phone, but it's locked and password protected."

"Let's see. It's listed under Sylvia Harding. I can look it up for you. I'd hate to worry her mother unnecessarily, but we need to know that she's okay."

"I agree. I'd rather be safe than sorry," Cameron stated.

"Okay, it's (812)555-8282."

"Got it," Cameron said, as he wrote the number down.

"Let me know what's going on once you talk to her mother," Phil said.

"I'll call you back in a few minutes." Cameron hung up with Phil and dialed Caitlyn's mother's number.

"Hello?" the woman answered anxiously.

"I'm trying to reach Sylvia Harding," Cameron spoke.

"This is she," Sylvia responded.

"Mrs. Harding, you don't know me, but I'm Cameron Spencer, a colleague of Caitlyn's."

"Yes, she's mentioned you. Have you seen my daughter?" she asked, her voice rising.

"No, and I'm getting a little worried about her," Cameron said.

"You're not the only one. She never called me. She was supposed to let me know when she got home. I've been frantic all evening. I'm so worried about her!" Mrs. Harding said.

"When did you talk to her last?"

"This morning. She told me that her flight would

arrive at 2:37 this afternoon. She promised to call, but I didn't hear from her. I've been calling her cell phone and her apartment all day. I just got home from checking her apartment, and there's no sign of her. I was just about to call my brother to see if he had another way of reaching her. My daughter never does things like this," Mrs. Harding said shakily.

Cameron could hear the strain in her voice as she fought back the tears.

"Please, don't panic. Her cell phone is here. I think she left it by mistake. I'm leaving tonight and I'll be home in a few hours," Cameron stated.

"I-I'm calling the police," she stated nervously.

"Please do. I'll be there as soon as I can," Cameron said, hanging up the phone.

Before leaving out of his room, he called David to have him and Linda to come over and stay with Rebecca for the night. He immediately got his bags together and took them downstairs. Rebecca was in the den.

"Son, what's wrong?" Rebecca asked.

"I have to leave for Indiana tonight. Caitlyn never made it back," Cameron said.

"What? How can that be? She left hours ago," Rebecca stated.

"That's what I want to know. I'm worried that something has happened to her. I have to go. I've called David, and he and Linda are going to come over and stay with you tonight."

"Sweetheart, that's not necessary. I'll be fine by myself," Rebecca said.

"No arguments, Mom. It's bad enough that Dad's in the hospital, now Caitlyn's missing. I will not take a chance that something could happen to you."

As Cameron was getting his things loaded into the car, David pulled up. He briefly explained everything to him as David got his and Linda's things out of the car. He explained to David that he didn't really want to leave his mother at home alone because he was worried about her. He felt that she

~ 257 ~

wasn't feeling well, but didn't want to worry him with it. He knew he'd never forgive himself if something happened to Rebecca. Cameron hugged his mother and got into the car and left.

On his way, he called Phil to let him know what he'd found out and that he was heading home. Cameron also mentioned to Phillip that Caitlyn had everything pertaining to the case. All of their files were supposed to be with her on the plane. Phil reassured Cameron that he would immediately contact the Kerrigan police, as well as Caitlyn's mother. Cameron suggested he check with the airlines as well to see if Caitlyn ever got on her plane. Phil told him that he would handle everything on that end, and that he should just get to Kerrigan as soon as possible. Cameron drove non-stop to Kerrigan, all the while praying that nothing had happened to Caitlyn. As he drove along, he thought about the way he and Caitlyn started off, and how she always seemed to get under his skin. He arrived home after 1 a.m., and went immediately to Caitlyn's mother's house after looking up her address, noticing the police car when he got there. Cameron pulled into the driveway and got out. He went to the door and rang the doorbell. A woman, whom he assumed was Sylvia, answered the door. Cameron noticed that she was an older version of Caitlyn.

"Hi, I'm Cameron," he stated.

"Cameron, please come in," Sylvia sighed, seemingly relieved that he was there. She looked as if she'd been crying. "Maybe you can talk to these officers."

"Mr. Spencer?" the first officer said.

"Yes, I'm Cameron Spencer."

"I understand that you were the last person with Ms. Frazier before she disappeared," the officer stated.

"I saw her earlier this morning. Caitlyn and I had been investigating a case in Kentucky, and my father became quite ill. She left Kentucky this afternoon heading back to Indiana to finish preparing for an upcoming hearing we're working on."

"Do you remember what Ms. Frazier was wearing?"

the second officer asked.

"Yeah. If I recall, she had on a pink blouse with blue jeans," Cameron stated.

"Did you take her to the airport?" the first officer asked.

"No," Cameron shook his head. "I went to the hospital to visit with my father before his surgery, and she said that she was going to catch a cab to the airport."

"Did she seem upset, or talk to anyone else that you know of?" the first officer asked.

"No," Cameron said, shaking his head. "She and I have been working on a case that has stressed her somewhat, but I can't see why she would–" Cameron stopped.

"What were you about to say?" the first officer asked.

"Serena," Cameron whispered.

"Who?" the first officer asked.

"Serena Felton. When we were in Illinois, I was drugged and a lot of our files were stolen concerning this case we're investigating. The woman's name was Serena Felton, or at least that's what she told me," Cameron stated. "She also contacted me a few days ago, but she refused to tell me how to get back in touch with her. She said she had vital information regarding our case, but she wouldn't say more; just that she'd be back in touch."

"Serena Felton," the first officer said.

"Yes," Cameron said. "I still have the phone number she called me from." Cameron immediately looked up the number on his cell phone and wrote it down for the officers.

"Thank you," the second officer said, retrieving the number from him. "Where was this woman from?"

"She said she was from North Carolina, but I'm sure it was a lie," Cameron said.

"Why do you say that?" the first officer asked.

"Because when she called back, she stated that she was the daughter of an alleged accomplice in the murder we're investigating."

"What else can you tell us about Ms. Felton? Can you describe her?" the first officer asked.

"She was about 5'5" and maybe 120 pounds. She had short, dark hair, and was a medium to light complexion."

"Mrs. Harding, do you have a recent picture of your daughter?" the second officer asked.

"Yes, I have one," Sylvia said, retrieving the picture from the fireplace mantle. She took the picture out of the frame and gave it to the officer, all the time crying as she did it. Mr. Harding held his wife, as he had tears in his eyes.

"We've checked her apartment, and we've talked with her boss. We've checked the airlines, and your daughter wasn't on any plane heading from Kentucky to Indiana. It doesn't look as if she rented any cars, or took the bus nor train. Her credit cards haven't been used. Is it possible that maybe she just wanted to be by herself for a couple of days?" the first officer asked.

"No!" Sylvia shook her head fiercely. "Caitlyn never does things like that! She always contacts someone. If no one else, she would tell me! I'm her mother!"

"I understand that, ma'am, but, sometimes–" the first officer started.

"Sometimes?!" Sylvia cut him off. "To hell with sometimes! I told you my daughter doesn't do things like that!"

"Mrs. Harding, you have to calm down. We're going to do everything we can to find her, but it hasn't even been 24 hours. Now, by right, you can file the police report, and we'll do what we can. But, honestly, it doesn't get serious until it's been a couple of days. People go off to be by themselves and may not want anyone to know. We see it all the time," the second officer shrugged.

"How dare you?! How dare you belittle the fact that my daughter is missing by saying she just went off to herself?! Now, you do your damned job and find her!" Sylvia cried.

"Honey, settle down," Mr. Harding said.

"No! I will *not* settle down! My daughter's been missing since earlier today and these officers are trying to shrug it off! Even if she wanted to be by herself, she'd tell me so I wouldn't be worried! But, if you won't do your damned

~ 260 ~

job, I'll hire my own investigator if I have to!"

"You have every right to do that, ma'am, but we're going to do our job," the second officer said. "Maybe your daughter didn't want to tell you anything this time. Now, you need to calm down about this situation. I'm only stating the facts about what we see everyday."

"And I've known my daughter everyday of her life, and I know what she will and won't do! Do you have children, officer?" Sylvia asked the second officer.

"Yes, I do, and that doesn't factor into this case," the second officer smiled slightly, shaking his head.

"Well, it's good to know that your child will never be in harm's way, but the rest of us aren't so lucky!" Sylvia spit out.

As Cameron listened to her, he saw where Caitlyn got her feistiness from. Caitlyn was her mother through and through. After several minutes of arguing back and forth, the officers left, stating that they would post Caitlyn's picture. Apparently, in the time it had taken for Cameron to drive from Kentucky, Caitlyn's mom had contacted a news reporter friend of hers, who would help get the word out about Caitlyn's disappearance. The police had come by earlier to take the initial report, and searched Caitlyn's apartment. They noted that her messages had not been checked all day. Cameron realized that Caitlyn's family was not one to be reckoned with. Alex Jacobs had been out of town, but he told his sister that the plane was going to fly him back and he'd be there in a couple of hours. He was upset by the fact that Phil had handled things and he'd not been contacted sooner. Sylvia explained to him that she'd gotten sidetracked before calling him.

Cameron stayed at Caitlyn's parents' home until after 3 a.m. He wouldn't have been able to sleep no matter how hard he tried. The love of his life was missing, and he didn't know what to do about it. He hated that it took something like this for him to put into perspective what was really important. He couldn't give up on her. He wished he'd been totally honest about his feelings for her. Now, maybe it was too late. When

Cameron got home, he called his parents' home to check on his mother. David answered the phone and told him that Rebecca was asleep. Cameron felt relieved knowing that David wouldn't let anything happen to his mother. He had no idea what had happened to Caitlyn. It had to have happened before she left Kentucky. Otherwise, she would have been on the plane, bus or train. There would be some sort of evidence that she'd left Kentucky. Wherever she was, Cameron had a sneaking suspicion that it had to do with the case they were working on. Was Serena really Dr. Varden's daughter? Was Serena behind Caitlyn being missing? She had to be. First the drugging, the theft, and then the mysterious phone call. She'd kidnapped Caitlyn. Caitlyn was right not to trust her. Cameron tossed and turned for the better part of the night, eventually falling asleep at almost 4:30 a.m.

Chapter
12

Despite his weariness, Cameron awoke with a start at 7 a.m. He realized that he'd not checked his messages. He had a message from Garret's parents that they wanted to meet with him as soon as he arrived back in town. After getting ready to go into the office, Cameron called the Marlows.

"Hello?" Mrs. Marlow answered.

"Mrs. Marlow?" Cameron responded.

"Yes?"

"This is Cameron Spencer."

"Mr. Spencer! We were hoping we'd hear from you! How are things going with my son's case?"

"They've been going extremely well. In fact, I'd like to meet with you today to go over what we've found so far."

"Um, I was watching the news last night. Is it true that Ms. Frazier has disappeared?" Mrs. Marlow asked.

"Yes, that's true, but the police are involved with trying to find her."

"I'm sorry about that. I know this must be a lot on you."

"It has been. But, don't let that bother you. It hasn't deterred me from the task of clearing your son. We will save your son from being executed," Cameron reassured.

"I believe you. What time would you like to meet with us?"

"How about 11 o'clock this morning?"

"That's fine. My husband and I will both be there," Mrs. Marlow said enthusiastically.

After hanging up with Mrs. Marlow, Cameron thought about his statement of reassurance. What if they couldn't clear him in time? What if they couldn't get a pardon? Then what? Garret's family would be devastated. Cameron felt as if he was being pulled in so many directions.

His parents needed him, the Marlows needed him, Caitlyn needed him. He cared about all of these people, but he could only do one thing at a time. Miracles happen everyday. Cameron was definitely praying for his share. The doctors were confident that Evan would be waking soon, and Cameron had enough evidence to go before the clemency board for a pardon. Cameron suddenly realized that all of the notes were with Caitlyn. All of the evidence, contacts, everything had left with her yesterday. What now? There was only so much he could do with nothing to go on. He knew he'd have to get to the office to see what he had there already, along with what he could remember. This was a snag that Cameron did not need. Not with everything going on.

Cameron arrived at the law firm at 9:30 that morning. He was driven by all the things that were going on in his life. He knew he had to find the love of his life, he knew he had to clear his client, and he knew he had to be there for his family. He didn't have a moment to waste. Caitlyn had been missing for an entire day. With a full day of no contact, the possibility was stronger that she might not be alive. No. Cameron refused to think that Caitlyn had been harmed. He had to keep a positive outlook on things. When Cameron arrived to his office, he was surprised to see a new secretary at Kristen's desk.

"Who are you?" Cameron asked.

"I'm Brenda, your new assistant," she smiled, standing to shake Cameron's hand.

"What happened to Kristen?"

"She quit," Brenda stated. "I'm with the temp agency."

Cameron smiled as he thought about the fact that now that Kristen was gone, something had finally gone right in his life.

"Welcome to the firm. I'm Cameron Spencer, by the way," Cameron stated.

He looked at her. She was at least fifty years old, and according to the pictures on her desk, seemed to be happily married with children and grandchildren.

"I know. It's a pleasure to meet you," Brenda smiled. "Has there been any word on Ms. Frazier yet?"

"You know about Caitlyn?"

"Yes, because there was an announcement by Mr. Larson this morning, and I'd been told that I would be working for her, so it piqued my interest. Besides that, there have been investigators here, and I think they've even called the FBI."

"I keep hoping something will turn up, but so far, it's as if she's fallen off the face of the earth," Cameron sighed.

"Well, I'm going to keep good thoughts," Brenda encouraged.

"Thanks. I think we could all stand to do that right about now. Any messages?"

"Yes," Brenda said, handing him a stack of messages. "Also, those boxes arrived this morning," Brenda stated, pointing to a stack of three boxes.

"Where did they come from?" Cameron asked, looking at them.

"They're from Ms. Frazier," Brenda murmured.

"Ms. Frazier?"

"It looks like she mailed them out before she left Kentucky to be delivered here."

"She was really thinking ahead," Cameron said. "This helps a lot. It's just so hard to concentrate without knowing whether she's okay or not."

"I hope everything works out," Brenda said.

As they were talking, someone walked up behind Cameron.

"Cameron," the woman called out.

Cameron turned to see who was calling him. It was Serena. What was she doing here? Why would she have the gall to show her face after all that she'd done? Was this just another one of her sick games?

"What the hell are you doing here?" Cameron yelled.

"Cameron, we really need to talk," Serena said.

"Brenda, call security," Cameron instructed Brenda, never once taking his eyes off Serena.

"Is everything okay?" Brenda asked.

"Just do as I say. I'm going to take Ms. Felton into my office." Cameron looked coldly at Serena.

"Cameron, please, there's no need for that," Serena pleaded.

"Wanna bet?" Cameron scoffed.

Serena reluctantly walked with Cameron into his office. Cameron closed his door forcibly.

"How dare you show up here? What have you done to Caitlyn?"

"Caitlyn? The attorney who works here? I swear I haven't done anything to her!" Serena said as she sat down.

"Don't play this game with me Serena! You drugged me, you stole my files on a very important case, you call out of the blue a few days ago, and now ironically, my colleague is missing. I know you've had something to do with Caitlyn's disappearance!"

"Caitlyn's missing?" Serena asked in a surprised tone.

"Like you didn't know! I've had enough of your games to last a lifetime. Now, tell me what you've done to her!"

"Cameron, if I had anything to do with her disappearance, would I be stupid enough to come to your office now?"

"I don't know, you might be!"

"Come on, give me credit for something! Look, I took

~ 266 ~

a huge chance showing up here today. You could have had cops waiting for me at the door. Besides, I wasn't even sure if I'd find you here or not. I showed up here as an act of good faith. I'd decided to go ahead and leave the journal in hopes that you would get it."

"Of course. The mysterious journal! The journal that's going to clear my client, right?"

"I feel bad about what I did, but I just had to know what you'd learned so far," Serena said.

"What did your father have to do with my client's wife's murder?" Cameron asked, as he sat on the edge of his desk.

"Let me explain. My real name is Serena Varden. Regina only knew me by 'Jessie' because of my middle name, Jessica. Felton is my married last name, although I'm divorced."

"Why didn't you just tell me who you were when we first met?"

"Like you would have helped me voluntarily!"

"I don't believe this," Cameron shook his head.

Serena went on to try to explain her reasons. "When my father was killed in that car accident years ago, I heard whispers from people that Regina Matheson was behind it, although she'd not worked for Daddy for over two years. My brother and I were children at the time, and I wasn't old enough to try to do anything about it. My brother admitted to me just a few years ago that Regina Matheson and Daddy were having an affair."

"So, what does that have to do with me?"

"I have a few connections, and I'd heard about this case concerning Garret Marlow. See, two years ago, when my mother died, my brother and I were clearing out a lot of her things, along with a lot of things that belonged to my dad that we'd never had the heart to get rid of, mostly because of Mom. Among my father's belongings was a journal. My brother never knew about the journal, but I found it, read it, and was totally amazed by the things my father revealed in it," Serena said.

"What did your father reveal?" Cameron asked. At that moment, there was a knock at Cameron's door. "Come in."

"Did you need some assistance, Mr. Spencer?" the first security guard asked.

"I might," Cameron said.

"Cameron, please. I'm not here to cause trouble," Serena pleaded.

"Is she bothering you? Do you need for us to escort her out?" the second guard asked.

"She could be very important to a case I'm working on. I need to question her further if you could just wait outside," Cameron instructed.

"Yes sir," the first guard said, closing the door behind him.

"Go ahead, Serena," Cameron encouraged.

"Well, as I was saying, in this journal, my father revealed some things about a murder that had taken place many years ago. I mean, it was like a confessional. He spoke about Regina Matheson and the part she played in it. Look, after what I did to you, I wanted to give you the journal to read. Learn about my father and what he did as well as why he was driven to do those things. He was being seduced by Regina," Serena stated, handing Cameron the journal.

"Why would you do this for me?" Cameron asked suspiciously, looking at Serena, then at the journal.

"I told you, I felt bad about what I did to you. And I want for you to catch Regina Matheson and bring her to justice. I believe she murdered my father and I know she murdered Victoria Marlow. I think it's time she paid for both crimes," Serena said.

"So this is just a matter of justice for you? How did you know so much about this case? How did you know we were at the hotel a couple of weeks ago?"

"Like I said, I have connections," Serena said.

"What does that mean? Look, if you want my help, you have to be completely honest with me. Who have you been working with?" Cameron asked.

Serena sighed. "I have a friend who works for Imperial Car Rental's corporate office. She heard Deanna Lassiter mention something about Regina Matheson, and her ears perked up. Deanna told my friend about it when they were on their break, that she was supposed to be meeting with a Cameron Spencer and Caitlyn Frazier concerning Regina Matheson. We knew that my father and Regina had rented the car from Imperial. My friend called me and I caught the first flight out from New York that same evening."

"So, you weren't from North Carolina?" Cameron asked.

"No, but I knew Gorham Software was having a conference there in the hotel because when I got there, I noticed all of the signs talking about the events for each day. Look, I'm sorry I lied to you, but I had very good reasons for everything I did."

"Spare me, okay? But, continue with what you were saying," Cameron said.

"I came down with my boyfriend, planted myself in the hotel, and met you. I knew you had vital information, and I needed to get it," Serena stated.

"How did you know what hotel we were staying in?" Cameron asked.

"That wasn't hard. I started with the best hotels in the city until I found the one with rooms registered to Cameron Spencer and Caitlyn Frazier."

"What were you hoping to gain from stealing my files?"

"Names, contacts, information. I wanted to find Regina Matheson. I hired a detective two years ago and the poor excuse couldn't find his hand if it wasn't attached to his arm. So, I had to find out what I could on my own."

"So, you drugged me, stole confidential information, and skipped town? So, what did you find out?" Cameron asked sarcastically.

"Unfortunately, I found myself at a dead end with the information you had. It didn't reveal much more to me than I already knew, until I found something in your notes about

Rachel Marlow. After digging a little deeper, I realized her brother was Roland Lyle. When I went to him, he and his wife refused to talk to me. By right, I didn't have a leg to stand on. After all, I'd obtained most of my information illegally. So, what's the connection between Rachel and Regina?" Serena asked.

"Don't you know? After all, you have every bit of information on the case," Cameron stated sarcastically. "But now I realize you're the other woman Mrs. Lyle mentioned. She said she'd refused to talk to the other woman about Rachel as well."

"Yeah, that would probably be me," Serena sighed. "I'm thinking that Rachel and Regina are one and the same. Am I right?"

"That's privileged information," Cameron stated.

"Come on, Cameron. Tell me."

"No, Serena! When I feel the time is right and I can trust you, I'll tell you everything, but until then, forget it!"

"Fair enough. Cameron, I know I'm not your favorite person right now, but we are both seeking the same thing: justice. Now, we may have different reasons, but the agenda's the same. Regina Matheson is the key. Let's find her together, and I will provide you with as much as I can to clear your client," Serena suggested.

What she was proposing was tempting. Cameron knew at this point, he was desperate.

"Fine. I'll read your father's journal, and if it reveals some of the things I feel can help my client, I will make sure that if I find Regina Matheson, I will do everything in my power to make sure she is prosecuted for the murder of your father. Fair enough?"

"I want to be totally involved."

"What?"

"I want to work with you on this case," Serena said.

"No way! I'm working this case with Caitlyn."

"But, she's missing, and you're in a race against time."

"You're not even an attorney!" Cameron argued.

"That's true, but I know that you have a clemency

hearing scheduled for tomorrow. I'll testify about the validity of my father's journal. I'll do whatever I can to help," Serena offered.

"I don't know," Cameron hesitated.

"Look, I have proven I'm a good detective. Let's face it, at this point, you need me. Your client is set to die from lethal injection in three weeks. You need all the help you can get," Serena acknowledged.

As much as Cameron hated to admit it, she was right. Against his better judgment, Cameron found himself agreeing to what Serena was proposing.

"Okay, Serena. I'll work with you, and I won't press charges against you for what you did in Illinois. Where are you staying?"

Serena provided Cameron with her hotel information, as well as her cell phone number. She continued to apologize for what she'd done, in hopes of getting Cameron to trust her. Cameron was still suspicious of her, but she could prove very helpful to his case. As he opened the door to let her out, he remembered that security was still waiting on him. He informed them that he didn't need them, and that everything was okay. When Serena left, Cameron sat in his office and perused her father's journal briefly. He also called Caitlyn's mother to see if there had been any word, and so far there was nothing. A little later, Brenda informed him that Mr. and Mrs. Marlow were anxiously waiting for him in the reception area. He didn't realize it had gotten to be so late, but it was almost 11 a.m.

"Mr. and Mrs. Marlow? Why don't you come into my office?" Cameron closed his door behind them. "Won't you two sit down? Would either of you like a cup of coffee?"

"To tell you the truth, we're about as alert as two people could be!" Mr. Marlow said happily. "No need for caffeine today, is there, honey?" Mr. Marlow laughed, looking at his wife.

"That's right. I told my husband that things were looking good for our boy. What can you tell us?" Mrs. Marlow asked.

~ 271 ~

"Mr. Marlow, I'm very encouraged that we can clear your son. I have substantial evidence that could be very helpful at the clemency hearing. It's quite evident that your son was framed for Victoria's murder. And, we have reason to believe that the one who murdered her and framed him was his ex-wife, Rachel."

"Rachel?" Mrs. Marlow's smile faded. "I knew it! I told Vicki not to trust her!" Mrs. Marlow cried.

"Excuse me?" Cameron asked.

"Vicki trusted Rachel. I told her to be careful of her!" Mrs. Marlow said, shaking her head. "I suspected that Rachel was up to something, but you obviously have more reason to believe there's some truth to it. What's happened?"

"We have a long list of witnesses who have stated things revealing her as a possible suspect. I'm confident that we have more than enough to establish reasonable doubt. A stay of execution would be a blessing at this point which should cause a delay, but I believe we have evidence strong enough to get a full pardon."

"You 'believe'? But, there is some doubt on your part?" Mr. Marlow asked.

"Mr. Marlow, nothing is guaranteed, but I have to believe that the legal system will not fail your son," Cameron reassured.

"It's failed him for 27 years. What if it fails him again?" Mr. Marlow asked. Cameron's face told the answer. "Then our son dies, doesn't he?"

"I'm sorry, Mr. Marlow. Unfortunately, I have to give you the bad news along with the good news. I don't want for there to be any surprises. But, please, please let's wait and see what the board has to say," Cameron encouraged. "I made a promise to you and I plan to fulfill that promise."

"Didn't you recently find out that Rachel's dead? If that's the case, how are you going to prove anything?" Mrs. Marlow asked.

"Mrs. Marlow, it's quite possible that Rachel Marlow is still alive."

"How is that possible?" Mr. Marlow asked.

~ 272 ~

"She faked her death, or so we believe."

"Does Garret know?" Mr. Marlow asked.

"No, not yet. I'm going to go and see him this afternoon. He needs to know exactly what's going on."

"Mr. Spencer, you said you believe Rachel faked her death. So, you're not 100% sure?"

"Not 100%, but we are 95% sure."

"My son can't gamble off of 95%. We need 100% proof that she's done these things you're saying. If this is just an educated guess that doesn't pan out, my son could pay for it with his life," Mr. Marlow stated.

"Mr. Marlow, I agree with you wholeheartedly. But, we have to do something, and right now, this is where my instincts are leading me as well as evidence. Let me show you something."

Cameron showed them the locket and explained to them that it belonged to Victoria, and that it was found in a rental car that was rented the same weekend that she was killed. Cameron asked if they recognized it. Both of them remembered when Garret gave the locket to Victoria, and how happy she was.

"He'd given one similar to it to Rachel as well," Mr. Marlow commented.

"Yeah, I heard about that," Cameron said.

"He felt so guilty about everything," Mr. Marlow said, shaking his head.

"Why would he feel guilty about the fact that Rachel couldn't have children?" Cameron asked.

"Well, Gary felt responsible," Mrs. Marlow said, with tears in her eyes as she stared at the locket. "Rachel had gotten deathly ill during her pregnancy, and was rushed to the hospital. She was near death, and the doctors told Gary that she'd lost the baby. They also explained that they'd have to give her a hysterectomy if she was to live. Gary knew how badly Rachel wanted a baby, but her life was more important to him, so he chose to consent for the hysterectomy. He hated what it did to her, but he had to save her life."

"I didn't know that. I was under the impression that

she'd never gotten pregnant at all," Cameron said.

He was starting to see things a lot clearer now. This could be a motive. Cameron continued in conference with Garret Marlow's parents for another 30 minutes telling them everything he'd learned so far, even mentioning the journal Serena had given him.

Cameron didn't have a moment to waste, so once again, he found himself utilizing the firm's plane to go and see Garret. Garret's parents wanted to accompany Cameron, but as they knew, they wouldn't be able to see Garret because of the strict guidelines about unscheduled visits. When he arrived at the airport, he went to the rental car agency located there because he still had the rental car. Thank goodness the local rental agency under the same name as the rental agency in Kentucky allowed him to leave the car with them for an additional fee, which he was able to charge to the firm. The plane then took him to see Garret.

"Mr. Marlow, we have a lot to discuss about your case," Cameron stated.

"What's happened?" Garret asked, sitting down.

"It seems we've come across witnesses who swear that your ex-wife, Rachel Marlow might have very well been the one to kill Victoria and frame you."

"Rachel? So, it's true? My first instinct was right," Garret said.

"Seems like it. She assumed a new identity and got help from a doctor in Illinois. He was almost the spitting image of you, and we are going on the assumption that he was her accomplice," Cameron stated.

"Why would she do that to me?" Garret asked.

"My guess is, because she could not have a child as a result of a hysterectomy that you consented to, and to add insult to injury, you married someone who could give you a child. Now, from what we've learned, she lived with her brother, Roland and his wife for a few months and she had a baby boy. It's a very good possibility that it was your baby boy that she had with her."

Garret smiled. "I have a son?"

~ 274 ~

"Now, we're still checking into all of that. Right now, I think I have enough evidence to present before the clemency board."

"That's cutting it pretty close isn't it? I mean my hearing's tomorrow."

"Mr. Marlow, if the evidence is compelling enough two hours before your execution time, it's not too late. I'm not giving up, and I need to know that you won't either," Cameron encouraged.

For reasons Cameron could not explain, he felt a deep connection to Garret. He truly wanted to see him cleared of the murder charge. Cameron conferred with Garret for another hour, filling him in on everything he and Caitlyn had discovered. He explained that it was possible that Caitlyn's disappearance had something to do with his case, but he wasn't sure. Afterwards, Cameron took the plane back to Kerrigan and left the airport in his own car, which was parked two cars down from Caitlyn's. He looked solemnly at her car briefly before getting into his own. He hoped that one day soon she'd be back in his arms. As he drove along deep in thought, his cell phone rang.

"Hello?" Cameron said hopefully. He was hoping it was good news about Caitlyn, but it wasn't.

"Mr. Spencer?" a woman responded.

"Yes?"

"This is Ashley Brierfield, from Lakeland Hospital in Illinois."

"What can I do for you?"

"You'd wanted a picture of Regina Matheson to be sent to you, is that correct?"

"Yes, it is. Do you have one?"

"Yes, we have a picture on file. I can fax it over to you if you'd like," she suggested.

"That would be great!" Cameron gave her his home fax number since that's where he was headed.

Ms. Brierfield promised to fax it to him that same evening. Soon enough, he'd be able to see how Regina Matheson looked. That would at least put them one step closer

~ 275 ~

to finding her. When Cameron returned home that evening, Serena was there waiting on him.

"What do you want, Serena?" Cameron sighed. "I told you, the minute I knew anything more about Regina Matheson, I'd let you know."

"I know what you said, but I wanted to talk to you," Serena said.

"Fine, come on in." They went into Cameron's apartment. "Have a seat."

"Thank you. Cameron, look, I know a little more about the case than I've let on," Serena said.

"What do you mean?" Cameron asked.

"Well, I know that Regina Matheson is living somewhere in Kentucky," Serena said.

"What? How do you know this?"

"Like I keep telling you, I have connections," Serena said.

"Where in Kentucky is she supposed to be?"

"That's what I'm not sure about. The detective I hired a couple of years ago said that a paper trail seemed to stop in Kentucky. That's where he lost her. It's almost as if she ceased to exist afterwards. My guess is she changed her name but she was still using credit cards that my dad had gotten her."

"I wonder if she's the one who's responsible for Caitlyn's disappearance. My home is Kentucky, and Caitlyn was abducted somewhere between there and here in Indiana. The police said she never got on the plane."

"It's quite possible," Serena shrugged.

"Hold on, I have to check my fax machine," Cameron said to Serena.

When Cameron went to his fax machine, the picture had come through, but it was dark and distorted. Cameron checked the ink cartridge, and it had leaked out into the machine.

"Damn it!" Cameron said in disgust. "Now what?" he sighed.

Cameron looked at the clock. It was almost 5:15 p.m.

Maybe there would still be someone in the hospital personnel department. Cameron dialed the number all the time feeling that it was too late in the evening. There was no answer, so he'd have to wait. Serena noticed his frustration after his phone call and fax. She saw the piece of paper he held in his hand and took it from him.

"What's this?" Serena asked.

"It was supposed to be a picture of Regina, but it came out distorted, courtesy of my fax machine ink cartridge."

"Where did it come from?"

"The hospital where your brother's office is located. It was supposed to help me to be able to identify her a little better."

"You mean all you need is a picture of Regina?" Serena asked.

"Yeah, it would be a big help," Cameron commented.

"Once again, I can save your ass," Serena sighed.

"What's that supposed to mean?"

"There are two pictures of Regina at our July 4th picnic. I don't think she realized they were being taken. Daddy always had a photographer to take candid shots during office luncheons and picnics. But, there's no mistaking it. She's definitely in the pictures."

"Where are these pictures?"

"They're at home. I can call my housekeeper and have her to overnight them to us. They can be here by tomorrow if you want."

"That would be perfect. I was going to call the hospital to see if they could do the same thing."

"Look, do you want to go out? Grab a bite to eat?" Serena suggested. "There's not much more we can do tonight anyway."

"No thanks, I'll pass. Besides, I have to read your dad's journal. I want to see what he had to say."

"Oh, you can do that later. Come on, let's go out."

"Serena, I am really not in the mood to have fun. I still have to clear Mr. Marlow, Caitlyn's still missing, and my father is still in the hospital. So forgive me if I don't see a

~ 277 ~

whole lot of reason to go out and party with you. You go on without me."

"Spoiled sport. I thought you'd be more fun than this."

"Serena, have you ever taken anything seriously in your life?"

"Of course I have. I take trying to find my father's murderer seriously, I take protecting my family seriously."

"Does your brother know what you're doing?"

"No. He'd kill me if he knew. He's always been so overprotective of me. I try to tell him not to worry, but it doesn't do any good."

"Were you in Illinois when we were there talking to your brother?"

"No, I was in Ohio, trying to find Regina, or rather Rachel's brother. Larry told me about your visit later on. He told me that you talked to Lauren about it. Believe me, if anyone knew anything about Regina, it was Lauren."

"Why are you so sure that she knew so much about her?"

"Because they were such close friends. Remember I told you about someone referring to Regina at Daddy's funeral? Well, it was Lauren and she made a comment about Regina finally doing him in."

"What did she mean by that?"

"Everyone suspected my dad and Regina were having an affair," Serena sighed. "Everyone knew except my mother, which I'm thankful for. Lauren and Regina used to talk, until they had a falling out about something. At Daddy's funeral, I heard her talking to one of the other nurses who worked with them. She told the nurse that my father was always treading on thin ice dealing with Regina, and that if anyone wanted to see him fall through that thin ice, it would be Regina. I was never able to find out what exactly happened between those two."

Cameron knew what had gone on, but he refrained from saying so to Serena. Serena sat there for the next ½ hour trying to convince Cameron to go out with her, when she finally gave up and decided to go back to her hotel, telling him to call her there if he changed his mind. With peace and quiet after Serena's departure, Cameron settled down to read about Dr. Varden.

"Now, let's see what you were up to, Dr. Varden," Cameron said to himself.

The things he read that night were astounding.

'July 1, 1983

Regina is still set on going through with her plan. I'm not comfortable with it, but Regina has a hold on me like nothing I've ever experienced before. She wants a life with me, but I love my wife. Why do I keep giving in to this temptation? I know she's dangerous, but isn't that the thrill of it? She wants a baby so badly, but is it really worth it to do what she wants to do? If we get caught, there could be hell to pay. I could lose my family, my practice, even my freedom. How do I say no to this woman?'

"Man, didn't you have any type of backbone?" Cameron said. He turned the page to read more.

'July 2, 1983

Well, the plan is set. Regina said Victoria's shower is set for Friday evening at Calamar's Restaurant in Indiana. Everything's supposed to take place afterwards. If all doesn't go well, if everything's not perfect, Regina could really go off the deep end. I'll do whatever it takes to please this woman, even if it means what we're about to do. I keep hoping there's another way, but it seems this is it.'

Cameron flipped through the pages. He went to July 4th.

'July 4, 1983

Regina talked to Marianne today at our Independence Day picnic. I was a nervous wreck. Having my lover and my wife see each other face to face again like that was really unnerving. Marianne doesn't suspect a thing I don't think. The children don't seem to like her. Although, usually Larry

~ 279 ~

and Jessie are pretty easy to get along with anyone. She keeps thinking that she'll be their mother one day. I keep trying to get through to her that I will not leave my wife. She was clearly upset about it, but Marianne is better suited for the children. I get the feeling that Regina has a lot of demons inside that are just waiting to come out.
'July 5, 1983

Today couldn't have been worse. Larry, Jr. walked into my office and found Regina and me in a very compromising position. I yelled at him when I shouldn't have. He was so excited about hitting that home run in today's game. I hate my patient load was so heavy that I couldn't be there to watch him. He and my little Serena are the most important people in the world to me. What am I doing to them? I have to end this thing with Regina. Now that my son knows, I can't take the chance of hurting the rest of my family as well. I apologized to him, but I don't think he's forgiven me yet. He even told me that Regina said she'd be his mom soon, and that she'd do whatever it took to do so. He was just upset. There's no way Regina would have told him such a thing, although she's mentioned it to me on more than one occasion.
'July 6, 1983

We're leaving tonight heading to Indiana. I don't know what's going to happen, but I get the feeling something is going to go wrong. Regina wants for me to perform a C-section on Victoria after drugging her. The whole plan is simply to get the baby. What if something goes wrong? I'm afraid I might be in over my head by doing this. Regina seems so calm about it. We're going to rent a car today from Imperial. They're a little shoddy, but Regina wanted to use a place that wouldn't require a credit card, somewhere we can pay cash. She doesn't want for this to be connected to us in any way. She'll probably use a fake name. I don't even want to know. The more I know, the more involved I'll be. We'll drive to Indiana, and tomorrow, Regina will go and see Garret during Victoria's baby shower to distract him long enough to drug him. I assume she wants to drug him so he won't realize his car is gone. She still has a copy of his car keys from when they were married a few years ago. We're going to follow Victoria from the shower and kidnap her so that I can perform a C-section and deliver the baby. Regina's manipulated her enough to know that she's bad about not locking her doors so at the first available moment, I'll climb into her backseat. I'll have a mask and gun anyway if I have to use them to scare her. I have to keep Victoria drugged long enough so that she won't remember who she was with. If she can identify us, all bets will be off.'

Cameron noticed the next entry was not dated until July 9th.

'July 9, 1983

My God, what have we done? Why didn't Victoria cooperate? I had no idea she was going to come around so soon after I knocked her out. I never had a chance to administer the medication for the spinal block. Everything went wrong. We had to tie Victoria down, and I gave her a local anesthetic while I performed a C-section. I know it wasn't enough, because she winced with pain. She was screaming and I was afraid the other hotel guests would hear her. Regina stuffed a towel in her mouth and taped it down to gag her. After I'd successfully delivered the baby, I looked into Victoria's crying eyes. She was so afraid. She looked pleadingly at me, and then at Regina. Victoria still seemed as if she was in a daze. She'd not completely come from under the drug I'd given her. Regina started yelling about how she'd ruined her life, and now she was going to ruin hers. Regina turned into a crazed monster, and raged out at Victoria. I had no idea she'd kill her. She started stabbing her, and wouldn't stop. I had to quickly put the baby down and pull Regina from Victoria. It took everything in me to get the knife she wielded angrily at Victoria. Everything went wrong. After Regina killed Victoria, she took the baby and wrapped him up. Victoria's lifeless body lay on the bed in a pool of blood, and Regina had no conscience about what she had done. I soon realized when we went outside, that Regina had it planned this

~ 281 ~

way the entire time. She'd gone to Garret's house supposedly to distract him. He let her in and she drugged his beer, causing him to sleep through the entire thing so that he wouldn't have an alibi. Now I see why we took his car and brought it back to the hotel. We were at the Cannon Hotel on Bryer Street. She wanted for me to drive Garret's car back to their house and she'd follow me in the rental car. I asked her what were we going to do about Victoria's body and car. She told me we'd just leave the car there, and she heartlessly said that eventually someone would find the body when it started to smell and that she wasn't about to clean up the mess. Regina cruelly snatched Victoria's locket from her dead body, claiming Garret never should have given Victoria something so similar to what he'd given her when they were married.

She'd even planted $10,000 in Garret's home to make it look as if he'd sold his own baby. Which explains why she wanted for me to withdraw such a large sum of money. She wanted to frame him for Victoria's murder, so she hid the knife in his trunk, wrapped in one of his t-shirts she'd retrieved from their house. All this time, Garret's been thinking of Regina as a friend he could trust, when in reality she's been setting him up. When we took the car back, it was getting close to 4 a.m. Those kids saw us; I'm just hoping they couldn't identify us. The girl thought I was Garret. I'm an accessory to murder now. How do I live with what I've done?'

Cameron couldn't believe it. A full confession right here. He noticed there was a picture in the back of the journal. It was Dr. Varden, and a lady, whose back was to the camera. He wondered if this was his wife or Regina Matheson.

"Oh my God!" Cameron picked up the phone to call Serena.

"Wellington Suites," the woman answered.

"Room 324 please," Cameron said.

"Hello?" Serena answered.

"Serena, my God, do you realize you've been sitting on the confession we've been looking for? How could you keep something like this?" Cameron was clearly upset.

~ 282 ~

"I'm sorry, Cameron. Look, you have it now, so use it. Find Regina Matheson, clear your client."

"No doubt about that."

"What else can I do?"

"Nothing at this point. I'll let you know when Regina comes into play. One question: who's this on the picture with your father?"

"Oh, that's Regina. I know, it's of her back, but it was tucked into the pocket of the journal, so I decided to leave it there."

"This journal could have cleared my client a long time ago," he sighed. "Look, I have to go. I have a lot to do."

"Call me if you need me," Serena offered.

"I will. Bye, Serena." Cameron hung up the phone.

This woman has had a confession from her father all this time, and Garret Marlow has been rotting away in a prison cell on death row. Although he could throttle Serena for withholding this information, he could also hug her for coming forward with such an important piece of evidence. Cameron read through more of the journal throughout the night. All he had to do was present this at the hearing. He knew that they'd want to have the handwriting in the journal authenticated, but this could be just what he needed to have Garret Marlow cleared of the murder charge. He hated to get his hopes up, but Garret could very well be released over the next few days or so. Cameron continued to read, for his curiosity was definitely piqued about what else Dr. Varden had to say.

'July 13, 1983

Regina has decided to take the baby and go away. I signed a blank birth certificate for the baby. Regina filled it out entirely, so I honestly have no idea what she put on it. I don't know what she named the boy, or anything. I even helped her to get a new birth certificate for herself so it would authenticate her new identity. I get the feeling that Regina planned all of this when she met me at the medical conference. That she was just using me all the time. She knew I was an

~ 283 ~

obstetrician, and that I'd have the ability to deliver a baby, and the authority to sign a birth certificate. She should be leaving soon, but not soon enough. After seeing what she's capable of, I think I'm better off without her. I'm glad I had the good sense not to leave my wife for her. They arrested Garret today, right after his wife's funeral. I can't believe it. It's been all over the news since Victoria's body was found on Sunday. I want to go forward and admit what we did, but I can't. I'll lose everything if I do that. Besides, they probably won't convict. Surely his attorney will be able to get them to clear him of the charges. Now I have to wonder if Regina will come after me. After all, I've done everything she wanted me to do, and I know too much.
'July 15, 1983

Regina left today. Thank God. I've never been so relieved to be rid of a person as I am to be rid of her. She's moving to Ohio, and she said she was going to try to start over there. I gave her money to get on her feet. What difference does it make? I've been keeping her all along anyway. I've been paying for her apartment in Indiana, paying for her apartment here, and giving her the money she used to frame Garret. I gave her $25,000 to get started. No price is too high if it'll get rid of her. I'm just glad she's gone. She told me her brother cheated her out of the money he got from the sale of their parents' home by gambling it away, but he's offered her a place to stay. I don't care as long as she's not my problem anymore. Now, maybe my life can get back to normal, with my practice and my family. I never realized how much I loved Marianne until I started going through these changes with Regina.'

Cameron noticed there were no more relevant entries for another few months. Mostly just talk about his family life. Then he started again about her that following January.

'January 25, 1984
Regina contacted me today. She threatened to make sure I went down with her if I didn't help her. She needed

~ 284 ~

money again. For what reason, I don't know. All she said was that she and her brother had a falling out and she's 'burned that bridge.' I'm not sure what she meant, but knowing Regina, it wasn't good. I told her that if I gave her money this time, it would be the last time, and no more. She's supposed to contact me tomorrow concerning where to meet her. She doesn't want for me to know where she's going to be, and quite frankly, I don't want to know. I can see right now that Regina is going to be nothing more than a money pit. I would like to see the baby though, to make sure he's okay. Maybe I should just turn myself in.

'January 26, 1984

I met with Regina this afternoon. She was staying at a hotel here in town. I gave her another $25,000. I can't believe how weak I was. I slept with her again, and I regretted it after it happened. She told me that I'm the one who gives mixed signals and that being with me has really confused her. She said she's missed me and regrets that we're not together anymore. I knew she was manipulating me, but I gave in anyway. The baby looks like he's being taken care of. I asked her what name she gave him, and she refused to tell me. I'm not sure why she's being so secretive. I've been there through everything she's done so far. What is it about this woman? Why do I give in to her? I thought I was over her. After seeing her brutally murder someone, I should be repulsed by the thought of even being around her. But, I'm not. I wonder if I'm in love with this woman? Couldn't be. How do you love someone like her?'

After that, there were no more entries about Regina, until close to the end. Dr. Varden didn't write every single day, but he wrote about relevant events that happened in his life. Cameron scanned through it and ran across another entry about Regina. It was over a year and a half later.

'September 12, 1985

Just when I thought things were going good, she did it again. Regina contacted me. I'd not heard from her in over

~ 285 ~

six months. She only contacts me when she needs money, and like an idiot, I keep giving in to her, sexually and financially. I know I've not written about seeing her in over a year and a half, but I've not wanted to be reminded of the fact that I'd been with her again. She contacted me a year ago, telling me she'd found a house she wanted for me to rent for her and the baby on the other side of town. I helped her to get settled in, and continued to have an affair with her for the next few months. After only four months, she was gone. I don't know where she went, but she left. I felt like such a fool, and now she wants to see me again. I wonder what this is all about. I'm going to see her tomorrow.
'September 13, 1985

Regina informed me that she's met someone else, and that she's getting married. Maybe now, she'll leave me alone. The baby's two years old. She calls him Ricky. He seems so well-behaved. No one would ever believe he's got a psychopath for a mother, who really isn't his mother. She said some things to me that make me fear for my life. I told her that what we did was wrong and maybe we should try to set things right. She told me if I ever told anyone about what we did, that she'd kill me. She even commented that I'm dispensable now, because she's found another patsy to take care of her. She told me this as we were lying in bed, after I'd slept with her again. I don't know what's going to happen, but I'm worried about what she might do. Maybe I should just go to the police. But, so much time has gone by. I'd be convicted right along with her for sure. I haven't heard too much about Garret lately. Last I heard, they'd denied him bail and he was still waiting on a trial date. If this thing continues like it has, I'm going to go to the police, to hell with what Regina says.'

That was the last entry in Dr. Varden's journal. According to Serena, her father's fatal accident took place two days later. Cameron shook his head in disbelief. How could anyone be this cold-hearted? What was even more unbelievable was that she'd gotten away with it. Obviously, this was absolute proof that she'd not gotten killed. According to the Lyles, she was killed within a day or so after she set fire to their home. This had to be the same person. Cameron checked the journal thoroughly to see if Dr. Varden ever mentioned what name Regina had changed her name to. She obviously had three identities: Rachel Marlow, Regina Matheson, and Ellen Harwood, but was that it? Cameron wondered if Dr. Varden knew about the fact that her name wasn't really Regina, and that it was Rachel. After all, Lauren had overheard her exchange with Alice Cramer who referred to her as Rachel. He never made it known if he did. This was also absolute proof that the murder that took place at the Cannon Hotel on Bryer Street was committed by someone other than Garret. This was so overwhelming for Cameron. Before going to bed, he called to check on his father. The nurse told him that he was improving, but still had not awakened yet. He also called Caitlyn's mother to see how she was holding up. Mrs. Harding was a very strong woman, who would not give up hope that her daughter was alive. They all were sitting vigil by the phone waiting for news, just as Cameron was doing.

Chapter
13

Cameron tried to get some rest that night, but mostly he tossed and turned, his head filled with unsettling dreams. He woke up in a cold sweat and looked at his clock. It was only 5:30 a.m. He knew he'd never get back to sleep, so he decided to work out in his apartment's gym. He lifted weights, ran on the treadmill, did a complete workout for over an hour. It gave him a lot of time to think about Dr. Varden. What type of spell did Rachel have over him to make him do the things he did? Cameron felt bad that he'd gotten killed, but in a way, dealing with Rachel was a way of writing his own death warrant. She was trouble and he should have known better.

By the time Cameron returned to his apartment, he was too revved up to relax. It was almost 7 o'clock, so he turned on the news. The first thing he saw was a story about a woman's body that had been discovered locally. The description of this woman was general: a woman in her mid-twenties, slender build whose body had not been identified. She didn't have any identification when she was found. Cameron immediately panicked. What if it were Caitlyn?

Before Cameron could entertain the thought further, his phone rang. It was Caitlyn's mom.

"Hello?" Cameron answered.

"Cameron! I've been watching the news! They found a body here in Kerrigan! Please tell me it's not Caitlyn! Please!" Mrs. Harding said tearfully.

"Please, Mrs. Harding. Don't panic." Cameron couldn't believe he was trying to reassure her when he was having the same horrific thoughts. "Now, it's true, they've discovered a body here in Kerrigan. But, it's almost impossible that it's Caitlyn. They would have contacted you if it were her. So, please, just calm down, okay?"

"Why haven't the police called me?" Mrs. Harding asked.

"Probably because they don't think it's her. Now, the FBI, the police and our firm's detectives are on it. With the pictures of Caitlyn circulating, Kerrigan Police would most likely know if it was her or not."

"I hope you're right. I'm so on edge right now. Caitlyn is my child, and I don't know what I'd do without her," Mrs. Harding sobbed.

"Neither do I," Cameron murmured.

"You're in love with my daughter, aren't you?" Mrs. Harding asked.

"Yes, I am. I just don't know how deep her feelings go for me," Cameron stated.

"When we get her back safe and sound, the two of you really need to figure that out. You're a sweet guy and I think you'd be good for her. She's been searching for happiness for a long time. Maybe you're just the one she's been looking for," Mrs. Harding said.

"I really appreciate hearing that," Cameron smiled. "We just have to keep good thoughts that the body discovered wasn't Caitlyn."

"It's crazy isn't it? Whoever that poor girl is that was killed was someone's daughter. All I can think of is the fact that I pray she wasn't my daughter. Doesn't that sound awful?"

"No, not at all. You're only human. Don't worry because we will find Caitlyn. She's strong and she can handle a lot," Cameron reassured.

After hanging up with Caitlyn's mom, Cameron took a shower and got dressed for work. He needed to get started on making sure all of his affidavits and depositions were ready to be presented. He and Caitlyn had already worked non-stop on getting ready for the hearing. Witnesses were allowed to attend the hearing, so they already had some of the witnesses scheduled to testify. Amanda Warren assured them that she would be there. One of the paralegals made sure that Amanda Warren's statement was signed and notarized. None of the witnesses from Illinois would be able to be there on such short notice. Cameron had already gotten their sworn affidavits to present to the board. Serena wanted to testify as well to corroborate that the journal was the authentic work of her father. Cameron had to keep busy so he wouldn't think of Caitlyn. He felt helpless, because he had no idea where she was. She had to turn up somewhere. The question was, where? And would she be alive? Is this the sort of torture Garret Marlow went through during the two days his wife was missing?

Cameron arrived at his office shortly after 8 a.m. and went over notes and evidence. During that time, Victoria's parents called and insisted upon speaking out on behalf of Garret. Cameron felt that this could go a long way considering what evidence they had so far. When Cameron had a break, he called to see if his father had made any improvements, and much to his dismay, there had been very little change. Garret didn't have to be at the hearing, which was probably for the best. The hearing was scheduled for 10:30 a.m. When Cameron arrived at the hearing accompanied by two paralegals and two law clerks who'd been helping him to do research, Garret's parents and in-laws were already there, as well as Serena and Amanda. When the hearing was called to session, and Cameron was asked to come forward to give opening remarks, Garret's parents couldn't have been more confident.

Cameron opened about all of the new evidence he and

Caitlyn had discovered over the past few weeks, presenting all of the signed affidavits as well as the journal. During the hearing, Amanda Warren, Serena and Victoria's parents all testified. Cameron tried desperately to read the expressions of the nine board members, but they were unreadable. All he could do was pray that he'd presented enough compelling evidence and testimony to argue Garret's sentencing. Although Cameron had given a compelling argument, the prosecution was allowed to tell their side as well, painting Garret as nothing short of a monster. After a couple of hours, the board members dismissed them, stating that they would take all testimonies and new evidence into consideration. They also stated that they would check the journal for authenticity.

"What happens now?" Clinton Marlow asked.

"We wait. We've done all we can at this point. Hopefully, that journal will be enough to clear your son's name, along with Mrs. Warren's testimony. Right now, it's just hard to say." Cameron wanted to be as honest as he could with the Marlow family.

"Well, you did your best. That's all we can ask for," Clinton Marlow said. "How soon will we know?"

"In about a week. The board will make recommendations to the governor, and he has a right to follow those recommendations or to make his own independent decision," Cameron explained.

"Mr. Spencer?" someone was standing behind him.

Cameron turned to see who it was. "Mrs. Warren, thank you so much for coming," Cameron said.

"I'm glad to do it. Mr. Marlow, Mrs. Marlow? You may not remember me, but I was your son's neighbor years ago," Amanda stated.

"I remember you. I met you once a long time ago when we were visiting Garret and Victoria one day. Thank you so much for coming forward," Mrs. Marlow smiled.

"You're welcome. I just wish I'd come forward sooner. I really hope all of this works out for all of you," Amanda said.

"I do too. At this point, there's nothing more we can do. It's always been in God's hands, and I know He'll do what He sees fit," Mrs. Marlow stated.

"Well, I'm going to be praying for you," Amanda said. She then looked at her watch. "I really need to get going. Mr. Spencer, please let me know if I can be of any more help. I'm sorry my husband was so difficult before. Even if I can't help, will you let me know how things turn out?"

"Of course. And thanks again for all of your help. Your account of what happened was a pivotal turning point in my client's case," Cameron said.

"You're welcome. Good luck to you," Amanda said.

Serena came up next. "So, do you think Daddy's journal will help?" Serena asked Cameron.

"I hope so. It's our strongest piece of evidence. Without it, I don't think we'd stand as good of a chance to clear him."

"Mr. Marlow, Mrs. Marlow, I'm sorry for whatever part my father played in putting your son through this. Nothing will ever make up for the time you've missed with your son and grandchild. I hope that someday all of you will be reunited," Serena stated.

"Thank you Mrs. Felton. Right now, I'm afraid to put the wagon before the horse. I'm going to keep an open mind until we hear from the governor," Clinton Marlow stated.

Cameron talked to Victoria's parents briefly, telling them how sorry he was that they were still going through so much concerning Victoria's death. Serena asked Cameron out to lunch, and this time, he agreed. He couldn't do much more for Garret except wait it out now. Serena took Cameron to a very nice restaurant for lunch. They talked, and for once, they were finally able to be comfortable around each other. Cameron asked her about the boyfriend who'd helped her at the hotel. She explained that he was more or less someone she had an 'understanding' with, although he wanted it to be more. She made it quite clear to Cameron that her attraction to him was not acting.

"Serena, I think you're very beautiful. And quite

~ 292 ~

honestly, if I'd met you three months ago, I would probably be more open to seeing where things could go, but. . ."

"You're in love with Caitlyn, aren't you?"

"Yeah, I am. I don't think I realized how much until after she disappeared. She didn't deserve this, and I'm going to make sure I find whoever is responsible for doing this to her and make them pay."

"What if you can't find them?"

"I'll never stop looking."

"What if Caitlyn's dead?"

"Then I know I'll never stop looking until I find them."

"Caitlyn's a lucky girl. How come guys like you are always taken?"

"We're not always taken. We usually just don't look appealing until someone else has us," Cameron smiled.

"You know, maybe you're right. Because even with knowing you're in love with Caitlyn, I'm finding myself extremely attracted to you."

"Serena–" Cameron sighed.

"I know, I know. Just forget I ever said anything and enjoy lunch. Deal?"

"Deal."

They enjoyed the rest of the meal over idle conversation, with Cameron telling Serena about how he and Caitlyn managed to connect Rachel and Regina. Then, Cameron took Serena back to the hotel. She informed him that the picture of Regina should be there. She left instructions for the desk clerk to accept the package and she'd pick it up when she got back in. The desk clerk told her that he'd already sent it up to her room. Serena invited Cameron up to look at the pictures. When they walked into her room, he noticed that her bags were packed.

"Are you leaving?" Cameron asked.

"I'm going back to New York," Serena said. "I've done what I came here to do."

"I appreciate all of your help, despite our initial encounter," Cameron smiled.

"You're rapidly becoming a good friend, Cameron

Spencer," Serena smiled.

"You, too. I'm going to miss you," Cameron said.

"Will you miss me enough to give me a ride to the airport? I have a 5 p.m. flight back to New York."

"Sure," Cameron smiled. "Let's load your luggage now." Cameron lifted her two suitcases. "What did you pack? Rocks?" Cameron joked.

"No, just the essentials that every girl needs," Serena smiled. "By the way, I've arranged for all of your notes to be returned to your firm. They should be there by now."

"Thanks, Serena," Cameron smiled. Cameron saw a bellhop with a luggage cart in the hallway as he was about to walk out with Serena's luggage. "Can I get a little help here?" he asked.

"Sure, Sir," the bellhop said, taking the suitcases and loading them. The bellhop offered to take the luggage down to Cameron's car, so Cameron gave him the valet ticket.

Cameron then went back into Serena's room. "Thanks for everything you did today, Serena."

"Hey, we're friends now. We have to keep in touch. Besides, when you catch Regina Matheson, or Rachel Marlow, whoever she really is, I'll be back to help drive the nails into her coffin," Serena said.

"Speaking of Regina," Cameron reminded her.

"Oh, I suppose you want the pictures! The clerk said they left them on the desk," Serena said, going to the desk. "Here they are." She opened the envelope. "Here's one at the 4th of July picnic, and here's another one at an office luncheon." She handed the pictures to Cameron.

Cameron looked alarmingly at the face smiling back at him. Cameron shook his head in disbelief. There had to be a mistake.

"Th-this isn't Regina Matheson," Cameron said, looking at Serena. "What is this? Some sort of joke?" He was shouting angrily.

"What do you mean? That's Regina Matheson," Serena argued.

"No it's not, dammit!" Cameron yelled.

~ 294 ~

"Cameron, I swear to you, that's the woman who worked for Daddy. That's Regina Matheson."

"This can't be happening! This is a mistake! This can't be her!"

"Yes it is. I know how the woman looks. It's definitely her."

"No, no, no, no," he started to cry out. "Oh, my God! It can't be!"

"Why are you so upset?!" Serena asked.

"Serena, this is my mother!" Cameron cried.

Serena covered her mouth. "Oh, my God. Cameron, I'm so sorry," Serena whispered, touching Cameron's arm.

He jerked away from her. "You stay away from me! You're lying! What kind of sick game are you playing with me!?"

"I'm not playing games! This is the woman who worked with my father!"

"Then she couldn't be the monster we think she is! My mother would never do those things!"

"Dammit, Cameron, it's time to face reality. If this is your mother, she's a cold blooded killer!"

"No, she isn't! No! Rebecca Spencer would never do the things Regina Matheson has done!"

"I wish I could tell you differently, but let's face it, if that's your mother, she needs help."

"Rachel Marlow! My mother is Rachel Marlow! I can't believe this! How could she? How could I have been raised by such a monster!" Cameron's heart was racing.

"Cameron, calm down. The only other possibility is if it's someone who bears a striking resemblance to her," Serena suggested. "There has to be another way to find out if it's her or not."

Cameron thought for a moment. "There is. Come on."

On his way, Cameron called the prison to see if they would allow him a short conference with Garret. He had to find out if this woman was his mother. After pleading with the warden, he was finally given the okay to have 30 minutes with Garret. Afterwards, he called the airport to see if the firm's

~ 295 ~

plane was available to fly him to see Garret. As luck would have it, one of the senior partners had just arrived back from a short trip, so the pilot was still there.

Cameron drove directly to his apartment, and retrieved the pictures of his mother and headed straight to the airport. If there was one person in the world who could prove if these two women were the same person it would be Garret. When they arrived at the prison, Cameron waited for what felt like an eternity before Garret came through the door. Serena was with him, so Cameron had to tell them that she was assisting him in order for them to let her in. She insisted upon being there, and considering all she'd done, Cameron didn't think it would be fair to keep her out of anything. Garret came through the door, looking as if he'd gotten very little sleep.

"Cameron, I didn't expect to hear from you until a decision had been made. Did the governor make his decision already?" Garret asked.

"No, Mr. Marlow. He's not rendered a decision yet. I came here to discuss another matter with you. This is my friend, Serena Felton. She played a major part in new evidence in your case, and she really wanted to meet you."

"Hi, Mr. Marlow, how are you holding up?" Serena asked.

"About as well as can be expected," Garret sighed. "Thank you for coming forward when you did."

"I'm just sorry you've lost so much of your life because of my father," Serena said.

"Your father wasn't the only one to blame. My ex-wife seems to have played a pretty big part as well," Garret stated.

"Garret, that's what I wanted to talk to you about," Cameron said.

"What is it, Son?" Garret asked.

The word 'son' hit Cameron like a ton of bricks. The realization hit him that he was possibly Garret and Victoria's long lost son. He started thinking about the dates, and his birthday was coming up in a few days, or at least the birthday his mother gave him. Some birthday present. He was

~ 296 ~

absolutely speechless for the first time in his life. Garret looked at him, very concerned all of a sudden. Cameron stared in a daze at Garret.

"Cameron? What's wrong?" Garret asked.

"Um, Garret, we think we were finally able to track down a few pictures of Rachel. Can you look at these and tell us if you think they could be her?" Cameron showed him the pictures that Serena had given him.

"Yeah, that's Rachel alright. I'll never forget that birthmark on her arm," Garret stated.

When Garret mentioned the birthmark, he remembered that his mother also had a birthmark. Upon closer examination of the photo, Cameron noticed the birthmark as well. Cameron then showed him the other picture.

"What about this one," Cameron said, slightly holding his breath. He showed him the one from his apartment.

"Man! That's her! She's just a little older. It looks like she's held her youth pretty well. Where did you get this picture?"

"Um, I'd rather not say right now. There's something I have to go and take care of," Cameron said, almost in a trance-like state.

"Cameron, are you okay?" Garret asked.

"Yeah, I'll be fine." Suddenly, Cameron seemed to come back to reality. "Listen, we really need to talk about some things."

"Okay. I know we probably still owe you guys a lot of money, and if I'm released, I'll do everything I can to pay every cent," Garret promised.

"No, no, no, no, it's not about money," Cameron reassured. "Please, don't worry about that. I have to leave town, but I will be back in a couple of days and I'll explain everything to you then. In the mean time, you keep praying for a good outcome. I know I will be," Cameron whispered.

Was this his father? Was the man sitting before him the man who was partly responsible for Cameron's existence? Garret looked strangely at Cameron.

"Cameron, are you sure you're okay?" Garret asked.

"I-I'll be fine," he reassured, standing from his chair. "I have to leave town, but I promise I'll be here when we find something out about your clemency hearing."

"Thank you, Cameron, for everything you've done," Garret said, standing as well and patting Cameron on the back.

Cameron stared at Garret. How does he tell him? Cameron decided to keep quiet for now. Nothing was definite yet because he had to do more investigating to find out if he was really Garret's son. Ironically, the son who was taken from him years ago could possibly be the one working on his case today. What are the chances of that happening? Cameron didn't know whether to laugh or cry after the life-altering day he'd had. His life had taken a completely different turn. Cameron left, wondering how to handle the situation that faced him. How could he look his mother in the face without hating her? She'd ruined so many lives, and never thought twice about it. Serena noticed how deep in thought he was as they drove along.

"Cameron, what are you going to do?" Serena asked.

"I have no idea. I know that I have to get to Kentucky as fast as I can. I'm going immediately there after we get back to the airport. You go ahead and catch your flight and I'll call you when I have some news."

"No, I'm going with you," Serena said. "I can fly out tomorrow."

"No, Serena. This is something I need to handle myself."

"Cameron, after everything I've done for you, I have a right to be there. You owe me this."

Cameron was so tired he didn't even want to argue. Maybe Serena would help him to keep his sanity. So, he agreed to let her accompany him. When they landed in Kerrigan, Cameron and Serena got into his car and headed straight for his hometown. During the time, Cameron was going over what must have happened. His mother, Rebecca Spencer, was really Rachel Marlow as well as Regina Matheson and Ellen Harwood. She'd murdered her own niece, tried to kill her brother and sister-in-law. She'd murdered

Cameron's real mother, Victoria, she'd framed her ex-husband to take the fall for it. She'd most likely murdered Dr. Varden, Rosemary and the body found in the well. Even her own mother; she'd tried to hurt her own mother.

All this time, Cameron saw his mother as a martyr and it was all a lie. She'd been the perfect mother: God-fearing, faithful to her husband, a community worker, a loving housewife, vice-president of the PTA, everything a mother should have been and more. How could she? How could she get away with it for so long? She had no conscience about the fact that she deprived Cameron of his family or that she'd hurt so many other people. And why? Just because she wanted a child? Why not adopt? Why ruin so many lives to get her way? Cameron realized that he'd been living a lie all his life. He'd always respected everything she ever said. He trusted that whatever she told him had to be the truth.

Suddenly, he thought about Caitlyn. Did she know something about Rebecca's involvement? Was Rebecca responsible for Caitlyn's disappearance? Was Caitlyn the reason it took her so long to come back to the hospital on Monday? Was the cabin fire accidental or on purpose? What was Evan trying to tell him? Cameron had a million questions racing around in his head. Who was this woman? Rebecca was a complete stranger to him. How could he look at her without seeing Rachel or Regina? Cameron thought about Garret and his family. Was that why Cameron felt such a connection to this family, why this case was so important to him?

Cameron wondered should he call George to tell him what was going on. He decided against it, because he really wanted to talk to Rebecca. Maybe it wasn't her. Who was he trying to kid? Deep down, Cameron knew that his mother was the woman he's been looking for over the past few weeks, the woman he'd come to despise the more he learned about her. If Rebecca was responsible for Caitlyn's disappearance, what had she done to her? Had she killed her? Obviously, she had no qualms about committing murder to cover her tracks. After they'd been driving for over two and a half hours, Serena,

~ 299 ~

who'd been napping, interrupted his thoughts.

"Cameron, are you okay?"

"What do you think?" Cameron snapped back.

"Sorry. I was just concerned, that's all. You don't have to bite my head off. Your mother's the murderer, not mine."

Serena's words really stung, but they brought him to the reality that the woman he's known as his mother is a murderer. He still hated the way Serena never minced words.

"Do you have to be so callous about the way you say things? Do you realize what I've just learned? Now, while I appreciate everything you've done, it doesn't give you the right to say something like that to me."

"Oh, and you're a lot better, I see. I can't say how I feel, but you can snap at me when the urge hits you!" Serena yelled. "I didn't do this to you, she did."

"Serena, look, I'm not blaming you for everything, but there were some things you had full knowledge about for a while, and you didn't come forward. When you did, you drugged me and stole from me! You had no regard for what I was trying to do, because you were obsessed with your own revenge!"

"Cameron, I've apologized to you a thousand times! I'm helping you now! Doesn't that count for something?"

Cameron thought for a moment. He wasn't mad with Serena, he was mad with Rebecca and he was mad with himself for not realizing it sooner. "Of course it does. Look, let's just take a step backward. I'm sorry for snapping at you. I'm just really confused right now," Cameron said.

"I know you are. I'm sorry, too for what I said. Despite everything that Regina has done, she's still the only mother you've ever known and you love her. I should have been more tactful about the way I said things. Can we call a truce?"

Cameron smiled. "Of course, we can," he said, glancing in Serena's direction.

"So, what are you going to say to her?"

"I have no idea," Cameron sighed. "I mean, they don't

teach you about this in law school. How do I question the woman I thought was my mother about something like this?"

"I don't know. But, I will be there for you, okay?" Serena reassured.

"Thank you, Serena. You know, for someone who drives me insane half the time, you're really helping me to keep it together," Cameron smiled.

"Thanks, I think," Serena smiled back.

"You know, my birthday is in a few days," Cameron commented. "Or at least I think it is."

"Well, happy birthday in advance," Serena said.

"What's happy about it? I just found out that my mother's probably not really my mother, which means my birthday is probably today. How ironic is that, huh?"

"I wish I could make this easier on you," Serena murmured.

"Just being here helps a lot," Cameron said.

They drove along for another 20 minutes talking back and forth when Cameron's phone rang. It was the hospital.

"Hello?" Cameron answered.

"This is Karen O'Reilly with Ludwick Memorial Hospital. I'm trying to reach Cameron Spencer," the woman stated.

"This is Cameron Spencer."

"I'm your father's nurse at Ludwick in the intensive care unit. We wanted to inform you that your father has awakened."

"Really!? Is he okay?" Cameron was relieved.

"He's still a little groggy, and his speech is somewhat difficult to understand, but he seems to be doing better," the nurse said. "He's been trying to ask for you. I've been trying to reach your mother, but I'm not getting an answer at your home."

"Has my mother been there at the hospital?" Cameron asked.

"Not really," the nurse stated. "She was here once yesterday, and she was very upset and felt that she wasn't given enough privacy with her husband. She complained that

~ 301 ~

we were always around and she couldn't visit with him privately. We tried to explain to her how critical it is that we take care of her husband, but our words seemed to fall on deaf ears."

Cameron thought about her obsession to want to be alone with Evan. Evan knew something and she wanted to stop him.

"I'm on my way to the hospital. If my mother gets there before me, do *not* leave her alone with my father," Cameron instructed.

"Yes, sir."

Cameron hung up with the nurse. "My father is awake!" Cameron smiled.

"That's great!" Serena said.

"I knew this wouldn't keep Evan Spencer down."

"That's your dad's name? Evan?"

"Yeah, why?"

"No reason. I'd just never heard you mention it before. Are we going to the hospital first?"

"Yes. I have to see him."

He started understanding more and more now. His mother was so upset when she couldn't be left alone with Evan. She was going to try to kill him. She knew Evan didn't want any extreme measures to be taken to save his life. Therefore, if she stopped his breathing, they wouldn't try to bring him back. So much was starting to make sense. When Cameron stopped by the hospital to visit with Evan, Serena waited on him in the waiting area. Cameron went into the room and noticed that Evan was sleeping. Cameron talked with the nurse for the first fifteen minutes, as she informed him about the progress Evan had made over the past few days.

"Dad?" Cameron called gently, waking him.

"C-C-Cameron," Evan stammered.

"Dad, I'm here. You're going to be okay," Cameron soothed. Cameron wondered if Rebecca had caused his father's illness.

"I-I-I hhhavve s-s-something t-t-to t-t-tellll y-y-you." Evan was clearly struggling with his words.

"Shh, Dad, don't try to talk."

"Y-y-you hhhavvve t-t-to ssstttop h-h-her. Sshhe's n-not who y-y-you th-think sh-she isss."

"Are you talking about Mom?"

"Y-y-yes," Evan said.

"Dad, I'm going to ask you some questions, and I want for you to blink once for yes, and twice for no, okay?" Cameron instructed.

"O-okay."

"Is Mom really Rachel Marlow?"

Evan blinked once.

"Is that what you were trying to tell me the night of your stroke?"

Evan blinked once.

"Is that what you were arguing about?"

Evan blinked once. Then, he spoke again.

"L-l-locket."

"The locket?"

Evan blinked once.

Cameron realized what was going on. "She has the other locket?"

Evan blinked once.

Cameron couldn't believe it. It was really true. Rebecca was Rachel. "Dad, I'm going to go and take care of some things, and I'll be back later, okay?" Cameron said.

"B-be c-caref-ful, s-son," Evan said.

"I will. I love you, Dad," Cameron said.

"I l-love y-you t-too."

Cameron left out of Evan's room and went to the waiting area to get Serena. She wasn't there, so Cameron assumed that maybe she'd gone to the restroom or to the snack machine. He waited a few minutes, and she never returned. He went to the nurses' station.

"Can I help you?" the clerk asked.

"I have a friend who was with me when I came in," Cameron said, describing Serena. "She was about this tall," Cameron said, holding his hand up. "Medium complexion, short, dark hair."

~ 303 ~

"Oh, yes. She came up to the desk and wanted a phone book. I gave her one, and she looked up a number and address, wrote it down, and left."

"What address?" Cameron had the sneaking suspicion that Serena was going to go looking for Rebecca.

"I don't know. She closed the phone book, so it could have been just about anything," the clerk said. "Oh, but she did ask me for the number to a cab, and I dialed it for her. She asked them to meet her out front."

"How long ago was that?"

"Oh, 15-20 minutes maybe. She came up here as soon as you went back to visit with your dad."

"Thank you." Cameron rushed out.

He got to his car and sped out of the parking deck. Was Serena going to confront Rebecca? If his mother was the person who he was starting to find out she was, Serena could be in a lot of danger. He called David upon impulse.

"Hello?"

"David, it's me, Cameron."

"Hi, Cameron. What's up?"

"Have you seen my mother lately?"

"No, I haven't. In fact, I haven't seen her since I left your house yesterday. Why? Is something wrong?"

"A lot's wrong. David, I need your help. I think my mother is the woman I've been looking for."

"What do you mean?" David asked.

"You know, my client's ex-wife," Cameron stated.

"The killer?"

"Yes. Rachel Marlow."

"No, way. That's impossible."

"It's definitely possible, and it's looking more and more like it's true. I'm just leaving the hospital. There's a woman who was with me, and I think she may be on her way out to the house to confront Mom. You're closer than I am, so I need for you to go to the house and check on things. I'm on my way."

"Cameron, if this is the woman you think she is, don't you think you'd better call the police?"

"Dave, she's my mom. I can't just turn her in yet. I love her. I at least want to see if she can explain any of this."

"I understand, but, Cameron, be reasonable."

"Look, I don't have time to argue about it, please just head over to my parents' place."

"I'm leaving now," David said.

"Thanks." Cameron hung up the phone. As luck would have it, he was stopped by every traffic light in town. Finally, Cameron pulled into the yard, and noticed David's jeep was there along with Rebecca's car. He saw David on the front porch ringing the doorbell. Cameron ran to the door.

"Hey, Cameron. No one's answering. Do you have your key?"

"Yeah." Cameron opened the doors, and as they walked through the foyer, he heard voices. It was clearly Serena and Rebecca arguing.

"You killed my father!" Serena yelled.

"Your father deserved to die! He was a fool! He never loved your mother, he never loved you nor your brother! He would have done anything I wanted him to do!"

For the first time, Cameron heard the real Rebecca. Rebecca spoke with such hate and cruelty. Nothing like the Rebecca he knew and loved. They'd not heard him come in. Then, he remembered his father telling him a few weeks back that he had to fix the doorbell on the front door. They'd not even heard David ringing it. Cameron listened further, and peeked around, to see Serena holding a gun on Rebecca. He whispered to David to go back out to the car and call the police. David went outside.

"He was so good to you! He helped you, and you betrayed him! You got him to help you commit murder! What kind of animal are you!?" Serena cried.

"It got me what I wanted. Look, don't take it personally. I cared about Larry. Now, Jessie, don't you think you should put the gun down? It's not going to solve anything by killing me. It won't bring your father back, now will it?"

"Just admit that you killed him!" Serena yelled.

"Okay, okay, okay. So I killed him. I killed a lot of

people. I would do whatever it takes to protect my son."

"You mean to stop him from finding out the truth about who you really are!"

"Cameron loves me!" Rebecca exclaimed. "He'll understand I did all of this for his good. Victoria would have been an awful mother! He needed someone who could shelter him from Garret and Victoria! I had to kill Victoria! Garret took everything from me when he let them operate on me, then Victoria took him from me. Now, doesn't that say to you who the real victim is?"

"Surely you don't mean you!? You've never been a victim your entire life! You're a predator!"

"Not this time. I could never bear children again thanks to him. I deserved to be happy, too. Now, let's be reasonable. Put the gun down." Rebecca started to speak in the same soothing tone she always did.

"Serena, put the gun down," Cameron said, calmly.

Serena turned to look at him. She shook her head as the tears rolled down her face. "No, Cameron! Sh-she killed Daddy! You'd never make her pay! You'd stick her in a mental institution somewhere and she'd never get what she deserves!"

"Serena, no I won't. Please. Put the gun down," Cameron said, walking slowly towards her. Although Serena still had the gun shakily pointed at Rebecca, she was looking at Cameron. As he was trying to convince her to put the gun down, two shots rang out, and Serena fell to the floor. Cameron stared in disbelief.

"Serena!" Cameron rushed to kneel down to her. He pulled the throw cover from the sofa to try and stop the bleeding. Cameron looked up, and his mother was holding a gun. "Mom, put the gun down."

"Son, I loved you! I did all of this for you!" Rebecca cried. "She wanted to kill me, to break up our home! I had to do it! Please say you forgive me and you still love me!"

"Mom, I love you. But, you've got to put the gun down. Please. Enough people have gotten hurt." Cameron stood slowly and walked towards Rebecca.

"You're going to send me away, aren't you?" Rebecca cried, the gun shaking in her hand.

"Mom, I'm going to get you the help you need. Now, please, give me the gun."

Suddenly, Rebecca moved the gun to her own chest. "If you don't love me, I can't live!"

"Mom, please! Don't do it! Please! I won't send you away! Give me the gun."

"Y-you p-promise not to send me away?" Rebecca said, as tears rolled down her face.

"I won't send you away. Come on, Mom, give me the gun."

Rebecca was just about to lower the gun when she heard the police sirens in the distance.

"No! You called the police! I'm going to kill myself, here and now!"

"Mom, please! Please don't! Give me the gun. We'll talk about it."

"Make them go away," Rebecca cried.

"Okay, I'll make them go away." Cameron eased towards her. At that moment, the sirens stopped, and Cameron knew they must have been outside. "See? The sirens are gone. Now, give me the gun, and let's talk about it."

Rebecca finally lowered the gun, and fell sobbing to the floor. As she did this, Cameron retrieved the gun from her, and three police officers burst in to apprehend her.

"Cameron! I had to kill her! Victoria would have never been a good mother to you! You were my son! She just carried you!" Rebecca was yelling as they were escorting her out.

Cameron stared in disbelief. He checked on Serena. Blood was pouring from the wounds in her chest and stomach. He checked her pulse. It was very weak. He heard the other officer calling for a paramedic to be sent out.

"Serena? Serena can you hear me?" Cameron pleaded, trying desperately to save her life. David came rushing into the house.

"Cameron are you okay?" David asked.

"Yeah, I'm fine. I have to stop the bleeding. I need a towel!"

"I'll get you one," David said, rushing to the linen closet. He quickly brought back a towel and gave it to Cameron. Cameron applied pressure to her wounds.

"Serena, can you hear me?"

"C-Cameron, w-we d-did it. W-we got her," Serena whispered as she smiled weakly.

"Serena, you're going to be okay."

"I-I-I can rest in peace now," Serena said, as her body went limp.

She died there in Cameron's arms. Cameron cried over the loss of his new friend. Serena had helped him so much, and Cameron had come to trust her. Why did she have to go looking for Regina on her own? When the paramedic arrived, it was too late. Cameron looked out the window, and Rebecca was in the back of one of the many squad cars that were there. He went outside, where George was talking to another officer.

"Can I talk to her for a minute?" Cameron asked. He had to find out where Caitlyn was.

"Just for a minute, then we've got to take her in. Cameron, I'm sorry about all of this. I was starting to get a little suspicious of your mother, and I had a check ran on her this morning. Your mother's been under five different identities in the past 27 years. It's a wonder she's gotten away with it for so long."

"Five?"

"Yeah, Rachel Marlow, which is actually her name, Regina Matheson, Ellen Harwood, Alice Cramer, and Rebecca Marrick Spencer."

"I can't believe it. How did you find out?"

"We ran her prints through, and she came back under all these different identities."

"How did you get her finger prints?" Cameron asked.

"Yesterday, I came by to visit your mother, and before I rung the bell, I could see from the window that she was sitting at the kitchen table looking at the locket," George explained. "When I rang the doorbell, she jumped slightly and

~ 308 ~

put the locket in a drawer before letting me in. When I walked in, she seemed nervous, not really wanting for me to be there. Apparently, David and Linda had left a little while before I got there. I asked her what she was looking at when I came in. She told me it was an old gift she'd gotten from her deceased husband. I asked if I could see it, and hesitantly, she showed it to me. I commented that it was a beautiful locket. I noticed the inscription we were talking about and the special markings."

"What happened then?"

"I couldn't do anything until I had a little more proof, so I asked her for a cup of water to go, and she fixed one for me. I brought the cup back to the station, and had her prints lifted from it. Her prints came back, because apparently, your mom has served jail time a few times. Mostly minor stuff, like theft and a couple of DUI's."

"I-I don't even know her," Cameron said, shaking his head.

"None of us did, Cameron," George said. "Do you want to represent her, or should we get public counsel?" George asked.

"I-I don't know," Cameron sighed. "How do I defend her?"

"I'll take care of getting her public counsel, and if you decide to take her case, you can discuss it with them."

"Thanks, George." Cameron walked over to the squad car and got in beside his mother. He looked at her, and she seemed dazed, as if she had no idea what was going on or where she was. Cameron knew he had to try to get through to her because he needed to find Caitlyn. "Mom, how are you?"

"Oh, Cameron! When did you get home?" she smiled.

"Not long ago." Cameron realized she was clearly not in her right mind. "Um, Mom have you seen my friend, Caitlyn?"

"Caitlyn? Caitlyn's gone," Rebecca smiled.

"Gone where?" Cameron asked.

"I put her away, where she can't hurt you anymore. She was a bad girl and needed to be punished for what she did to you. I told you I'd always take care of you."

"Yes, Mom, you did. How did you punish Caitlyn?"

"Does it matter?" Rebecca said calmly. "I told you I'd take care of you."

"Mom, please tell me, what did you do to Caitlyn?"

"I torched her," Rebecca said, laughing hysterically.

George came over to the door and opened it.

"Cameron, we've got to take her in. I'll keep working on her."

"Give me a minute George. Mom, what did you say? Did you say you torched her? Was Caitlyn in the cabin?" Cameron asked fearfully.

"Of course she was, Cameron," Rebecca smiled calmly. "I killed her for you."

"Oh, my God! Mom, what have you done?!" Cameron yelled. He grabbed her by the shoulders and shook her fiercely. "You killed her?!"

It took two officers to pull Cameron away. At that moment, one officer got in beside Rebecca.

"Cameron, don't leave me! Help me! I-I did it for you! Tell them to let me go! Cameron! Ricky! Richard! Richard! Daddy! Daddy, please help me! Don't let them take me, Daddy! Daddy, help!" Rebecca was screaming hysterically.

"Oh, my God!" Cameron screamed. David was close by, trying to hold him back. "She killed her, David, she killed Caitlyn!"

"Come on, Cameron, it's going to be okay," David said calmly.

Cameron turned towards his best friend. "She's gone! David she's gone!" Cameron sobbed.

"Mr. Spencer?" an officer called to Cameron. "I know this is hard for you, but we need to get a statement about what went on. The cabin is being combed now to see if Ms. Frazier's body is in there. But, we have to know what went on with Ms. Felton."

"I-I can't handle this now," Cameron cried, holding his hands up and walking away.

"Mr. Spencer? Mr. Spencer?" the officer called after him.

"Give him time," David said. "He's just had a few devastating blows. It's not that easy to take it all in."

Things were really chaotic for the next hour, during which time they came to pick up Serena's body. How would he go on without Caitlyn? Was Rebecca telling the truth? How would he call her mother and break the news to her. He was also faced with the dreaded job of calling Serena's brother to tell him that his sister was dead. How could he do it? This day had gotten to be more than he could bear. He went into the house, which was officially considered a crime scene. He sat on the sofa with his hands clasped together under his chin staring at Serena's bloodstains. David came in and placed his hand on Cameron's shoulder.

"How are you holding up?"

Cameron shook his head. "I-I can't believe all of this. Oh, God! Caitlyn! What will I do without you?!" Cameron sobbed.

"Are you sure she wasn't just talking crazy? There's no definite proof that Caitlyn was in the cabin," David reasoned.

"No, I think for the first time she may have actually been telling the truth. She's kept me from my real family. And she's harmed the woman I love. How do I forgive her?"

"Cameron, look, you're very emotional right now. Come on over to our house, so we can talk. If you want to sit up and talk all night, that's fine, if you want to lie down and get some rest, that's fine. But, you've got to get out of this house," David suggested.

"I'm not going anywhere until we know if Caitlyn's body is in that cabin."

"They'll call us, Cameron. You've got to get away from here tonight."

"No! If the love of my life is in there, I want to know." Cameron got up and went to the backdoor where he watched helplessly as a crew went through the ruins of the fire.

"Don't put yourself through this. Come on home with

~ 311 ~

me and they'll call as soon as they know something. Agreed?"

"I'm not leaving, David!"

"Oh, yes you are! Dammit, Cameron, you've got to get away from here. What do you want? To see them bring her body out?!"

"Damn you, David! How could you say such a thing!?"

David turned Cameron towards him. "Because you need to be realistic. I've known you since we were five. You don't need to see what they bring out of those ruins!" David said, shaking Cameron.

Cameron knew that David would be stubborn, and there was no need to argue with him. Cameron finally conceded and went home with David. He had to call Dr. Varden anyway to tell him the news. He wanted to wait before calling Caitlyn's mom. He had to hold out hope that she was still alive. They drove to David's house in silence, with the day's events reeling through Cameron's head. What now? What could Cameron do now? Did Rebecca really kill her? When they pulled up at David's house, Linda met them at the door. She hugged Cameron.

"Cameron, I'm so sorry. If there's anything I can do, let me know," Linda said.

"Thanks, Linda. I don't know what to say or do right now. I can't believe all of this has happened." In one day, Cameron's entire life had changed. David and Linda showed him to the guest room that Linda had already gotten prepared for him. When Cameron was alone, he knew it was time to make the dreaded phone call. He looked into his wallet and retrieved Dr. Varden's personal card. As he dialed the number, he practiced what he would say.

"Hello, Varden residence," a woman said.

"I'm trying to reach Dr. Lawrence Varden."

"May I ask whose calling?"

"Cameron Spencer."

"Dr. Varden is at the hospital, but Mrs. Varden is here. Would you like to speak with her?"

"Yes, please." Cameron waited while the housekeeper

got Dr. Varden's wife to the phone.

"Hello?" the woman answered.

"Is this Mrs. Varden?" Cameron asked.

"Yes it is. What can I do for you?"

"I'm Cameron Spencer, and I'm an attorney. I met with your husband a couple of weeks ago."

"Yes, Larry mentioned that. What is this concerning?"

"Mrs. Varden, this is concerning his sister, Serena."

"What about her?"

"Mrs. Varden, I hate to be the one to tell you this over the phone, but Serena was killed this evening."

"Oh, my God!" Mrs. Varden yelled, dropping the phone.

"Mrs. Varden? Mrs. Varden?" Cameron called out. He could hear Mrs. Varden crying hysterically, calling out Serena's name.

Eventually, the maid retrieved the phone. "Mr. Spencer, Mrs. Varden is very upset. Let me take down a number where Dr. Varden can contact you, because he will want to talk to you."

Cameron gave her his cell number as well as the number at David's house. Cameron hung up with the maid and looked at the clock. It was after 10:30, and Cameron was exhausted. His mind went to Caitlyn. He felt as if his heart was breaking into a million pieces. He sobbed loudly, calling out her name. He remembered their last meeting and how he was too stubborn to tell her how much he truly loved her. He wanted to spend his life with her, and now it was too late. He wanted to punch something, break something. Anything to relieve him of the hurt. When he couldn't think anymore, he decided to take a shower to try to wash away his tired senses. He had no idea what was going to happen now. Caitlyn's dead. No matter how much he wanted to believe she wasn't, Rebecca admitted that she did it. On top of everything else, he had a family that he knew absolutely nothing about, and a mother who he thought he knew but really didn't. After Cameron got out of the shower, and climbed into bed, his cell phone rang. It had to be Dr. Varden returning his call.

"Hello?"

"Mr. Spencer? Is-is it true? Is Serena dead?"

Cameron could tell he had been crying.

"I'm afraid so."

"How?! What happened?!"

"She was shot."

"By whom?!"

"Dr. Varden, your sister was murdered by the woman you knew as Regina Matheson."

"What?"

"It's true. There was a confrontation, and Regina shot her. This may not be of much solace to you, but the police have Ms. Matheson in custody."

"In custody? That bitch should be dead! Where are you? Where's my sister?"

"We're in Kentucky."

"Tell me where, and I'm taking the first flight out."

Cameron told Dr. Varden exactly where they were. Cameron knew that Dr. Varden would have a million questions for him when he arrived. Cameron tried to sleep after hanging up with Dr. Varden. He had Caitlyn on his mind, and the idea that she was gone got to him for the better part of the night. Every time he closed his eyes, he saw Caitlyn's beautiful smile and her haunting eyes. He wanted to see her in his mind, but then, he thought of what she might have gone through in her death. This was enough to cause him not to sleep a wink.

Chapter
14

After a restless night, Cameron got up early the next morning. After getting dressed, he knew he had to know if they found anything in the cabin. Was Rebecca telling the truth? Did she kill Caitlyn? Before he could call the Fire Marshall, David and Linda's phone rang. There was news from the fire site. David knocked on Cameron's door.

"Cameron, it's Steve," David said, giving him the phone.

"Thanks," Cameron said. He inhaled deeply and closed his eyes. "Hello?"

"Cameron?"

"Yes, Steve?"

"There was a body in the cabin," Steve said.

"Oh, God! Caitlyn!" Cameron sobbed. He dropped the phone, and David picked it up from the floor.

"Steve? He's going to call you back," David said. David hung up the phone. "Come on, Cameron, sit down. Linda!" David yelled.

Linda came rushing into the room. "What's wrong?"

"Help me with him," David said.

"Come on, Cameron, sit down," Linda said gently, leading him along with David to the bed.

"She's gone! David, Rebecca killed Caitlyn!" Cameron cried.

Linda hugged him to her. "Shh, it's all going to be okay. We're here for you."

"Oh, God, Caitlyn!" Cameron yelled through his tears. He broke down and cried as his life shattered before him.

Linda and David stayed with Cameron as long as necessary. After about an hour, Cameron managed to get his bearings. At that point, he and David went back to his parents' home. Cameron didn't know why he wanted to go back to the scene of the crime. Not only did Serena die there, so did Caitlyn. When they arrived, the house was sealed off. Cameron went in because no officers were there at the time to stop him. When he walked into the living room, he once again saw the blood stains from Serena's body on the carpet. He knew he could never live in that house again, and he didn't figure Evan would want to either. He had to make some major decisions about his father. He was going to be in rehab for the next few months, and Cameron knew Evan would need him. Cameron had to figure out how to get on with his life. He had to face the reality that it would be without Caitlyn. He realized he'd not had the heart to call her family to let them know. He knew they had a right to know, but he knew that once he told them, it would make it a reality that he wasn't ready to accept. Upon impulse, Cameron went upstairs to the room that Caitlyn was using.

When he walked in, he looked around and sighed. He looked over to the dresser and noticed her charm bracelet. He picked it up and caressed it. Once again, he started to cry just thinking about her. He wondered what happened to her luggage and decided to look in the closet. There were both of her suitcases and carry bag neatly tucked away. Rebecca had managed to hide them probably thinking she'd have time to dispose of them later. A few minutes later, David knocked on

~ 316 ~

the door and walked in.

"Hey, you okay?" David asked.

"I wish I could say I was," Cameron said quietly.

"Cameron, let's get out of this house. You don't need to be here," David sighed.

"Where else am I supposed to go?" Cameron asked.

"Anywhere but here," David advised. "Come on, you've got to get out of here."

"Fine," Cameron sighed. He looked at her charm bracelet again. "Caitlyn, I'm so sorry. I'm sorry I couldn't save you."

"I talked to George this morning," David said, as they walked down the stairs.

"What did he say?"

"Rebecca doesn't even realize what's going on." David shook his head. "She was right on the edge, Cameron. There's nothing you could have done."

"I couldn't protect my own mother, I couldn't protect the woman I love."

"Cameron, she did this to herself."

They were interrupted by Cameron's cell phone ringing. "Hello?" Cameron answered.

"Cameron?" George responded.

"Hi, George. Is everything okay?"

"Cameron, I've got some important news to tell you," George sighed.

"Oh, no, what now?" Cameron sighed. Things were already bad enough.

"First of all, your mother has escaped."

"What?! How did that happen!?"

"I had a guard with her around the clock. She was sitting handcuffed at one of the desks wanting to make a phone call, and she asked if she could go to the restroom."

"Didn't a guard go in there with her?"

"Yes, a female guard. Unfortunately, she's new, and when they got in there, Rebecca over-powered her and knocked her out. She climbed out of the window. Apparently, she stole the keys to the cuffs and her gun, and got away.

~ 317 ~

She's probably heading your way, Cameron. She's so out of touch with reality, I don't think she even cares anymore."

"I'm going out to look for her," Cameron said.

"Don't do anything alone. She's upset and out of control."

"But, I'm her son. She won't hurt me."

"Don't be too sure. Let us handle it," George said. "Not to mention Caitlyn--"

"No, George! Your 'handling it' is what caused my mother to escape in the first place! I'll find her myself!"

"Cameron, don't do anything stu-" George started. Cameron hung up on him before he could finish.

"How did Rebecca escape?" David asked.

"An incompetent guard! She's killed Caitlyn, so why does she insist upon making it worse for herself? Why didn't I see it? I get the feeling she's going to try to come to me."

"Cameron, let the police handle this," David advised.

"Hell no! If they find her, they'll kill her! I'll never forgive her for killing my real mother and Caitlyn, but I don't want her dead."

"They won't kill her if they can help it. You know George would do anything to avoid killing Rebecca," David reasoned.

"Who's to say he'll have a choice? Rebecca's sick, and out of touch with reality! There's been enough killing!" Cameron said, going into the kitchen. His cell phone rang again and he ignored it, noticing it was George.

David followed him. "Cameron, you have to calm down. You're not doing yourself any good by being irrational."

"I'm beyond irrational at this point! This is crazy! How could they let her escape?" Cameron yelled. "God, I need your help. Where is Rebecca? God, what has she done? Why did she kill Caitlyn? What more can she do?" Cameron said, as a tear rolled down his face.

A few moments later, there was a knock at the back door. David noticed it was Joe and let him in.

"Joe, where have you been?" Cameron asked. "I

haven't seen you. Where were you when the fire broke out?!"

"I-I'm sorry, Mr. Cameron. I've been at my sister's house. Can you come somewhere with me?" Joe asked.

"Where?" Cameron asked.

"I need you to come with me to my sister's house," Joe said.

"What's this all about, Joe?" David asked.

"Please, just come with me," Joe said.

"Does this have anything to do with Rebecca? She's escaped from jail," Cameron said.

"I haven't seen her, but you really need to come with me," Joe said.

"Fine," Cameron sighed. He was in such a daze until he didn't care anymore. "David, stay here just in case she comes here. If she does, call the police."

"Okay," David agreed.

He got into Joe's truck with him. Cameron couldn't figure out why Joe wanted him to go with him to his sister's home. He knew that Joe's sister was in her late fifties. Maybe she was sick and he needed help with her. When they were down the street from the house, they noticed it was in flames.

"Oh my God!" Joe said.

"Isn't that your sister's house?" Cameron asked.

"Yes, and she's in there with Miss Caitlyn!" Joe yelled.

"What?! How did that happen?" Cameron asked. Cameron immediately pulled out his cell phone and called 911. He quickly gave Joe's sister's address and hung up.

"We've got to get in there!" Joe said, jumping out of the truck.

Cameron jumped out as well, and stood frozen as he saw Rebecca holding a gas can with a smile on her face.

"Burn, you bitch!" she yelled.

"Ma, what are you doing?" Cameron asked calmly, walking in her direction. "Answer me!"

"Oh, hi, Son," she smiled. "I was just burning up a lot of dead weight."

"Put the gas can down," Cameron said calmly. He looked at the house, which was almost engulfed in flames.

"Mrs. Spencer, please! My sister's in there!" Joe begged.

"Then, she shouldn't have tried to save that bitch! She'll just have to burn with her!"

"No!" Joe said, running into the house.

"Joe! Wait!" Cameron then rushed towards the house.

"No, Cameron! Let them all die! It just needs to be you and me!" Rebecca pleaded.

"No, Mom! Enough is enough!" Cameron then rushed into the house.

Joe's sister was passed out in the hallway as the house was filled with smoke. Cameron tried to cover his face as he called out for Caitlyn.

"Joe, get her out of here," Cameron said.

"What about Miss Caitlyn?" Joe asked.

"I'll get her. Just get Donna out!"

Joe picked his sister up and took her to safety out the back door.

"Caitlyn!" Cameron called out. "Caitlyn, can you hear me!?"

"Help!" someone was screaming. He was relieved that it was Caitlyn's voice. "Someone, please help me!"

"I'm coming! Keep screaming, Sweetheart!" Cameron said as he coughed.

"Cameron!" Caitlyn screamed. "Save me, Cameron!"

Finally, Cameron made his way to the bedroom where Caitlyn was lying down. He lifted her into his arms and ran out of the room. He couldn't go out the back way as Joe had done because it was already engulfed in flames. He finally managed to make his way to the front as a beam fell behind them, barely missing them. He got her out and laid her gently on the ground. Caitlyn had blacked out and wasn't breathing. He immediately started mouth to mouth on her.

"No! Cameron, she's not worth it! Don't make me kill you!" Rebecca yelled pulling a gun out.

"Ma, you don't know what you're doing. You're not going to hurt me," Cameron said, still trying to save Caitlyn.

"I-I don't want to! I did all of this for you! You have

~ 320 ~

to believe me, Cameron! When I heard them at the police station saying they'd just found out that Caitlyn was safe here, I knew I had to come finish what I started. Let her die! She doesn't deserve you!"

"I have to help her!" Cameron argued, as Caitlyn coughed, to Cameron's relief.

"No! I'll kill you!" Rebecca yelled as a shot rang out.

Cameron felt the bullet pierce his shoulder, but he continued to help Caitlyn. She was pale and weak.

"Caitlyn! Are you okay?" Cameron yelled.

"Cameron! Help me!" she cried weakly. "I-I've been shot."

"I know, but you're going to be fine now," Cameron soothed.

"I-I thought I'd never see you again!" Caitlyn cried, weakly.

"Shh. I'm right here. You're safe now," Cameron soothed. "When did my mother shoot you?"

"A couple of days ago. Sh-She thought I was dead." At that moment, Caitlyn passed out again.

"Caitlyn!" Cameron yelled. He checked her pulse and breathing and both were fine. She'd passed out.

"Why did you save her!?" Rebecca yelled. "I'd gotten rid of her for you! You don't need her! I have to finish her off!" She then aimed the gun at Caitlyn.

"You need to put the gun down. You can't keep hurting people like this," Cameron tried to reason with her.

"Y-You left me, just like Garret!" Rebecca yelled. "I hate you!"

"No you don't. Please let me help you," Cameron soothed. He could hear the sirens in the distance. "Put the gun down."

"If I can't have you, no one can!" Rebecca yelled. Before Rebecca could shoot, a shot rang out and she fell to the ground.

Cameron saw George, who'd shot Rebecca in the leg. George rushed towards her with another officer, as he got the gun away from her.

~ 321 ~

"I did this for you!" Rebecca cried. "Y-You're going to leave me!"

George and another officer apprehended Rebecca, and put her in cuffs. Cameron was thankful that George shot her in the leg, because it could have been a lot worse. He looked at Caitlyn, who had already lost a lot of blood.

"Please, Caitlyn, don't die!" Cameron cried. "I can't lose you!"

Shortly afterwards, the firefighters and paramedics arrived and they immediately started to put out the fire and treated Caitlyn's wounds which had opened up again, and got her into the ambulance. They treated Rebecca's leg and Cameron's shoulder as well. Donna needed a little oxygen, but for the most part she was okay. They wanted to take all of them to the hospital to have them treated properly. Cameron refused to leave Caitlyn's side, as they put Rebecca in the squad car and drove off with her. Joe took his sister to the hospital in his truck, and the paramedic immediately rushed Caitlyn to the hospital, with Cameron riding in the ambulance with her. He held her hand the entire time. He watched her as if she'd disappear if he took his eyes off of her for a second. They arrived at the emergency room of the hospital and rushed Caitlyn in on a stretcher. Cameron was right by her side.

"Sir, you'll have to wait out here," the nurse told him.

"Please, save her," Cameron said.

"He needs to be treated for a GSW to the shoulder," the paramedic said.

They immediately rushed Cameron into an examining room to treat his shoulder. The bullet grazed his shoulder, and didn't leave any major damage. Considering how good Rebecca was with her target, he knew that Rebecca didn't really want to kill him. After sending him to radiology to have his shoulder x-rayed to make sure everything was okay, they gave him something for the pain and released him. When Cameron came out, David was there waiting on him.

"David, how long have you been here?" Cameron asked.

"I got here a few minutes ago. George called me and

~ 322 ~

told me what happened. Apparently, Joe called them right before coming to your house to tell you. He told George that Caitlyn was with his sister. When George called you, he was trying to explain everything to you, but you hung up before he could give you the news about Caitlyn. After I talked to him, I left immediately after that from your house."

"I'm so glad you're here," Cameron sighed. "Have they said anything about Caitlyn yet?" Cameron asked David.

"No, not yet," David said, shaking his head.

"I don't know what I'll do if I lose her. I just got her back. Do you have any idea how agonizing the past few days have been, not knowing if she was alive or not? And then, Rebecca saying she'd killed her. She's my life, Dave."

"I know she is. Everything's going to be fine. I honestly believe they got her here in time."

"What if Joe hadn't saved her? She would have been killed for sure. And she could still die from that gun shot. My God, what kind of person is Rebecca?"

"A sick woman, Cameron. Look, I'm here for you, okay?" David said.

"I know you are. Man, I don't know what I would have done without you over the past 24 hours."

"We're best friends for a reason. I'm going to go and call Linda. I'm sure she's worried by now since we haven't shown back up at the house."

"Okay. I'll be right here," Cameron stated. As if anyone could get him to leave Caitlyn's side. Cameron immediately thought of Caitlyn's parents, the detectives, and those at the firm who were concerned. He saw George by the nurses' station. He walked over to him.

"Where's Rebecca?" Cameron asked.

"She's been checked out here in ER for her leg wound, and she's in custody," George said. "How's Caitlyn?"

"I don't know. They haven't said anything yet," Cameron said. "I have to call her family and Phil to let them know what's going on. At least now I won't have to tell them that she died."

"Let me know if I can do anything. We're going to

~ 323 ~

have to do a police report. Do you have time to do that now? We need to know exactly what happened," George said.

"Sure. I'll tell you everything I can," Cameron agreed.

For the next few minutes, one of the officers on the scene took Cameron's statement. Afterwards, he remembered that he'd not contacted Caitlyn's family yet. He knew her mother was worried sick about her. Especially since he didn't call her the night before. Now, he was glad that he didn't since Caitlyn was still alive. He went back to the nurses' station to see if there was any word.

"No, Sir. They're still in with her. The doctor will come out and talk to you as soon as he knows something."

"I have a few calls to make. So, I'll be right outside. Please come and get me the minute they come out."

"Yes sir."

Cameron walked right outside the emergency room and called Caitlyn's mother.

"Hello?" Mrs. Harding answered anxiously.

"Mrs. Harding? This is Cameron."

"Oh, my. You have some news don't you?" Mrs. Harding said solemnly.

"Yes, I do. Caitlyn's been found," Cameron said.

"Oh, thank God! Is-is she okay? Is she alive?"

"She's alive. She's been shot, and we're here at the emergency room. The doctors are in with her now."

"Is she going to be okay?"

"Right now, I don't know," Cameron said despondently.

"I'll be there as fast as I can. Where are you?"

Once again, Cameron found himself explaining where he was. After hanging up with her, Cameron called Phillip to let him know what happened. Phillip couldn't have been more relieved to find out that Caitlyn was still alive. Cameron briefly explained to Phillip that his mother, Rebecca Spencer, was really Rachel Marlow. Phillip was shocked to say the least. He apologized to Cameron for all that he'd gone through. Phillip also told him that he would take care of contacting the clemency board to let them know about the new development, especially Rebecca's confession. After finishing his phone calls, Cameron went back inside to see what was going on. He saw David back in the waiting area.

"Anything yet?" Cameron asked.

"No, not yet. Where were you?"

"I had to make a few calls. What time is it?"

David looked at his watch. "It's almost 1 pm. Why?"

"Dr. Varden should be here soon. He's supposed to call the minute he gets here. He has my cell number as well as your number at home. The only problem is, he can't call me on the cell phone because I have to turn it off while I'm in the hospital."

"I'll call Linda back and see if he's called there."

"Thanks, Man."

While David was gone to use the phone again, the doctor came out to talk to Cameron.

"Mr. Spencer?"

"Dr. Moreland." Cameron shook his hand. He remembered him as the same doctor who treated his father a few short weeks before.

"Your friend Caitlyn is going to be just fine."

"Thank goodness! When can I see her?"

"Pretty soon. We were able to remove the bullet and we've done several x-rays, and the bullet missed all of her vital organs. It seems to have hit her on the lower left side of her torso. She lost a lot of blood, so we're giving her a transfusion now. It's a miracle she stayed alive for over two days. If Donna hadn't treated her, she wouldn't have survived. You have Donna to thank for saving her life. She's going to be on antibiotics because the wound is a little infected."

"And nothing vital was wounded?"

"No. She's going to be okay. She's going to have to stay in the hospital for a couple of days, but after that, she can go home."

"Thank you so much doctor. Can I go in and see her now?"

"In a little while. She inhaled a lot of smoke, so respiratory is with her now giving her another treatment," Dr.

Moreland explained. "She was complaining that she couldn't catch her breath a few minutes ago. So, I'd say in about half an hour you should be able to go back to see her. How's your shoulder?"

"It's fine. I'm just glad I didn't have to be admitted," Cameron said.

"Why don't you go and visit with your father, then come back?" Dr. Moreland suggested.

"Okay. That's a good idea. First, I have to find Donna to thank her."

"I think she's in Room Five," Dr. Moreland said.

"Thanks for everything, Dr. Moreland," Cameron smiled.

"You're welcome. I'm just glad this all had a happy ending," the doctor smiled.

Cameron then went into Donna's room, knocking slightly before going in. Joe was there holding her hand. She looked at Cameron and smiled.

"Is Caitlyn going to be okay?" Donna asked.

"She's going to be fine. I can't thank you enough. Either of you," Cameron smiled looking at Donna then at Joe. "Tell me what happened." Cameron sat down in a chair close to Donna.

"The other day, I came back a little early from an errand for Mr. Spencer," Joe said. "I had my truck parked out back, so Mrs. Spencer didn't see it. I saw Mrs. Spencer with a gun on Ms. Caitlyn, making her walk down to the cabin. I kinda hid 'cause I didn't know what was going on. Then, I saw Mrs. Spencer shoot Ms. Caitlyn. Mrs. Spencer then grabbed two gas cans and put them in the trunk of her car and sped off like crazy. I rushed up to the cabin and saw Ms. Caitlyn laid out on the floor. I picked her up, and put a blanket down in the truck and laid her down on it. I was scared to take her to the hospital, so I took her to Donna."

"When Joe got there, I didn't know what to think," Donna said. "He came telling me he needed my help. He brought Caitlyn in, and I treated her, but I couldn't remove the bullet. I wanted to take her to the hospital, but Joe kept telling

~ 326 ~

me that Rebecca would kill him. We kept her at my house, and I finally convinced Joe to call the police and tell you after we found out Rebecca had been arrested. When he called the police, he immediately left and went back to your house to tell you. About 20 minutes later, I heard a noise outside, and all of a sudden, I saw nothing but flames. I went down the hall to try to see if Caitlyn could walk okay, but the smoke got the better of me and I passed out. The next thing I remember was Joe shaking me as I was laid out in my back yard."

"This is all so unbelievable. I don't think I'll ever be able to repay either of you for what you've done," Cameron said. "If there's ever anything you need, let me know."

"Thank you, Mr. Cameron," Joe smiled.

"Donna, don't worry about your house, I'll take care of everything," Cameron offered.

"The house is insured, so you don't have to worry about it," Donna said.

"But, it was clearly arson. The insurance company may try to get out of paying. Please, let me do this for you," Cameron said.

"Okay, we'll talk about it all later. For now, go check on Caitlyn," Donna smiled.

"I am. The doctor said it would be a little while, so I'm going to go visit my dad for now," Cameron said.

As Cameron walked out of the room, he saw David. "What did the doctor say about Caitlyn?"

"He told me she's going to be just fine. At least something good has come from this," Cameron sighed.

"And what about Donna?" David asked.

"She's great. I can never thank her enough for what she's done," Cameron smiled. "She saved Caitlyn's life."

"Yes, she did," David smiled.

"I almost forgot to ask you. Did Linda say if Dr. Varden had called?"

"He's not called so far. But, she promised to have the hospital to overhead page me the minute he gets there."

"Good. I'm going to go and visit my dad. You want to come?"

"Sure. What are you going to tell him?"

"I've no idea. He already knows the truth about Rebecca."

"Come on. Let's go," David said.

Cameron and David walked over to the intensive care unit just as visiting time was about to begin. Cameron talked with the nurse who had Evan, and she told him that his father was progressing beautifully. She even informed him that Evan would be moving out to the step-down unit the following day. Nothing pleased Cameron more than finding out that despite what Rebecca had tried to do, his father and Caitlyn were going to be okay. Too bad he couldn't say the same for Serena. Cameron and David visited with him for the entire 20 minutes allowed, with Cameron filling Evan in on what had happened. As they were walking out, David heard his name paged to call the operator. When he dialed the operator from a guest phone, they told him that it was Linda. After hanging up with Linda, he told Cameron that the Vardens had arrived and were at the airport. They were renting a car and would be there in about an hour or so.

Cameron and David walked back over to the emergency room where they told him he could visit with Caitlyn. David agreed to stay in the waiting area, knowing that Cameron wanted some time alone with Caitlyn. He walked into her room, and noticed that her arm was bandaged up. The nurse explained that she had first degree burns on her arm from the fire. He walked over to her bedside. He looked at her and smiled, thinking about how only a few short weeks ago, he couldn't stand this woman. Now, he wanted to spend the rest of his life with her.

"Caitlyn?" he whispered, holding her hand. "Can you hear me?"

Caitlyn's eyes slowly opened. "Cameron? Is it really you, or am I dreaming?"

Cameron smiled. "It's really me. I talked with the doctor and he says you're going to be just fine."

"Oh, Cameron! I have so much to tell you!" Caitlyn started to cry.

"Shh. It's okay. I know the truth. I know about my mother and everything."

"I-I realized it when I saw the locket at the cookout."

"How did you know?"

"I saw the locket earlier on the day your father got sick while you and your father were outside," Caitlyn said tearfully. "The clasp on my charm bracelet broke again, and Rebecca told me she had something to fix it. She and I went into your parents' bedroom, and I saw the locket on a necklace in her jewelry box. I commented on how beautiful it was, and she told me it had been the last gift from your real father before he died. I examined it and noticed the inscription. She told me that he had an exclusive jeweler design it for her."

"I'm sorry Caitlyn that you've had to suffer like this!"

"The important thing is I'm okay now, and I'm here with you. Where is Rebecca?"

"She's in jail. So much has happened over the past couple of days. It's unbelievable. We've had so many people looking for you. Your family's on their way now."

"Joe saved my life. If it weren't for him, I would have died in that cabin."

"I know. I've been going crazy looking for you. Then, yesterday, Rebecca told me that she'd killed you and burned you in the cabin." Cameron caressed her hand as he spoke. "I felt as if my whole world had been destroyed. I hated her for what I thought she'd done. Then, when Joe came this morning to the house and brought me back to his sister's house, I still didn't realize it was because you were alive. When we saw Donna's house engulfed in flames, he told me what was going on. He ran in, and I noticed Rebecca standing in front of the house smiling as it burned. I ran in after Joe. Joe got Donna out okay. And I heard you scream out for help. Those flames weren't going to stop me from getting to you."

"Cameron, there's something I want to say to you."

"What is it?"

"I love you. When we first met, I fought it so hard. I was so mean to you because I didn't want you to see the real me. But, you did, despite all my efforts. Sometimes, I think

~ 329 ~

I've loved you since the day we met, and I swore that if I lived through this, I'd tell you the first chance I got."

"I said the same thing, that if I ever found you, I'd tell you just what you mean to me. Caitlyn, I love you, too."

Caitlyn smiled at Cameron as a tear ran down the side of her face. He smiled, and leaned down to kiss her. He never wanted to let her go. Shortly afterwards, the nurse came in to tell them that Caitlyn was being moved to a room.

"She'll be in room 326. You can stay with her as long as you like," the nurse smiled.

Shortly afterwards, they came in to transport Caitlyn to her room. Cameron went out to let David know that Caitlyn was going to be fine.

"That's good news, Cameron. Is there anything else I can do for you?" David asked.

"Dave, you've done so much for me already. But, if you can meet with Dr. Varden and take him to the police station, that would be great. Let him know that I'll talk with him later about everything as soon as I finish up here."

"I'll take care of everything for you. You stay with Caitlyn, and tell her I hope she recovers well."

"Thanks," Cameron smiled.

David left after that, and Cameron went to the third floor. Once again, he had to wait because they had to get her settled into her room. Cameron used that time to call George again.

"George, David is going to be bringing Dr. Lawrence Varden to see you. He's Serena Felton's brother. They'll probably be there in about an hour or so."

"Okay. I'll take care of everything," George stated.

Cameron hesitated briefly before asking his next question. "How's my mom?" Cameron asked.

"She's not good. She keeps asking what we've done with you. She's talking out of her head. Quite honestly, Cameron, I thought she was faking at first, but now I'm not so sure."

"Do you think she's really unaware of what she's done?"

~ 330 ~

"I don't know. Either she's a great actress, or she really is detached from reality. How's Caitlyn?"

"She's doing fine. The bullet didn't hit any vital organs, and she had a burn on her arm, but the doctor says she should make a full recovery, mostly thanks to Donna and Joe."

"Cameron, I'm going to need to get a statement from her, and actually Joe, too since he witnessed Rebecca shoot Caitlyn. Do you think Caitlyn's up for it today?"

"I'm waiting now to go in and visit her again. I'll ask her and I'll give you a call if she feels like it. Her family's on the way now. They should be here some time this afternoon."

"Good. I've talked with the detective they hired as well as the one that works for your firm. Everything has been squared away. The FBI will want to talk to Caitlyn as well. If we can both get her statement at the same time, it'll save her from having to go through the experience again more than once."

"George, I appreciate everything that you've done. And I'm sorry about the way I talked to you this morning when you called me about Rebecca. David told me that you were trying to tell me about Caitlyn too when I hung up on you. Please forgive me for that."

"Forget about that, Cameron. You were under a lot of pressure. I've known you practically all your life. You're a good man. And, despite the fact that Rebecca is obviously disturbed, she and Evan did a wonderful job of raising you. Speaking of which, how is your father?"

"He's doing good. He'll be moving to the step down unit tomorrow."

"That's good news. Liz and I visited him a few times. We've been praying for him to recover. In fact, the whole church has been concerned about him. Jim's been running their business, and he and Ann have been trying to be there for him as well. Son, I know you might feel alone now, but there are a lot of people in this town who love and respect you and your father. We're all here for you."

"Thank you for that, George. That's just what I needed to hear. I'm going to get in touch with Jim to see if he wants

~ 331 ~

to buy Dad's half of the business. There's no way Dad can continue with him."

"Well, I'm going to get to work and take care of everything on this end. And Cameron, I'm sorry about having to shoot Rebecca. "

"George, that's not your fault. I'm just thankful that you were able to avoid killing her. Any other officer would have taken her out."

"I've always thought the world of Rebecca. I can't believe she would do all of this."

"Neither can I. Once again, thanks, George for all that you've done."

"Anytime, Son. Oh, by the way, we got a definite ID on that body found in the well," George said.

"Oh? Was it who we thought it was?" Cameron asked.

"Yep. Oscar Lucas. His wife is still living and she didn't seem too broken up when we told her," George stated. "Apparently, he crossed Rebecca one too many times."

"Man, was there any end to her terror, or what she would stoop to in order to get her own way? But, wait a minute. Steve called this morning and said there was a body in the cabin. Who was it?"

"You mean he didn't tell you?" George asked in a surprised tone.

"No, I broke down in tears the moment he said a body had been found. Who was it?"

"We suspect its Rosemary. Nothing positive yet, but we'll know soon enough. The corpse has been in there for several years, buried under floor boards," George said.

"Rosemary? You mean Rebecca may have killed her?" Cameron asked.

"It's looking more and more like that's what happened," George said.

"This is really a lot to take in at one time," Cameron sighed.

"I'm sorry, Cameron. I wish I had something good to tell you," George said.

"I appreciate your honesty."

"Call me when you talk to Caitlyn," George said.

After hanging up with George, Cameron went to see if it was okay for him to visit with Caitlyn yet. They told him he could, so he went to her room. She was lying there looking like an angel, sleeping. Cameron sat in the chair and reached into his pocket and retrieved her charm bracelet. He looked at it and remembered the day when Caitlyn referred to the charm bracelet as a way of always having her guardian angel with her. Maybe Joe was her guardian angel that day. She must have sensed him in the room, because she stirred slightly and looked in his direction.

"Hey," she said groggily. She was still connected to an IV. "How long have you been here? I didn't hear you come in."

"I just got here. I didn't want to disturb you, and I guess I just wanted to watch you sleep," Cameron smiled, moving his chair closer to her bed. "How are you?"

"Better, now that you are here," Caitlyn smiled.

"Me, too. Caitlyn, the police and the FBI both need to talk with you about what happened. George is going to try to arrange it so that the FBI can be here with him so you can just give one statement if you're up to it today."

"That's fine. I'll tell them anything they want to know about that horrible woman." Caitlyn immediately thought about the fact that this 'horrible woman' was thought to be Cameron's mother. She saw the expression on his face. "Oh, Cameron, I'm sorry."

Cameron reached out to caress her hand. "Hey, that's okay. She is horrible for all that she's done, and she's going to have to pay for it. I'm just sorry that so many people had to be hurt because of her. I'm sorry that you almost died because of her."

"How are you holding up?" Caitlyn asked.

"I'm fine. It's hard, but I'll make it. Knowing you're okay, I can try to put my life back together. One good thing will come out of this. Garret will be cleared. Phillip's handling that as we speak."

"That's wonderful. I'm sorry you had to pay such a

high price for our client's freedom," Caitlyn said.

"Looks like it's my father's freedom," Cameron murmured.

"Yeah, she admitted it to me," Caitlyn stated. "Have you told him yet?"

"No, not yet, but we had the clemency hearing yesterday."

"How did it go?"

"It went well, despite the fact that all I could think about was you and whether you were alive or not. It was probably the hardest thing I'd ever had to do."

"But you did it. I'm so proud of you, Cameron."

"I'm proud of you, too. You held on and you made it through a terrible ordeal."

"My love for you kept me going," Caitlyn smiled. "I'm just glad the evidence we gathered helped to at least plant doubt in the board's mind."

"Actually, we got a mind-blowing piece of evidence."

"What do you mean?"

"Remember when Serena Felton resurfaced? Well, she came to the office the other day. And she was telling the truth."

"So, she really was Dr. Varden's daughter."

"She felt guilty about the fact that she had stolen our files. She explained that she was trying to find Regina Matheson. This journal she had that her father kept was one of our biggest pieces of evidence."

"Well, what did the journal say?"

"It was like he wanted to confess to everything. He said how he and Regina wanted to steal the baby, but he had no idea that Regina was planning to kill Victoria."

Cameron went on to explain everything that had transpired, including how he realized that Garret and Victoria were really his parents. Caitlyn continued to listen intently as he told her about the confrontation between Serena and Rebecca that resulted in Rebecca killing Serena.

"Oh, Cameron, you've gone through so much! Are you okay?"

"Yeah, I'm okay. Rebecca isn't even in her right mind right now. I don't think she's completely aware of all that she's done." Then, Cameron looked skeptical.

"What's with that look on your face?" Caitlyn asked, looking at him.

"George said something, and I have to be honest, I'm wondering about it myself."

"What is it?"

"I'm wondering if Rebecca is faking. I mean, she totally went off the deep end, but somehow, she's managed to hide this part of her life from us for so many years. I mean, when she shot me, she hit me in the shoulder because she really had no intention of killing me."

"There's no doubt that Rebecca is disturbed mentally. It takes a very sick person to do the things she's done. How do you feel about her now?"

"I still love her. How can I care about what happens to her? I mean, she killed my real mother."

"Sweetheart, she's still the woman who raised you. She's the only mother you've ever known. That's not going to go away overnight. Despite everything, in Rebecca's own sick way, she does love you and she really thinks she did what she did to protect you."

"Caitlyn, I hate to ask you this, but I need to know what happened. Tell me everything." Cameron climbed into the hospital bed with her, holding her.

"Are you sure you want to know?" Caitlyn asked, snuggling closer to him.

"Yes. I need to know. Can you talk to me about it?" Cameron stroked her hair.

"Yes I can." Caitlyn started to think back. "It all started the day I was scheduled to leave. I was so awful to you that day, but I had no idea how to handle things. I mean, how could I tell you that the woman we'd been looking for was your mother? The night before, I'd come downstairs to talk to you because I hated the way things were between us." Then Caitlyn smiled. "You looked so peaceful sleeping in the recliner. I couldn't resist covering you up with a blanket and

~ 335 ~

kissing you."

"You covered me?" Cameron smiled.

"Yeah, I did," Caitlyn smiled. "Then, the next day, I lost my nerve to talk to you about it, so I just shut you out. Funny, huh? When we first met, I didn't bite my tongue about anything."

"No, you didn't," Cameron smiled gently.

"Later, when you left your parents' house going to visit your dad at the hospital, I knew I needed to find out the truth–"

Caitlyn thought back to what happened:

Caitlyn stared silently as Cameron drove away. She knew she had to find out if Rebecca had the locket. The one Cameron had looked a lot like the one Rebecca showed her the day they arrived. It couldn't be. Surely it was another one of similar looks. The only way to find out would be to find the locket to examine it again. But, what if it was Rebecca? How could she tell Cameron that his mother was the woman they'd been looking for? Caitlyn was about to go into Rebecca's room when her cell phone rang. It was her mother calling her back. As usual, her mother wanted to hold a long conversation, despite Caitlyn's being distracted by the task ahead of her. She tried to cut the conversation short, reiterating to her mother that she would call once her plane landed. Yet, her mother insisted upon telling her everything that had happened over the past few days. Even though she was interested in finding out about her dogs, now wasn't the time.

After almost half an hour, she was finally able to get off the phone with her mother. Caitlyn immediately went into Rebecca's room to go through her jewelry box. She started rambling through frantically to see if it was there. There were two jewelry boxes, and she could have sworn she was looking in the right one. With no luck in the first one, she tried to find it in the second one. Finally, she found it. She looked at it in horror. It was the one given to Rachel. Rebecca had it. Maybe she'd purchased it at a pawnshop. Surely, this woman wasn't a cold-blooded murderer. There's no way Cameron's mother was this evil person and the truth never came out. Yet, she realized recently that Rebecca was a manipulator from the way she made Cameron feel so guilty. Caitlyn was so engrossed in her examination of the locket, until she didn't hear Rebecca enter the room.

"What are you doing?" Rebecca inquired.

"R-Rebecca," Caitlyn jumped. She gained her composure and smiled. "You caught me. I wanted to look at that beautiful locket of yours, because I'd love something like it for my mother."

"Really?" Rebecca smiled. "Why, that's a wonderful idea, Sweetheart. Did you find it?"

"Um, y-yeah, I did," Caitlyn stammered.

"Did you get a close look at it?" Rebecca asked, moving closer to Caitlyn.

"Y-Yes, I did," Caitlyn smiled.

Rebecca walked slowly toward Caitlyn, all the time smiling and staring eerily at her. "It's quite lovely, isn't it?" Rebecca said, retrieving it from Caitlyn's trembling hands.

"Yes, it is. So, where did you say you got this?"

"Cameron's father gave it to me." She stared into Caitlyn's eyes coldly. "And you know who Cameron's father is, don't you?" Rebecca asked calmly.

"Y-you told me it was the last gift you got from his real father who died years ago," Caitlyn said.

"No, I think you know better than that," Rebecca continued to smile.

"I-I'm afraid I don't understand," Caitlyn said, backing away from Rebecca.

"Funny how things turn out, isn't it? I mean, how ironic is it that my son is working on a case concerning my ex-husband?"

"Wh-what do you mean?" Caitlyn asked.

"You know, Evan and I had an enlightening conversation before he nearly checked out the other night. He told me that Cameron had a locket very similar to the one I have. Evan's a little too smart for his own good. He figured out that my locket is the one that you two are looking for.

~ 337 ~

Apparently, you're starting to get it, too," Rebecca smiled.

"I-I don't know what you're talking about," Caitlyn said.

"Now, Caitlyn, you're smarter than that. You know exactly what I'm talking about. Just like you know exactly who I really am," Rebecca smiled.

"I-I know you're Cameron's mother, R-Rebecca," Caitlyn smiled nervously.

"Don't insult my intelligence!" Rebecca yelled. Then, she smiled and extended her hand to shake Caitlyn's. "Hi, I'm Rachel Marlow. A pleasure to meet you."

"Oh, my God! It's true! You are Rachel!" Caitlyn's voice trembled. Caitlyn continued to back towards the door. She had to get out of the house.

"Very good, Dear. It's so nice to make your acquaintance. So, you and Cameron are trying to clear that son of a bitch Garret? You'll never prove that he didn't do it in time. I know he's set to die soon," Rebecca said calmly. "I covered my tracks pretty good after killing Victoria."

"Y-you killed Victoria Marlow?" Caitlyn stammered.

"Now you're getting it!" Rebecca said.

"B-But, why would you do such a thing?"

"I had to! I should have been the one having the baby, but no!" Rebecca yelled. "After I miscarried, Garret let them do that hysterectomy on me, leaving me unable to ever have children again! Then Garret no longer wanted me after I couldn't give him children, and he went back to Victoria. I hated her and I hated him. Victoria and Garret had to pay." Rebecca was nearly in tears as she spoke, but she regained her composure quickly.

"So, you decided to kill Victoria and frame Garret?"

"Yeah, with a little help from the good doctor, Larry Varden," Rebecca smiled. "See, I saw his picture at the doctor's office one day in a magazine about women's health and about some medical conference where he'd be head lecturer. Amazing, because he was almost the spitting image of Garret. All I had to do was place myself in his presence at the conference and get a job working for him. He was such an

~ 338 ~

idiot. It didn't take much to convince him to do it, just sleeping with him a couple of times. Like most men, he was so predictable!"

"Th-This isn't making any sense!" Caitlyn said, shaking her head fiercely.

"What doesn't make sense?!" Rebecca yelled. "That bitch stole my husband, and he let them take my baby! I would have been okay if he'd not let them do that to me! Garret and I could have still been together, happy if it weren't for Victoria luring him away! I know it was her who convinced him to let them take away my womanhood! So, they took my ability to have a child, I took theirs."

"Wh-what does that mean?"

"Well, I say 'an eye for an eye.' Garret let them take my baby, so I took his," Rebecca said.

Caitlyn suddenly realized what Rebecca meant. "Oh, no! Cameron! Cameron is Garret and Victoria's son!"

"No, you stupid bitch! Cameron is my son! Dr. Larry Varden even signed a birth certificate that says so," Rebecca smiled. "Victoria's body was just used to carry him. I befriended her, got her to trust me. After all, I couldn't have my baby coming into the world unhealthy. Larry did a C-section on her and my beautiful son was born."

"You need help, Rebecca," Caitlyn said.

"No, you need to die, Caitlyn."

"W-What?" Caitlyn cried.

"You know too much. You could ruin things for me."

At that point, Rebecca went into a nearby drawer and retrieved a gun. As she was occupied with getting the gun, Caitlyn ran out of the room. Rebecca went immediately after her.

"Hold it, or I swear I will blow your head off!" Rebecca shouted.

Caitlyn immediately stopped in her tracks and turned to face Rebecca.

"You'll never get away with this! Cameron will know something is wrong! Please, Rebecca, turn yourself in. Get some help."

"What, so you can bad mouth me to my son! No way! I'm just going to have to kill you. You're not the first, and for anyone else who tries to come between me and my son, you may not be the last," Rebecca said. "Come on, let's go."

"Wh-Where are we going?"

"You'll soon find out," Rebecca smiled.

"Cameron's coming back to take me to the airport!" Caitlyn lied.

"No, he's not," Rebecca smiled. "He just called me on my cell from the hospital as I was pulling into the driveway. I asked him would he be taking you to the airport, and he stated that you were going to take a cab, that your pride wouldn't allow you to let him carry you. So, you see? We're all alone."

"Cameron will know something's wrong," Caitlyn cried.

"Look, I'm losing my patience with you! Give me your cell phone," Rebecca demanded. Caitlyn hesitantly handed her cell phone to Rebecca. "You're going to 'conveniently' leave it here. That way, he won't be worried when he can't reach you on it. I'll tell him you forgot it. Come on!"

Rebecca pushed Caitlyn, forcing her to walk out the back door. They walked for a long time, and Caitlyn knew if she ran that Rebecca would kill her. They walked until they reached the little cabin on their property. Rebecca turned the light on, and pushed Caitlyn inside.

"Rebecca! Please! Don't do this!" Caitlyn cried.

"I heard you talking to my son the other night, trying to turn him against me!"

"No, I wasn't," Caitlyn cried.

"Oh, save it! I'll take care of you once and for all! This is such an inconvenience! I haven't had to kill anyone in a long time, now here I am having to take care of you and Evan!" Rebecca gave a frustrated sigh.

"Please, Rebecca don't do this!" Caitlyn pleaded.

"Don't do what? Kill you?" Rebecca laughed evilly. "Why not? The only reason you've lived this long is because I didn't want to destroy my beautiful rug. I'd rather kill you here in the cabin. Sweet dreams, Caitlyn."

"Rebecca, no!" Caitlyn screamed. She cried out, knowing that Rebecca was going to kill her.

Rebecca then smiled eerily and shot Caitlyn in the stomach. The hot bullet pierced her flesh and she fell to the ground. The only thing she could do is to let Rebecca think she'd killed her. She closed her eyes and tried desperately to hold her breath. At that very moment, Rebecca kicked her fiercely in the stomach. Caitlyn did everything she could not to move or react. She lay there in a pool of blood, praying that she'd make it out alive.

"You insufferable little bitch!" Rebecca yelled.

A few moments later, she heard Rebecca leave out, slamming the door shut. Caitlyn cried, hoping that she would survive. She struggled to turn over. Rebecca had left her there to die.

A few moments later, Caitlyn heard the door opening again, fearing it was Rebecca. She passed out, and the next thing she remembered was being in bed at Donna's house, with Donna by her side.

"Wh-where am I?" Caitlyn asked groggily.

"Hi, Caitlyn, I'm Joe's sister, Donna," Donna smiled. "I've been taking care of you since you were shot."

"Wh-what? Where's Cameron! I-I have to talk to Cameron!" Caitlyn screamed hysterically.

"Shh, you'll see Cameron soon enough. We have to get you well first," Donna soothed.

Chapter
15

Cameron was stunned at hearing about all of the things his mother had done. He stroked Caitlyn's hair as she cried softly in his arms.

"I didn't think I would survive that bullet wound. I was in so much pain, and Donna was so sweet," Caitlyn said, tearfully. "She was there with me the whole time, rarely leaving my side."

"Oh, Caitlyn, thank God for Donna! I can't believe you've gone through that," Cameron said, hugging her tighter, wiping the tears away. He noticed Caitlyn wince in pain. "Oh, I'm sorry! I almost forgot about your wound!"

"That's okay," Caitlyn smiled.

"Wait a minute. My birth certificate. I never thought about it, but it was signed by Dr. Varden. The light bulb never went on in my head. I should have put two and two together."

"Cameron, no one can fault you. I mean, how often do we look at our birth certificate?"

"I know you're right," Cameron smiled.

"I'm just glad to be here with you," Caitlyn said.

"Just know that you're safe now, and I'll never let

Rebecca or anyone else hurt you again," Cameron said. "I don't want anything else to do with her. She's hurt me in the worst possible way. All this time, she thought she was protecting me, but she was depriving me of a whole other family. I have relatives that I never even knew existed. All this time, there's been another side of my life that I don't even know about. Twenty-four hours and my life is completely different. It's true that things can change in the blink of an eye," Cameron said.

"Cameron, you're a strong man, and I'll be here to help you through all of this," Caitlyn whispered.

"You're the strong one. You survived for three days with a bullet wound. I know you were with Donna, but it still took a lot of strength on your part. My God, why didn't I see this in Rebecca? Sometimes, I just don't know anymore."

"It's okay now. I'm here with you, and life is going to be good again," Caitlyn said, looking up at him. "Something I'm wondering about, though."

"What's that?" Cameron asked.

"How did she find out where I was?"

"She overheard an officer talking to another one about the fact that you were at Donna's house. She made an excuse about having to use the restroom, and she overpowered the female cop who took her. She made it a point to escape and go straight to Donna's house. I saw her with a gas can, so that's probably what Rebecca used to start the fire."

"She was really determined," Caitlyn sighed.

"I'm never letting you go again," Cameron said, as he caressed her face with his hand.

"I like the sound of that," Caitlyn smiled. "When did you realize I was missing?"

"Well, I knew you were mad at me about something, but I knew you well enough to know that you would have called when you arrived home. I called and left you a message that night, but I had the nagging feeling that something was wrong. Rebecca tried to ease my mind by saying you'd forgotten your phone by mistake."

"Yeah, she made me leave it. And for the record, I

~ 343 ~

wasn't mad at you, I just didn't know how to face you. I was upset because I didn't know how to handle what I found out. I mean, how could I tell you the truth about Rebecca?"

"I understand," Cameron said. "I'm just glad to have you back." Cameron then leaned in to kiss her. They were interrupted by a brief knock and someone entering her room.

"Caitlyn?" the woman said.

Caitlyn looked towards the door. "Mom? Robert? You're here!" Caitlyn smiled.

Cameron immediately stood up from the bed.

"We're not interrupting, are we?" Mrs. Harding asked.

"No, we were just talking," Caitlyn said.

"Sweetheart! I'm so glad you're okay!" Mrs. Harding said, hugging her.

"We were so worried about you," Robert said, hugging her.

"Cameron, this is my mother and step-father, Sylvia and Robert Harding," Caitlyn said, introducing them.

"Cameron!" Mrs. Harding said, hugging him.

"Cameron, it's good to see you again," Robert smiled, shaking Cameron's hand.

"You act as if you all know each other," Caitlyn smiled.

"Cameron has been so supportive. This man has put everything he had into trying to find you," Mrs. Harding smiled.

"We were all worried about you. Mrs. Harding really handled the police that night we filed the report," Cameron said.

"Cameron, Mrs. Harding is my mother-in-law. Please call me Sylvia."

"Okay, Sylvia," Cameron smiled.

"Now, I've not been given any specifics about what happened. So, maybe now you can fill me in," Sylvia suggested.

"You're right. You have a right to know," Caitlyn said.

Caitlyn looked at Cameron. Sylvia looked at both of

them. "Is there something you two don't want to tell us?"

"Actually, there's a lot to tell you. There are some things that have shocked both Cameron and me," Caitlyn said.

"Well, what is it?" Sylvia asked.

"My mother was the one who was responsible for Caitlyn's disappearance," Cameron said.

"What? Wh-what happened?" Sylvia asked.

"Do you remember me telling you about the case we'd been working on?" Caitlyn asked.

"Yes, the one about Garret Marlow who was framed for killing his wife," Sylvia recalled.

"Well, the woman who committed the murder and framed our client is the woman who raised me as her son."

"How is that possible?" Sylvia asked.

"She murdered my real mother and framed my real father for it. She abducted me as a baby, and raised me as her own. I just found out yesterday."

"I realized it the same day she tried to kill me," Caitlyn said.

"How did you find out, Caitlyn?" Sylvia asked.

"The locket. Cameron was telling me about another locket," Caitlyn explained. "I'd seen the other locket in Rebecca's possession, and I realized it was the one Cameron was talking about. I wanted to find out if it was really the one before telling Cameron, just in case I was wrong. Before I could tell Cameron about it, Rebecca kidnapped me at gunpoint, shot me once we got to the cabin and left me for dead. She'd shown me the locket on the day we arrived, and Cameron's dad confronted her about it before he had a stroke. She caught me snooping through her jewelry and realized that I was on to her."

"I'll never forgive myself for what happened to Caitlyn," Cameron said.

"Cameron, it wasn't your fault," Sylvia said. "You had no idea your mother was like that. Where is she now?"

"She's in jail," Cameron said.

Caitlyn went on to explain once again everything that had happened. By the time she was finished, her parents were

~ 345 ~

totally amazed at how strong she was. She'd gone through a lot, but somehow she'd come through it okay. Cameron left Caitlyn and her family to visit with her for a while.

Cameron called David to get an update on Dr. Varden. David told him that he'd taken Dr. Varden and his wife to the police station to talk to George. David mentioned that Dr. Varden was anxious to meet with him, and that he was staying at a hotel that was only 10 minutes from the hospital. Cameron told Caitlyn that he had to go and meet with Dr. Varden, and that he'd be back at the hospital later. Cameron looked at the clock and saw that it was almost 3:30 p.m.

He caught a cab back to his parents' house to pick up his car, which had been there since the day before. He also needed to change. He still had on the blood stained shirt from earlier. After going into the house to shower and change, he went into the living room and looked at the bloodstain on the carpet again. He shook his head as he realized that the home he'd always loved was now nothing more than a painful memory. When he got into his car, he glanced at his backseat and realized he still had Serena's belongings. Cameron sat there and cried, as all of the events that had taken place over the past 24 hours overwhelmed him. He briefly wished he'd never been born. So many people had died at the hands of his mother, all because she wanted desperately to hold on to him. He knew he couldn't dwell on it forever, so after sitting for a few moments to gather his thoughts he left there heading to the hotel. He noticed his gas was quite low so he stopped at the local gas station to refuel. He went in and was greeted by Bob, whom Cameron had known for years.

"Hi, Bob," Cameron said, as he paid for his gas.

"Hey, Cameron. Is your car okay?" Bob asked.

Cameron was confused. "What do you mean?"

"Rebecca came in here the other day and said you'd run out of gas. She purchased two gas jugs full. You didn't have any problems with your fuel injection after that did you? You know those new cars never run as well when they run out of fuel," Bob shook his head.

"It-it was a rental," Cameron tried to smile. "But

thanks for asking."

"Anytime. I heard about all the problems with Rebecca. Is it true that she's not your real ma?"

"Yes, it's true."

"Well, what happened exactly? You know, I've heard stories, but you never know how much is true and how much is fiction."

"If you don't mind, Bob, I really would prefer not to talk about it," Cameron said.

"I understand. I didn't mean to pry," Bob said.

"No, I don't mean to be short with you. I've just got a lot on my mind right now. We'll talk later," Cameron smiled slightly.

"Okay, Cameron. I hope things get better for you," Bob said.

"Things will never be the same," Cameron said. "I'll see you later, Bob."

"Bye, Cameron." Bob looked concerned and shook his head as Cameron walked out of the store.

As Cameron pumped his gas, it occurred to him that the purpose of Rebecca purchasing the gas was to burn down the cabin with Caitlyn in it. She didn't realize that Joe had saved Caitlyn's life. After leaving the gas station, he went to the hotel readying himself for the dreaded task of meeting with Dr. Varden. Cameron saw him sitting in the lounge already. Cameron noticed that he looked as if he'd already had quite a bit to drink.

"Dr. Varden, are you okay?" Cameron asked.

"What do you think? I had to identify my sister's body. Do you know how hard that was?"

"I can only imagine," Cameron said.

"You know, I'm a doctor. I should be used to this," Dr. Varden said, as he started to cry. "My sister! My little Jessie's gone!"

"Dr. Varden, I know this is hard on you," Cameron said.

"Is it true? Is it true that your mother is the woman who's responsible for all of this? She killed my father, she killed my sister! I don't need any comfort from you! Your mother has done quite enough! How could you let this happen? How could you not know that your mother was a cold-hearted murderer?" Dr. Varden took another sip of his drink.

"Dr. Varden, please calm down. I want to explain to you what happened. You have every right to know."

Dr. Varden slammed his drink down. "You're damned right I have a right to know! How did my sister come to get involved in this investigation of yours? Why didn't you just leave us alone? You didn't have to involve her! You'd already talked to me! I told you not to involve her, but you did it anyway, didn't you? This is all your fault! Jessie would still be alive if it weren't for you!"

Dr. Varden was right. This was Cameron's fault. He should never have let Serena come along with him on the trip. If he'd insisted she go ahead with her plans to go back to New York instead of going with him, he could have gotten Rebecca into custody, and the entire confrontation wouldn't have happened. Dr. Varden wanted someone to blame, and Cameron didn't want to make things more difficult for him. Cameron decided not to tell him everything that had really happened. There was no need to mention how much could have been avoided if Serena would have been honest with him in the first place.

Cameron had the bartender to call up to Dr. Varden's room for his wife. When she came down, Cameron explained that her husband had drank a little too much. Cameron helped her to get him to their room. After getting Dr. Varden to his room, Cameron called a bellhop to retrieve Serena's luggage from his car to give to Dr. and Mrs. Varden to take back with them. As he was about to leave, Mrs. Varden came outside the door with him.

"Thank you so much for calling us. Larry is very upset, and he has a right to be. We're leaving tomorrow. Serena's body will be brought back home tomorrow as well and we will have her funeral in a few days," Mrs. Varden said.

"I'm so sorry for your loss," Cameron said solemnly.

~ 348 ~

"I know you are. Look, I know what we've been told, but I also know that Serena can sometimes be very hot-headed. I loved her like she was my own sister, but I have to ask you something."

"Sure. What would you like to know?" Cameron asked.

"How much of my sister-in-law's death was her own fault?"

"Excuse me?" Cameron asked surprisingly.

"Look, Mr. Spencer," Mrs. Varden sighed. "Serena told me about the journal. She didn't tell Larry because she didn't think he'd deal too well with it. She told me that she wanted to find the woman who was responsible for their father's death. I know Serena well enough to know that she probably did more than her share of something she shouldn't have been doing."

"To be honest, Serena went to confront my mother once we'd found out who she was. I had no idea she would run off and try to find her. She held my mother at gunpoint. I tried to talk Serena into dropping the gun. Unfortunately, when Serena turned towards me, my mother pulled out her gun and shot Serena twice."

"I kind of had the feeling it was something like that. And you didn't tell Larry?"

"No, I didn't. I don't think he needs to know what part she played. I think Serena should rest in peace."

"You're a very nice man, Mr. Spencer. Thanks so much for everything. Word of advice."

"What's that?"

"Don't feel guilty about Serena's death. It's not your fault. Serena was an adult, and she knew better. I tried to talk her out of whatever she was planning, but when Serena gets an idea in her head, there's no stopping her. From what I've heard, this Regina Matheson was not stable and was an extremely dangerous woman. I know she is your mother, but it's just my opinion."

"I perfectly understand. I'm sure I will hear her called a lot more terrible things than 'not stable' or 'dangerous.'"

~ 349 ~

"Just know that you didn't do anything wrong."

"Thank you so much for talking to me about this. Let's just keep this between us, okay?"

"That's fine," Mrs. Varden smiled, then her smile faded. "You know, Larry's going to have to know at some point. He's going to pursue your mother's conviction for Serena's death."

"I know he will. When the time is right, he will find everything out. Now's just not the time," Cameron stated.

"Goodbye, Mr. Spencer."

"Goodbye, Mrs. Varden."

Cameron left the hotel with so many mixed emotions going through his mind. What should he be feeling right now? How can so many good and bad things happen all at once? Every last one of them has affected his life dramatically. All because of one woman. The woman he's known his entire life as his mother. She's murdered, she's kidnapped, she's lied. She's committed just about every crime there was to commit. Cameron needed to do a lot of soul-searching. Did he want to defend her? She was going to need a good defense attorney. But, how could Cameron defend this woman? Would it destroy his relationship with those closest to him? Cameron knew that deep down he still loved Rebecca, but, she had to pay for her crimes. He realized that he couldn't defend her, in or out of court. He really just wanted to wash his hands of the entire situation, but he knew that would not be possible. He was too tied to her for that. Cameron drove in silence back to the hospital. He went to visit with his father first, since the visiting time was restricted to only a few short minutes. Cameron thanked God that Evan was getting stronger everyday. Despite Rebecca's efforts, he would still survive.

"Hi, Dad," Cameron smiled.

"H-hi s-son," Evan smiled.

"Remember, blink once for yes, twice for no. Are you feeling okay?"

Evan blinked once.

"Dad, I want to talk to Jim about his buying your ½ of the business. Is that okay with you?"

~ 350 ~

Evan blinked once.

"Do you want for me to sell the house?"

Evan blinked once.

"Do you think I should defend Mom?"

Evan blinked twice.

"Dad, I think she is just unstable. She may not even know what she's done. She needs someone to help her."

"N-not y-you," Evan said.

"She's my mother."

Evan blinked twice.

"I know that biologically she's not, but, still. The two of you raised me. How can I turn my back on that?"

"She b-brought th-this on h-herself. G-go on w-with y-your l-life," Evan advised.

"How do I do that? I love her."

"I-I know y-you do. B-but sh-she's d-done s-some b-bad th-things."

"And you feel like she needs to pay for those things?"

Evan blinked once.

"I agree, but I still feel sorry for her."

"Sh-she c-could h-have d-done d-diffferently. B-but sh-she d-didn't."

"I know, Dad. I have a lot to think about."

"H-how's C-Caitlyn?"

"She's fine. She's downstairs on the third floor," Cameron smiled.

"Sh-she s-seems n-nice," Evan said.

"She is. The nurse told me earlier that you're going to start your physical and speech therapy soon."

Evan blinked once.

"Before you know it, you'll be walking out of here," Cameron encouraged.

Evan blinked twice.

"Dad, you can't give up. We'll do whatever it takes to take care of you."

Evan blinked twice.

"Don't you want to get better?"

Evan blinked twice.

"Why not?"

"I-I'll b-be a b-burden. S-so it w-would b-be b-bet-ter if I w-were d-dead."

"Dad, you'll never be a burden on me. Now, I don't want to hear you talking like that, okay?"

Evan blinked once.

"Now, are you going to fight to get better?"

Evan blinked once.

"That's better. I love you," Cameron smiled. Shortly thereafter, they announced that visiting time was over. "They're kicking the visitors out," Cameron smiled. "I have to go, but I'll be back at the next visit, okay?"

Evan blinked once. Cameron left Evan's room and went straight to the gift shop. He realized he'd not gotten Caitlyn any flowers. He purchased two dozen long-stemmed roses in a vase, along with a ½ dozen Mylar balloons. He took them to her room, and the smile on her face told him that she was pleased.

"Oh, what beautiful roses!" Sylvia said.

"Cameron, that's so sweet of you!" Caitlyn smiled. Cameron placed the roses on the table and let the balloons float to the ceiling. He leaned over and kissed Caitlyn.

"We were just about to leave," Sylvia said. "We're staying at the hotel near here."

"Do you need for me to show you out?" Cameron asked.

"No, we'll be fine. We'll be back tomorrow morning. The doctor came by and said that if she continues to do well, she should be released in a couple of days," Sylvia said.

"Yeah, that's what they told me earlier," Cameron said.

When Sylvia and Robert left, Cameron told Caitlyn that they had a lot to talk about. Before they had a chance to discuss anything, George and the FBI agent came by to take Caitlyn's statement. The reporters had been swarming as well, but the hospital PR person had taken care to protect Caitlyn from them. After Caitlyn gave her statement, both George and the agent left, leaving her alone with Cameron. Cameron knew there was a lot to be done, a lot of loose ends to tie up.

He also knew that he wanted his home to be Indiana, not Kentucky. They discussed the possibility of moving his father to Indiana to continue his recovery.

When Cameron talked to Phillip, he told Cameron that the state was granting Garret a full pardon since it was quite obvious that Rebecca was the murderer. Phillip also stated that the journal was compelling enough to clear him by itself. Phillip told him that Garret's family was throwing him a welcome home party and they wanted him and Cameron both to come, and he'd explained that Cameron was tying up some things in Kentucky about the case and wouldn't be able to make it. Phillip also reassured Cameron that he'd not told Garret the truth about his being Garret's son. He felt it was something Cameron should do himself.

The next few days were really hectic. Evan was moved into the step-down unit for a couple of days and then into a room, and the doctors informed Cameron that he would probably be there for another week or so, and at that point would go to a rehabilitation facility in the nearby city. Cameron made it clear that he was planning to take his father back to Indiana with him. Caitlyn was feeling much better, but was going to have to be watched carefully. Although the bullet didn't hit any vital organs, they still wanted to keep an eye on her. The doctors had arranged for her to follow up with her doctor in Indiana. Although he'd wanted to, Cameron was unable to attend Serena's funeral, so he sent a nice floral arrangement and card expressing his condolences. Donna's insurance did pay for her home after learning the circumstances. In the meantime, Cameron helped her financially until the rebuilding of her house was complete. As hard as it was for Cameron to do, he put his parents' home up for sale. He also gave Joe a year's salary to live off until the sale of the house, at which point, he stipulated that Joe be re-employed there. He knew he never wanted to live there again, and considering Evan's condition, he wouldn't be able to live there alone. As sad as it was to think about, Rebecca would probably never see the outside world again. Cameron had always wanted to protect his parents, especially his mother, but in this case, her fate was in the hands of a judge and 12 jurors.

During the time they were in Kentucky, the body found in the remains of the cabin after the fire had been positively identified as Rosemary. Apparently, Rebecca had killed Rosemary, because Rosemary's parents had left her a great deal of money. Under one of her many assumed names, Rebecca appointed herself as Rosemary's overseer of the money she received. Rebecca ended up embezzling $75,000.00 from Rosemary's estate. Rosemary didn't understand a lot of what was going on, and she trusted Rebecca. Unfortunately, she was also a threat because Rebecca was afraid that someone would find out the truth one day. All those years they'd enjoyed the cabin, how did he not discover her body buried beneath? Rebecca was sick enough to bury her in a place that Cameron always thought was special between them.

Cameron and Caitlyn remained in Kentucky for the next few days, going back to Indiana on the following Friday. Cameron tended to her, and refused to let her out of his sight again. After he'd gotten Caitlyn settled, he decided that he would talk to Garret the next day. Cameron had been at Caitlyn's apartment more than his own. They still had not made love yet, and Cameron was okay with that. He wanted to wait until the time was right. Caitlyn was still recovering from her ordeal, and Cameron was not about to pressure her about intimacy. Early Saturday morning, Cameron drove to Garret Marlow's home. Garret's mother answered the door, and told him that Garret was out on the patio. She was so happy to see Cameron. How would she feel towards him when she found out that he was her grandchild? Cameron stared at her and smiled. He had the feeling she'd be happy about it. She showed him to the patio.

"Cameron! I'm so glad you called and wanted to come out and talk!" Garret said, shaking his hand. "Sit down. Would you like a cup of coffee, or anything?"

Cameron sat in the chair next to him. "No, sir. Thanks anyway. Um, there are some things that we really need to discuss."

"Sure. Anything for you. What is it?"

"Garret, there have been some amazing revelations over the past week and I think they will shock you to say the least."

"What's going on?"

"Gosh, I don't even know where to start," Cameron smiled shyly.

"Cameron, what's on your mind?"

Cameron sighed. "Well, I guess there's no easy way to say this, so I'm going to just come right out and say it." Cameron took a deep breath. "Garret, I'm your son."

"Wh-what did you say?" Garret was understandably shocked.

"I'm the child Victoria gave birth to 27 years ago. You're my father." Cameron stood from his chair.

"Oh, my– how is that possible!?"

"Rachel Marlow kidnapped me, and raised me. She'd changed her name to Rebecca Marrick, and she married my stepfather, Evan Spencer when I was two. Dr. Varden helped her to pull it off. I had no idea because I'd never seen a picture of Rachel Marlow. So, when we realized she and Regina were the same person, and Serena remembered she had pictures of Regina, she had them sent here. When I saw the pictures, I was totally shocked."

"Is that why you were asking the questions when you showed me the pictures?" Garret asked, standing beside his son.

"Yeah."

"Why didn't you tell me then?"

"I was in shock. I wanted to make sure it was absolutely true before telling you. It's definitely true. I'm your son."

"My son!" Garret smiled tearfully. Garret immediately drew Cameron into an embrace, as both of them cried. "I never thought I'd see you!"

"I was stunned to say the least about everything I learned. Fate really has a way of bringing people together," Cameron said through his tears.

~ 355 ~

"I'm actually here, talking to my son! So many times since I've talked to you, have I thought to myself that there was some sort of connection with you. I guess now we know why."

"If you'd like, we can have a DNA test to confirm everything," Cameron offered.

"Is that what you want?" Garret asked.

"Although I believe with everything in me that I am your son, it would be nice to confirm it, beyond a doubt."

"Well, let's do the test. There's nothing I'd like more than to prove that you are the child Victoria gave birth to," Garret smiled.

"Fine. We can go Monday, if it's convenient for you," Cameron said.

"Just tell me where and what time," Garret said.

"There's a DNA lab downtown that can see us Monday at 8:30 a.m., if that's okay."

"I'll be there."

Cameron looked at Garret, not once thinking that he couldn't be his son. Because of this, he wanted to know everything.

"Garret, what was Victoria like? I mean, I've read reports about her during the case, but, I want to know what the woman who carried me for nine months was really like. And I think only you can answer that for me."

"I could talk about Victoria all day and never get tired," Garret smiled. He shook his head, as he seemed a million miles away. "She was a beautiful woman, inside and out. She was kind-hearted, accepting of just about anyone. She was so excited when she found out she was pregnant with you. I was scared at first after Rachel's near-death experience with a pregnancy. But, there was no doubt that I wanted you. We had so many plans. So many hopes and dreams for you. It looks like you turned out better than we could have ever hoped for," Garret said proudly. "You followed my footsteps and became an attorney."

Cameron and Garret continued to talk for the next three hours, with Cameron telling Garret about all that had happened over the past couple of weeks, as well as other things that had gone on in his life. Garret told Cameron about his family, and how happy they would all be to meet him. While they were laughing about how nervous Garret was when he proposed to Victoria, Jean came out to let them know that lunch was ready and to see if Cameron would join them.

"Mother, I think you'd better sit down for this," Garret smiled.

"What? What's going on with you two? You've been out here all morning," Cameron's grandmother said.

"Jean Marlow, I'd like for you to meet your grandson, Cameron Spencer," Garret smiled.

"Gr-Grandson? Wh-What do you mean?" Mrs. Marlow asked.

"Cameron is the baby that Victoria gave birth to."

"Oh my! You're kidding! How is that possible?"

"Fate. We're going to have a DNA test Monday to confirm it, but this is most definitely my son."

"A part of me knew there was something about you, Cameron. That first time I laid eyes on you, I couldn't explain it. My grandson!" Mrs. Marlow hugged Cameron as tears rolled down her face.

Cameron stayed there and visited with his father and grandmother for the rest of the afternoon. When Garret's father came home, he was told the news about Cameron, and couldn't have been more delighted. Cameron had a family. There was so much he wanted to know, so much he wanted to do. He had no idea where to even start. Cameron left there with a new lease on life. Victoria's parents still didn't know the truth, so Cameron and Garret decided that they would tell them together. The following Monday, Cameron and Garret went to the DNA lab to have the test done. They were told it would be a couple of weeks before they had the results.

After leaving the genetics lab, Cameron and Garret went to Victoria's family and told them who he was. He was accepted instantly by Victoria's family, who wanted to know all about what had happened. When Cameron explained everything about Rebecca, Victoria's father wanted to see that she was put to death, but Victoria's mother told him that it was time to let Victoria rest in peace. After all, this was someone their grandson cared about.

They wanted Cameron to meet the rest of his family, so they planned an impromptu family reunion. Cameron had such bittersweet feelings about all of it. On one hand, he was learning about these two wonderful families that he belonged to, and how great it would be to get to know all of them. But, on the other hand, what about Rebecca? What about Evan? Was he to just forget about the fact that they'd raised him? He and Garret sat down and talked about it one day and Garret told him that he would always respect the fact that Evan had been a father to him, and that he'd be forever grateful knowing Evan loved Cameron the way he did.

Over the next week, Cameron went back to work, and started on other cases that had been piling up. Caitlyn still wasn't ready to return to work, but she was getting stronger everyday. The following week, Evan was transferred to Conley Rehabilitation Center in Kerrigan. Cameron wanted Evan close to him, and this was the best Rehab facility in the state. Cameron went to visit with him everyday, and kept in close contact with the doctors. They told him that his recovery time would probably be a few months. Cameron had already put their house on the market and was drawing up the paperwork for Jim to buy Evan out of the business. Cameron wanted to use the money from the sale of the house as well as the business, along with what his parents had in stocks, bonds and their savings, to take care of Evan. Evan's medical insurance thankfully paid for all of his medical bills, including up to a year in a rehabilitation facility.

Cameron decided that he wanted to be there for Rebecca, but he would not represent her. So, he agreed to pay for her legal expenses. Caitlyn understood why he did it, but she wasn't totally in agreement. In fact, at first, she was disappointed knowing he would do that after everything Rebecca had done to her. After a while, she realized that Rebecca was still Cameron's mother, no matter what. They decided that this would be something about which they would agree to disagree.

Cameron thought a lot about the fact that he'd been with Kristen and that he couldn't have a real future until he knew he was okay. He felt it was his responsibility to get himself checked not only for his wellbeing but for Caitlyn's as well. He was relieved to find out that everything was fine when his doctor called him to let him know that all of his tests had come back negative.

Two weeks and two days after having the DNA test done, Cameron and Garret went into the lab together to get their results. The results proved beyond a shadow of a doubt that Cameron was Garret's son. They knew deep down that it was true, but now, there were no doubts, and they could really bond as a family. To celebrate, they went to play golf together. Cameron wanted to visit Victoria's grave, so that was something that they did together. Cameron decided to bring flowers to his mother's grave once a month to honor her. Cameron and Garret talked about everything together, trying to make up for a lost twenty seven years.

Chapter
16

After Caitlyn had been home for about a month, Cameron decided to start shopping for an engagement ring. He knew he would only have one chance to do it right, and he wanted everything to be perfect when he proposed to her. Upon instinct, after searching for two weeks, Cameron visited Hallinger's Jewelry to see what he had to offer. He told Garret that was where he wanted to look for Caitlyn's ring. Garret went with him and was able to become reacquainted with an old friend at the same time. Cameron found the perfect ring, and had it engraved with 'C loves C forever.' It was a two carat pear-shaped solitaire with three small diamonds on each side of it. Cameron knew that Caitlyn would love it.

Cameron thought about how he'd wanted to propose, and he decided to get a very special gift for her as well. He thought about the clarinet he'd found while they were investigating his father's case, so he contacted the pawn shop to purchase it. It was delivered to him a few days later, just in time for the evening he had planned for Caitlyn.

He'd planned to take her out to dinner to propose. She was starting to feel more like her old self, and she was healing beautifully. She still wasn't in the mood to be around a lot of people, so Cameron had the perfect plan. He hired a limo and told Caitlyn to be ready at 7:30 one Saturday evening. When she asked what she was supposed to wear, he told her to dress formal. Cameron rented a penthouse suite at the best hotel in town, which overlooked the city. He had dinner catered just for the two of them. The music and the candlelight provided the perfect background for their special evening. He wanted everything to be just right.

When she arrived, she was brought up to the 35th floor of the hotel by a private elevator. Cameron was standing there waiting on her. When she stepped off the elevator, Cameron couldn't believe his eyes. She was absolutely beautiful. Her hair was up, with whispers of it flowing down her neck and around her face. She had on a beautiful black strapless evening gown. He thought before laying eyes on her at this moment that she couldn't be more beautiful than she already was. He was wrong. The woman standing before him was breathtaking.

"You're beautiful," Cameron whispered, hugging her.

"Thank you. You look quite handsome in a tux. So, is this a special occasion?" Caitlyn smiled.

"Very special. Come on, sit down."

Cameron gently took her hand and escorted her to the sofa and poured two glasses of champagne. Shortly after, someone called up to see if they were ready for dinner to be served. Caitlyn told Cameron that she was starving, so he instructed them to bring it up. They had a romantic dinner by candlelight out on the terrace overlooking the city complete with the soft jazz playing in the background. After dinner, they danced to the soft music, feeling as if they were the only two people in the world. As they danced, Cameron looked into Caitlyn's eyes, as city lights twinkled behind her. All he could think of was how beautiful she was. Afterwards, they went inside and sat down on the sofa. He reached for a beautifully wrapped box and handed it to her.

Caitlyn looked at the box. "What's this?" Caitlyn gave a half-hearted smile.

He knew she couldn't have thought it was an engagement ring, which was exactly what he wanted her to do.

"Open it up," he smiled.

"Pretty big for a ring box," she muttered.

"Ring box? Who ever said anything about a ring box? Wait a minute. Did you think this was a proposal?"

"W-well, I-I guess I thought–"

"Caitlyn, my life has been turned upside down lately. The last thing on my mind is marriage," Cameron lied.

"I'm sorry, Cameron. I just thought--"

"Just open the box," Cameron instructed.

Caitlyn sighed. She looked disappointed as she opened the box. Underneath the tissue paper was a Bastionne 450 clarinet.

"It's really sweet," Caitlyn smiled, trying not to show her disappointment. She leaned over to kiss Cameron. "Thank you, Cameron."

"You're welcome. I know how much the one you had as a child meant to you, and I wanted to do something special for you. Well, come on, play something for me."

"Now?"

"Yes, now. What better time? We're here to celebrate your getting healthy again, and for me to thank you for always being there for me."

"You're welcome," Caitlyn half smiled. "I haven't played in a long time, but, what would you like to hear?" Caitlyn asked despondently.

"You choose," Cameron smiled.

Caitlyn lifted the clarinet to her mouth and started to blow once she'd positioned her fingers properly. As she blew, Cameron stopped her.

"Wait a minute. It looks like something else is in the box," Cameron said in a surprised tone. "What's this?" Cameron asked. It was a small ring box. "Now how did that get in there?"

Caitlyn inhaled deeply, dropping the clarinet as she covered her mouth with her hand. Cameron reached for Caitlyn's hand.

"Oh, my God!" Caitlyn smiled, as tears streamed down her face.

"You didn't think I spent all this money on the evening just to give you a clarinet, now did you?" Cameron smiled, as he was getting on one knee.

"I-I didn't know what to think! Oh, Cameron!"

"Caitlyn, I know we've only known each other for a short time, but I feel like I've known you my entire life. I can remember very little that went on in my life before you came along. I remember the day I fell in love with you, and I knew I couldn't settle for less than spending the rest of my life with you. So, Caitlyn Frazier, will you do me the honor of marrying me?" Cameron asked, as he pulled the ring out of the box.

Caitlyn smiled, as a tear ran down her face. "Oh, Cameron! Yes, yes, I'll marry you!"

Caitlyn was crying and smiling at the same time as Cameron slipped the ring on her finger. Caitlyn leaned down happily to hug him. The two of them kissed passionately as Cameron still remained on one knee. He got off of his knee and sat next to her, holding her hand.

"You've made me the happiest man on earth."

Cameron leaned in slowly to kiss Caitlyn again, this time with more passion than the one before. Cameron caressed her arm as he kissed her neck. Both of them knew that this would be the night they would be intimate for the first time.

"Cameron, make love to me," Caitlyn whispered.

Cameron lifted Caitlyn into his arms, and carried her to the bedroom. Cameron had waited so long to hold her like this. He laid her gently onto the bed, as his manhood yearned to enter her. He had to take things slowly. He didn't want to rush the night, or cheapen it. They sat up on the side of the bed. As he kissed her, his hand gently reached back to unzip her dress, and caressed her bare back. He slowly leaned her back on the bed, as he joined her. Caitlyn unbuttoned Cameron's shirt to expose his chest. Cameron's mouth slowly moved from Caitlyn's lips, to her neck, down to her breasts.

His tongue was like a raging inferno, sending them both to heights they'd only dreamed about since their first meeting. His hands explored his future wife's body, getting to know her as his lover for the first time. Caitlyn slowly reached down and unzipped Cameron's pants. As they completely undressed each other, Caitlyn caressed his manhood, causing Cameron to want to enter her right then and there.

'*Take your time, Cameron, you have all night,*' he had to remind himself.

He pulled her to him and kissed her passionately, reaching up to let her hair down. Her body was perfect, everything he'd imagined and more. As passion ignited more and more between them, Cameron knew he had to have her right then, as he entered her. As Cameron made love to Caitlyn, he knew that he would never forget the night they were intimate for the first time. Neither one of them were virgins, but Cameron felt something he'd never felt before. He felt a passion that he never knew existed. They made love into the wee hours of the night. As they basked in the afterglow, Caitlyn lay in Cameron's arms looking at her ring, smiling.

"I can't wait to become Mrs. Cameron Spencer."

"Thank you, Caitlyn."

"For what?"

"For being in my life. For agreeing to marry me." Cameron kissed her again.

"I can't believe you had me going about the clarinet. When I saw that big box, my heart sank."

"That's exactly what I wanted to happen."

"You little schemer, you!" Caitlyn smiled, playfully hitting him in the chest.

Cameron laughed as he pulled her into a tight embrace. As they lay there, they talked about their future together, and then they made love again, only to eventually fall asleep in each other's arms. The night was perfect; more perfect than Cameron ever could have hoped. He wanted her to be in his arms forever.

****

On Labor Day of that year, Cameron's family got together and planned a cookout for him. Victoria and Garret's family wanted him to know how welcome he was. The cookout was a huge success, with Cameron and Caitlyn announcing their engagement. His entire family was supportive and offered to do whatever they could to help with their plans. Cameron and Caitlyn hadn't even set a date yet, and his family was offering to pay for the entire wedding. They wanted to make up for lost time. Victoria's family felt that he was their link to Victoria's memory and wanted to have him in their lives for as long as possible. It did make Cameron and Caitlyn decide on a wedding date: January 7th.

Caitlyn had always dreamed of a 'Winter Wonderland' wedding. Now that the date was set, they had to have all plans in place in the next four months. Caitlyn and Cameron both decided that they didn't want a huge wedding party, wanting only a maid of honor, a best man, three bridesmaids and three groomsmen. They wanted to keep the guest list to a minimum, with no more than 150 people. Cameron couldn't decide whether to let Garret or David be best man, but Caitlyn knew she wanted Marie to be matron of honor. One day, while they were out for a drive, Caitlyn spotted the perfect place to hold the wedding reception. It was in the ballroom at the botanical gardens. They'd already decided that the ceremony would be held in Caitlyn's church.

Caitlyn returned to work a week after Labor Day. Her desk was piled up with welcoming work, and she couldn't have been more pleased. She seemed to be getting along better with the people at the firm, no doubt due to the happiness she was experiencing with Cameron. She was not as much of a viper as she'd been in the past, and everyone noticed it. It finally was revealed about the fact that Alex was her uncle. It was also realized that Kristen had been the one to start the rumor in the first place about the two of them having an affair. She wanted to get the gossip off of her, after people started to suspect something between her and Eric. So when she noticed how close Alex and Caitlyn were, she got the idea to start telling everyone that it was how Caitlyn got her job.

One morning in September, when Cameron got to work, he had a message from the prosecutor's office. As a favor, the DA called him and told him that he was going to seek life imprisonment for Rebecca. Cameron knew that would be a far cry better than what she deserved, because she'd done enough to warrant the death penalty. Rebecca had been transferred to Kerrigan, to await trial for Victoria's death. She was also going to go on trial for kidnapping Caitlyn. Serena's death was ruled self-defense, thanks to Rebecca's lawyer. Serena had been on Rebecca's property intent upon doing her bodily harm. She had several other counts of murder going against her, so even with that charge being dropped, she still had a long way to go.

Roland wanted nothing to do with her, and he gladly testified against her when questioned about his daughter's death. She was to be held accountable for Rosemary, Rosemary's parents, Oscar Lucas, Dr. Varden, Lisa Lyle, Alice Cramer, Jennifer Creighton and Victoria Marlow. They exhumed the supposedly dead Rachel Marlow's body and identified her as Alice Cramer, Rachel's college classmate. Apparently, Rachel had murdered Jennifer Creighton, a college rival in a jealous rage because Garret had taken Jennifer out when he and Rachel broke up briefly, just as Hallinger told Cameron. Jennifer's murder was never solved because Alice knew about it, but was willing to provide Rachel with an alibi on the night of the murder. Jennifer had been stabbed six times. When Alice started to have money trouble, she tracked Rachel down and started demanding money from her in order to keep quiet. Rachel killed her and took over her identity for a brief period of time, just long enough to get lost in the paper trail leading to her.

Dr. Varden's son really wanted revenge after it was determined that she would not be on trial for Serena's death, but his wife talked him out of going after Rebecca again. She convinced him that he'd still won because she would be punished for his father's murder. Cameron had been in touch with Rebecca's lawyer concerning the other charges, and he told Cameron that they were going to plead insanity. Cameron figured just as much, but he wondered if an institution would be punishment enough for what his mother had done. He still loved her, but he knew that she'd done a lot to hurt a lot of people, including him. In the mean time, Cameron was in the middle of finalizing his father's business partner taking over their business, as well as selling his parents' home. Amazingly enough someone was interested in purchasing the house and land after less than two months on the market. They were willing to pay the full asking price of the house.

Thanks to Evan's foresight about planning for his and Rebecca's retirement, Cameron had enough money set aside to take care of Evan. He started checking into an assisted living facility for Evan once he was released from rehab. Evan was getting much stronger, so by the time Evan had been in rehab for three months, his speech had remarkably improved. He was almost sounding like his old self again. Cameron hoped he would be well enough to attend the wedding.

For the Christmas holidays, Cameron and Caitlyn decided to throw a party, inviting his family as well as Caitlyn's family, so that they would have a chance to meet each other. Caitlyn wanted for everything to be perfect, so they planned it for the Saturday, a week before Christmas. All of Cameron's relatives came into town, as well as Caitlyn's. They'd gotten in over their heads, because they ended up with almost 100 people between the two families. Everything was going along perfectly for Cameron, and he and Caitlyn couldn't have been happier.

On January 6th, the day before Cameron's wedding, Rebecca's attorney called Cameron and told him that a trial date had been set for her. Her trial was going to start on February 20th. Cameron was relieved, because that meant that soon they could put all of this behind them.

On Cameron's wedding day, Garret was there in the dressing room with him. He told Cameron a couple of months before that he should let David be best man because he knew that David was his best friend. He wanted to just enjoy being father of the groom. Garret just wanted to help him get ready for his big day.

"Are you nervous?" Garret asked.

"More than you could imagine," Cameron said. His hands were shaking as he tried to button his shirt.

"This is a special day, and I thank God I'm able to be here with you. I know I've missed out on so much of your life, but I'm glad I could be here for this," Garret said.

"I wouldn't want it any other way, Dad," Cameron said. Cameron had not even paid attention to his words.

"What did you say?" Garret asked.

"What?" Cameron asked.

"You called me 'Dad,'" Garret smiled.

Cameron smiled. "Yeah, I guess I did. Do you mind?"

"Son, that's something I've waited on for 27 years," Garret said, hugging him. "I'm so proud of you." Cameron could see tears of joy in his father's eyes. "Um, I've got a very special gift for you," Garret said, reaching into his pocket.

"What is it?" Cameron asked.

"It's your mother's wedding ring. I still had it because she wasn't able to wear it during the last couple of months she carried you. Her fingers had swollen, and it became uncomfortable for her. I should have given it to you months ago, but I wanted to do something special on your wedding day. You don't have to give it to Caitlyn right now. I'll leave it up to you."

"It's beautiful. I'll cherish it, and I'd be honored to give it to Caitlyn now." Cameron smiled.

The ring he'd purchased for Caitlyn didn't compare to this one. They'd purchased each other's rings separately, because they wanted for the other one to be surprised by what they each picked out.

"Thanks, Dad."

"You're welcome, Son," Garret smiled.

At that time, David knocked at the door, and walked in. "The bachelor party wasn't too much for you last night, was it?" David laughed.

"Nope. Steady as a rock," Cameron demonstrated by holding his hand out. "It's a good thing I'm only getting married once. I don't think I could handle all you guys threw at me a second time in my life," Cameron smiled.

"Are you about ready?" David asked.

"About as ready as I'll ever be."

Cameron had decided to ask two of his first cousins and Caitlyn's cousin to be groomsmen. He chose one from Garret's family, one from Victoria's family as well as Aaron, Caitlyn's cousin by marriage. Over the course of a few months, he'd gotten to know Aaron quite well, who was married to Caitlyn's cousin Penelope. Caitlyn asked Penelope, Linda and a close college friend to be bridesmaids. Linda had just given birth to a set of twin girls in November, so she was able to travel for the wedding. Of course, Caitlyn's friend Marie was going to be matron of honor. Everything seemed to work out perfectly. Cameron had wanted Evan to be there, but his doctors weren't sure if he'd be ready for such an event.

"Only one thing would make this day complete."

"What's that?" Garret asked.

"If Evan could be here," Cameron said. "I mean, I love that you're here, but he means a lot to me."

"I understand. Don't worry. Everything will be okay," Garret smiled, patting Cameron on the back. "I'm going to go and take my seat."

As Cameron and David walked down the hall, they met the pastor in his study so that they could walk into the sanctuary together. Cameron had not even seen how the church was decorated, because Caitlyn had overseen the entire thing, telling him just to make sure his tux fit and to be there on time. Cameron couldn't have thought of a better arrangement. There were candles up and down the aisles. She'd used a midnight blue and silver as their colors. Everything from the candles to the flowers blended just right.

When Cameron looked out into the church packed from front to back with guests, he looked over to where Garret was sitting in front. To Cameron's surprise, right next to Garret was Evan. He was in a wheelchair, and completely alert. Cameron looked at them and smiled, and realized life couldn't get much better, having both of his fathers there on his big day. Evan smiled at him. Cameron looked at Garret, and realized Garret had made it happen. He smiled and mouthed the words 'thank you' to Garret. Garret smiled and nodded proudly, as he was finally able to do something for his son.

The entire wedding ceremony went perfectly. Cameron felt that Caitlyn had done a wonderful job decorating the church, although nothing compared to its beauty until he saw Caitlyn walk down the aisle. Cameron felt the tears welling up in his eyes. Something about the candlelight sent a special glow to Caitlyn. Or maybe her beauty just lit up the room. Cameron didn't know what it was. He did know that he was a blessed man to have a woman like Caitlyn. Everyone else in the church seemed to fade. Cameron felt that he and Caitlyn were the only two people in the world. When she reached him, he smiled at her.

"Every time I think you can't get more beautiful, you find a way to amaze me and do just that," Cameron whispered.

"Thank you," Caitlyn blushed, smiling at the man who was about to become her husband.

The ceremony was perfect, as they quietly reaffirmed their love for each other. Everyone in the church was touched by the special vows they presented to each other. After the ceremony, everyone went to the reception where there was a big celebration until late that night. After celebrating with family, friends and co-workers, which incidentally went well over the 150 limit they were trying to set, Cameron and his new bride rode around in a horse and buggy that night, even though it was January. They'd decided to honeymoon in Hawaii, wanting to get away from the cold for a while. They stayed in Hawaii for two weeks, which resulted in Caitlyn becoming pregnant. She didn't realize it until after they'd been home for almost three weeks.

Considering the fact that they now had a baby coming, they knew they definitely needed a bigger place. They found the perfect house in Crescent Hills, which was a family-oriented community just being developed. The four bedroom three and a half bath house was being built, which gave

Caitlyn the opportunity to go in and add her special touches. She was able to choose paint colors, carpet colors, even the types of the kitchen and bathroom cabinets. They knew the baby would be due in early October, which was enough time to get decorated and settled into their new home. There was a pool, and a huge backyard, perfect for their two dogs. The home had a huge den and formal living and dining room. There was a deck that connected to the patio, which surrounded the pool. Cameron would even have his own 'man cave' downstairs, complete with surround sound, a pool table and big screen TV, for whenever Cameron invited the guys over. Cameron and Caitlyn's life was perfect.

When Rebecca's trial started, Cameron contemplated going to the courtroom. He decided against it because he felt it would only encourage her. He'd only been to see her twice since her arrest. His visits seemed to be unhealthy for the both of them because she felt that he was going to get her out. The first time he went to see her was a complete disaster. She started yelling for him to get her out, because they had her trapped and were abusive to her. Cameron's heart went out to his mother, but knew that Rachel deserved what she was getting. How could he go on after that? He made one other attempt to see her before her trial started. She was still the same. She felt as if the world had betrayed her, and that Cameron hated her. He realized that it wasn't doing either one of them any good by his going to see her. Even the psychiatrists who'd been assigned to her case felt the same way.

By the end of June, they were moved into their new house, and getting prepared for the baby's arrival. Caitlyn was coming along right on schedule, with her due date fast approaching. Cameron enjoyed being able to participate in everything with his wife, as they waited with anticipation on their baby's arrival. For the 4th of July, they were able to have a cookout, and invited Caitlyn's parents, Garret, and both sets of Cameron's grandparents, as well as Evan. Evan was getting better, and he was finally able to use a walker to assist him. He was happy and content in the assisted living facility where he was residing. He commented that it was like a resort all year round, just with nurses. Evan said he never knew relaxation could be so much fun.

After several weeks of a grueling trial and a week of deliberation, the jury finally reached a verdict. Rebecca was sentenced to life in prison without the eligibility of parole, in a maximum security prison. It was obvious that the crimes Rebecca had committed had been with full knowledge about what she was doing. The judge stated his surprise at the fact that the prosecutor was not going after the death penalty. No doubt, if they'd gone after it, she would have gotten the death penalty. Cameron was just glad it was over. Rebecca's attorney stated that he was going to file an appeal, which Cameron expected. She had a right to that. A part of Cameron felt that it was money going down the drain, because no court would reverse her sentencing. Rebecca refused to give up. She wanted to appeal, which of course, was her right. Cameron knew deep down that she would never get a reversal of the verdict, because the end result would always be life without the eligibility of parole, possibly worsening the situation with the death penalty next time. Because he felt somewhat responsible, he agreed to continue paying Rebecca's legal expenses.

Although she appealed, Rebecca began serving her sentence on August 10th. Cameron thought about her all the time, although he never mentioned anything to Caitlyn about it. Cameron had such mixed feelings about everything that had happened. How could he turn his back on her as if she didn't exist? No one understood the position Cameron found himself in, because no one else was living it, except maybe Evan. Cameron wanted to just get on with his life.

Garret was also getting his life together. He opened up a restaurant, which became an instant success. He'd always dreamed of owning a restaurant of his own along with being an attorney. He and Victoria were making plans for that before her death. He was able to use the money from Victoria's insurance. What he'd never known was the Victoria's parents had put the money in a trust after making a couple of smart

$\sim 372 \sim$

investments, allowing it to grow interest over the years. Because of that, $250,000.00 had ultimately turned into over $1,500,000.00. They wanted to give it to Cameron, because they'd always hoped he would be found. Cameron and Victoria's family discussed it, and decided that the money would best be used if Garret could use it to get on his feet. Garret refused the money at first, but Cameron insisted. Garret decided to take ½ of the money, and put the other half in a trust fund for his grandchild on the way. Garret also was awarded by the state a sum of $520,000.00 for wrongful imprisonment.

Since Evan was starting to regain all of his faculties, he was getting restless. Garret and Evan had become good friends over the months, so Garret offered him a partnership in the restaurant, which Evan eagerly accepted. The two of them worked side by side, calling the restaurant Victoria's, in honor of Cameron's mother. The irony behind it all was how the one person who was devious enough to ruin so many lives, was also the reason such a good friendship was formed.

Life was good for Cameron and his family. Finally, after months and months of waiting, on September 25th, after 14 hours of being in labor, Cameron and Caitlyn welcomed their first child into the world. It was a girl. Caitlyn and Cameron decided to name her Victoria Sylvia Spencer, after Cameron and Caitlyn's mothers. She weighed exactly seven pounds, and was 19 inches long. She had 10 perfect fingers, and 10 perfect toes. This was perfection. Cameron had his beautiful wife, his beautiful daughter, a happy home, and the big family he'd always wanted. Not only that, he had a job he loved. Although at times, Cameron knew he'd been wrongfully taken from his family without parental consent, he owed Rebecca a debt of gratitude. Had he not gone through those things, would he have been able to appreciate what he had at this point? Cameron knew he'd never really know, but he'd like to think that deep down somewhere, there was a good person inside of Rebecca. After all, she was worthy of Cameron's love, a love that he would forever feel for the woman he knew as his mother.

Epilogue

While Cameron and Caitlyn were celebrating their first Christmas as husband and wife, and as first time parents, Rebecca was plotting. Even in a maximum security prison, it wouldn't be hard to escape. Rebecca knew she needed to see her new grandchild. She knew if she got to the infirmary, she'd be home free. So unsuspecting, so easy to overthrow, especially around the holidays. People were always in such a festive mood, so they tended to let their guards down. Not only that, she had the help of two willing accomplices. It was now or never. Rebecca knew they were keeping Cameron and her granddaughter from her. She read about it in the celebrations section of the newspaper. Caitlyn was trying to keep her son from her. She'd pay for that. They'd all pay for keeping Cameron and his daughter from her. After orchestrating a perfect escape and stealing money from the nurse and guard she murdered, Rebecca found herself on a bus.

"So where are you headed?" the man asked, as they rode along.

"To Kerrigan, to see my new granddaughter," Rebecca smiled.

If you want to know what happens next, be sure to purchase the sequel, *Without Cameron's Consent* when it comes out. . .

Here's a little teaser about what to expect. . . .

The hazy, overcast sky fit the woman's mood perfectly. She felt a slight mist of rain as she stared at the grave's headstone. Filled with memories of everything that had happened over the years, she was drawn to Victoria's grave. Her only true comfort was that despite everything Victoria had done, she came out on top, even now at the point of being able to stand on top of Victoria's grave.

"You ruined my life, Victoria," the woman said in a frustrating tone. "I hope you rot in hell!"

Her helpful companion, without whom she wouldn't have had the nerve to come this far to reconnect with her family, placed her hand on her shoulder.

"You have to let this go," Kristen sighed. "It'll eat away at you if you don't."

"I know. Coming here helps," the woman smiled. "I wish you were with my son instead of What's-her-name."

"She ruined both of our lives with her lies," Kristen said in a frustrating tone. "But, don't worry, this will soon be a brand new year, and things are going to be better. We'll expose her for her lies once and for all."

"What would I do without you?" the woman smiled.

"You'll never have to know," Kristen said. "I'll always be here for you, Rachel."

"Are you sure your friend is okay with all of this? I don't want to impose," Rachel said.

"Charles is more than happy to help," Kristen smiled. "He's willing to help you with whatever you need."

"Is he meeting us here?" Rachel asked.

"Yes," Kristen said, turning slightly. "There he is now. Come on."

Rachel turned slowly to walk away. Looking ahead, she noticed a distinguished looking gentleman walking towards them. He was handsome, looked to be in his mid fifties. She was mesmerized by him. So mesmerized in fact, until she almost tripped and would have fallen if it were not for her handsome, mysterious knight in shining armor. He reached out quickly and broke her fall.

"Are you alright?" he asked.

"Yes, I'm fine. Thank you," she smiled.

She noticed another woman observing them as they talked. The woman was placing flowers on a grave.

"You're welcome. You have to be careful around here. The ground is unsteady, and a pretty lady like you could lose her balance," the man said.

"I suppose it was a good thing you were here to rescue me. My hero," she smiled.

"Rachel, this is Charles, Charles, this is Rachel," Kristen introduced him.

"Rachel, I've heard so much about you," Charles smiled, extending his hand.

"Same here. Kristen can't say enough nice things about you," Rachel said as she shook his hand.

"This is a rather strange place to meet. Is there a reason for meeting in such an odd place?"

"Had to pay a visit to an old enemy," Rachel commented.

"I've heard all about your situation, and I'm here to help you undo some of what this woman has done," Charles said, looking at her.

"Thank you," Rachel laughed slightly. "She only ruined my life and turned my family against me. How can you undo that?"

"I can at least help where your son is concerned, can't I?" Charles asked.

"I hope so," Rachel smiled.

"Rachel's been through so much over the past year. Charles, you have to help her," Kristen spoke up as they walked towards Charles' car. "Rachel, why don't you ride with Charles? I'll follow along in my car."

"I don't know. We don't know each other," Rachel commented.

"That's the purpose of riding together. We can get to

know each other," Charles smiled.

"Well, I suppose if Kristen trusts you so much, so should I," Rachel smiled.

"Kristen knew exactly who to call to help you," Charles smiled.

"Thank you for doing so much," Rachel said. "Most people wouldn't be so kind as to help someone in my situation," Rachel said, noticing the car, which was quite expensive. Charles opened the door for her. "Such a gentleman."

"I try to be," Charles smiled.

"I'll follow you," Kristen said, getting into her car.

Rachel leaned back onto the soft, luxurious leather and sighed. Maybe her luck was about to change with this handsome stranger.

As they drove along, the ride was somewhat quiet, as Charles broke the silence. "So, how was your trip?"

"A little uncomfortable, but I won't complain," Rachel said. "I appreciate the bus ticket."

"Any time. I wish I could have sent my plane for you, but considering the circumstances, I wasn't able to do that," Charles said.

"That's okay. The most important thing is that I'm here, because I want to see my new little granddaughter."

"You know you can't just go and knock on their door, right?" Charles asked.

"I'm willing to be adventurous," Rachel smiled. "Besides, the surprise on my daughter-in-law's face will be satisfying enough!"

"I don't know. Are you sure you can trust her? She's already done so much to you," Charles reminded her.

"That's why I have to talk some sense into my son. Kristen's the one he should have been with. She's been there for me through everything this past year, while my daughter-in-law has kept my son from me."

Rachel thought back to the last time she was in Kerrigan, and wondered if much had changed. She was glad she'd missed her son's wedding, because he shouldn't have

~ 3 ~

married her anyway. She regretted missing the birth of her granddaughter more than anything. The baby should be three months old now. Her son's wife was always unfit. Rachel sometimes feared that maybe the baby wasn't his. He'd be heartbroken if he knew that little tramp had cheated on him.

Her thoughts were interrupted by Charles. "A penny for your thoughts."

"Oh, I think you can afford a little more than a penny," Rachel smiled.

"True, very true," Charles said.

"I was just thinking about my son. Kristen didn't tell me if you were married or not. Your wife won't mind your bringing a strange woman home, will she?" Rachel probed.

"I'm a widower," Charles said. "My wife died five years ago, so it's just me."

"I'm sorry to hear that," Rachel commented.

"It gets better over time," Charles shrugged.

"I suppose that's true," Rachel said.

Ten minutes later, they arrived at Charles' lake house, which wasn't very modest. It finally occurred to Rachel to ask Charles exactly what it is that he does for a living. Not very many people could afford such an opulent place by the lake. Kristen said he had money, but she didn't expect this. She looked around in amazement.

"So, what do you do, Charles?" Rachel asked, smiling.

"I dabble in a little of this and a little of that. Mostly real estate. I hope you'll make yourself comfortable," Charles smiled.

"Do you have someone who keeps house for you?"

"Yes, but she's out of town on vacation. She won't be back until next week," Charles said.

As they all went into the house, Rachel looked at Kristen and smiled. "Why didn't you tell me how handsome and obviously rich your friend is?" Rachel whispered to Kristen.

"I wanted to surprise you. This is the kind of man who can get things done," Kristen whispered back. "I want your son. I help you, and you help me."

~ 4 ~

"You've got a deal," Rachel smiled.

"What are you two whispering about?" Charles smiled.

"Just girl talk," Kristen said, as they went into the den. "Charles, Rachel came here with very little. You think you can help?"

"Of course I can," Charles smiled. "In fact, we can go today to get a few things. I know if you're going to be seeing your new granddaughter, you want to be dressed for the occasion."

"I don't know, Charles. We really don't know each other. I just met you an hour ago. I wouldn't feel right accepting gifts from you."

"Nonsense. I won't accept no for an answer," Charles insisted. "We can go today."

"I told you he's a great guy, Rachel," Kristen reassured. "Let him take care of you."

"That's very sweet of you," Rachel smiled. "I just still feel like I'm imposing."

"You're not. Why don't you go and freshen up, and we can go when you're ready," Charles suggested.

"You're the boss," Rachel smiled.

Rachel went to the bathroom after Charles showed her where it was to freshen up. She looked at herself in the mirror and noticed the tired lines underneath her eyes. After splashing cold water on her face, she patted it dry, worrying about how Cameron would receive her being there. She couldn't believe they would name the baby Victoria, of all things. They were determined to put that undeserving woman on a pedestal. She was hurt to learn about it from the newspaper. Caitlyn probably wanted it put into Rachel's local paper just to bother her. So many things had happened, and Rachel wondered if she and Cameron would ever have the relationship they had before he married Caitlyn.

After coming out of the bathroom, she went back into the den where Kristen was sitting reading a magazine.

"Aren't you coming?" Rachel asked Kristen.

"No, I'll stay here. You two will be fine," Kristen smiled.

"Don't worry. I won't bite," Charles smiled.

"Strangely enough, I feel I can trust you with my life," Rachel commented.

"You can," Charles said.

They rode along in silence at first, with Rachel deep in thought. Charles glanced in her direction.

"So, what are you thinking about?" Charles asked, breaking the silence.

"The usual. My son," she sighed.

"Are things really that bad between the two of you?" Charles asked.

"In a way," Rachel shrugged. "We used to be so close. He just doesn't need me anymore."

"I'm sure that's not true," Charles disagreed.

"Do you know how I found out about my granddaughter?"

"How?"

"From the Celebrations section of my local newspaper. Why would they have it put into my local paper unless they were trying to make a statement? It was just another cold, calculated move orchestrated by my daughter-in-law."

"That is a pretty impersonal way to find out you're a grandmother," Charles agreed.

"Well, I'm here to claim what's rightfully mine. I have rights, you know," she chimed.

"I agree. Maybe shopping is just the thing you need right now. I'm glad you agreed to let me pamper you today, Rachel," Charles smiled as they drove along.

"I'm still not too comfortable with letting you do this for me," Rachel said. "It just doesn't feel right."

"Would you stop feeling guilty? It's a pleasure helping you. Being here for you is just as important to me as it is for you after knowing what's happened in your life," Charles said.

Shortly thereafter, they pulled into the parking lot of a very elegant women's clothing store. Apparently, Charles had already called them, telling them he was bringing in a friend, and to pull out some of their best attire for her to see. She marveled at how much this man was able to get done by a simple phone call.

"Hello, Charles," an elegant woman in her fifties smiled as she greeted them.

"Hi, Naomi. This is my friend, Rachel, who I was telling you about. Rachel, this is Naomi, and she'll be taking care of you today."

"Hello, Rachel," Naomi smiled, extending her hand.

"Hello, Naomi," Rachel smiled.

"Why don't you follow me? After Charles called, I pulled out some of my best ensembles for you to try on," Naomi said, as they walked towards the dressing room.

"Are you the owner?" Rachel asked.

"Yes, I am," Naomi smiled.

"Well, when Charles does something, he goes right to the top," Rachel commented.

"That's the only way to do it," Naomi smiled. Naomi then looked her up and down. "Let's see. It looks like you're about a size eight."

"Boy, you're good," Rachel smiled.

"That's my job," Naomi smiled.

Rachel looked in awe as she tried on several outfits, most of which cost more for one item than she'd pay for an entire wardrobe. Naomi had also picked out shoes and purses to match each outfit. She couldn't believe how beautiful she looked in such elegant clothes. They seemed to take years off of her. She felt like Cinderella right before the ball. Rachel didn't want to be greedy, so she decided to pick two out of the ten she tried on. When she decided on which two she wanted, Charles looked at her.

"Why are you only picking two outfits?" Charles asked.

"Charles, these outfits cost a small fortune. I can't ask you to purchase more than that. You're already being overly-generous."

"Naomi, we'll take them all, shoes and purses, too," Charles instructed, giving her his credit card.

"Yes, Sir," Naomi smiled.

Rachel's mouth dropped. She tried to argue, but

Charles insisted. She wondered if people were really this nice. Why would a rich, handsome stranger do all of this for her? What was his agenda? What would he want in return? Why was he so willing to help her all because Kristen asked him to? If he was sincere, he was so different from Evan and Garret. This was a man who knew how to take care of a woman. He looked at her and smiled as Naomi handed him the receipt from the purchase to sign. Why wasn't he married? It wasn't as if he couldn't get another woman. Men like this are rare, so why would he take up so much time with a fifty-something twice-divorced woman? Rachel knew this was someone she should have met years ago. One of the store clerks helped them to carry the things out to Charles' car. Rachel looked at him as they drove away.

"I can't thank you enough, Charles, but you really shouldn't have gotten me all of those things," she protested.

"Rachel, I have more money than I'll ever spend. Besides, I haven't brought anything for a beautiful woman in a long time. Consider it an early Christmas gift."

"That's very sweet," she said.

"Just accept it, and know that there's no hidden agenda. I like you, Rachel. I want to help you. You're a breath of fresh air for me," Charles said, as they drove along. "Now, you're armed and ready to face anything. I'll do whatever I can to help and protect you."

"You really are a good man, aren't you?" Rachel smiled.

"I try to be. When we get back to the house, we'll fix a nice dinner and try to come up with a plan to help you."

"You've done so much for me. At least let me fix dinner for you," Rachel offered.

"You have a deal," Charles smiled.

Shortly afterwards, they pulled up at Charles home. He helped her to get out her new purchases. She smiled and thought that this man was first class all the way. When they got into the house, they noticed that Kristen was gone. She'd left a note that she wanted to give them a little time to get to know each other and she'd be back the next day. Charles showed Rachel to one of the guest bedrooms for her to take a bath and change. When Rachel walked into the room, she closed her eyes as she inhaled deeply. She put her many packages on the bed and went into the bathroom. There was a large jetted garden tub in a bathroom that was larger than any bedroom she'd ever had. She immediately ran water to fill the tub, as she noticed some bubble bath on the counter. She'd not had a bath since the day before, so this would be welcoming. After inspecting the outfits Charles had purchased for her, she chose one of the more casual outfits to put on. After luxuriating in a bath for almost an hour, she realized that she was drifting off to sleep, so she got out.

She immediately went downstairs after putting on her clothes, and noticed Charles had already started dinner. She looked at him in amazement as she smelled the aroma coming from the stove. He was chopping tomatoes for a salad.

"Will you ever cease to amaze me?" Rachel smiled. "I thought I was supposed to be cooking dinner for you."

"You'll get your chance," Charles smiled.

"I'm going to hold you to that. So, what are you preparing, anyway?"

"The only thing a man knows how to cook: pasta."

"My favorite dish," she smiled.

"Good," Charles smiled, continuing to cut the vegetables for the salad.

Rachel looked on the counter and noticed a bottle of wine; a very expensive bottle from what she knew about wine.

"May I?" she asked, referring to the wine.

"Please, be my guest," Charles insisted.

"Thank you," Rachel smiled, opening the bottle with the corkscrew.

"You know, I could get used to this," Charles smiled.

"What do you mean?"

"Having a woman around the house."

"Proposing so soon?" she joked as she poured two glasses of wine.

"You never know," Charles laughed slightly. "I suppose we should know each other a full 24 hours first."

~ 9 ~

"It's a deal," she said, as she sipped her wine. "So, what made you get into real estate?"

"My father. He owned a couple of rental properties years ago. He always stressed to me about how important owning real estate was. I bought my first rental property when I was 20 years old."

"Impressive," Rachel commented.

"After buying a rental house, I kind of liked the ease of profit, so, when I could afford to, I purchased another house. I also developed a shopping center on the east side and I developed a community of high rise condos and a community of expensive homes. When my father died, he owned four luxury apartment buildings, and he left them all to me."

"What about your mother?" Rachel asked.

"She didn't want to be bothered with it. She lives in a retirement home now, and she loves every moment of it."

"Did you have any sisters or brothers?"

"No, unfortunately, I'm an only child," Charles answered. "But, I do have a lot of people that I'm close to."

"Well, I hope I'll be one of them," Rachel smiled.

"From the looks of it, you will be," Charles smiled, as they clinked glasses.

A few minutes later, the two of them sat down to a nice, quiet dinner, with soft jazz playing in the background. She knew she could get spoiled to this type of lifestyle. She had a lot of hurdles to overcome before she could even entertain the idea of having a future with this man whom she'd just met. She had to try and focus on what was important: her relationship with her son. Charles proved to be funny and entertaining throughout the evening, and she couldn't remember the last time she'd laughed so much. After she loaded the dishwasher, they sat on the couch and talked for the better part of the night. Eventually, Rachel decided to turn in so that she could get an early start on her day. She had to find a way to see Cameron. She knew she couldn't avoid him. After all, she'd come this far. There was obviously no turning back now.

Rachel was restless, probably because of the change in

environment. She decided to go downstairs for a glass of wine, in hopes that it would calm her so that she could get a good night's sleep. As she went downstairs, she heard the television, and assumed that Charles was watching it. The closer she got, the more she could hear. She stood outside of the den and listened:

"People, please beware. This woman is dangerous. She is a known felon who has escaped from prison. If you see this woman, please call 911 immediately. I repeat, she is armed and extremely dangerous. She may be using several aliases, including Ellen Harwood, Alice Cramer, Regina Matheson or Rebecca Spencer. Her real name is Rachel Marlow. This woman may use other names as well, so please study her picture posted here, and if you have seen this woman, please do not hesitate to call. I cannot stress how dangerous this woman is," the man's voice said.

Rachel saw her face on the television for several seconds. She then walked further into the den and looked at Charles.

He turned towards her and smiled. "Looks like you've made the evening news."